RISE

OF THE

ALPHA

By

BEX GOODING

Rise of the Alpha

Book 3 of the Lycan Angel Trilogy from the Wolfangel Chronicles

ISBN: 9798580805764

DEDICATION

For my family, now and always.

XMLMLMWX

CONTENTS

ACKNOWLEDGMENTS

For Peter, my Editor and loving husband for all his hard work editing and proofreading my manuscript and whose constant encouragement, support and love enabled me to write this book and complete the whole trilogy.

Thank you to my daughter Elena and her 'eagle eyes'!

Thank you to those who have walked this path beside me.

PREFACE

Arcane looked at the boy as he stood before him trembling, his eyes full of terror and pleading. The two vampire guards held him between them, their supernatural strength easily keeping him in place.

The boy was part Fey, Arcane could sense it, possibly an earth element but too young for his powers to have manifested and Arcane wanted him for his collection. He stood in front of the boy, dark and imposing and looked into his frightened eyes. He could feel the power of the Fey running through the boy's veins and he subconsciously put his hand to his throat, his long slender fingers closing around the amulet.

'Excellent work!' said Barumar pushing Arcane aside.

Barumar, the Vampire King had arrived quicker than Arcane expected, the boy was *his* prize after all.

Using the power of the delusional, Barumar spoke softly to the boy until he stopped shaking. He stroked the boy's face with his left hand in a comforting, almost loving gesture and the boy smiled. Perhaps on some level the boy thought he was saved. Like the cobra who uses its movements to hypnotise its prey before striking, Barumar spoke gentle, reassuring words to the boy and smiled exposing his razor sharp, white fangs. Using his right hand, he extended his nails, plunged his hand into the boy's chest and ripped out his heart. For a fleeting second, the boy's eyes registered shock and betrayal before the light faded and his eyelids closed for the last time.

Arcane watched in disgust as Barumar ate the boy's heart, his teeth ripping at the muscular flesh, blood running down his chin. This was the King's monthly ritual, the Lunar Hunt and Arcane had been too slow to discover the boy's supernatural heritage and had been denied the chance to take the essence of the Fey before the boy died. He cursed himself for his error but philosophised that there are always lessons to be learned and the next time he would have the elemental power before the Vampire King realised anything had happened.

Arcane's power was growing in tandem with the King's insanity and he had plans to overthrow the monarchy and rule the City. He looked at the King as he wiped the blood from his mouth with a white silk handkerchief.

He'll never see it coming. Arcane thought to himself and smiled.

BRAEDEN

Roman stood in the shop doorway; his large six feet and five inch frame filling the gap blocking off all evidence of the shop that had sold digital goods, before the pulse had rendered digital technology obsolete.

People recognised him as the tall man with the open top vintage car that drove tourists around the city with himself pointing out the sights. In appearance he was about forty years old although his slim, muscular physique only added more deception to the visual puzzle as he was in fact much older. It was his alert brown eyes and friendly smile that people remembered however and before the pulse he had earned a fairly reasonable living. These days however the numbers of tourists were in a real decline and Roman had his suspicions as to why.

He watched from the doorway as a man handed out leaflets to anyone passing by. The man had bloodshot eyes and a defeated air about him. Indeed he emanated sadness and Roman felt a great pity for the man who was trying to find his missing son. He shook his head as he thought that this missing boy would most likely be found in a week or so with the dead body left at the edge of the forest. It would be made to look like an animal attack but he knew better. This poor boy would have been the latest victim of the Vampire King's 'Lunar Hunt' as he liked to call it. At least another two or three bodies would be found before the three nights of the full moon were over. Everyone would blame the wolves; they always did. The truth however was that vulnerable werewolves were just as likely to become prey in this madness. As Alpha, Roman was concerned for his pack, especially the young and inexperienced. There were also always those who were on the cusp of puberty and about to undergo their first change. A werewolf was incredibly vulnerable at this time.

He pushed himself off of the doorway and growled inwardly as he walked along the street heading towards Mike's Cafeteria.

He had lived in Braeden for a long time and had watched the city fall further into darkness since the pulse. Up until then the wolves had maintained the balance and although a truce of sorts existed between the vampires and the werewolves of this city, it was a very fragile one at best.

The wolves protected the people in the city and surrounding forest and the vampires stayed on the other side of the river, or at least they were supposed to. Things had become far worse since the king had appointed a new adviser for his court. Even the vampire Sheriff Reidar was concerned with the escalation of the king's progressive and erratic behaviour. This recent and reckless Lunar Hunt had pushed him to approach Roman to talk the situation over with him. As Alpha of his pack, Roman would speak for the wolves.

He continued on his way to Mike's Cafeteria, following the familiar streets. His senses were sharp and alert as he acknowledged Karayan and Lorcan. Karayan was sitting on a torn sleeping bag, her head slightly bowed, posing as a homeless woman and Lorcan was in his wolf form posing as her dog. Although he was too big to pass for a domestic canine, he was able to disguise his size as he lay next to Karayan by having a blanket draped over his back. In recent times the Vampire King had influenced the City Officials to pass a law prohibiting large dogs on the streets and so the wolves had to be extra careful when in wolf form not wanting to fuel eager hostilities between these two races of supernatural beings. Of course there were always isolated incidents but those were just par for the course in this dark city. Roman passed them by with a cursory nod. Most people simply ignored them for fear of being expected to part with their money and hurried by. As Alpha, he liked it that way. Hiding in plain sight had become one of the wolves most powerful assets in these dark times.

Mike's Cafeteria was set back off the main thoroughfare in a south facing courtyard that always benefited from the sun whenever it was out. Roman didn't know who Mike was, or why the cafe was named such. Perhaps the original owner was named Mike. Whatever the reason, the cafe had a reputation for serving good food and good coffee in a relaxed atmosphere, something lacking in the rest of the City.

An ancient looking tree grew in the centre of the courtyard, its roots deep in the earth at the convergence of energy lines. These energy lines were commonplace in the city of Braeden, the largest and capital city in the Republic of Bohem, and home to over a million people. It was known by many as the City of a Thousand Spires, and with its arches, vaults and asymmetrical structures it had spawned many stories and legends throughout the centuries. To the werewolves however, it was the vampire capital of this world. The cellar of the cafeteria had been built around the roots of the tree and the restaurant and bar above were incidental. The courtyard itself was protected from dark magic by a very ancient power, so old in fact that no one knew of its origin. Although a strong physique was still superior to a weaker one, the magic of Mike's Cafeteria did much to put all supernatural creatures on a more equal footing. It was a favoured safe zone of the werewolves. It was also the place where the vampire Sheriff Reidar was to meet with Roman.

Roman pondered upon whether Reidar's actions would be considered treasonous or not, quickly deciding that it was not his problem in any event; he had enough to worry about. As he stepped through the door of the restaurant he was greeted by the aroma of fresh coffee. Matyas nodded to him and Roman slid into his usual booth facing the door and waited for Matyas to bring over his coffee and daily report.

Matyas had the appearance of a man of average height though being a werewolf lent him a broadness to his shoulders with black hair that was streaked with grey, dark brown eyes and a scruffy greying beard. He was a serious looking man and his expression rarely changed. Having seen too much horror as a young wolf he rarely spoke aloud now, not because he couldn't, but because he preferred to listen and mostly communicated with Roman through werewolf telepathy. Roman knew that the atrocities he had seen still haunted him and visitors to the cafe assumed he could not speak their language and merely accepted his strange silent ways. Although there was once a time that he could have become Alpha, he was much more content to support Roman, who was a natural leader in his eyes. He had been Roman's general for more than four decades now.

Roman looked out of the window and watched the people milling around the courtyard, the positive energy from the tree lifting their spirits as they passed through. Some stopped to chat; others merely cut through to the parallel streets. A large mug of hot black coffee was placed in front of him as Matyas took the empty chair opposite him.

'Another boy's gone missing.' Roman gruffed.

Matyas nodded and spoke telepathically.

He was part Fey. Matyas replied.

'Are you sure?'

Matyas frowned. Roman knew better than to question Matyas on his facts and he cursed himself that they had been unable to save another innocent.

What time is the meeting? Matyas asked.

'After sunset.'

The Sheriff must be nervous. Something must be seriously wrong if he's prepared to come here.

'We'll find out soon enough.'

Roman sipped his coffee. It was strong and he enjoyed the bitterness of the beans Matyas used in the restaurant. He added three heaped teaspoons of sugar and Matyas frowned at him again.

'I like the conflicting taste of the bitter beans and the sweet sugar!' he said defensively. 'I like strong, sweet coffee.'

Matyas raised one eyebrow and almost smiled.

'Anything further to report?' Roman asked, getting back to business.

Apart from the hunt and losing the boy it has been fairly quiet. Matyas replied.

'What's the word on the street?'

Matyas paused before responding.

I've heard people say they feel like there's something coming; like a shadow moving over the city. We've picked up snippets of conversation and people are concerned. The older folks are saying they haven't felt this way since the war.

'That was over seventy years ago.' Roman said. 'Most of those still alive were only small children then.'

It's more a sense of foreboding. Matyas replied. *The younger folks are saying they feel the same way they did when the pulse hit.*

'What they felt was Azrael.'

Matyas shrugged.

They're more aware of their gut feelings now that they're not distracted by technology. Though I suppose the missing teenagers and dead bodies piling up isn't helping either.

'Maybe the Sheriff can enlighten us about his king's plans eh?'

Grimlock sent word. He wants to see you.

Roman rolled his eyes.

Do you know what it's about?

'The same thing as always, the vampire truce, you know how much he hates the arrangement.'

Don't we all, but he may have found something in the histories.

'Possibly.' Roman said. 'But it's more likely that he wants to berate me again. No doubt Yendor is getting on his nerves and Grimlock wants to shout at someone.'

Why do you bother?

'Because he's one of us, no matter how difficult he can be….no-one should be alone.'

Matyas nodded, the corner of his mouth moved into a half smile and his voice mimicked Grimlock's.

I will only follow an alpha worthy of my allegiance.

Roman laughed. Matyas spoke aloud as he stood up.

'Breakfast?'

Roman nodded as he smiled, he smelt the glorious waft of bacon and responded.

Please.

*****

Reidar had been the Sheriff of Braeden for over a century and had been instrumental both in negotiating and keeping the truce with the wolves. He considered himself to be somewhat of a visionary and understood that the survival of any species depended on its ability to adapt and vampires were no different. He considered the truce and how Roman the Alpha wolf had compromised by allowing the vampires to feed on human blood; he was aware of the difficulties Roman still faced from the pressures of his pack. Vampires were allowed to seduce and feed but not to kill. Tourists were the choice victims as they attributed any fatigue and illness they felt to the change in food and water. Victims were left weakened and slightly anaemic but they were left alive and as long as his kind adhered to the ruling, the wolves would not seek retribution.

The vampire population of Braeden was higher than any other city in the known world and many possessed strength of age. The wolves, although few, represented a powerful counterbalance, but the recent influx of new vampires was dangerously close to tipping that scales in their favour. Some vampires were ancient and possessed immense power and knowledge but Reidar was still reluctant to see such power put to the test in some needless supernatural war.

Many younger vampires were unhappy with this compromise and ignored the rules set down and on many occasions the fragility of the truce hung by a thread about to snap due to their arrogance and refusal to follow the agreed code. Of course there was punishment to be set and the Vampire King seemed to care not who suffered, he merely enjoyed it, as if the very suffering of others fed and sustained him in the way blood did for the rest of them. It had been quite some time since the last execution but since that time, the vampires kept to the west side of the Nejelski river which now housed Government Officials who ran the day to day business from the old Palace building.

The river spouted almost as many legends as the city itself did. Running beneath the Draven Bridge its dark waters were said to cross a powerful focal point of energy lines where one legend told of a woman consumed by dark forces who drew on the energy to fuel her evil magic. It was said that she caused terrible pain and suffering to the people in the city. She became a thing of nightmares who disappeared before her capture by transforming into a four legged beast and vanishing into the surrounding forest. There were yet others who said she threw herself from the bridge and disappeared into the dark waters. One thing that all the legends agreed upon however was that she was not gone and watched from the shadows and would continue to do so until times were at their most dark and dire.

Inside the palace grounds stood an old cathedral, closed to the public but unable to be demolished due to legislation protecting the architecture where the Vampire King resided. An undead, evil being living in a former place of worship to the Divine was a contradiction and an irony the Vampire King enjoyed. King Barumar controlled the politicians by manipulating them through their love of power and feeding their greed with money.

The king had always been a bit of a loose cannon but over the last ten years Reidar had observed his increasingly erratic behaviour. The Vampire Queen, Thana was also worried and had met Reidar in secret to discuss her fears and suspicions. Their clandestine meeting had confirmed what he had thought for some time, that the king was no longer in control. The real power in Braeden was the king's advisor Arcane, what some might refer to as a 'snake in the grass.'

Since the pulse, people were returning to older ways especially where transportation was concerned and Reidar delighted in his preferred method of travel which was a horse and carriage, a more common sight in the city now. He thought hard about his current situation and his decision to meet with the Alpha Roman. This action would be considered treason and if found out, he could lose his head or be forced to walk in the sunlight. He shuddered at the thought; something he had not done for an age and left for the meeting.

THE TWINS

Shayla stood looking at her son her green eyes blazing, Max stared back defiantly.

'Well?' Shayla said. 'I'm waiting for an explanation!'

The sound of a stifled giggle drew her attention to her daughter Elena.

'You think this is funny?' Shayla asked giving her daughter a withering look.

Elena stopped laughing and looked at her mother, her expression serious.

'No mum, I'm sorry.' Elena said casting a sideways glance at her twin brother.

Shayla regarded the twins standing before her, alike in so many ways with their blond hair and blue eyes, but equally as different in others. Neither one of them had inherited her hair and eye colouring, they both looked more like their father. They were a complicated mix of werewolf, angel, Fey and human, and had frequently delighted and exasperated Shayla over the last thirteen years.

Max was every bit his father's son, born of an alpha wolf he showed all the signs of following in his father's footsteps and becoming a great leader. He was slow to anger and showed a wisdom beyond his years and Shayla assumed it was the angel part of him that attributed to his patience and understanding but like his father, he was fearless and coupled with the impetuousness of youth Max would try anything especially if it promised to be fun and contained an element of risk.

Elena kept pace with her brother and was as feisty as any other wolf although she gave the outward impression of being a quiet and reserved girl.

Their latest escapade and for which they silently stood before her was for jumping from the first floor balcony of the house into the river. Both children could swim but the water was deep and dark covering the rocks below.

'I've told you time and time again not to dive into unfamiliar waters, haven't I?' Shayla said. 'You could have broken your necks on the rocks.'

'But we didn't.' Elena said.

'The water's deep enough for a grown up to dive in safely.' Max said.

'You know that now.' Shayla said. 'But you didn't know that when you jumped off!'

'We did.' Elena said enthusiastically. 'Dad does it all the time, oh!'

Elena clapped her hand over her mouth and Max dug his sister in the ribs.

'Shut up!' Max said through gritted teeth.

'Does he now?' Shayla said putting her hands on her hips.

Neither child responded. Shayla looked at her children and sighed.

'You can both help me clean the house.' Shayla said. 'That way I can keep an eye on you.'

The twins groaned.

'Perhaps you can think about how dangerous the consequences of your actions could have been while you work.'

'But…' Max began.

'You can start in the kitchen.' Shayla said firmly.

Shoulders slumped, the twins walked away muttering. Shayla sensed

Peter's presence but didn't turn around.

'I told you not to dive off the balcony.' Shayla said. 'They've seen you do it and now they've copied, this is all your fault.'

'Their wolf DNA would have healed any injuries.'

Shayla spun around to face him and Peter held up both hands in surrender.

'That's not the point!' Shayla exclaimed. 'Both of them follow your lead and whatever you or the other wolves are doing they want to do it too, especially if it looks dangerous. They're....they're fearless and.....adrenaline junkies!'

'They're wolves.' Peter laughed.

'They're also my children.'

'Mine too.' Peter replied, his tone more serious.

'You're content to let them run off half cocked!'

'That's not true, or fair.'

Shayla paused and rubbed her eyes, the beginning of a headache was threatening.

'They're thirteen.' Peter said taking a step towards Shayla. 'On the verge of adulthood in some cultures.'

Peter opened his arms and Shayla stepped inside and hugged him. Peter held her close and inhaled her scent, the subtle change told him there was an underlying fear and there was more going on than what she was saying.

'What's really bothering you?' Peter asked.

'This whole rite of passage ritual.' Shayla said. 'I'm not happy about it, Max is too young.'

Peter took a step back and held Shayla at arm's length.

'He's a wolf, he *has* to do this. The pack will never fully accept him if he doesn't.'

'He's half angel too.'

'But unlike Elena he's always manifested as a wolf and therefore he has to be tested. It's the only way he can obtain the crystal he needs to help him when he changes. Without going through the rite of passage he will never be able to take his place as alpha.'

'He may not want to become an alpha.'

Peter raised one eyebrow and Shayla looked away, she knew in her heart that following in his father's footsteps was everything Max wanted, but he was her son and she still saw him as a child.

'Maybe he can do it next year?' Shayla said.

'No.' Peter replied firmly. 'It has to be in his thirteenth year. The ritual has to be done on the day of the autumnal equinox when the day and night are in equal balance and this year the harvest moon falls on the same night.'

'Perhaps if I knew more about it.'

'Like what?'

'Like.....what he'll have to do and what he'll be facing.'

'You know I can't tell you that.' Peter said. 'Every wolf's journey is different.'

Shayla walked away from Peter and paced around the room. He watched as she struggled with her feelings.

'Tell me as much as you can.' Shayla said.

'Again?'

Shayla nodded; Peter sighed.

'The wolf being tested must enter the cave alone. One of the pack will wait outside to make sure he doesn't come back without the crystal.'

'You mean to make sure he goes through with it.' Shayla said.

'If you like.' Peter replied. 'Rufus will go with him.'

'Why aren't you doing it?'

'I'm the Alpha.' Peter said. 'And his father, I'm not permitted.'

'And then what?'

'Uri will call upon the spirits of the elders who will be waiting for him. They'll look into his heart and know what he fears, from this they will create a scenario for him to work through. Once he completes the task he'll be able to pass through to the spirit world, which will leave a mark on him and collect a crystal.'

'What sort of a mark?'

'It's the spirit world and it leaves its mark.' Peter replied vaguely. 'The crystal will become the charm that he will carry and which will enable him to keep his clothes when he changes from human form to wolf form and back again.'

'Ok.' Shayla said. 'What else?'

'That's it.'

Shayla looked at Peter and he held her gaze, it was Shayla who broke eye contact.

'I know that's not everything.' Shayla said. 'You're not lying to me, but you're not telling me everything either.'

'The scenario he'll be in and the creatures he may have to face can be pretty scary.'

Shayla looked at Peter again knowing that he was keeping the details from her, but also knowing that he would never tell her either. It was a wolf thing and she would never understand. At least that's what he told her on every other occasion she had asked him. She tried a different approach.

'I'm not sure Max is ready for this.'

'I *am* ready!' Max said stepping into the room.

'*You* shouldn't be listening!' Shayla said. 'This conversation is between me and your father.'

'Wolf senses mum, there's nothing wrong with my hearing.'

There's that defiance again. Shayla thought.

'I *want* to do this and I'm going to do this.' Max said unwavering determination in his voice.

Peter looked at his son and felt himself swelling with pride, he was an alpha in the making.

'And *you* can't stop me.' Max said with an attitude typical of a young teenager.

'Enough.' Peter growled. 'Watch your tone with your mother.'

Max lowered his eyes and nodded.

'I'm sorry.'

'Come with me.' Peter said. 'I need to speak with you.'

'Mum said I have to clean the house.' Max replied sourly.

'Go with your father, I don't need two wolves under my feet.' Shayla said smiling at her son.

Max smiled and went to his mother who embraced him. He was already as tall as she was and would undoubtedly be over six feet tall by the time he was a fully grown man. Shayla kissed the top of his head before pushing him towards his father.

'Go, before I change my mind.' Shayla said.

Max walked towards his father and Peter winked at Shayla, a look of understanding passed between them.

'Elena!' Shayla said. 'I know you're outside listening.'

As Peter and Max left the room, Elena came in grinning at her brother as they passed each other.

'Go and see if Milly is free to train with you.' Shayla said.

'Really?' Elena said, her face bright with enthusiasm.

'Yes, really.' Shayla said. 'I know how much you enjoy your karate.'

'It's Lupinedo mum.' Elena said. 'It means "the way of the wolf".'

'I know what it means.' Shayla said. 'I know a little bit myself. Anyway, it's good for you to stay fit and learn how to defend yourself. It's also too nice outside for any of us to be stuck indoors, the housework can wait.'

'Thanks mum.' Elena said as she began to walk away.

'Hold up Missy!' Shayla said.

Elena stopped and turned back to her mother, frowning quizzically.

'You have to give me a hug and a kiss.' Shayla said. 'It's the law.'

Elena didn't hesitate and ran back to her mother and hugged her. Elena was not as tall as her brother and the top of her head still sat snugly under Shayla's chin.

'Is it really the law?' Elena asked her blue eyes wide with wonder.

'It's my law.' Shayla said kissing her daughter on the forehead. 'Go, have fun.'

Shayla watched her daughter as she ran from the room and her eyes filled with tears. Turning to look out of the window Shayla saw Peter and Max walking across the clearing adjacent to the house. Peter had his arm around his son's shoulders and they were deep in conversation. Elena quickly caught up and ran passed them on her way to find Milly, she was all legs and blond hair. At thirteen years old they were still children, but they were no ordinary children and she knew she would have to start letting them go, but she was determined to hold on for a little longer.

Titan, her ever faithful halo hound had silently walked into the room and stood behind her. He grew in size as only his kind could and put his head on her shoulder and spoke in her mind, his tone comforting.

The twins are exceptional. Titan said

Shayla raised her right hand and stroked his soft furry face.

I know.

*****

Peter walked with Max across the clearing, his arm around his son's shoulders.

'There's nothing wrong with your mother's hearing either.' Peter said. 'We'll talk further away from the house.'

'I'm sorry I spoke out of line.' Max said. 'I didn't mean to be disrespectful.'

'I know.'

Peter looked at his son from the corner of his eye, nothing in Max's face betrayed his fear, he was strong.

Max walked with his father, deep in thought. He didn't like to see his mother upset and he could understand her fears but he was prepared and determined to take the test, both his father and Rufus had reassured him he was ready. Approaching footsteps distracted him from his thoughts and Elena ran past, evidently released from her domestic chores. Max knew exactly where she was going; she was on her way to find Milly. They had been training together since Elena discovered that only Max would be taking the test.

Max recalled how Elena had thrown a terrible tantrum and demanded to be allowed to take part in the rite of passage arguing that her wolf DNA was proof enough that she should be included. It had been their father's unenviable duty as Alpha to inform her that she was not permitted to take the test as she had never fully manifested wolf traits in the same way as Max. Elena's anger had triggered a change in her eyes to an animalistic yellow customary to wolves, her nails had grown into long, sharp claws and her teeth had slightly elongated as she ranted. All of these things notwithstanding, Peter had denied her demanded request making it clear that the discussion was over.

Elena had burst into tears and threatened to run away but Milly had come to the rescue by offering to train her to fight and defend herself so that Elena would at least go through the same rigours as her brother. The final test would be the only thing in which she could not partake. This appeased Elena for which Shayla and Peter were thankful, it was not the last time they would see her volatile temper.

'She really wants to take the test.' Max said to Peter, his eyes following Elena as she ran off. 'Even though she knows it's impossible.'

'She's been training as hard as you, and your mother and I have a crystal pendant to present to her at the feast in recognition of her hard work.'

'She'll like that.'

'I hope so.' Peter said watching his daughter.

Peter thought about how different the twins were and wondered why the wolf DNA was more dominant in Max than in Elena. His daughter had yet to display her dominant gene but her temper and the physical changes that accompanied it clearly showed that the wolf was there. Whatever they grew to become it didn't matter, he loved them, plain and simple. Reaching the edge of the clearing and far enough away from the house to speak freely, Peter turned to his son.

'Has Rufus explained the ritual to you?' Peter asked.

'Yes.' Max nodded. 'Uri also went through it with me, and Sandy and Scara. Flint even mentioned it the last time I saw him.'

'That's good. So you know what you have to do, but do you fully understand what's going to happen.'

'Not entirely.'

'You will enter the cave.' Peter began. 'And pass through the veil into the spirit world. You may have heard it referred to as the afterglow.'

'Uri called it the afterglow.'

'Once you pass through, you will be on your own.'

'What's in there?' Max asked.

'I don't know.' Peter replied honestly. 'It's different for every wolf.'

'Then how will I know what to do?'

'Trust your instincts. The afterglow will look into your heart and see your deepest fear, whatever that may be and use that fear to test you.'

'What did you see?'

Peter thought back to the time of his testing. Until he entered the afterglow he did not realise that his greatest fear was to lose his sight. The afterglow had temporarily taken his vision and plunged him into darkness forcing him to focus on his other senses. He recalled his initial panic but then his acute hearing and sense of smell had enabled him to detect the vampire as it moved to attack. As a young boy of twelve he would have presented as easy prey for a vampire. Although unable to hear any breathing, especially from one of the undead, Peter heard the soft whisper of cloth as the vampire moved and felt the changes in the air around him and as he fought his adversary, Peter had forgotten about his eyes and used all of his other senses, his third eye enabling him to see in a different way. He had fought to the point of exhaustion sustaining many injuries before finally prevailing and destroying his enemy. The vampire had tried to eviscerate him and Peter still carried the scar on his lower abdomen. Injuries sustained in the afterglow left a permanent scar.

'Dad?' Max said breaking into Peter's reverie.

'What I saw won't be the same for you.' Peter replied.

'If I die in the afterglow, do I die here too?'

'Yes. The test is not an illusion, the afterglow is a real place, it's the spirit world, but you're not going to die.'

Max chewed his lower lip, it was the first time he had displayed any nervousness and Peter watched the varying emotions move across his son's face.

Peter put his hand on his son's shoulders and looked him in the eye.

'Believe me when I say that you are strong, fearless and more than capable of defending yourself. Trust your instincts, listen to your heart and you will defeat whatever the afterglow sends to you. You're no ordinary young man, you're a wolf. You're also my son, first born of an Alpha, born of a royal blood line, a descendant of the Silver Claw.'

'Does that mean I'm awesome?' Max said.

'Absolutely!' Peter replied.

ARCANE

Before the pulse Arcane had spent a lot of time in and out of various institutions where good people had tried to help him to become a normal functioning human being and he smiled as he recalled the time he had spent "battling his demons". They had no idea that he was the demon. Over the last two decades Arcane and the demon that lived within him had settled into a symbiotic relationship and had manipulated their way through society and into positions of power.

Arcane had been born into darkness. His mother had been unfortunate enough to pique the Shadow Lord's interest when he came through the gateway decades earlier to conquer and rule her world. Arcane was the result of the Shadow Lord's pleasure and her terror, even his name meant mysterious, secret, dark. Arcane never understood why his mother had kept him, surely he was a constant reminder of her terrifying experience but perhaps only another mother could truly understand a mother's love. His mother had believed in nurture over nature and ignored his origins. She tried to raise him to be a good boy, respect others and be kind, but her efforts were in vain. Arcane acted on impulse doing good things if he was feeling good and bad things if he felt negative. His behaviour grew worse as he got older, the bad deeds outweighing the good.

His mother became exasperated with him and took him to different Doctors and other healthcare professionals to see if any of them could help her son. She was concerned for his mental well-being. The truth was that his mother feared him and she was right to. As a boy and then a young man before the pulse people had labelled him as a psychopath rather than give a name to the thing he truly was; Arcane was a sociopath and he was evil.

As a young man Arcane had an easy going style that exuded confidence and people found it easy to trust him. He gave no outward sign of his evil intent and hid his true nature well which only made him more dangerous. Arcane used people to get what he wanted. He didn't waste time with anyone who was not in a position to help him and once he got what he wanted, he discarded them without a second thought.

Perhaps it was his inherent evil from the Shadow Lord that made him search out darker practices. Before the pulse that brought about an end to the digital era, Arcane had a skill with computers. The Underworld was part of the information network where certain sites could hide beneath layers of code. In the Underworld, assassins advertised their services, companies offered live human hunts in secluded forests with no fear of prosecution. Other sites offered various outrageous practices, virtual temples to the Deceiver and sites with video footage of unspeakable acts of wickedness. These were places normal people would not consider searching for, but were a psychopath's dream.

During these searches and guided by his dark impulses, Arcane had discovered the existence of a book said to contain exceptional power within its pages. He felt drawn to the book and searched for months trying to discover its whereabouts. Eventually he found it. The book had been sold to a collector of rare artefacts. Using his computer skills, Arcane had tracked down the courier service being used to transport the book and had broken into the courier's warehouse with the intention of stealing the book and unlocking its secrets.

Arcane had been disappointed to see strange hieroglyphs and words on the pages and had almost discarded it. It was only through the genetic memories of his father that he had been able to read the words and discovered that it was a prison for a demon and in that moment, Arcane understood that he had the knowledge and the power to release the demon and possibly use it for his own ends. He remembered the exhilaration of tracing his finger over the dry parchment pages and softly whispering each word. As he spoke the ink lifted off the page and soaked into his fingertips leaving the pages blank. He had set the demon free from its imprisonment, although his possession by said demon had been an unexpected oversight.

The demon and Arcane's own psychotic personality battled for supremacy. Only after absorbing the demon did Arcane throw the book away but breaking into the postal service warehouse had triggered the alarm and he was arrested before he left the building thereby marking the start of his criminal career. Over the years that followed Arcane was arrested several times, offences ranging from theft to computer hacking crimes but always he successfully managed to avoid prison. His volatile nature, unpredictability and erratic behaviour ensured he was always detained in secure medical facilities. It had taken years for Arcane to learn how to hide his true nature beneath the surface and say what professionals wanted to hear until he was free to walk among the masses again.

Arcane stood at the window looking out over the river and City beyond. He ran his index finger across the surface of the crystal at the centre of the amulet he wore around his neck. The discovery of the amulet and its power to extract and collect supernatural power had been another turning point in Arcane's life and he had the demon within to thank for that.

The demon was obsessed with the Fey and his need to destroy anyone with Faerie blood was sometimes overpowering, but the demon's obsession paralleled his own desire to find and destroy the Angel-Fey hybrid and those who protected her. The Fey Princess had sent the Shadow Lord to the Oblivion which in Arcane's mind was as good as dead. Therefore he held the half angel responsible for the death of his father and revenge was a powerful motive. Eliminating his equal and opposite was his life's ambition and if he could extract and collect her power he was convinced that he would become invincible.

The sound of marching footsteps heading towards his room broke into Arcane's thoughts and he sighed impatiently, the Vampire King Barumar was on his way. Arcane closed his eyes and composed his features to disguise his true feelings. He was facing the door as the King entered, his face expressionless.

'I sent for you.' Barumar said without preamble.

'I didn't get the message.'

'Where have you been?'

'Here my Liege, in my room.'

'I should not have to come and find you. I am the King.'

'My apologies.'

'How can you bear it in here?' Barumar said looking around disdainfully, the austerity of the room was at odds with the rest of the palace.

'It suits my needs.' Arcane replied.

'So you need nothing?'

The King was in a mood, that much was obvious, sometimes it was as if he ran on cold malice alone. Had he been human, doctors would have described him as having a personality disorder, every time he smiled his features lit up, but always in the wrong way.

Arcane said nothing and Barumar looked around the room again. He looked at the narrow bed on the far wall and swept his gaze over the small writing desk and chair near the window. Arcane watched as the King appraised his room. There had been many times when he thought about how easy it would be to break a leg off the chair and stab the King through the heart with it, ending his maniacal reign, but he was patient and his time would come.

'The effects of the blood obtained from the last hunt are dissipating already.' Barumar said finally, his dark eyes boring into Arcane.

'The boy was only half Fey.' Arcane replied. 'I *did* explain….'

'Silence! I'm seriously wondering what use I have for you.' Barumar said.

Arcane paused and waited. The King's madness was escalating, perhaps the loss of his head at the hands of a werewolf following the defeat of the Shadow Lord and the reanimation process had not been a total success. Arcane knew only too well that he had to tread carefully. The Shadow Lord's memories came to Arcane in the form of dreams and he had seen Barumar bowing and scraping at his father's feet and he despised him, but Barumar was useful, even as an insane figurehead. The people believed it was the King that ruled the City, though the reality was that it was in fact Arcane who ruled through the King and he played his part well in the charade of faithful and obedient servant.

'Find a way to prolong the effect or you'll find yourself a participant of the hunt and I'll find myself a new adviser.'

'As you command.' Arcane replied.

Arcane bowed before the king but kept his head up, his eyes fixed on Barumar. He would never bow his head in subservience to a creature he despised.

Barumar stared back at Arcane and waited for him to lower his gaze. Arcane stared back defiant. It was Barumar who broke eye contact first feigning dismissal of an insignificant human, but the vampire had seen something in Arcane's eyes, a fleeting change to black which was instantly gone.

Barumar turned and left the room, leaving the door open. The exchange had unnerved him and he wasn't entirely sure the decision to leave the room had been his own. He scoffed at the thought of anyone having the power to use a skill like the delusional, especially on him and dismissed the idea. He turned his thoughts to Arcane's position and wondered again whether he had any further use for his insubordinate advisor

As the sound of Barumar's footsteps faded, Arcane bowed his head almost imperceptibly and the door closed on its own.

* * * * *

Eversor, the destroyer, the demon within, watched the Vampire King through Arcane's eyes and hated him. Eversor hated everything, or did it? It had waited patiently, trapped within the pages of a book of the Fey and contemplated what it felt. Hate was the opposite of love and it had never loved, therefore it could never hate. Eversor was indifferent, cold, malicious and evil. Once freed from the book it planned to take its revenge but control of the host had not been forthcoming and Eversor was enraged and fought against Arcane for control of his mind and body. It used Arcane's hate to fuel his dark impulses bringing some sense of satisfaction. Eversor learned that Arcane did not need a lot of persuasion to do terrible things and instead of fighting, it encouraged and motivated Arcane into taking action with an emptiness that cared not if others suffered.

It was Eversor that led Arcane to the amulet and unlocked the secrets of extracting the supernatural power from individuals and Arcane had embraced that power viewing it as a means to an end.

Eversor had been brought to life by the Deceiver, created from the fiery wastelands, its only purpose was to destroy. Eversor had been instrumental in the fall of many realms over the millennia, but it had underestimated the Fey and forsaken by its creator, found itself trapped and imprisoned. Time had no meaning for Eversor, surrounded by a darkness so complete and impenetrable it waited. The blackness of its prison was as liquid, thick and sticky with a pungent smell of ink and blood and Eversor quickly stopped fighting, instead it listened. As the pages of the book aged and the ink dried, sounds began to filter through the darkness. Eversor listened and knew that the darkness of his inky prison would not be eternal, and so Eversor waited for the one who would release it, hiding in plain sight. Once free it would no longer wreak chaos in the world, it would destroy it from within.

With nothing to destroy and no obvious way out Eversor spent the time in its prison contemplating its purpose. It wondered why the Deceiver allowed people to live, he was a fallen angel and had the power to destroy them in an instant. Eversor did not understand why his master wasted time whispering to the minds of people encouraging them to do whatever they wanted and disregard the consequences, until the Deceiver spoke directly to Eversor in soft whispers through the void. He explained that it was simpler and much more fun to delude the minds of people; to feed their greed and stimulate their selfishness so they would eventually destroy themselves. The Deceiver said that receiving tormented souls was much more enjoyable and worth the wait.

He also explained how easy it was to convince people that loving things and using people rather than the other way around was the best way to live and that everything they did was because of their own efforts and had nothing to do with the Divine. He corrupted the influential giving them power so that they could persuade the masses into believing that they alone were the centre of the universe.

The more Eversor listened, the more it understood the genius in the subtlety of the Deceiver's ways and listened to how people had been coerced into believing that they worked too hard and laziness was good and taking narcotics was acceptable, until every man, woman and child was tranquillised by pills and too lethargic to care about the world, if others were starving, then that was someone else's problem. He told stories of how he had sent other demons to possess and influence them into killing their enemies and their friends, how to sow discord, trouble and dissension until they spiralled further into darkness.

But what would become of Eversor when the Deceiver had destroyed all worlds?

Eversor had spent an interminable amount of time herding tormented souls to the Deceiver, but had no desire to return to guard the gates of the fiery wasteland.

Eversor had expected complete control of the host once freed but Arcane has been created by a disciple of the Deceiver and had many unexpected gifts and strengths. The Deceiver had whispered instructions on the art of manipulation and Eversor knew how to cause chaos from within and eventually it learned to live within Arcane.

They discovered they had a mutual goal and would use any means to achieve it, which had finally led them to accept each other and share the confines of one body and mind. This symbiosis suited them both for the time being, but ultimately Eversor was created to destroy, and destroy it would.

Since being with Arcane, Eversor had discovered the existence of a half angel and it wondered if it was possible to possess a full angel. Its thoughts often dwelled on whether it could infiltrate and control a half angel, then maybe it really could do the same with a full angel. If possession of such magnitude were possible then Eversor could control the Deceiver and put an end to everything.

Is it possible? Eversor wondered.

PREPARATIONS

'Do you remember when you used to flinch?' Milly asked Elena as they circled each other.

'That's before I got used to a hit in the face.' Elena replied.

'I needed to un-flinch you.'

'You did!'

Milly feinted a punch and Elena moved to block it, dropping her guard and leaving herself wide open. Milly rewarded her with a cuff around the ear.

'Ow!'

'Don't drop your guard.' Milly said. 'I catch you every time with that move.'

Elena rubbed her ear that was already turning red and scowled at Milly.

'Trust your instincts. You've done really well with the training and you're incredibly fast.'

'Not fast enough.'

Milly laughed.

'I've got the speed and experience of a nine hundred year old vampire and with Gaolyn's memories there's not much I haven't seen. Don't be so hard on yourself.'

'Do you miss him?' Elena asked in her usual straight forward, innocent way.

Milly looked away, her expression unreadable.

'More than you can imagine.' Milly whispered. 'And more than I expected to.'

Elena bit her bottom lip, something she always did when she was thinking.

'Scara said that he's part of you, is that right?'

'Yes, he is.'

'What does that mean?'

'I was badly injured and Gaolyn gave his blood to me so that I could live.'

'All of it?' Elena asked, her eyes wide with astonishment.

Milly nodded.

'And he died?'

'Yes.' Milly replied. 'But his blood carried his memories and I remember things now that I know I haven't done.'

'Gaolyn's memories?'

'Yes. Which makes him a part of me.'

'Wow!' Elena replied. 'Do you think I'll ever meet somebody who loves me that much?'

Milly laughed, grabbed Elena and hugged her.

'You're very young, I don't think you need to worry about finding true love just yet. There's plenty of time.'

'But do you think it's possible?'

'I'm sure when you're older, you'll meet somebody who loves you completely and unconditionally.'

'I like the sound of that.' Elena said her arms still wrapped around Milly's waist in a tight squeeze. 'Do you know, you're the coolest Aunty anyone could *ever* have.'

'I like the sound of that.' Milly echoed holding Elena at arm's length.

'I love you.' Elena laughed.

'And I love you little pup.' Milly said kissing Elena on the forehead. 'Enough training for today, go and have some fun.'

Elena hugged Milly one more time before running off to find her brother. Milly stood at the edge of the clearing and watched Elena as she raced across the grass towards the river.

'How long have you been there?' Milly asked without turning around.

'You know how long I've been here.' Uri said stepping out of the shadow of the trees. 'That conversation could have been awkward.'

'I told her enough to satisfy her curiosity.' Milly replied.

Uri walked towards Milly and looked her in the eye.

'What?' Milly asked.

'I'm waiting for you to tell me.'

'How do you do that?'

Uri raised one eyebrow quizzically. Milly sighed, there was no point trying to avoid Uri's question, since losing most of her sight and becoming an Elder, Uri seemed to know everything. Milly wondered, and not for the first time, whether Uri had mastered the art of clairvoyance.

'Do you remember what I was like in the beginning?' Milly asked averting her eyes and avoiding Uri's question.

'All too well.' Uri replied. 'I spent most of my time in the afterglow talking to the spirits for guidance!'

'It wasn't entirely my fault.' Milly laughed. 'I couldn't think clearly.'

'Your brain was trying to make sense of the new memories. You remember the computers before the pulse and how they slowed down when too much information was downloaded?'

Milly nodded.

'Our bodies are like an organic computer.' Uri continued. 'And your brain is like a hard drive. When Gaolyn gave his life for you, all of his memories and skills, the very essence of who he was, was all downloaded into your brain, it was an information overload. Your brain had to write new pathways to cope with all the data.'

'It's strange to hear you use computers as an analogy.' Milly said. 'I thought you hated technology?'

'I did, I still do, but just because I don't like something, doesn't mean I don't know how it works. Know your enemy, that's one of the first lessons I ever taught you.'

'I only felt like myself when I was in wolf form.' Milly said her eyes focused on something over Uri's shoulder, as if recalling the memory.

'It took a while for your brain to process the new data.'

'It took even longer for me to get used to the changes. For a long time I had no desire to hunt with the pack.'

'I'm pleased that was only temporary.' Uri said.

'Me too.' Milly said smiling.

'Let's walk.' Uri said taking the lead.

Milly paused for a second before following. The two women walked in silence away from the clearing and headed in the direction of the cave where the rite of passage would be taking place later that evening.

'I don't think I'll ever get used to being cold.' Milly said wrapping her arms around her body.

'Do you feel cold?' Uri asked.

'Only to the touch. I was always warm as a wolf, but now I'm much cooler, like a vampire, I suppose.'

'For a long time it was difficult for me to look at you and see Gaolyn's blue eyes, but I'm used to it now.'

'You can see my eyes?' Milly asked.

'My vision is blurred by these infernal cataracts but I'm not completely blind.' Uri replied. 'I see enough. You're still my little Milly, you always will be.'

Milly smiled and slipped her arm through Uri's as they walked and Uri patted her hand affectionately.

'Sometimes, when you talk, you sound like Gaolyn. Your syntax is different.'

Milly spoke in a different language and Uri glanced at her as they walked.

'Gaolyn's mother tongue?' Uri asked.

I can understand you because you think the words before speaking.

That's cheating!

'It's a wolf thing.' Uri said laughing.

'Do you know, I look at Gaolyn's broadsword and know exactly how to use it?'

'That's a very useful skill.' Uri said. 'Peter's the only other one of us who can use a sword.'

'I didn't know that.'

'You've seen him use a staff.'

'Yes, he's started teaching Max how to use the smaller staff.'

'The principle's the same.'

'I recall the details of battles I…I mean Gaolyn fought and feel the exhilaration of wielding his Greatsword and killing my…I mean his enemies.'

'Don't try to separate one from the other.' Uri said. 'They're *your* memories now. I know what you mean and so does everyone else in the pack.'

They walked on and Uri waited for Milly to speak.

'The change to wolf form's no longer painful.' Milly said. 'It hasn't been for a while.'

'I envy you.' Uri said ruefully. 'I think we'd all like a bit of that!'

'And in warrior form I'm sure I'm taller!'

'Perhaps you are.' Uri laughed. 'But that's nothing new is it?'

'No.'

'Do you still see him in the mirror?'

'Yes.' Milly hesitated. 'How did you know about that?'

Uri waved her hand dismissively.

'And?'

'We talk, as if he's standing right in front of me, but I'm the only one who can see him.'

'I see.'

'No you don't!' Milly said. 'I can have a full on conversation with him and he answers but only I can see him and hear him. Anyone seeing me talking to the mirror would think I'm schizophrenic and speaking to one of my other personalities!'

'You are.' Uri said. 'In a manner of speaking. What does it matter what others think?'

Milly didn't reply, she fell silent and thoughtful and Uri walked beside her waiting patiently, but she didn't speak again until they reached the cave.

'There's something new.'

'I know.' Uri said. 'I sensed something different about you.'

'It's better if I show you.' Milly said.

Milly stood directly in front of Uri.

'Can you see me?' Milly asked.

'Of course.' Uri replied. 'Like I said, I've got cataracts but I'm not blind!'

Milly's face took on a look of concentration and a mist started to rise from beneath her feet, only it wasn't beneath her feet. Milly's whole body began to fade and dissolved into a fine mist, her blue eyes were the last to lose colour and definition. The mist swirled in front of Uri and encircled her, it moved with purpose and as Uri stretched out her hand to touch it, the mist moved out of reach and swirled in a slow vortex behind her before coalescing into a shimmering shape and fading back into the form of Milly. Uri turned around to face her.

'That's a vampire trait if ever I saw one.' Uri said putting her hand on Milly's shoulder.

'It's a powerful vampire skill.' Milly replied. 'Only very old vampires can shift into a mist and then not all of them.'

'Gaolyn was a very old vampire, only time will tell what other skills he had that may manifest in you.' Uri said. 'How long have you been able to shift like that?'

'A week or two. During one of the dream states.' Milly said. 'I don't dream about him every night, but the last time he taught me how to shape shift into mist. He said it's useful for infiltration, or escape.'

'He obviously felt you needed to master that skill.'

'Why?' Milly asked.

'I'm not sure.' Uri said suddenly overwhelmed with a sense of foreboding. 'But I have the feeling you'll find out soon enough.'

Uri looked thoughtful and Milly changed the subject.

'Is everything ready for tonight?'

'I'm ready. Max is nervous, but he doesn't need to be. He's strong.'

'He'll be fine, we've all done it.'

'I need you to watch Elena.' Uri said her tone serious. 'She's desperate to be a part of the ritual and I know she's going to try and sneak into the cave. You have to make sure that doesn't happen.'

'I agree. I'll watch, and keep her away.'

'Good. Now I need to prepare.' Uri said looking around.

'I'll leave you to it.' Milly said.

'Don't ever be afraid to tell me when you discover new skills.'

'I…'

Uri looked directly at Milly a small smile playing on her lips and waited for her to deny it.

'In future, I'll come straight to you.' Milly said.

* * * * *

After talking with his father, Max decided to look for Rufus and made his way to the lodge where Peter had lived with the pack before the pulse. Max found Rufus in the shed he used as a workshop next to the dwelling tinkering with his motorbike and thought that it was the cleanest, most well-oiled machine he had ever seen.

'You don't get to ride as much as you used to, do you?' Max said.

'Sadly.' Rufus replied.

Rufus and his best friend Andy used to love taking the bikes out for ride but since Andy's wife Lori had the baby she wasn't keen on Andy going out on the bike with Rufus. On the rare occasion they did go out, Andy was reluctant to drive at any speed or take chances. Rufus understood why, humans did not heal as well or as quickly as wolves, but he still missed the old days.

'I could ride with you.' Max enthused.

'Your father might say yes.' Rufus laughed. 'But your mother would never allow it, she'd kill me if she found out and I'm not brave enough to chance it!'

'She doesn't need to know.'

'Trust me buddy.' Rufus said. 'She'd know.'

Max looked thoughtful and watched Rufus as he worked.

'Is this your favourite bike?'

'I love all my bikes.' Rufus replied. 'But if I had to choose a favourite it would be this one. The off-road bike is great fun and I built it myself.'

'Whoa! Really?'

'Yep, from the tyres up.' Rufus replied.

Rufus wiped his hands on a rag and looked at Max.

'Do you want to learn?' Rufus asked.

'Yes please, there's so many tools, where do I start?'

'Come closer and I'll show you. You may have your own bike one day and it's good to know a few basics.'

Max was an enthusiastic student and listened as Rufus explained how to check the tyres, change spark plugs, air filters, fuel filters and on some engines oil filters too.

'Why has this bike only got one spark plug?' Max asked

'It's a small off-road bike.' Rufus replied. 'It's not for travelling long distances, it's more for fun, like riding through the forest and jumps and stuff. Less to go wrong too.'

'And no lights?'

'We don't need them with our eyes.'

'And no speedometer?'

'Feel the wind in your face, that tells you how fast you're going.' Rufus replied.

After a couple of hours Rufus had shown Max how to service a small bike and both of them were smeared with oil. Rufus took the bike off the work bench and placed it on the ground in front of Max.

'Do you want to start her up?'

'Can I?'

'You've done most of the work.' Rufus said. 'Let's see if you've done a good job.'

Max sat astride the bike, his hands on the handlebars.

'Now give the lever a good solid kick and gently pull back on the throttle as you do it.' Rufus said. 'You've seen me do it, go ahead.'

After a couple of kicks Max was finally rewarded with the spluttering hum of the two-stroke engine as it burst into life. Max smiled from ear to ear as he gleefully pulled the throttle, revving the engine. There was something about the sound that really appealed to him.

Rufus detected a familiar scent and raised his voice over the sound of the motorbike engine.

'Excellent work Max, thanks for your help.'

Rufus leaned forward and turned the engine off suddenly, Max frowned at him until he too detected his parent's scent, although he couldn't see them.

'As I said earlier, bikes are very dangerous.'

By the time Peter and Shayla walked past, Max was standing next to the bike. They glanced at him but said nothing. Peter knew the act was purely for Shayla's benefit and smiled to himself.

Rufus exhaled a breath he didn't know he was holding.

'That was close.' Max whispered. Rufus nodded.

'Do you like this bike?' Rufus asked.

'It's great.' Max replied.

'I was going to wait until later, but….what the heck, it's yours.'

'For real!' Max exclaimed.

'For real.' Rufus replied.

'Wow! Thanks Rufus.'

Max held the bike firmly and hugged Rufus with his free arm.

'You're welcome.' Rufus said moving to the back of the workshop.

Rufus wheeled out another off-road motorbike and stood beside Max. He handed him a crash helmet and a pair of gloves.

'Do you wanna learn how to ride?' Rufus asked raising one eyebrow.

'But I thought you said you weren't brave enough?' Max said putting on the crash helmet.

Rufus sat astride his bike, kicked the lever and started it first time.

'What's life without a few risks?' Rufus said.

RITE OF PASSAGE

Eversor had the ability to look into the spirit world, which some enlightened souls referred to as the Afterglow, and while Arcane slept it watched as the She-Wolf made her preparations. This was the opportunity it had waited for and it returned its attention to Arcane rousing him from his slumber.

Arcane stood in front of the mirror and looked at his reflection, women had always said he was a good looking man, boyish with a certain something.

'Boyish!' Arcane said to his reflection.

The whites of his eyes turned a pure black, his iris glowed red and his features contorted into a malicious sneer. His stare was piercing, this reflection was the presence of Eversor.

'We have an opportunity.' Eversor said. 'To bring the half angel here.'

Arcane's eyes and face reverted to its boyish good looks and his features switched from his normal outward appearance and back to the demonic stare of Eversor as he conversed with his own reflection in the mirror.

'How?' Arcane asked.

'I know! Listen and do as I say.'

Arcane waited.

'The wolves have a rite of passage that takes place within the afterglow.' Eversor said. 'One of the half angel's children will take part in such a ritual tonight. Bring the child here and the mother will follow.'

'Excellent.'

'Find the crone, you will need dark magic to transport the child here. Be quick, the ritual takes place when the moon is at its highest point in the night sky'

'And when I have her, I will take her power, then kill her and her half-breed child to avenge my father.'

Eversor did not respond. It had a different plan.

* * * * *

Uri was aware of the spirit demons moving in the Afterglow, they were evil and cunning and she had taken every precaution when preparing for the rite of passage that young Max would take that evening. She had the sensation of being watched and although no demon manifested Uri was certain that an ancient presence lurked in the deeper shadows.

Most of the pack had gathered for dinner at the lodge, even Sandy had come to share in the celebration. At six feet seven inches tall with broad shoulders and a larger than life personality he could fill a room by himself. His unkempt red hair and shaggy beard made him a distinctive figure in the City. He was well known in the bars and used this infamy to his advantage. With his werewolf metabolism, alcohol had little effect on him and he could often be found singing loudly and acting drunk but in reality he was watching, listening and hiding in plain sight. Many a foolish opportunist had waited for him outside various bars and tried to rob him, to their detriment.

A knock on the door signalled the arrival of Mackie. Like most of the male wolves, in human form he stood at around six feet tall. Mackie was muscular with dark skin, brown eyes and a winning smile and Scara brightened when he arrived. Mackie preferred to travel rather than settle in any one place but he was a faithful pack member and regularly checked in with Peter and if asked he would return immediately in a crisis. Peter embraced Mackie and welcomed him home.

The pack crowded around the table and on Peter's signal began eating, the wolves were always hungry but Shayla couldn't fail to notice that Max only pushed his food around the plate while his sister Elena seemed to be trying to keep up with the other wolves. Shayla had little appetite herself and looked around the room. Uri was absent, she had been fasting for the last twenty-four hours in preparation for the ritual. Sheba and Marty had not made it back in time; car trouble had slowed them down and they would not arrive until the following morning. Titan was also absent, the noise and chaos of too many people irritated him; he preferred the company of Shayla alone and chose to stay outside. He would return later when things had quietened down or when everyone went to bed.

The moment Shayla was dreading finally arrived, dinner was over. Peter stood up, followed by Rufus and Max; it was time. Shayla fought back her tears so as not to embarrass her son. She hugged Max and whispered in his ear that she loved him and then stood back with Peter and the rest of the pack as they watched Max and Rufus walk away in the direction of the cave. She desperately wanted to go with him, but pack law was clear and only the elder, the initiate and the advocate were permitted anywhere near the cave.

'I'd say it's time for a drink!' Sandy announced.

'You always think it's time for a drink.' Mackie replied.

Sandy's booming laugh filled the air and he grabbed Mackie in bear hug and squeezed.

'Get off me you big lump!' Mackie said, not unkindly.

Sandy released Mackie and clapped him on the shoulder.

'Do you want some ale or not?' Sandy asked.

'Why not.'

'Good lad.'

Sandy and Mackie went back into the lodge and the others followed leaving Peter and Shayla alone.

'He'll be back before you know it.' Peter said putting his arm around Shayla.

'I know.'

Everyone was staying at the lodge that night, it was nearer to the cave and there was plenty of room. Shayla went back inside and busied herself clearing up. When she ran out of things to clean she turned her attention to her daughter who was listening raptly to Mackie telling stories of his travels.

'Elena, it's late. Time for bed.'

'But I want to wait up for Max.'

'He won't be back for several hours. I'll wake you when he returns.'

Elena was about to argue, but the warning look on her mother's face was enough to stop her. She sighed loudly.

'Not fair.' Elena muttered as she walked away.

'Come and sit down.' Peter said.

Shayla joined him on the sofa and tucked her feet up so that Titan could sit next to her. He had wandered back into the lodge after Max and Rufus had gone.

'He'll be fine.' Peter said.

Shayla said nothing; Titan rested his head on her legs and she stroked his soft velvet ears. It was going to be a long night.

* * * * *

'You didn't eat much at dinner.' Rufus said to Max as they walked away from the lodge towards the cave.

'No appetite.' Max shrugged.

'You should always eat when food is offered.' Rufus said putting his arm around Max's shoulder. 'You never know when the enemy is gonna strike.'

'That's a comforting thought.'

Rufus laughed and Max smiled.

'Just a figure of speech, but I love food and it's a good motto to live by.'

They walked the remainder of the way in silence as the moon made its way across the sky. Before long they both detected the familiar scent of Uri. Max was afraid but his features remained relaxed, his eyes steady as if he were heading out to nothing more serious than meeting a friend from school; Rufus was proud of his self-control.

'Come on buddy.' Rufus said. 'Let's do this.'

Uri waited a short distance from the mouth of the cave already in a semi-trance state.

'Maximus.' Uri said. 'Are you ready?'

'I am ready.' Max replied.

'Advocate.' Uri said to Rufus. 'Are you prepared to do what is necessary?'

'I am ready.' Rufus replied.

Uri nodded and swept her hand towards the cave indicating that Max should proceed alone.

'In your own time Max.' Uri said. 'And remember who you are.'

Max nodded, he knew that being brave wasn't the absence of fear but he was still afraid. All the lessons his father had taught him suddenly came to mind as he walked towards the cave, clenching and unclenching his fists.

'Bravery and fear go hand in hand.' Peter had said. 'Never let the fear rule you, face it and defeat it.'

Max took a deep breath and set his mind to facing the unknown within the cave. His heart was beating fast and his fingers were tingling from the excess of adrenaline, but he was a wolf and a warrior. Without hesitation he stepped into the cave and into the afterglow.

Rufus watched as Max disappeared from sight. He sniffed the air and turned around to see Milly standing a few feet away from him.

'What are you doing here?' Rufus asked.

'Waiting to catch Elena.' Milly said. 'She's going to sneak out of bed. I'm here to.....'

'She's coming.'

'Told you.'

Milly stepped to the side of Rufus and back into the shadow of the surrounding trees. Elena crept towards the cave keeping upwind of Rufus and finding a suitable view point she crouched down and smiled, pleased with herself. Milly grabbed her by the arm and yanked her upright.

'You were told to stay away!' Milly said sharply.

'But..'

'Don't say another word! It's forbidden for you to be here.'

Elena went to speak.

'Quiet!' Rufus said. 'Something's not right.'

Milly looked around and sniffed the air.

'I don't see or smell anything.' Milly said, still holding Elena by the arm.

'There's something wrong in the afterglow.' Rufus said. 'I can see it.'

'The afterglow?'

'Yes, I can see into the afterglow with one eye and I'm telling you something's not right.'

Rufus glanced at Milly.

'Don't frown at me.' Rufus said. 'You have your vampire abilities, but I'm not without gifts myself.'

'I don't doubt that brother.'

'What is it? What do you see?' Elena asked her voice trembling with fear.

'The afterglow looks darker than it should, like a black mist and.....'

'And what?' Milly asked.

Rufus sniffed the air.

'Malevolence. I can smell the bitterness in the air.'

'You can smell evil?' Milly said.

'Seeing into the afterglow and smelling evil, or evil intent, are two of the gifts I've developed since the pulse and I'm telling you that black mist is full of hostility.'

'My brother's in there!' Elena exclaimed. 'Max!'

Elena wrenched her arm out of Milly's grasp the way she had been taught, and ran towards the mouth of the cave.

'Elena!' Milly shouted running after her.

Neither of them noticed Uri's unconscious body.

Black mist began to pour from the mouth of the cave separating into long oily fingers that probed the air, searching. Elena ran towards the mist and into the cave calling to her brother.

Rufus followed Milly, both of them fearful for Max and Elena. Rufus sniffed the air, the pungent smell of mordacity assailed his nostrils. Beneath the hateful smell was the scent of an unfamiliar street, food and the stench of a river and rats and vampires. Rufus tried to capture as much of the detail as possible and send a message to Peter as he ran.

*Cobbled street, river...vampires...*Rufus thought as he ran.

Back at the lodge Peter and Titan sat upright simultaneously.

'Something's wrong.' Peter said leaping to his feet.

'Max?' Shayla asked but Peter was already heading for the door.

Peter and Titan ran in the direction of the cave, Shayla followed her stomach knotted in fear for her son, not knowing that her daughter was also caught up in events. Before they reached the cave the black mist retreated drawing everything in the surrounding environment towards it and with a sound resembling a sharp intake of breath the mist disappeared taking the twins and Milly and Rufus with it.

Peter skidded to a halt when he reached Uri, she was awake but she was babbling and shaking. He looked at Uri and ran into the cave.

'Max! Max!'

The cave was empty and cold, nothing of the afterglow remained.

Peter returned to Uri and knelt beside her holding her arms, she was still in a half trance.

'What's happened? Peter demanded. 'Where's Max?'

'…spirit demon….'

'Is Max in the cave?' Shayla asked already knowing the answer.

Peter shook his head.

'Spirit demon….witch….' Uri said.

'What about the spirit demon? Uri!' Peter shouted.

'Don't shout at her!' Shayla said taking Uri from him. 'We need to bring her out of the trance.'

Shayla sat beside Uri and put her arm around her. She spoke softly and gently stroked Uri's face until she stopped shaking. Uri took a deep breath, her eyes focused on Shayla and she smiled sadly.

'The twins have been taken.' Uri whispered.

'I don't understand.' Shayla said. 'Elena's at the lodge.'

Uri shook her head vehemently.

The rest of the pack arrived and Sandy and Mackie checked the cave just as Peter had done.

'Elena's not in her room.' Scara said. 'I checked, I wasn't going to leave her alone.'

'Elena was here at the cave watching, Rufus and Milly tried to save her and Max, they've been taken.' Uri said.

'Taken where? Uri, you're not making any sense.' Shayla said, although every instinct told her that her children were somehow gone.

'Where's Milly and Rufus?' Peter asked

'Gone.' Uri said. 'Help me up.'

Peter helped Uri to her feet, she was shivering and Titan stood beside her for warmth and support.

'Gone!' Shayla said, her panic rising. 'Gone where? Who's taken them?'

'Let's get back to the lodge.' Peter said.

'No!' Shayla said rounding on him. 'We need to look for the children. They must be lost in the dark among the trees! We'll search.'

'Not here.' Uri said. 'The twins have been taken.'

'Titan and I will look.' Shayla said turning around in circles.

'Shayla!' Peter said firmly. 'They're not here.'

'But…'

'I know their scent, they're my children. If they were anywhere nearby I would know.'

Peter stepped forward and tried to take Shayla's hand but she shrugged him away.

'No! I'm not leaving. Go back to the lodge if you want to. I'm going to find them!'

'Shayla.'

'No!'

Peter stepped forward again and wrapped his arms around Shayla, she struggled and tried to hit him but he held her tightly until she stopped fighting and collapsed in tears against his chest.

'We'll find them.' Peter said. 'I promise, but we need to know where to start.'

'Do you have any clue where they might be?' Sandy asked.

'Rufus said something about cobbled streets, a river and..' Peter hesitated, he didn't want to upset Shayla further by mentioning vampires. 'And rats. Let's get back to the lodge and try to figure this out.'

* * * * *

The crone flung her head back and cackled, Arcane winced, he hated the sound of her voice.

'Did it work?' Arcane asked looking around at the witch's paraphernalia that had been cast aside in disarray.

'It worked.' the hag replied her mouth spreading into a smile revealing her ruined teeth.

'Where's the child?' Arcane demanded.

'Children.'

Arcane grabbed the crone by the front of her dress and lifted her up to face him.

'Listen to me you old hag!'

'Desistum!' the crone said raising her right hand.

Arcane was forced to release her and step back with his arms outstretched.

'You need to learn respect.' the crone said. 'You're going to need my help.'

'What do you want?' Arcane asked, his body held by the witch's command.

'An apology.'

Arcane inhaled and exhaled slowing regaining his composure. In that moment he decided that complying would be his quickest course of action.

'I apologise. Now release me.....please.'

With a flick of her hand the witch released him.

'My name is Thebe. I have not brought the child here.'

'Wha...'

Thebe raised her hand again to silence Arcane's protest.

'I have done something better.' Thebe paused for dramatic effect. 'I have brought the half angel's *children* here.'

Arcane's eyes widened in delight.

'I thought that would please you.' Thebe said, smiling again to reveal her rotten teeth.

Eversor took control of Arcane's body and grabbed the witch by the throat. Thebe tried to raise her hand but she was paralysed, Eversor could not be controlled like Arcane.

'You will serve us.' Eversor said. 'You will live only as long as you obey. Never try to control this body again.'

Eversor pulled the witch close and looked into her eyes, the red irises glowed menacingly and Thebe shrunk back in fear.

'Do you understand?'

Thebe nodded. Arcane's face reverted to his usual outward appearance.

'Where are the children?' Arcane asked.

'They're here.' Thebe's voice croaked. 'In the City. They're here in Braeden.'

TAKEN

Max walked into the cave and within a few paces the roof lowered and he had to stoop to pass below the hanging rock. He walked hunched over along a narrow passageway towards twinkling lights. As he drew closer the cave opened up into a huge, round cavern. He felt a shift in the air around him and knew he had stepped into the afterglow. The spirit world existed alongside the normal world, and although it looked similar it had subtle differences. In the normal world the inside of the cave was a large empty space with hard rock faces, cold and a little damp, but in the afterglow the walls were filled with brightly coloured crystals. If one had the skills, it was possible to walk in the spirit world alongside a person in the normal world and remain unseen.

The first thing Max noticed was that the afterglow was mostly black, white and shades of grey with only certain things brightly coloured, himself included. He walked towards the crystals intending to take one as quickly as possible and complete the ritual. However, when he touched the wall the crystals reverted to grey stones and when he removed his hand the coloured crystals reappeared.

Great. Max thought. *No shortcut, it was worth a try.*

He looked around and saw passageways leading off from the main chamber like the spokes of a wheel and assumed he had to choose one. He walked a full circle, peering into each chamber and sniffing the air, but they were all virtually identical. Only the entrance to the large chamber was different and Max thought how easy it would be to become disorientated and forget which one was the exit. He made a decision; he would take the passageway directly opposite the entrance.

He took a step forward and stopped, the air changed and a black mist started seeping out of each passage. Max stepped back into the centre of the chamber and looked around.

This must be part of the test. Max thought.

'Max! Get out of here!'

Max whirled around to see the spirit of Uri shimmering near one of the passageways, her hands out in front of her like she was indicating for something to stop.

'Is this part of the test?' Max asked.

'No Max, something's wrong.' Uri said. 'This isn't my doing. Get out of here! Run! Now!'

Max looked around frantically, unsure of which way to go. The black mist filled the chamber and he had trouble seeing which was the exit.

'Max! Max!'

'Elena?' Max shouted.

He was confused, why would his sister be calling to him. Suddenly she burst into the chamber and ran to him.

'Elena! You're not meant to be in here.'

'There's something wrong.' Elena said. 'I came to get you out.'

'Run!' Uri said, her spirit form pushing against the black mist. 'Both of you!'

Within the swirling mist, Max saw the shimmering figure of an old woman standing directly opposite the spirit of Uri her ugly face partially hidden in the darkness of the mist and beneath a tangled mop of thick wiry grey hair. Her skin was coarse and wrinkled and Max thought she resembled an overgrown toad with hairy warts. Her small black eyes glittered above a bulbous and deformed nose. Her mouth, puckered from years of scowling spread into an evil smile as her lips muttered the spell that created the mist. Max stared at the crone; she was hideous, her outward appearance reflecting the twisted personality within and Max was certain he could smell her rotten breath as she cackled.

The crone was standing in a stone room surrounded by candles and strange objects. Bolted onto the wall behind her Max thought he could make out the presence of chains and wrist cuffs, it was a dungeon.

'Run!' Uri shouted again breaking through the twins fear induced paralysis.

Max and Elena turned and ran towards the exit but the black mist thickened and stretched out towards them like long clawing fingers. They both moved back to the centre of the chamber as the mist encircled them. The crone was pulling them towards her and the dungeon and Uri was trying to stop her.

The mist began to clear again and Max and Elena could see unfamiliar streets, gothic looking buildings and a stone bridge with a tower at either end and gargoyles and statues on both sides. Max and Elena could feel themselves being pushed towards it and Max planted his feet trying to stop the forward momentum but with nothing to hold onto it was pointless and his shoes scrapped against the stone floor of the cave. Uri's voice sounded in Max's head.

Can't pull you back….spell is too strong…..

The strain of fighting the crone was taking its toll on Uri and she struggled to communicate, her physical body outside had already succumbed to exhaustion and lay inert on the floor.

Push you out of reach……..run…..hide…..

'We have to run!' Max said to Elena grabbing her hand.

Elena didn't argue, she trusted her brother. They both ran into the mist towards the cobbled street and the stone bridge.

* * * * *

Milly entered the inner chamber of the cave, Rufus was right on her heels. They could see Uri's spirit form stuttering and fading in and out as she fought an unseen assailant.

Hurry…

Was the only thing Uri managed to say to Milly and Rufus as she pushed them towards the black mist which opened up to reveal a town square.

Rufus tried to take in as much of the detail as possible in order to convey to Peter where he was going. He could make out winding lanes running off the square, part of a clock tower and the silhouette of a church. Many houses fronted the centre, their architecture unfamiliar to Rufus and he knew the place was hundreds of miles from home in a different country. The aroma of food, refuse, filth and vampires filled his nostrils and he communicated as much as he could to Peter before he and Milly ran into the mist.

*****

From the clock tower, the vampire guards saw the night sky light up in the direction of Draven Bridge seconds before another flash of light blossomed at the edge of the closed up market stalls. The Captain of the Guard sent a runner to inform the King of the arrival of not one, but two supernatural disturbances in the City and despatched guards to the Bridge and the market area to apprehend the new arrivals.

*****

Milly and Rufus exited the mist in a flash of light and found themselves near the middle of a town square facing the clock tower. By happenstance, the clock was striking the hour and presenting its hourly show of moving figures. The people milling around were distracted by the clock and did not turn to look at the flash of light, instead they watched the little figures as they moved in and out of the clock tower, one the representation of death in the form of a skeleton which struck the time.

Rufus turned a full circle and saw clearly the church he had only seen in silhouette, its doors locked. In the distance he saw the outline of what appeared to be a palace brightly lit against the night sky and beyond the palace, the delineation of a cathedral, dark and foreboding.

'This place is vampire central!' Rufus said sniffing the air.

'I know.' Milly replied. 'There's too many of them and only two of us.'

'We need to get off the street or we're dead.'

'I agree, but where are we and where are the twins?'

Rufus shook his head and continued looking around, his eyes scanning their surroundings.

'There's wolves here too.' Rufus said. 'Their scent's coming from that direction.'

Rufus pointed to the mouth of one of the winding streets leading off the Town Square.

'Let's go.' Rufus said. 'We can ask *them* where we are and ask them to help us find the twins.'

Milly hesitated.

'What?' Rufus asked. 'They're wolves, like us.'

'It's their territory.'

'And? I'd rather take my chances with the Alpha than hang around here waiting for the vampires. We can't find the twins if we're dead!'

'You're right.' Milly replied. 'Let's go.'

Rufus and Milly hurried towards the narrow street, following the scent of the wolves, both aware of the presence of more than a few vampires closing in on their position. The scent of the wolves grew stronger as they approached a restaurant.

Mike's Cafeteria was set back off the street in its own courtyard. There were tables and chairs outside for customers to enjoy their beverages and meals during clement weather, but only one table was occupied. Rufus estimated the man was slightly taller than himself at six feet three inches and two hundred and ten pounds of mostly muscle. His brown shoulder length hair was pulled back into a low ponytail and his beard was neat, he stood up as Milly and Rufus approached.

'We're here to check in with the Alpha.' Rufus said.

The man looked at them and said something in a different language.

'Are you the Alpha?' Milly said in the same foreign language.

'You speak his language?' Rufus asked Milly.

'I understand him. Gaolyn must have known it.'

'Werewolves.' the man said in the common tongue, looking from one to the other. 'But something else, she smells different.'

'She's my sister.' Rufus replied. 'We're both wolves.'

Before the man could respond, two other men stepped out from the restaurant and looked them over, one a wolf, the other a vampire.

'I am Roman, the Alpha. This is Jedrek.' Roman said in the common tongue, indicating to the first man they had met. 'State your business here.'

'When do wolves socialise with vampires?' Rufus asked acerbically.

'You are a long way from home wolf, things are different in this City.' the vampire replied.

'I can see that.' Rufus replied.

'Reidar?' Milly said taking a step forward. 'Your name is Reidar, isn't it?'

The tall blond haired vampire looked at Milly and took a step towards her, his green eyes searching her face.

'How do you know me?' Reidar asked.

'Gaolyn Lancing.'

Reidar's eyes widened in surprise.

'Oh my life!' Reidar whispered looking at Milly's blue eyes. 'How?'

'The Sanguinaria ritual.'

Reidar stepped forward and embraced Milly. She stood stiff and erect and allowed the vampire to take her in his arm and inhaled her scent.

'My old friend.' Reidar said. 'It *is* you.'

Reidar thought about his old friend Gaolyn Lancing. They had not parted on the best of terms and Reidar regretted not making peace before Gaolyn left Braeden. They had been through so much together, young soldiers barely out of boyhood fighting in the Crusade Wars, the difficulty of adjusting to vampire life after being turned, hiding from the humans and finally working towards a state of repentance that most believed to be a myth.

Reidar held Milly at arm's length and looked into her blue eyes.

'You must tell me everything.' he said.

'Somebody needs to tell me what's going on!' Jedrek snapped angrily.

'Not out here, everyone inside.' Roman said.

Roman turned to look at Rufus.

'As Alpha you have sanctuary in my territory.'

'Thank you.' Rufus replied bowing his head respectfully.

Roman nodded then led everyone inside the restaurant, Reidar still had his arm around Milly, Rufus followed and Jedrek brought up the rear closing and bolting the door behind them.

* * * * *

Max and Elena ran out of the mist straight onto the stone bridge with a bright flash of light that did not go unseen. They stood blinking, momentarily blinded by the flash of light and took in their surroundings. Max sniffed the air and tried to identify the many aromas around them.

'You shouldn't be out at night.'

Max and Elena turned quickly to face whoever had spoken. Max instinctively dropping into a fighting stance and stepping slightly in front of his sister.

'It's dangerous for people like us.'

The boy was younger than the twins, around eleven years old. He was dirty, his clothes too big for him and torn in places; he was a street urchin. He spoke in his native language but the twins understood his words and he theirs when Elena replied.

'What do you mean, people like us?'

'Kids'

'If it's so dangerous, why are you out?' Max asked.

'Ratman sent me. He said you would be here.'

'Who's Ratman?'

'My friend. He knows things. He told me to come and get you.'

Max and Elena exchanged a glance.

'Where is Ratman?' Elena asked looking around. 'And how did he know we'd be here?'

'I don't know.' the boy shrugged. 'I'm Yosef.'

'Elena.'

'You're pretty.' Yosef said smiling brightly at Elena.

'Er...thanks. This is my brother Max.' Elena said blushing.

'I didn't expect you to understand me.' Yosef said.

'Why not?' Elena replied.

'Cos you're not from here and you speak a different language.'

'How do you know we're not from around here?' Max replied.

'I know all the kids and I don't know you.'

There was an awkward silence as Max and Yosef looked at each other.

'You're speaking our language.' Elena said.

'No. You're speaking mine. Doesn't matter.' Yosef said. 'You're special, that's why you can understand me. Ratman said you were special, that's why he sent me to meet you.'

Yosef looked around suddenly, his movements quick and furtive. Max caught a scent in the air and both boys looked at each other.

'We can't hang around here. I know a safe place.' Yosef said. 'Quick, follow me.'

Elena started to follow and Max grabbed her arm.

'What?' Elena said.

'Should we trust him?' Max said quietly.

'What does your gut tell you?'

Max said nothing.

'Exactly.' Elena said. 'Our angel DNA is making it possible for us to understand each other and I don't get any bad vibes from him. Do you?'

'No.' Max said shaking his head. 'But we need to be careful. We don't know anything about him, or this Ratman.'

Their senses detected the presence of something evil closing in.

'Are you coming?' Yosef said urgently.

Their instincts told them to follow the boy. Uri's command to run and hide still ringing in their ears, they hurried after Yosef.

Yosef took them towards the tower at the end of the bridge closest to the City. There was a tower at either end and both had been built so that they were illuminated by the first light of dawn. The far tower stood dark and imposing.

Max noticed two statues at the end of the bridge and at first glance he thought they were dogs, but drawing closer to the tower brought them clearer into view. They were wolves, their motion caught at the precise moment of leaping at their prey, large jaws open revealing sharp stone teeth. Max thought the detail was incredible as if real wolves had been frozen in time and turned to stone. Yosef saw Max staring at the statues.

'They guard the City.' Yosef said matter-of-factly.

Max said nothing. He stared at the wolves a second or two longer before following Yosef and Elena.

Yosef led them to a set of worn stone steps at the side of the tower. The steps led down, away from the street, towards the river.

'Where are you taking us?' Max asked.

'Storm drain.'

'Storm drain?' Elena said.

'Don't worry, it doesn't flood….not very often.'

'Wh…?'

'And the old sewer pipes haven't been used for years.' Yosef said. 'Upgrades. That's what Ratman said.'

'Do you live in the sewers?' Elena asked.

Yosef nodded and smiled.

'It's the safest place.' he said quietly. 'The smell of the river hides our scent from the cold ones, so they can't find us.'

'Who?'

'The cold ones with sharp teeth.' Yosef said. 'They take a lot of people.'

'Vampires.' Max said.

Yosef nodded but said nothing more. He led the way down the steps and Max and Elena followed. Two large, brown rats standing at the top of the steps, looked at the trio as they approached; their small eyes peered at them out of furry faces, sensitive whiskers twitching on their fleshy blunt muzzles. The rats stood up on their hind legs using their densely haired tails for balance and sniffed the air.

'Ew!' Elena said wrinkling her nose at the rats.

'Don't mind them.' Yosef said. 'They're friendly.'

'Is one of them Ratman?' Max asked.

Yosef gave Max a patient look but said nothing. The rats decided the trio were of no interest and scurried away.

The stone steps ended abruptly at the water line, the river's dark waters churned ferociously and thundered past them as they stood together on the bottom step. Yosef pointed to the entrance of the storm drain that opened up almost two meters from the bottom step.

'How are we supposed to get in there?' Max asked raising his voice over the noise of the water.

'Jump.' Yosef said.

'Are you mad?' Elena said incredulously.

Yosef laughed and pointed to the storm drain.

'Do you see it?'

'What?' Elena said.

'The handle.'

Max looked, the darkness making no difference at all to his sharp wolf eyesight. An old maintenance ladder had once clung to the stone wall giving access to the storm drain. A lone metal rung and a few rusted brackets was all that remained.

'Do what I do.' Yosef said.

Yosef stepped back and rocked back and forth on his feet before leaping off the step into the air, his arms outstretched. He grabbed the metal rung with both hands, his body swinging like a pendulum. Holding onto the rung with one hand, Yosef stretch his other arm to the mouth of the storm drain and pulled out the end of a thick rope. Transferring both hands to the rope and with a practiced swing, he landed on both feet just inside the edge of the storm drain.

'See!' Yosef said 'Easy. Now you.'

Max sniffed the air and hesitated.

'What is it?' Elena asked fearfully.

Max shook his head, his expression telling her danger was close.

Elena took one step back and jumped grabbing the metal rung with both hands. Yosef swung the rope towards her and as she swung towards the storm-drain, Yosef pulled her in to stand beside him.

'Cold ones.' Yosef said looking up at the bridge.

Max jumped and copying Yosef and Elena's movements he swung into the mouth of the storm drain. Yosef pulled the twins back into the shadows and put his finger to his lips.

Two vampire guards looked over the edge of the bridge as the three youths disappeared into the shadows.

'Anything?' one said.

'Nothing. But they were here.'

'How many?'

'Two and a human boy.'

'Where are they?'

'They must have gone back into the City.'

'What are they?'

'Not sure. Wolf. Fey and something else.'

'We'd better report back.'

DARK CITY

Peter stood next to Shayla his arm around her shoulders, she had hardly said a word since they returned to the lodge. Shayla's arms were folded in front of her as if comforting herself, she had stopped crying and stared straight ahead, her eyes unfocused. Titan stood the other side of her protectively. Having grown in size to stand at shoulder level, he too stared straight ahead.

Uri sat at the table twisting the water glass in her hands. Earlier the pack had enjoyed a meal together but now the mood was much more sombre as they gathered again.

'Tell us what you remember.' Peter said.

'It all went wrong so quickly.' Uri said. 'As soon as Max crossed into the afterglow. It was as if the witch knew he'd be there, she came right for him.'

'Can you tell us anything? What did you see? Maybe give us some clue as to where they are.'

Uri shook her head and rubbed her temples with her fingertips.

'It isn't anywhere I recognise.' Uri said.

'Rufus said something about cobbled streets.' Peter said.

Uri looked up.

'That's right, cobbled streets.' Uri repeated. 'And a river, yes, a river. I recall the smell of a river and food, spoilt food, from street vendors I'd say.'

'That's good.' Peter encouraged.

'It could be any city, anywhere.' Sandy said.

Peter gave him a withering look; that sort of negativity was unhelpful.

'And.' Uri paused and looked at Peter. 'Vampires, their scent was strong, even through the mist.'

Shayla started and looked at Uri.

'I'm sorry Shayla.' Uri said. 'I didn't want to say anything……I didn't want to make things worse.'

'Right now I don't think I could feel any worse.' Shayla replied. 'I was against this stupid ritual all along and now both my children are lost, who knows where!'

Uri nodded, the pain evident in her eyes, but said nothing, she already felt responsible for the twins disappearance having opened the way to the afterglow for the ritual. Shayla closed her eyes and took a deep breath, none of it was Uri's fault.

'But you pushed them away from the witch.' Shayla said. 'I know you did what you could.'

Shayla managed a weak smile and Uri appreciated the gesture.

'Anything else?' Peter said trying to focus the conversation on finding a solution.

'A bridge.'

'Footbridge?'

'Stone bridge. Big enough for cars, but I didn't see any cars. And statues, lots of statues.'

'At the end?'

'Down the side.' Uri said closing her eyes trying to recall the images her spirit self had seen. 'On both sides.'

Mackie suddenly sat forward.

'Uri. The bridge.' Mackie said. 'Did it have a tower at either end?'

'Possibly.' Uri said.

'Can you show me what you saw?'

'What are you thinking?' Peter asked.

'I think I know the place.' Mackie replied. 'If I see the images, I'll know for sure. The bridge sounds like Draven Bridge.'

Shayla looked at Peter who shook his head, Draven Bridge was not familiar to him either.

'I can try.' Uri said anxious to discover the location of the twins.

Mackie moved and sat beside Uri, she turned to face him and put her hands either side of his face and moved forward so their foreheads were touching.

'Relax.' Uri said. 'And let the images flow, don't try to latch onto any one in particular.'

Mackie closed his eyes and breathed deeply. The rest of the pack watched in anticipation, all of them offering silent prayers to the Divine. After a few minutes, Uri released Mackie and they both opened their eyes. Mackie smiled broadly.

'Well?' Peter asked, unable to contain himself. 'Did you recognise it?'

'Yes.' Mackie replied. 'They're about a thousand miles east of here, in Braeden.'

'You're sure?'

'Absolutely.' Mackie said. 'It was definitely Draven Bridge.'

Peter exhaled and squeezed Shayla's shoulders, she leaned into him.

'We know where they are.' Peter said kissing the top of her head.

The whole pack seemed to breathe a sigh of relief now that the location of the twins and Milly and Rufus had been discovered.

'When did you go you Braeden?' Sandy asked.

'Years ago.' Mackie replied. 'Before the pulse. I was working, you know, blending in with humans. One of the guys was getting married and had his stag weekend in Braeden. They asked me to go, so I went. It was fun.'

'Stag do eh?' Sandy said wiggling his eyebrows. 'Were there lots of women?'

Mackie laughed. The laughter was good and eased the tension in the room.

'Is that all you think about?' Peter said rolling his eyes.

'No.' Sandy replied putting his hand on his chest in feigned offence. 'I think about hunting, beer *and* women! But mostly women.'

'Me too!' Scara said.

More laughter ensued, but not from Shayla and Peter watched her carefully in his peripheral vision. Peter knew that Shayla and Titan communicated telepathically, he had suspected from the time they first met but had never said anything. Titan had a special bond with Allandrea, Shayla's mother, but when he met Shayla Titan had imprinted on her. Not in the way newborn animals imprint on the first creature they see, Halo Hounds imprinted on a deeper level. Titan and Shayla were soulmates. Titan would never leave her side and would do whatever it took to protect her.

Over the years it was evident in the way Shayla and Titan interacted with each other they communicated and Peter knew they were conversing now while the rest of the pack laughed

Shayla blinked and Titan twitched his ears, the movement almost imperceptible but not to Peter who also knew his wife well enough to know she was planning something reckless.

I can take you there now. Titan said breaking into Shayla's thoughts. *We can be there is a few hours.*

Do you know the way?

Head east, towards the stench of the vampires.

Let's go.

Peter still had his arm around Shayla's shoulders and held her firmly. He turned his head to speak directly to her.

'We'll go to Braeden together, find them and bring them home. But we need to make a plan.'

Shayla looked at him, her eyes searching his.

'You can't go off by yourself.' Peter said quietly. 'Neither can you go with alone with Titan. We do this *together*.'

'How long have you known?'

'That you and Titan talk to each other?'

Shayla nodded.

'Always.'

Shayla smiled.

'I want them back.'

'We'll get them back.' Peter said. 'I promise.'

Peter turned his attention back to the pack and addressed Mackie.

'Tell me what you know about Braeden.'

'It's a dark city.' Mackie said.

'Dark, how?'

'It's run by a council of people of course, but they're controlled by the vampires.'

'How does that work?' Shayla asked.

'They're clever about it, but people know they're not safe at night.' Mackie replied. 'The streets and bars were packed with tourists when I went, most locals stay at home, especially families.'

'How come the vampires don't run riot?'

'Discretion is the key to their survival.' Uri said. 'Too much exposure and they'd been hunted and killed. Humans greatly outnumber supernaturals, we've all learned to blend in and not draw too much attention to our own kind.'

'There must be wolves in Braeden.' Peter said. 'To keep the balance.'

'There are.' Mackie said. 'When I was there, the first thing I did was check in with their Alpha Roman.'

'Tell me about him.'

Mackie went on to tell Peter the little he knew of Braeden, the wolf pack and where to find the Alpha. Peter stepped away from Shayla to address the whole pack.

'Shayla, Titan and I will go to Braeden and bring back the twins and Milly and Rufus.' Peter said.

'I'll come with you.' Sandy said standing.

'Me too.' Mackie said. 'I've been there before, I know my way around a bit.'

'No.' Peter said. 'I need you both here to take care of things.'

Both wolves started to protest and Peter held his hand up commanding silence; they both obeyed. Peter looked at Scara who nodded her understanding.

'Scara is the alpha female and will lead the pack in my absence.'

Peter moved towards Sandy and put his hand on the big man's shoulder.

'I need you to stay here and help Scara protect the pack.' Peter said. 'Rufus is my second in command but as he's not here I need you to step up. Can you do that for me?'

'I won't let you down Alpha.' Sandy replied bowing his head.

'Mackie.' Peter said turning to Mackie and placing his hand on his shoulder. 'Scara and Sandy will need you here. We're already missing two wolves and we need every warrior we have. It won't take long before word gets around that I've left the City. You may get a few challenges to our territory.'

'We'll take care of everything and keep the pack safe.' Mackie replied inclining his head.

'I know you will.' Peter replied.

'I trust you all with my life.' Peter said stepping away from Mackie.

'Peterus.' Uri said. 'I would speak with you.'

Uri stood up from the table, no trace of her ordeal evident in either her manner, nor her movements. Peter kissed Shayla on the lips and lingered slightly longer before turning to Uri.

'Walk with me.' Peter said.

Uri followed him through the lodge and they stood outside.

'We should walk far enough to be out of earshot.' Uri said.

'Agreed.' Peter replied. 'If I can hear them, they can certainly hear us.'

Peter and Uri walked for a while in silence.

'If you are to go to Braeden.' Uri said. 'A city crawling with vampires, then it will be useful for you to know and master certain inherent abilities.'

'What kind of abilities?'

'You are descended from the first Alpha.'

'I know.'

'The first wolf was given the gift, or ability I should say, to command vampires to sleep.'

Peter looked surprised; Uri smiled.

'Why didn't I know about this?' Peter asked.

'Had you been raised by your wolf parents I expect they would have told you. As it is, I only know because the spirit elders have told me and I tell you as much as I know. I'm sorry.'

'For what?'

'That there's so much I don't know about you.'

Peter stopped walking and turned to face Uri.

'Uri, you've always been there for me and given me everything.' Peter said. 'You took me in and cared for me after my parents were killed.'

Uri looked flustered.

'Well, it's a difficult skill to master.' Uri said brusquely to cover her embarrassment.

'How do I do it?' Peter asked smiling.

'Speak the words *Mortem Dormitabius.*'

'Mortem Dormitabius.' Peter said. 'That's it?'

'No! That's not it!' Uri snapped. 'If it was just a case of saying two words don't you think we'd all be doing it?'

Peter laughed at Uri's return to form.

'Pay attention!' Uri frowned. 'The words have to be spoken using the warrior voice.'

'Oh.'

'Indeed. You have to be in warrior form and somehow speak the words clearly and directly at the vampire, or vampires.'

'In warrior form the vocal chords aren't designed for speech.'

'You must learn to speak the words in that form, even though the mouth isn't designed to speak, only roar and howl.' Uri said.

'And the first Alpha could do this? Actually speak in warrior form? Like a ventriloquist?'

'Apparently so.' Uri replied tersely. 'The first Alpha was able to speak in warrior form, not full conversation but a few words. The spirit elders say that his bloodline also possess this ability and when the two words are spoken clearly, any vampire close enough will feel the need to go to ground and sleep like they do at dawn. They seem to know when the sun's about to rise.'

Peter tried to speak without moving his lips.

'Ordis norditadium.'

'What was that?' Uri asked.

'My first attempt.' Peter said.

'Pitiful.'

'Ordis…'

'Practice on the way.' Uri said cutting off Peter's words. 'The ability to do this *is* in you. You only need to master it.'

'Anything else?' Peter asked.

'Your claws can transform into silver, if you wish it. It's a natural gift of the Silver Claw Tribe.'

'I know that.' Peter said looking uncomfortable. 'I discovered that many years ago.'

'When?'

'I…..um…was a lot younger and couldn't control my rage like I can now and….um…'

'No need to elaborate.' Uri said raising her hand to stop Peter from saying anything further. 'I don't want to know.'

Peter nodded, grateful that he could keep the details of the fight to himself.

'Did you know you can become living silver?' Uri said.

Peter's eyes widened; Uri looked sad.

'I've done my best, but there are some things I just didn't know and I'm sorry you're only learning about them now. Had your wolf parents not died they could have instructed you…'

'Uri.' Peter said putting his hands on both of her shoulders. 'You are my friend, my counsel and my guide. I couldn't have asked for a better mother.'

Uri put her hand on Peter's cheek and smiled. It was rare for her to speak so unguarded.

'You're my son.' Uri said. 'The fact I didn't give birth to you is irrelevant. I'm so *very* proud of you. Your parents would have been too.'

Peter put his hand on hers for a second before moving the conversation back to business.

'Tell me more about the living silver.' Peter said.

'You are descended of the Silver Claw and you were born under a full moon which gives you certain abilities that you need to master. The sleep command is one, living silver is another. The full moon also gifts the power of the fire walker.'

'I can walk through fire?'

Peter looked down at his scarred right hand, a constant reminder of the injury he suffered as a wolf cub.

'That would have been useful back then.' Peter said.

'It wasn't *your* fire.' Uri said. 'You would still have burned.'

'I don't understand.'

'You can alight any part, or all of your body and remain unharmed while the fire burns.'

'Like one of the Elementals?'

'Exactly. If the need arises you can ignite a flame within you and set your whole body on fire and be completely impervious to its effects.'

'So if I run into a burning building I'll still get burnt?'

'Yes, but if you ignite your internal fire and burn you can walk through the flames.'

'Right.' Peter said slowly. 'It'll take a while to get my head around that.'

Peter looked thoughtful.

'What is it?' Uri asked.

'All these abilities I have in my blood and I have no idea how to use them, apart from the silver claws.'

'The silver claws are the first step to living silver and you now know the words of the sleep command, you just have to practice.'

'These talents take years to practice.' Peter said exasperated. 'Shayla wants to go to Braeden tonight!'

'You need to prepare for this journey.' Uri said. 'Shayla knows that too. It's a mother's instinct to want to rush to her babies aid. As much as she wants to climb onto Titan's back and fly to Braeden, she's sensible enough to know you need to be equipped and ready. Meditate with me and we'll commune with the spirit elders. They can tell you more about your gifts than I can.'

JOURNEY EAST

'You need to meditate.' Uri said to Peter.

'I'll meditate on the ferry.' Peter replied. 'We've got a couple hours, I'll do it then.'

Uri was unhappy that Peter had decided to leave as soon as possible to journey to Braeden, although she understood his urgency, she worried that he was ill equipped to survive in a City run by vampires.

Uri hugged Peter and whispered in his ear.

'You already possess these abilities. You only need to unlock them. Promise me you'll meditate and speak with the spirits.'

'I promise.'

Peter turned to Sandy who jangled a set of car keys in front of him.

'Thanks for lending us your car.' Shayla said opening the passenger door and getting in.

'Are you sure this thing's reliable?' Peter asked. 'It looks a bit old.'

'It'll blend in and it's got the latest upgraded engine.' Sandy replied. 'Runs on petrol and has the new solar power converter.'

'Where are the solar panels?' Peter asked taking in the car's shabby appearance.

'The roof's been adapted to a solar panel which charges a power cell in the engine. Trust me, it won't let you down *and* it's a four wheel drive.' Sandy said. 'You'll need that, if it snows.'

'It's a bit early for snow, even in Braden.' Mackie said handing Peter a roughly drawn map. 'I've sketched it as well as I can remember and written the name of the Alpha and where you can find him on the back.'

'Thanks.' Peter replied. 'I think that's everything.'

'I'll take care of things in your absence.' Scara said stepping forward.

'I know you will and the pack will follow your lead.' Peter said.

'You should be able to communicate with Rufus and Milly the closer you get to Braeden.' Uri said. 'Safe journey.'

Titan was already in the back of the vehicle spread out along the back seat, his eyes closed feigning sleep.

We need to get moving. Titan said impatiently.

Soon. Shayla replied.

Peter got into the driving seat and started the engine, a healthy rumble filled the air. He raised his hand and drove away from the lodge. Uri and Scara went inside leaving Sandy and Mackie watching the four-wheel drive vehicle until it disappeared.

'I didn't know you owned a car.' Mackie said turning to Sandy.

'I don't.' Sandy replied. 'I don't even have a licence.'

'Wha..?'

'Borrowed it.' Sandy said.

'From who?'

'The guy won't be needing it for a while.'

'What guy?' Mackie asked incredulously.

'Mackie my son.' Sandy said putting a big arm around Mackie's shoulders. 'Ask me no questions and I'll tell you no lies.'

'Won't the Police be looking for it.'

'Probably. But things aren't digital anymore and it'll take a few days before it's reported missing. By then Peter and Shayla will be out of the country.'

'What if the guy comes looking for you?' Mackie asked.

'I'll handle it.' Sandy replied. 'Let's get a beer.'

'It's too early for beer.'

'It's *never* too early for beer.' Sandy laughed.

* * * * *

At the same time as Peter, Shayla and Titan embarked on their journey to Braeden, the Vampire Queen Thana was pacing her room unable to sleep. Although the windows blocked all daylight from her chamber, the Queen was unable to rest and after three days, she was beginning to feel the effects of the insomnia. Her skin was always pale beneath her long black hair but she was beginning to develop darker circles under her eyes and her energy level was low enough for her to be overpowered by a human, if one had the courage to try.

King Barumar's behaviour had driven her to a state of melancholy that she was struggling to shake off and she questioned how he had ever charmed her into marrying him. Thana and Reidar had been together for centuries and had almost reached the vampire state of true repentance where they could regain their humanity, if not their souls and finally embrace death and peace. Not a day went by when Thana did not regret setting Reidar aside for Barumar and his fake charm. A knock at the door drew her attention from her dispirited thoughts.

'Who is it?' Thana asked.

A servant opened the door carrying a silver tray with a single crystal goblet filled with blood.

'Take it away.' Thana said.

'Majesty, you must drink.' the servant replied.

Thana turned her head away and waved her hand to dismiss the servant; the servant lingered.

'Anything else?' Thana asked.

'Sheriff Reidar to see you, Majesty.' the servant replied.

'Is the King asleep?'

'Yes my lady.'

'Bring Sheriff Reidar here, to my rooms.'

The servant hurried away leaving the goblet of blood on a side table and seconds later when Reidar arrived at the Queen's door and stepped into the room, Arcane moved from his spying position and headed to the King's chamber.

'Thana.' Reidar said looking at the Queen and frowning. 'You look unwell.'

'It's dangerous for you to be here.' Thana said. 'Close the door.'

Reidar's eyes went directly to the goblet of blood.

'Why are you not drinking?'

'I'm tired of this life.' Thana said sadly looking Reidar. 'I didn't think vampires experienced regret.'

'We were close to the state of repentance.' Reidar replied gently. 'All human emotions returned.'

'I don't feel most of them anymore, only the regret and sorrow.'

'Thana….'

'I hate being Queen to a mad, sadistic King.' Thana said cutting off Reidar's words. 'I want it…' She paused. 'I want it to end.'

'Starvation is not the way.' Reidar said picking up the goblet and holding it out to Thana. 'Drink.'

Thana shook her head.

'I don't care anymore.'

'But *I* care.' Reidar said taking a step forward and touching Thana's hand.

Reidar looked at Thana; tall, slim and beautiful, her long black hair framing her face. Her pale, white skin was almost transparent and her eyes were black as ink. Her lips usually full and red as roses were pale and set in a thin line hiding the smile that Reidar had fallen in love with.

'You did not come here to discuss my health.' Thana said snatching her hand away.

Queen Thana turned her back on Reidar and the proffered drink, so that he would not see her pained expression or the regret in her eyes.

'You have information?' Thana asked.

'Indeed.'

Reidar put the goblet of blood back on the tray, his hand lingering on the glass. He did not believe that Thana no longer felt any other emotion beyond regret. Having almost reached the enlightened state and regained their humanity it was not possible to return to feeling only the hunger and bloodlust, but this was not the time for such a discussion or thought.

'I thought you would want an update.'

'You've risked being out in the daylight. It couldn't wait until tonight?' Thana asked.

'No.'

'It must be important.'

'It is.' Reidar replied his face still smarting from the brief exposure to the daylight when he stepped from his closed carriage and into the palace.

'Last night two wolves were transported to the City by supernatural means.' Reidar said.

'Witchcraft?'

'Yes. They live about a thousand miles west of here. Arcane is behind this. I know it. I've seen his type many times throughout my extremely long life, manipulating their way to positions of power.'

'What use would he have for wolves other than the Kings lunar hunt? Besides, there are wolves already in the City, why bring others in from outside?'

'They weren't the intended victims.'

'Who then?' Thana asked intrigued.

'The wolves were intentionally vague, as you would expect around a vampire.' Reidar replied. 'But as they obviously need the help of Roman and his pack they had no choice but to reveal a few of the details whilst I was there.'

Reidar paced the room, his eyes frequently straying to the goblet of blood.

'The wolves were caught up in the spell whilst trying to rescue a set of twins. There must be something particularly special about them for Arcane to employ the services of a witch to bring them here.'

Thana's memory cast back eighty years to the time of one of the human wars and thoughts of another set of twins came to mind. The General on one side of the conflict, fascinated by the occult, commissioned a scientist called Dr Mordred to perform experiments on his prisoners in the hope of finding the secret of immortality. At the time Thana thought the solution was simple, the General could have been turned into a vampire, but the General didn't want to be solely a night creature. During the war many vampires used the cover of conflict to feed. Thana posed as a nurse, a ruse she had first employed during the Crusade Wars and visited the wounded during the night, telling herself that she was being merciful by easing the soldiers' suffering and sending them on to whatever afterlife they believed in.

It was during one of her late night rounds that she discovered the twins. Drawn by the sound of their suppressed crying Thana went to investigate and found a boy and a girl aged around six years old, emaciated, covered in dirt and blood and dressed in rags locked in a basement room in the hospital. Thana never fed on children but she felt drawn to the twins, with their beautiful blue eyes large and frightened staring out of their thin faces. Perhaps because she had been made a vampire as a young woman, a part of her yearned for the children she would never have. Whatever the reason, Thana knew she had to try and save them.

They huddled together in the corner of the room shivering and shaking with cold and fear. Thana had heard the stories of Dr Mordred and was incredulous how humans could label her kind and others they couldn't comprehend as monsters when evil clearly walked among them, many holding positions of power.

The twins were anaemic, not from any cut or wound but from systematic exsanguination. Dr Mordred was draining them.

'Come little ones.' Thana said holding out her hands towards them. 'Are you hungry?'

The twins nodded, but remained huddled together in the corner.

'I'm not going to hurt you.' Thana said.

Thana could see they were traumatised and wouldn't be easily persuaded to trust her, she would have to use the vampire delusional and coerce them into following her. Thana crouched down in front of the twins and looked into their eyes, speaking words of encouragement in soothing tones. They both smiled at her and stood up on their skinny legs, both as unsteady as new born foals.

When her heart clenched at the sight of the twins, Thana knew she had entered the final stages of the repentance, the feeling was both a shock and a revelation. Thana scooped the twins up in her arms and inhaled their scent. The twins clung to her, she could feel their bones as brittle as birds and for the first time in centuries, Thana wanted to cry. She headed for the door, her intention to take them as far away as possible, but she stopped short. It was snowing outside and although Thana did not feel the cold, the twins would surely die quickly from hypothermia in their current state.

'Stay right here.' Thana said. 'I'll fetch a blanket.'

The twins reluctantly let go of Thana and stood side by side.

'I'll be right back.' Thana said. 'I promise.'

Thana returned with a blanket in less than two minutes, when she entered the room, the twins were gone. All that remained was the scent of Dr Mordred and his guards.

'Thana?' Reidar said breaking through her thoughts.

'Perhaps they're Fey.' Thana replied shaking off the painful memory. 'Barumar's got it in his head that if he drinks enough blood from other supernaturals he'll become impervious to sunlight.'

'Possibly.' Reidar said. 'But I think there's more to it.'

'I'm guessing Arcane doesn't have the twins.'

'No.' Reidar said shaking his head. 'The wolves said their elder fought against the spell and pushed the twins out of reach. They suspect, and I agree with them, that the twins are hiding out somewhere in the City.'

'If Arcane is behind this as you suspect, we must ensure he doesn't get hold of these twins. At least, not until we know who and what they are.'

'And what Arcane wants with them' Reidar said.

Thana turned her head quickly towards the door.

'Barumar.' Thana said.

'And Arcane.'

King Barumar opened the door without knocking, it swung back and slammed against the wall. Arcane stood behind him in the doorway.

'Am I interrupting?' Barumar said looking from Thana to Reidar.

'Not at all my King.' Reidar said. 'I was giving my report to the Queen.'

'As your Queen I am perfectly capable of receiving the trivial daily reports.' Thana said. 'Had Reidar something important to say, I would have sent the servants to wake you.'

Barumar looked disarmed and paused; Arcane scowled, his expectations of finding the Queen in a compromising position dashed.

'There is no uprising in the streets and the wolves are keeping to their designated areas.' Thana said. 'Apparently nothing interesting happened last night.'

Thana looked directly at Arcane who stared back defiant and with equal loathing.

The King regained his composure, the momentary confusion in his eyes gone.

'You're right, of course my love.' Barumar said smiling at Thana. 'These are trivial matters. However, in future, I would prefer if Sheriff Reidar did not come to the Palace during the day. I don't want to risk losing such a loyal subject to the sunlight.'

'That will be all Sheriff Reidar.' Thana said.

Reidar nodded to the King and Queen and left the room, the sub-text of the Kings words was not lost on either Reidar or Thana.

'You look unwell.' Barumar said looking Thana up and down.

Thana picked up the goblet of blood and drained the contents in a single swallow.

'I'm fine my King.' Thana replied suddenly feeling energised by the infusion. 'Go back to sleep my love.'

Barumar paused.

'You will not see the Sheriff again, is that understood.'

'As you command, your majesty.' Thana replied.

'His reports can wait. We will talk again later.'

The King turned and left the room, Arcane moved to fall in step behind him.

'Arcane!' Thana called. 'A word, if you please.'

Arcane stopped and exhaled slowly to control his impatience and anger.

'Majesty?' Arcane said.

Thana moved with lightning speed and pushed Arcane against the wall holding him tightly by the throat. Arcane used both hands to pull at her fingers in a theatrical display of weakness and futility refusing to draw on Eversor's strength so as not to expose the presence of the demon to the Queen.

'If you *ever* try and set the King against me again, I'll rip your throat out.' Thana said. 'Do you understand?'

Arcane nodded. Eversor remained silent inside, full of loathing.

'You may have the King's ear, but trust me, I can be much more persuasive than you. It would be easy for me to encourage the King to have you beheaded.'

Thana squeezed Arcane's neck to emphasise her point, then released her grip and threw him along the corridor. There was something in his eyes that unnerved her, a look of hatred and menace.

'Get out of my sight.' Thana said.

Arcane picked himself up and stood defiant, resisting the urge to rub the skin on his bruised neck. Thana looked at Arcane and saw his eyes change to completely black then back to normal. The change was quick, but so was the Queen's perception. Arcane stared back at the queen holding her gaze. Eversor spoke in Arcane's mind.

Why do you play their game? Crush them!

In due time. Arcane replied.

Find the children.

Arcane turned on his heel and strode purposefully along the corridor, promising himself he would find the children before nightfall.

GUARDIANS OF THE CITY

When Tempest arrived at Mike's Cafeteria at seven in the morning to start work the wolves were still gathered around one of the tables talking. Milly and Rufus sat side by side opposite Roman and Jedrek. Matyas had gone to the kitchen to start cooking their breakfast. Mike's Cafeteria and Tempest in particular, had a reputation for cooking the best breakfast in the City and regular customers who worked early shifts had already started to wander into the cafe looking for their eggs and sausages. Tempest also cooked food to attract the tourists and soon the savoury aroma of bacon and freshly baked bread filled the room.

Tempest was a wolf and part of Roman's pack and knew exactly what the two strangers at the table were. In human form she was an attractive woman in her late fifties, five feet nine inches tall, slim, with short blond hair and a disarming smile that reached her light blue eyes. The freshly cooked food was not the only reason a lot of local workmen came to Mike's Cafeteria. Over the years many men had attempted to win her affections but Tempest only had eyes for the strong, stoic Matyas.

'You two on holiday?' Tempest asked Milly and Rufus as she placed a pot of coffee, a plate of warm bread rolls, butter and a selection of preserves on the table.

'My cousins from the country.' Roman said loud enough for the other patrons to hear. 'I'm going to show them the sights after breakfast.'

'Ah, I see.' Tempest said smiling. 'Welcome to Braeden.'

'Thank you.' Milly said.

'Don't forget to take them up around the palace.' Tempest said to Roman.

'I won't.'

'Looking forward to it.' Rufus said.

Some of the locals had cast surreptitious glances at the table, but turned back to their own conversations when there appeared to be nothing interesting going on. Tempest walked over to an occupied table and took their breakfast order.

'She's.....' Milly said.

'One of the family.' Roman replied sitting forward in his seat. 'We need to speak carefully. You never know who's listening. Anyone of the people in here could be spying for the King.'

'There's plenty of regular people in the City willing to do their dirty work during the day.' Jedrek said.

Rufus and Milly nodded.

'Help yourself.' Roman said pushing the plate of bread rolls towards them. Rufus took a bread roll and poured a cup of coffee.

'Interesting situation you've got here in the City.' Rufus said quietly.

'It's not ideal, but it's the best we can do in the circumstances.' Roman replied. 'There's not enough of us to rid the City of its parasite problem.'

'Can the Sheriff be trusted?'

'Can any of them?'

'Some of them.' Milly said helping herself to coffee. 'Gaolyn was a man of his word and I believe the same to be true of Reidar. He's a man of honour, very old and if memory serves, he was almost at the point of regaining his humanity.'

Milly glanced at Rufus.

'What?' Milly asked taking in her brother's strange expression.

'If memory serves?' Rufus said. 'You sound like Gaolyn.'

'Do I?' Milly replied blushing.

'I thought the vampire repentance was a myth.' Jedrek said.

'No, it's real.' Milly said. 'Some vamp…some people like Gaolyn and Reider have lived for so long they're tired and seek to be at peace. The real death can give them that.'

'I can give them real death and peace.' Jedrek said laughing.

Rufus laughed politely; Milly didn't.

'There's good and bad in all of us!' Milly said sharply.

'The best vampires are dead ones.' Jedrek replied.

'Keep your voice down.' Roman said. 'There are other customers here.'

The two wolves glared at each other across the table, Jedrek bared his teeth and Milly extended her claws.

'Stop it! Both of you.' Roman said firmly. 'I won't have our kind fighting each other.'

'She's not one of us.' Jedrek said standing up, the anger evident in his voice.

'Watch yourself.' Rufus said, his hackles rising.

The exchange had drawn attention to the wolves at the table.

'Silence!' Roman hissed. 'Jedrek! Calm yourself.'

Jedrek bowed his head to Roman and marched out of the cafeteria almost bumping into another customer as he came through the door. Roman took a deep breath and tamped down his own anger.

'What's his problem?' Milly asked.

'He hates vampires.' Roman replied. 'His younger sister was killed by vampires about ten years ago.'

'That explains his anger towards me.'

'It's not only that.' Roman continued. 'She was on the cusp of her first change and vulnerable, as most young wolves are. Jedrek blames himself for not protecting her, so he's angry all of the time.'

'Survivor guilt.' Milly said. 'I know something about that.'

'Probably doesn't help that you look a bit like her. I think it's the blue eyes.'

Milly thought about the irony of Roman's last statement.

'Enough about Jedrek.' Roman said to Rufus and Milly. 'You came to me for help. Tell me about the twins and how you came to be here. This time, leave nothing out.'

Milly and Rufus looked at each other and back to Roman.

'Tell me exactly who and what these children are. I need to know so I can try and work out how the….residents in this city will react and what the King wants with them. I can't help you if I don't know the facts.'

'We didn't want to say too much in front of the Sheriff.' Rufus said.

'I understand.' Roman said.

'Just because I know who the Sheriff is, doesn't mean I reveal information freely.' Milly said . 'We need to be cautious.'

'Agreed.' Roman said. 'Do you feel you can trust me?'

Milly and Rufus looked at each other again.

'We do.' Rufus replied.

'The twins belong to our Alpha.' Milly said.

'So they're like *us*.' Roman said, the emphasis on his words clear that he meant wolves.

'Not entirely.' Rufus said. 'Their mother is half Fey.'

'I would have thought such a union impossible, given the strength of our kind.' Roman said.

'She's not half human.' Rufus said.

'She's half angel.' Milly whispered.

Roman paused before speaking.

'The prophecy?' Roman said.

'Possibly.' Rufus said.

Roman sat back in his seat and reached for his coffee.

'I can't believe it!' Roman said. 'Are you sure about the mother's heritage?'

Milly and Rufus both stared at Roman but said nothing.

'Of course you are.' Roman said shaking his head in disbelief. 'Stupid question.'

Roman paused before recalling the words of the prophecy.

'Lycan angel's greatest light.' Roman said.

'You know the prophecy?' Milly asked.

'I know the words.' Roman said. 'But not the whole meaning.'

'How?'

'Finban told us of the prophecy many years ago. He suggested that we may have a part to play in the future.'

'Who's Finban?'

'He's…..how does he put it?' Roman said looking to one side as he tried to recall the details. 'Complicated.'

Rufus and Milly sat forward simultaneously.

'Do you mean Fishbone?' Rufus said. 'Tall guy, a bit scruffy looking who always seems to know everything but tells you nothing?'

'Could be?' Roman asked. 'The name could be lost in translation.'

'Have you seen him recently?'

'Not for many years.'

'Neither have we.' Milly said.

The wolves were silent for a few moments, each lost in their own thoughts. It was Roman who spoke first.

'How old are these children?'

'Thirteen.' Rufus said.

'What are their names?'

'Max and Elena. Why?'

'At that age they wouldn't think to use an alias. If anyone has seen them, they will know them by those names.'

'Max also means greatest.' Roman said. 'And Elena means sun beam.'

'Or light.' Rufus said. 'Yes we know.'

'Do you think the "greatest light" in the prophecy means Max and Elena?' Milly asked.

'I don't know.' Roman said. 'But it's a hell of a coincidence.'

Milly nodded.

'I used to think the words were like an angel, as in angel-like.' Rufus said. 'But now I see it's Lycan as in wolf. Lycan angel's greatest light, could well mean the wolf and the angel's children, Max and Elena.'

Rufus went quiet and contemplated the magnitude of his deduction and the possibilities laying out in front of him.

'Peter must know that's what it means.' Milly said.

'Peter is your Alpha?' Roman asked.

'Yes. Peterus Maximus.'

'Maximus.' Roman said. 'Named after the first alpha.'

'Named after his ancestor.' Milly said.

Roman nodded.

'Your Alpha would definitely know the meaning.' Roman said.

'He'll be on his way here, once he discovers where the twins are.' Rufus said.

'We have to find them.' Milly said earnestly.

'Before the King does.' Jedrek said having suddenly returned to the cafe to stand at Roman's side.

'Or Arcane.' Roman said. 'If he gets hold of them, he'll kill them for sure.'

'This is *your* City.' Rufus said to Roman. 'Where do we start?'

'*We* don't do anything.' Roman replied. 'I'll speak to Lorcan and Karayan. They're the pack's eyes and ears on the streets. Then I'll speak to

Grimlock.'

Roman drained the last of his coffee and stood up.

'I'd like to go with you.' Rufus said standing up.

'No.' Roman said. 'You both need to rest. Jedrek will accompany me.'

'I don't need to rest.'

Roman looked directly at Rufus. 'This is not a request.'

Rufus said nothing. Roman nodded to Tempest who returned to their table.

'Take care of Milly and Rufus.' Roman said as he turned away. 'Make sure they have enough to eat and take them downstairs to our room so they can rest in safety.'

'I'll take care of it.' Tempest replied.

'Get some rest.' Roman ordered. 'I'll be back in a couple of hours.'

Rufus was reluctant but nodded his acquiescence to Roman. He was the Alpha of the Braeden pack and Rufus knew that he and Milly had no choice but to obey.

Milly and Rufus watched Roman and Jedrek leave the cafe. Roman spoke to a few of the customers on his way out. The wolves spoke to each other in their minds.

It's odd taking orders from another Alpha. Milly said.

I know. Rufus replied. *I don't like it.*

At least he's going to help us.

Rufus shrugged.

'Can I get you anything to eat?' Tempest asked.

'No thanks.' Milly replied.

Rufus also shook his head. Both wolves had a typical healthy wolf's appetite but circumstances had robbed them both of their usual enjoyment of a good meal.

'Follow me.' Tempest said. 'I'll show you where you can rest.'

Milly and Rufus followed Tempest through the cafe and out towards the kitchen area. At the back of the kitchen she unlocked a wooden door and indicated for Milly and Rufus walk ahead of her. On closer inspection Rufus could see the door was reinforced with a thick metal panel and the wooden appearance was only a facade.

'Don't touch the metal on the door.' Tempest said stepping through and closing the door behind her. 'It's silver.'

Tempest switched on a light and the three wolves stood together on a small landing at the top of a set of wooden stairs.

'Vampires hate silver as much as we do. This way.'

Tempest led them down a short flight of stairs to the basement. The room opened up much wider than the footprint of the cafeteria above. At the far end of the basement the roots of a tree grew down from the courtyard above, through the basement and deep into the earth below.

'This basement takes in the whole of the courtyard as well as the cafe.' Rufus said picturing the area in his mind.

'It does.' Tempest said. 'The struts used to reinforce the walls and ceiling were taken from ash trees.'

'I can smell lemons.' Milly said.

'Citronella.' Tempest replied.

'Vampires hate it.' Tempest and Milly said simultaneously.

'We find that most of the things that repel mosquitoes, repel vampires too.' Tempest laughed.

'Those roots are from the tree in the courtyard.' Rufus said.

'It's a rowan tree.' Milly said.

'That's right.' Tempest said. 'You already know about the things in nature that protect against vampires. Are you an elder in your pack?'

'No, but I'm learning.' Milly said.

Milly paused and looked at the tree's roots, Gaolyn's knowledge came to mind.

'I know quite a bit about the things that repel vampires.' Milly said. 'The rowan tree was held in high esteem in this part of the world for its power against evil, including vampires, witches and other supernatural creatures.'

'That's right.' Tempest said. 'What else do you know?'

'What I've read over the years in folklore and what our pack Elder has told me.' Milly replied.

Milly looked past Tempest to the rowan tree.

'According to mythology.' Milly continued. 'There was a goddess of youth, who dispensed rejuvenating ambrosia to the gods from her magical chalice, but she was careless and lost the cup to demons, the other gods sent an eagle to recover the cup. The feathers and drops of blood which the eagle shed in the ensuing fight with the demons fell to the earth, where each of them turned into a rowan tree. Hence the rowan derived the shape of its leaves from the eagle's feathers and the appearance of its berries from the droplets of blood.'

Tempest looked at Milly and frowned.

'Did you swallow that text book?' Rufus said staring at Milly, his wide eyes conveying a warning.

'At least that's what I remember.' Milly said hurriedly, suddenly aware of her Gaolyn-style speech.

Old head on young shoulders. Tempest thought. *Who is she?*

Tempest moved closer to the tree and gently placed her hand on one of the large roots.

'If you listen carefully.' Tempest said. 'You can hear what's going on above. Try it.'

There was a challenge in Tempest's tone and Milly accepted. She stepped forward without hesitation and placed both hands on the roots of the tree. Milly felt no repulsion from the tree other than a tingling on her skin as she made contact with the wood. After a few seconds, she stepped back.

'That's incredible.' Milly said. 'You can feel the vibrations. It's like you can hear what the tree is hearing.'

'That's why we use this room for pack meetings.' Tempest said. 'And storage of course.'

'If the vampires attacked there's only one way in and out.' Rufus said looking around the room.

'Look behind the roots.' Tempest said. 'Under your feet.'

Rufus looked down and saw a well disguised trap door set flush with the floor with small hinges on one side and no handle. He knew it was the entrance to the drains that ran beneath the City and assumed that in an emergency the strength of wolf claws could easily lever the door open.

'It's made from ash wood.' Tempest said.

'And reinforced with silver?' Rufus said.

'Yes.'

'Where does it go, into the sewers?'

'Yes, but it's like a labyrinth.' Tempest said. 'You could be lost for days down there, if you don't know your way around.'

'Thank the Divine for citronella.' Rufus said. 'I can smell the sewer from here!'

'You should get some rest.' Tempest said. 'There are a couple of old chairs down here you can sleep on, Roman won't be back for a few hours. If you need anything just ask, I'll be listening and I'll hear you.'

Tempest walked back towards the stairs.

'Are we prisoners?' Milly asked.

'No, but you're strangers and we have to be careful. If Roman said he'll help you, he will, but you have to do as he says and he's told you to wait. Waiting down here is the safest place for you right now. I'll come back with some food and water, you really *should* eat. You'll need your strength.'

Without another word Tempest climbed the stairs and left the basement locking the door behind her.

Rufus sat on the floor, he had always been able to sleep anywhere and did not seek the creature comforts humans looked for like a chair or a bed.

'Ask me.' Milly said as she moved an old packing crate to reveal an old chair.

'Ask you what?' Rufus replied.

'The question that's been on your mind since we got here.'

Rufus said nothing; he watched Milly clear the remaining items off the chair and sit down. She sat with her legs crossed, her hands in her lap.

'I don't know what you're talking about.'

Rufus looked away, refusing to make eye contact and picked at a piece of sacking on the floor next to him.

'OK.' Milly said. 'I'll ask the question for you. Am I still me, or am I Gaolyn Lancing?'

Rufus looked at his sister. She hadn't really changed but he found her blue eyes disconcerting, they were Gaolyn's eyes.

'I'm still *me*.' Milly said with emphasis. 'But I'm *him* as well. I have his memories, knowledge and some skills, but I'm still your sister, your twin.'

'I know.' Rufus said. 'I see you, but sometimes it's like I don't recognise you.'

Milly sat upright, waiting for Rufus to speak, but Rufus had known her long enough to see that she was upset and fighting to keep her composure.

'I'm not trying to be mean here.' Rufus said gently. 'When you recognised the Sheriff, that was…'

'I understand.' Milly said. 'And I can't explain it either.'

'Your syntax is different, but not all the time. It comes and goes. It's weird hearing you speak, you sound just like him.'

'It sounds strange to me too.' Milly paused. 'I don't think about it, the thoughts and the words just flow and I hear myself sounding like Gaolyn.'

'Very proper.' Rufus said with a smile.

'Indeed.' Milly replied.

They both laughed.

'What does it feel like?' Rufus asked.

'Touching the rowan tree?' Milly smiled, teasing her brother was part of their relationship.

'No! Being part wolf and part vampire?'

'It was *really* hard at first.' Milly said looking down at her hands. 'I didn't want to hunt, or change into a wolf, or eat. I was worried that I was more vampire than wolf.'

Rufus sat quietly and watched Milly as she tried to articulate how she felt.

'I felt guilty at first.' Milly said finally.

'Why?'

'Because I survived, I should have died from my injuries.'

'But you didn't.' Rufus said. 'I never really warmed to Gaolyn, but I'm eternally grateful that he saved your life. Although, I'm not saying I'm glad he's dead.'

'I know. It's hard to get my head around it. It felt wrong that I should be here and he's not.'

'He loved you.' Rufus said, his tone implying that Gaolyn's feelings for Milly explained everything.

'And I loved him.' Milly said smiling. 'Even though it's wrong for our kind to love a vampire.'

'All things considered.' Rufus said. 'I think when it comes to matters of love, the lines of right and wrong are often blurred.'

'That's very philosophical.'

Rufus raised one eyebrow and grinned.

'Speaking of love.' Milly said.

'Were we?'

'Idiot! What happened with you and Molly?'

Rufus paused and looked away.

'Didn't work out.' Rufus said finally.

'Evidently. Why not?'

Rufus paused again for a moment, his thoughts momentarily lost in his past until finally he turned back to Milly and spoke.

'As much as she said she loved me, I never felt I could tell her who I really was.'

'Maybe you need someone a bit different.' Milly said. 'Someone who would understand.'

'You mean another supernatural?'

Milly nodded.

The click of the lock on the basement door brought Rufus and Milly to their feet.

'Probably Tempest returning with food.' Rufus said.

'Do you *always* think about food?' Milly asked.

'Not always but often.'

The door opened and a beautiful young woman walked through the door carrying a tray of food. She was a wolf and a member of Roman's pack. Rufus stared at her as she walked down the stairs. The woman appeared to be the same age as Milly and Rufus, she was slim, average height, with dark skin, brown shoulder length hair and green eyes.

'Hello.' she said. 'I've brought you something to eat. You must be hungry. We're *always* hungry right?'

'Starving!' Rufus said.

'You speak the common tongue very well.' Milly said.

'I've travelled.'

'Before the pulse?' Rufus asked.

'And since.' the woman said smiling at Rufus.

'Let me help you with that.' Rufus said taking the tray. 'I'm Rufus. This is Milly.'

'I know. Tempest told me.'

'Right.'

Milly watched her brother and intuitively knew what was happening between the two wolves. Not only because they were twins, but with the knowledge and insight of someone who had lived almost a millennia and seen nearly everything, Rufus was smitten.

'My name is Willenetta.' the young wolf said. 'But everyone calls me Witty.'

'Witty.' Rufus beamed.

RATMAN

Yosef had led them to a sub-level below the City where the tunnels were dry. He had told Max and Elena that it was safer for him to live in the sewer system than out on the Streets. Above ground he said he would be easy prey to those he referred to as "the cold ones". The tunnels stretched for several miles beneath the whole city, some serving as foul drainage, others as storm drains and some, where Yosef lived, were access tunnels for maintenance, always dry and relatively warm compared to the open streets above.

As they walked Max and Elena asked Yosef many questions about where they were going and the mysterious Ratman.

'Where are you taking us?' Max asked.

'To Ratman.' Yosef replied.

'Who is Ratman?'

'A friend.'

'Does he live in the sewers?'

'He lives wherever he wants to.' Yosef said. 'Wherever he's needed. At least that's what he says.'

Max glanced at Elena, his line of questioning was getting them nowhere.

'How can we be sure Ratman won't hand us over to the vampires?' Elena asked.

Yosef stopped in his tracks and looked at Elena and Max, his face serious and his tone of voice full of indignation.

'Ratman sent me to help you.' Yosef said. 'Why would he do that? He could have left you to be captured.'

Elena looked at Max abashed but said nothing.

'Ratman knew you were coming.' Yosef said. 'He knows things. I don't know how, but he does. Trust me, he's not evil.'

Yosef continued to lead the way and Max and Elena followed in silence. Before long they were sitting together on one side of an old metal dustbin that served as a brazier in one of the dry tunnels. The sconces burning in the passageway provided light and the fire in the brazier supplied a small amount of heat. The stone floor had been cleared of rubbish, some of which was piled in a corner and the twins balanced on either end of an old, dented metal box, once used for tools, long since scavenged.

As soon as they had reached their destination and before introductions were made, Ratman had put his hand on Yosef's shoulder and whispered something to him. Yosef nodded.

'Stay here. I'll be right back.' Yosef said.

'Where are you going?' Max asked.

'We need more wood for the fire.'

'We'll come with you.' Max said standing.

'Stay.' Yosef said. 'You're safe here.'

Yosef quickly disappeared down one of the tunnels leaving Max and Elena alone with Ratman. Max could see that the small fire in the brazier was insufficient and more fuel was needed. So far Ratman had not spoken to them and Max wondered why this mysterious man had sent Yosef to save them if he had no intention speaking. Ratman sat opposite the twins whittling a small log with an exceptionally long fingernail.

As Max looked into the flames, he thought about how close he and Elena had come to being caught by the vampires and was grateful they had met Yosef who had led them to safety through the labyrinth of the storm drains. Ratman had said nothing to the twins since their arrival and Max decided to try and break the awkward silence.

'What are you making?' Max said.

'Making up my mind.' Ratman said looking up from his work.

'About what?'

'Not what.'

'Who?' Max asked.

'*Whom.*'

'Pardon?'

'It's *whom* not *who.*'

'To *whom* are you referring?' Elena asked trying to hide the irritation in her voice.

'You.'

'What about me?' Elena said.

'Exactly.' Ratman said returning his attention to the log he was whittling.

Max put his hand on Elena's arm as she was about to speak and shook his head.

'Leave it.' Max said.

Elena sighed impatiently and nodded. Max looked around and wondered if he would be able to find his way out of the sewers without Yosef's help and concluded that he probably couldn't even with his heightened wolf senses. A distant squeak and scrape caught his attention and he turned his head towards the sound.

'Fish oil.' Ratman said.

'Excuse me?' Max asked.

'Fish oil.' Ratman said again. 'For the wheels on the sack truck.'

'Right.'

'Listen.' Ratman said. 'You can see without eyes, if you listen.'

Elena looked at Max who shrugged, but as he concentrated on the sound he discovered he could visualise the sack truck, its hard wheels crunching and crushing small stones as it wheeled its way towards them.

'What do you see?' Ratman whispered.

'A heavy load.' Max replied. 'Unbalanced.'

'What else?'

'Nothing.'

'You have six senses. Sight is only one.' Ratman said sharply. 'Tell me what you see.'

Max inhaled and concentrated on his sense of smell.

'Wood, burning in the brazier.'

'Rubbish!' Ratman said. 'A human baby could smell burning wood. What else?'

Max stood up and thought about his other senses.

Sight: he couldn't see around corners or through walls.

Hearing: he could hear the grinding wheels of an unbalanced sack truck and assumed it was Yosef returning with more logs for the fire.

Taste: Max stuck out his tongue to taste the air and detected salt, ash and dust.

Smell: The tang of sweat and adrenaline filled his nostrils.

Instinct: the natural and intuitive way of thinking.

'The river.' Max said. 'I can smell the river, even from down here, and....Yosef...he's being followed....and it's not friendly.'

The activation of all his senses was overwhelming and Max put his hand on the tunnel wall to steady himself.

Touch: the vibrations in the stone wall completed the picture and in his head.

Max saw Yosef moving as quickly as he could along the tunnel, the sack truck loaded and unbalanced with wood, blankets and food. Yosef was limping, he must have stumbled on uneven ground, sweat beaded on his brow from fear and exertion. Two vampires pursuing him from a calculated distance, the same two that looked over the Bridge when he and Elena first arrived, both waiting to strike.

Yosef hurried into the light, his own instincts quickening his pace. He was breathless from running, his eyes wild. He tried to speak but his throat constricted in fear.

The two vampires burst into the tunnel, sharp fangs exposed, hungry for blood.

Elena screamed.

Max saw, heard and sensed Ratman move and turned to face him.

'Catch!' Ratman said tossing the whittled object into the air.

Max leapt up and caught the wooden stake in his right hand as one of the vampires lunged towards him. Using his downward momentum, Max stabbed the vampire through the heart stopping him dead.

Ratman threw a second stake straight into the heart of the other vampire impaling him against the tunnel wall.

Both vampires turned to ash and exploded into a cloud of dust in the air.

'You knew!' Max said rounding on Ratman. 'You knew all along! Why else would you whittle stakes?'

Max could feel his heart beating in his chest as if it wanted to break free from his rib cage. He looked around, every colour was suddenly brighter, every sound louder. He felt as if his blood was on fire as the adrenaline coursed through his veins.

'Breathe Max.' Ratman said. 'Concentrate on your breathing.'

'What's happening?' Max gasped as pain flared in his body.

'The change.' Ratman said. 'Killing the vampire has triggered the change. There's no stopping it now.'

'Max!' Elena shrieked.

Terrified for her brother, Elena ran towards him. Ratman threw off his long coat and moved quickly to intercept her. He wrapped his big arms around Elena and held her tightly.

'Stay back!'

'It's killing him!' Elena screamed.

'No. It's who he is.'

Max's cried out in pain and fear and stared at Ratman.

'Don't fight it.' Ratman said taking a few steps backwards and pulling Elena with him. 'Let the pain wash over you. Go with it.'

Max fell to the ground on all fours as a fresh wave of pain ripped through him, the sound of bones snapping and reshaping filled the air. He looked down, his fingernails grew into sharp claws, the skin peeled back on his fingers and toes as his hands and feet transformed into paws. Silver-grey fur sprouted all over his body, his mouth extended into a snout and his teeth grew into sharp pointed fangs.

The change took less than a minute but to Max if felt like an eternity of pain. When the transformation was complete, Max stood before Ratman and Elena in full wolf form. His wolf instincts took over, he lifted his head and howled, the sounded echoing through the underground tunnels.

Yosef, who had been stood to one side of the tunnel paralysed by fear, took one look at the huge grey wolf and fainted.

Ratman smiled and released Elena who ran towards her brother.

'Max.' Elena said holding out her hand tentatively towards her brother.

The silver-grey wolf sniffed her hand and Elena knelt in front of him looking into his eyes. Max tilted his head to one side and looked back at his twin. In the commotion of the vampire attack and Max's ensuing transformation, Elena has undergone a change of her own. Her eyes had changed from blue to an animalistic yellow. Her face retained its shape but her teeth had extended into sharp fangs and the fingernails had extended on her hand into long, razor sharp talons.

'I know you can understand me.' Ratman said to Max. 'Focus on your breathing.'

Ratman looked at the twins, his gaze lingered on Elena.

'When you're both calm, you'll be able to change back.'

Max shook his furry head, turned in a circle and sat down. Elena sat beside him, her arm over his back.

'Breathe deeply.' Ratman said. 'Both of you.'

Ratman looked at Yosef's prone body and shrugged. Having decided to leave the boy where he was, Ratman returned to where he had been sitting and produced a third stake, longer than the other two, opened a paper packet beside him and produced four small fish. He pushed the sharp end of the stake through each fish and set it atop the brazier.

'When Yosef wakes up we'll all have something to eat.'

The aroma of fish cooking on the brazier roused Yosef from his sleep and he remained perfectly still savouring the enticing fragrance of grilled fish.

'Don't pretend to be asleep!' Ratman said. 'Sit up and join us.'

Yosef sat up slowly, his eyes searching his surroundings. Ratman was sitting back in the shadows as usual, but the large silver wolf was still there, the girl Elena looked different from when he had first met her, she had larger teeth, and claws instead of fingernails and her eyes had turned yellow. The memory of the events leading up to his fainting flooded back and he inhaled sharply. Yosef scuttled backwards on his bottom trying to get as far away as possible from the wolf and the girl.

'Yosef!' Ratman said. 'You're safe. Trust me. Look at me.'

Yosef looked at Ratman and back to the wolf and finally back to Ratman again who smiled and held out his hand.

'Come and sit beside me.' Ratman said, his voice gentle. 'There's no need to be afraid. You know there are men and women in the City who can change into wolves and back again?'

Yosef nodded.

'Max is one of them.'

Yosef felt Ratman's words calming him, more in the way they were said than the actual words. It was as if Ratman had wrapped Yosef in a blanket of concern and Yosef moved towards Ratman and sat beside him with complete trust. Ratman put his hand on Yosef's head and muttered something only the boy could hear.

'What does that mean?' Yosef asked looking up at Ratman and frowning.

Ratman patted Yosef on the head and smiled, but said nothing.

'Will he change back into a boy?' Yosef said finally looking at Max and pushing himself closer to Ratman.

'He will once he's calmed down.' Ratman said putting his arm around Yosef's shoulders.

'What happened to Elena's face?'

'She's like Max with the wolf thing, but…um…not so much.' Ratman said.

'I can speak for myself.' Elena said. 'Yosef, it's still me.'

Yosef glanced at Elena who smiled, but her new fangs made her look more ferocious. Yosef gulped and Elena turned her face away at his reaction, her eyes filling with tears. Elena's earlier fear and anger was replaced with remorse at scaring her new friend and her body responded accordingly. The claws changed back into fingernails, her teeth shrunk back to normal size and her yellow eyes reverted to their usual blue. Elena felt the changes and turned her face back towards Yosef and smiled again. This time he responded with one of his own.

'Your body reacted to your emotions.' Ratman said in explanation. 'Usually a wolf learns to anticipate the feelings and master the change, but circumstances forced Max's first change to a wolf and as his twin, you reacted in sympathy.'

Elena was about to ask how Ratman knew they were twins, but concern for her brother was a more pressing question. The fact that Ratman knew their names without introductions did not cross her mind at that point.

'Will he be able to change back?' Elena asked stroking her brother's furry head.

'He will.' Ratman replied. 'The smell of food should help.'

Max sniffed the air, turned his snout in the direction of the fish cooking in the brazier and licked his lips. Yosef edged closer to Ratman who patted his shoulder gently.

Max stood up and turned in a circle, Elena backed off to give him more room, she could sense that he was about to transform. The sound of snapping and cracking bones filled the air and Max's bones moved beneath his wolf skin and fur, contorting his body as they re-shaped. The silver fur receded into his skin and disappeared, his paws once again resembled hands and feet. His face, the first and last thing to change, reverted to human form and Max stood up, once again a young man. His clothes had been shredded during his transformation to wolf form and forgotten, consequently he was completely naked. Ratman handed Max his own long coat which he had cast to one side earlier and Max quickly covered himself.

'You also must be hungry.' Ratman said.

'Starving!' Max replied self-consciously. 'But I have questions.'

'I'm sure you do.' Ratman replied. 'Eat first. Then we talk.'

*****

Above the sewers on the streets, Roman and Jedrek walked side by side in the general direction of the library.

Jedrek stopped suddenly as his acute hearing heard the howl.

'Was that an Alpha's call?' Jedrek said turning to Roman.

'I don't know.' Roman replied a chill running down his spine.

*****

Grimlock paused, his hand hovering over the old document he was copying. He tilted his head to one side listening, but the howl did not repeat.

An Alpha? Grimlock thought to himself.

Yendor his long suffering human assistant interrupted his thoughts by dropping a large tome on the end of his desk. The book slammed down disturbing Grimlock's other papers; Grimlock growled.

'This is the only one I can find.' Yendor said sheepishly.

Grimlock had a vicious temper and Yendor was often on the receiving end of it, frequently receiving a cuff around the ear for not moving, or imparting information quickly enough.

'Where was it?' Grimlock asked, glowering at Yendor.

'In the folklore section.'

'Leave it with me.' Grimlock said.

Yendor nodded and turned to leave.

'Yendor.' Grimlock said. 'Did you hear anything just now?'

'No Sir.' Yendor said shaking his head. 'Only the ticking of the clock.'

'Right. Yes.' Grimlock said. 'That'll be all Yendor. Thank you. I'll look through this book, if it doesn't have what I'm searching for, I'll return it myself.'

*****

King Barumar's eyes snapped open.

It was dark inside his coffin and he had only just settled down to sleep. He was troubled by thoughts of Reidar and Thana and wondered if they were plotting against him. Arcane had alerted him to the Sheriff's presence in the palace but he doubted his advisor's loyalty as much as anyone else's around him. The King was seeing conspirators in every corner and now the sound of an Alpha wolf's howl had woken him, or was it part of a nightmare, an echo from a different time in his life, decades earlier?

Barumar listened in the darkness; nothing.

With no heartbeat and no breath, the silence was deafening, Barumar liked that. Satisfied that the howl had been nothing more than part of a vivid dream the Vampire King closed his eyes and settled once again to sleep.

*****

In the basement below Mike's Cafeteria, Witty paused mid-sentence. Rufus and Milly looked at each other. All three had heard the howl.

Witty made a hurried excuse to leave as if she suddenly remembered something important.

Rufus turned to Milly.

'That was Max.' Rufus said. 'He's undergone his first change. We have to find him.'

'Agreed. We have to get out of here.'

Milly looked at her brother. 'We need a plan.'

Rufus glanced at the floor towards the trapdoor and back to Milly.

*****

Peter and Shayla had been on the road heading east for a couple of hours. Peter was driving and Shayla had fallen asleep in the seat beside him. Exhaustion had taken over and Peter could hear her even breathing as she sat with her head leaning against the window. Titan had been sleeping since they left home.

The roads were fairly quiet and Peter kept the car at a steady speed. The last thing they needed was to be stopped by the Police for speeding. Every second was precious and every minute was a minute too long away from his children.

Sharp pain ripped through his whole body and Peter tightened his grip on the steering wheel. He felt on a molecular level that his son was in pain and although he could not hear him, when Max howled in the sewers of Braeden, Peter felt it and knew subconsciously that Max had undergone the transformation. Another wave of pain lanced through him, his own body responding to Max's howl by commencing his own transformation. Peter glanced in the rear view mirror, Titan was awake, fully alert and staring back at him.

He felt it too. Peter thought.

'Max!' Shayla gasped, startled from sleep.

'I know.' Peter replied.

'Are you alright?' Shayla asked, frowning at Peter.

'No! I need to pull over. Fast!'

Shayla understood what was happening to Peter and scanned both sides of the road as it rolled out before them.

'Over there!' Shayla said. 'There's a lay-by, pull over!'

Peter pulled the car off the road and switched off the engine. He sat holding the steering wheel, his knuckles white, his breathing ragged.

'Can you stop the change?' Shayla asked.

Peter made no reply, he stared straight ahead, his hands clenched, the force threatening to crush the steering wheel. Shayla put her hand on Peter's arm and squeezed gently, trying to bring his focus back to her.

The touch of Shayla's hand on his arm brought Peter's attention back to his surroundings and he felt the change receding like an ebb tide. The initial pain that washed over him subsided and he finally released his hold on the steering wheel and flexed his hands before placing one hand over Shayla's.

'Max has undergone his first change.' Peter said, sadness creeping into his voice. 'Did you feel it too?'

'Is that what I felt?' Shayla asked. 'I was aware of Max and Elena, but Max was in pain. I heard him cry out, that's what woke me, but I couldn't possibly have heard him.'

You heard him howl. Titan said. *An Alpha's howl on a Divine frequency.*

'What's he saying?' Peter asked looking at Titan in the rear view mirror.

'He said that I heard Max howl on a divine frequency.'

'You're his mother and half angel.' Peter said. 'It makes sense that you would feel something, they're part angel, like you.'

'How do *you* feel?' Shayla asked.

Peter looked away, his emotions shifting from pride, to guilt and then sadness.

'Proud. Guilty for not being with him. Sad.'

Shayla squeezed Peter's arm again and he looked up at her and smiled. He leaned forward and kissed her.

'I'm fine.' Peter said turning back in the driving seat. 'I'll be fine. We should get going.'

Shayla nodded. Peter started the engine and pulled out onto the motorway to resume their journey.

'I bet he's magnificent.' Peter said.

'He is.' Shayla replied. 'Just like his father.'

Peter smiled and pressed his foot harder on the accelerator.

DAY TO DAY

With Witty's quick exit from the basement at hearing the sound of the Alpha's howl, Rufus and Milly wasted no time.

Transforming their fingernails into claws they levered the heavy trapdoor enough to put their fingers beneath it. Gritting their teeth against the burn of the silver they heaved the trap door and pushed it to one side. There were no hinges on the ash wood door, instead it sat on a solid silver lip just inside the edge which allowed it to sit flush to the basement floor.

'Is there a ladder to climb down?' Milly asked as Rufus peered into the darkness of the tunnel.

'No. I'll jump down and take a look.'

'You don't know…'

Rufus jumped down into the tunnel.

'…how far down it is!' Milly said rolling her eyes.

'About seven feet.' Rufus called up from the darkness. 'Just above head height.'

'For you maybe!' Milly said looking down at Rufus who was looking back up at her.

'Pull the door near to the edge and come down.' Rufus said. 'I'll reach up and drag is back into place.'

Rufus stepped further into the tunnel out of the way to allow Milly to jump down. The tunnel was narrow and the wolves changed positions to allow Rufus to move back to the tunnel entrance and pull the trap door back into place. The light died as if it had been swallowed and the tunnel smelled of the earth.

'There's plenty of silver in that thing to bite at your hands!' Rufus said.

'Suppose it wouldn't be much of a deterrent if there wasn't.' Milly said. 'I can't see a thing!'

Normally dark spaces were no problem for werewolves with their keen eyesight, but the trap door had sealed off the light from the basement leaving the tunnel completely black. Milly closed her eyes in the darkness to heighten her other senses. She could feel the heat radiating off Rufus as he stood next to her and detected a faint scent of the river.

'I guess we follow our noses.' Milly said.

'Follow me.' Rufus replied. 'I can see.'

'How?'

'I can see into the Afterglow with one eye, I *told* you that last night.'

'Right.' Milly said processing the information. 'Is it like trying to watch two different TV shows at the same time?'

'No.' Rufus laughed. 'Do you remember those early three dimensional movies and everyone had to wear cardboard glasses to watch them, one red lens, the other green?'

'Yes.'

'The brain compensates for the differing images and you see one big picture, same sort of principle.'

'Wow.'

'Yeah, I know.' Rufus said. 'The walls are shored up with timber.'

'Ash wood, I'd guess, like the trap door.' Milly said.

'The floor looks pretty even and well-trod. There shouldn't be any tree roots to fall over.'

'We should get moving.'

'We'll follow the tunnel away from here.' Rufus said. 'It obviously comes out somewhere.'

Rufus took the lead and the wolves moved at a brisk pace along the tunnel in single file.

'We're heading downwards.' Milly said. 'I can feel it.'

'It was probably dug that way to stop it from flooding.' Rufus replied. 'I think this tunnel links to the sewers, at least that's what my nose is telling me. Come on.'

The wolves quickened their pace and ran along the dark tunnel for about a mile.

'Is there light up ahead?' Milly asked. 'The darkness doesn't seem quite so complete to me?'

'Yes. It must be where the tunnel meets the sewer.'

The dim light from the sewer grew brighter turning the blackness in the tunnel to a dark grey. The definition of the timber on the walls began to take shape and Rufus no longer needed to look into the Afterglow to see where they were going. The tunnel dipped once more and widened enough for the wolves to walk side by side.

'Careful!' Rufus said putting his arm across Milly to stop her.

The floor had been cut down and four stone steps led them to a round opening approximately five feet in diameter, barred by a portcullis. The gate consisted of a latticed grill made of wood and metal with spikes at the bottom that slid down into grooves in the floor.

'More ash wood and silver.' Rufus said.

'And I'm guessing the spikes are solid silver.' Milly said. 'Can you see a mechanism to open it?'

Rufus looked around the opening and felt the walls for any hint of a lever.

'Nothing. I'm going to try and lift it.'

'Together.' Milly said squeezing in next to her brother and putting her hands on the grill.

Milly hissed as the silver burned the palms of her hands.

'There's not enough room for both of us.' Rufus said. 'Let me try it by myself.'

Rufus bent his knees and put all weight into lifting the gate. He grunted and sweat beaded on his brow but the gate remained solid. He tried again drawing on his werewolf strength but the gate was immobile. He stood up and rubbed his burnt palms on his jeans.

Milly thought about using the vampire ability to turn into mist and move through the gate but that would leave her brother stranded on the other side. Equally, Milly wasn't sure what affect the silver bars would have on her in that form. The gate was designed to be vampire-proof and she imagined the builders had taken all vampire abilities into consideration. There had to be a way to open the gate.

'It's an escape route.' Milly said. 'So it must lift up somehow. There's got to be a hidden lock.'

'Somewhere difficult to reach perhaps?' Rufus said looking up at the ceiling that was now more than four feet above his head. 'Up there. I can see a recess, there has to be a lever inside.'

'Give me a leg-up.' Milly said. 'I'll be able to reach it.'

'This escape was designed by werewolves to be vampire proof it's not going to be that easy.'

'Good point.' Milly said.

'It'll take strength to open it.' Rufus said. 'I'm going to have to be in warrior form to reach it.'

'Do it.'

Rufus concentrated and began the transformation from human to warrior form. The familiar sound of bones snapping as his body grew and reshaped itself and his cries of pain at the process, filled the tunnel and in less than two minutes Rufus stood at nearly nine feet tall, in full warrior form, the pain of the transformation manifesting as rage. He looked at Milly, she was part vampire and Rufus detected her scent. He snarled, saliva dripping from his teeth.

'Rufus! The lock!' Milly commanded. 'Find the lock!'

Rufus controlled his primal instinct to fight the vampire, he recognised his sister and did as commanded. He looked up at the ceiling and saw a lever deeply recessed above his head. He reached up and pulled, the lever resisted and Rufus growled deeply, the anger fuelling his strength. The lever yielded springing the lock. Rufus stepped forward and put one of his huge hands on the grill, lifting the gate up to chest height allowing Milly to stoop beneath it and step out into the sewer. Milly stood the other side of the gate and held it with both hands straining against the weight while Rufus dropped to all fours and crawled out of the tunnel. Milly released the portcullis as soon as Rufus was clear and it dropped back into the grooves with an echoing clang. Rufus transformed back into human form and remained on all fours breathing hard.

'Are you ok?' Milly said putting her hand on Rufus's shoulder.

'Yep. I heard the lock click back into place as the gate slammed to the ground.' Rufus said between breaths. 'Good design.'

Rufus stood up, ran his fingers through his hair and wiped the sweat off his brow with the back of his hand. Although his clothes were still intact thanks to the crystal charm that he and all fully fledged wolves wore to retain their clothing during their change, they were rumpled and dirty and Rufus smoothed them down as best he could.

'Let's move.' Rufus said.

'Which way?' Milly said.

'I believe this is an escape route that heads north towards the forest. I can smell it faintly over the stench of this place, it makes sense that it would take you right outside the boundaries of the City and into the safety of the forest.'

'I smell it too.' Milly said. 'We need to get above ground. The sewers must branch off and come up at various points in the Town.'

'We should follow the smell of the food.' Rufus said. 'We can get lost among the crowds.'

'Agreed.'

The wolves ran along the sewer tunnel heading north until it split into two where they took the east passage away from the scent of the forest and back towards the centre of town.

The passage began to narrow and Milly and Rufus knew they were heading towards another dead end, although this tunnel had no portcullis barring the way. The darkness gathered around them and Rufus took the lead, looking into the Afterglow for a clearer view of his surroundings. He led his sister along the tunnel eventually stopping beneath another ash wood and silver trapdoor.

'Wherever this comes up, it's not as secure at the cafe.' Milly said.

'It's closer to the centre.' Rufus replied. 'I can hear voices.'

'Not directly above us.' Milly said.

'Probably outside the building. Let's go.'

Rufus put both hands on the underside of the trap door and pushed, the silver burning his hands as he manoeuvred it to one side of the opening. Weak daylight and the smell of petrol and engine oil filtered down into the tunnel.

'Give me a boost up.' Milly said.

Rufus cupped his hands around Milly's foot and lifted her up until she was head and shoulders into the basement above.

'It's a garage.' Milly said placing her hands either side of the opening and pulling herself the remainder of the way in. She stood to one side to allow Rufus access to the garage.

'Who's gonna give me a leg up?'

'Idiot.'

Rufus jumped out of the tunnel and put the trap door back in place. He looked around and stared at the gleaming white paintwork of a classic car.

'Whoa! Nice car.' Rufus said.

'It's beautiful.'

'It's a vintage Silver Cloud drop-head coupe.'

'Really.' Milly said without interest.

'Nineteen sixty I'd say.'

Rufus stepped closer to the car.

'Do you know this engine is a hundred and fifty-five horse power, six cylinder unit with inlet over exhaust valves, twin carburettors, four speed transmission with a top speed of a hundred and two point nine miles per hour. Nought to sixty in thirteen point five seconds. She's absolutely stunning.'

Rufus gently ran his hand along the body of the car.

'Do you two need a moment?' Milly said.

'Now who's the idiot?' Rufus said smiling at his sister.

Rufus looked around the garage, it was pristine with every tool in place on a rack fixed to the wall.

'The owner loves this car, it looks like it just rolled off the production line.'

'It belongs to Roman.' Milly said.

'I know.' Rufus replied. 'I detected his scent when we first came up.'

'Let's get out of here before he comes to check on his car and finds us!'

'Bye gorgeous.' Rufus said running his hand along the car one more time.

Rufus grinned at Milly who rolled her eyes again at her brother.

Access in and out of the garage was either via a sturdy roll up shutter, wide enough for a car or a small door set to one side. Milly turned the handle; it was locked, as expected. She looked at Rufus and shook her head.

'Let me take a look.' Rufus said. 'I could pick it, if I had a paperclip.'

Milly looked at her brother and raised her eyebrows. Rufus shrugged but said nothing. He turned the door handle slowly and firmly past the point of resistance and broke the lock leaving the handle loose. The garage opened into a quiet side street and Rufus opened the door carefully and peered out.

'We're good.' Rufus said stepping out. 'I don't think this street gets much passing foot traffic.'

Milly followed her brother and pulled the door closed behind her.

'The main square is that way.' Rufus said pointing to the end of the street. 'I can hear people and smell food.'

'I can hear them.' Milly said. 'Probably a market.'

The wolves headed towards the noise of the people and the aroma of cooked food. They paused at the end of the street to survey the scene. The outside of the square was crowded with market stalls, some selling packets of dried fruit and nuts, while others had meat roasting on skewers. Visitors to the City strolled casually browsing while locals hustled and bustled, and haggled over the price of the vegetables and other merchandise.

Milly and Rufus headed towards the throng and tried futilely not to bump into people. Their keen sense of smell caught the metallic scent of freshly slaughtered meat hanging from hooks and their stomachs rumbled in response. The smell of freshly baked bread and other baked goods wafted towards them as they walked and even the rancid smell of body odour did nothing to stop them salivating.

Rufus stepped away from the stalls towards the centre of the square away from the crush of people. Milly stood next to him.

Rufus watched an old lady with a walking stick as she walked from east to west away from the market stalls, her shopping bag heavy and bulging with vegetables. He looked the other way and saw a young man moving west to east, his path taking him on a direct intercept route towards the old lady. His hat was pulled down over his ears, his scarf covering his mouth and the collar of his coat turned up hiding his face, Rufus knew instinctively from the man's quick, agitated movements that he intended to rob her.

'What now?' Milly asked but Rufus's attention was elsewhere and she followed his gaze.

The young man quickened his pace and ran straight into the old lady, wrenched the bag from her hand, knocking her to the ground and ran towards Rufus. The old lady shouted and passers-by rushed to her aid helping her to her feet. Two men began pursuing the robber, but the young man was quick and would disappear into a side street before they could catch up with him, unless someone slowed him down.

'Don't get involved.' Milly warned.

Rufus took a step to the side as the young man drew level and bumped shoulders with him. The impact knocked the robber to the ground, the shopping bag spilled its contents sending carrots and onions rolling. Rufus grabbed the collar of the man's coat to detain him giving his pursuers the extra few seconds they needed to catch up. The two men nodded to Rufus and hauled the young man to his feet. Two local Policeman who must have been patrolling the market square approached Rufus and Milly.

'That's all we need.' Milly said through gritted teeth.

Before the Police could ask any awkward questions the old lady, who seemed fully recovered, pushed past them and stood in front of Rufus. She was old but clearly fighting it every step of the way, at five feet tall she was much shorter than Milly and she looked up at Rufus with clear brown eyes full of gratitude. She reached up and put both hands either side of Rufus's face and began talking in her own language. Rufus looked at Milly for assistance.

'She's saying thank you.' Milly said. 'She said you're a wonderful young man.'

'Tell her she's welcome.' Rufus said.

Milly translated and the old lady smiled at Rufus again and pulled his face towards her, planting a kiss on his forehead. Rufus blushed and nodded at the old lady. Milly scooped up the errant vegetables and the old lady's purse and handed it to her. The old lady rummaged around in the bag, pulled out a note and thrust it at Rufus.

'No, no.' Rufus said. 'That's not necessary. Tell her Milly.'

Milly translated and the old lady shook her head and held the money out again to Rufus.

'She said she can see you're homeless and down on your luck.' Milly said with a smile. 'She thinks you may be a bit simple because you can't understand what she's saying. She wants me to promise to take you for a hot meal. I think she thinks I'm your carer!'

Rufus looked back at the old lady and smiled. He put his hands together in front of him in supplication and inclined his head towards her. She understood the gesture and put her hands around his. Her hands were wrinkled but strong and she squeezed Rufus's hands. Rufus bent his head and kissed the old lady's hands, she giggled. Rufus looked in her eyes and saw the girl she was all those years ago, the girl shc still was beneath the wrinkles and the grey hair.

A younger woman stepped forward, possibly a relative and took the old lady's arm gently pulling her away from Rufus. The old lady looked back once as she walked away and smiled at Rufus. The local Police had momentarily lost interest, and Rufus and Milly slipped away into the crowd.

HIDING PLACE

The wolves moved as quickly as possible away from the local Police. They were both hungry and decided to use the money from the old lady to buy food and a hot drink. They needed to blend in, but the money wouldn't stretch far enough to buy clothes. Instead, Milly coerced a vendor of scarves, wraps and hats into giving her a thick brown shawl which she used to cover her head and shoulders and a dark blue woollen hat for Rufus. They also bought two meat skewers and hot, black coffee.

Towards the far end of the square, the market stalls were more spaced out and Rufus saw a young boy, not much older than Max on his hands and knees between two stalls. His head was bowed, almost touching the floor, his hands red and raw from the cold, holding out an empty paper cup; he was a beggar. The boy lifted his head and looked up at Rufus, his lips were tinged blue. Rufus stepped towards the boy and offered him the skewer of meat. The boy sat back on his haunches and looked at Rufus warily. Rufus smiled and held out the cup of hot coffee with his other hand. The boy hesitated for a second before taking the cup and skewer. He ate quickly, his eyes constantly moving, checking his surroundings.

'Hey!' Milly cried as Rufus snatched the skewer of meat from her hand.

'He needs it more than you.' Rufus replied handing it to the boy. 'Ask him if he has somewhere safe to go at night?'

Milly looked at the homeless boy sitting on the cobbled stones, she sighed and offered him her coffee, he took it and nodded gratefully. She asked him if he stayed on the street all night and he shook his head saying that he had a place that was dry and safe.

'He's off the streets at night.' Milly said to Rufus. 'But he's not willing to give the details. Understandable. What are you thinking?'

'That maybe the homeless have given Max and Elena shelter.' Rufus replied.

'I could coerce him to tell me, if you want?'

'Or you could leave the boy alone.'

Milly looked around at the sound of Roman's voice. He and Jedrek were standing on the other side of the square watching. Her wolf hearing enabling her to hear the Alpha speak. She glanced at Rufus who shrugged. Rufus dug into his pocket for the last of the money the old lady had given to him and dropped it into the boy's paper cup. Rufus and Milly left the boy to enjoy his food and crossed the square to join Roman and Jedrek.

'You were asked to wait.' Roman said.

'We heard Max howl.' Rufus said. 'He's undergone his first change, alone, that shouldn't have happened. I wasn't going to sit around and do nothing!'

Roman sighed patiently before speaking.

'As you're so keen to do something, you may as well come with us to the library.'

'Why the library?' Rufus asked.

'Grimlock's at the library. If anyone knows how the twins have been brought to the city and why, it'll be him. He'll also know a bit more about the prophecy. It's a good place to start.'

'Nice car, by the way.' Rufus said.

Roman smiled.

From the shadow of a nearby building, the witch Thebe watched the strangers interact with the homeless boy. She too thought the twins were sheltering in the city, it was the only explanation as to why they had not been apprehended the previous night. She decided to question the boy and headed towards him.

From his begging position, the boy looked at the dirty black boots and sensed that the person in front of him was not friendly.

'Look at me boy.' Thebe said. 'Tell me what you told the strangers. Tell me everything.'

Although reluctant, the boy had no alternative but to do as commanded.

* * * * *

Following the meal of cooked fish Max suddenly weary from the ordeal of the transformation, stared at the flames in the brazier with heavy eyes. Movement to the side of Ratman caught his attention and he sat bolt upright and sniffed the air.

'Is that a rat?' Max asked.

'Where?' Ratman said.

'Beside you!' Elena said pointing between Ratman and Yosef.

Ratman looked down and picked up a large brown rat. It was huge, for a rat, almost the size of a domestic cat, with intelligent eyes and a twitching nose. Ratman stroked the rat's head affectionately.

'This is Pickens.' Ratman said.

'Your pet?' Max asked.

'Pickens is no pet! He's my friend.'

'Does he bite?' Elena asked.

'Do you?'

Max and Elena exchanged a glance. In the short time since meeting the mysterious Ratman they had learned enough to know that he never fully answered a question, nor did he give a straight answer.

'Get some rest.' Ratman said. 'Pickens and I will keep watch. There'll be no more unpleasant visitors today.'

'Are you sure?' Max asked.

'Quite sure. Sleep now, you'll need your strength.'

'For what?'

Ratman made no reply.

In the tunnels, the twins had no idea whether it was night or day, and Max was too tired to pursue the matter. The stone floor was hard but Max and Elena were exhausted and they laid down side by side.

'Tell me about the other wolves.' Ratman whispered.

Elena was soon snoring and Max was vaguely aware of Ratman speaking, and wondered if the question was directed at him or Yosef or the rat called Pickens. In the end he gave into sleep and Ratman's voice faded away.

'They'll sleep for a few hours.' Ratman said to Pickens. 'Now tell me about the other wolves.'

Satisfied that the children were asleep, Pickens moved away from Ratman and sniffed the air in much the same way as Max had done. His body twitched and he grew in size, his small bones snapping and reshaping, his fur retracting into this body and in less than a minute a small thin man stood before Ratman; a were-rat.

'Here.' Ratman said offering a piece of fish to Pickens. 'You must be hungry.'

Pickens nodded and took the food, he was a man of a few words.

'The wolves?' Ratman prompted.

'Two of them. Male and female, but the female is something else.'

'What do you mean?'

'She smells like a vampire.' Pickens said licking the fish oil from his fingers.

'When did they arrive?'

'Same time as the children, more or less. Popped up right in the middle of the square!'

'Where are they now?' Ratman asked.

'With Roman and his pack.' Pickens paused.

'What else?'

'The witch is searching for the children. I've seen her hiding in doorways and in the shadows, only glimpses. You know how she moves about, but my eyes don't miss much.'

'She cannot be allowed to get hold of them.' Ratman said.

'You'll have to keep them hidden, she has spies everywhere.' Pickens replied.

Pickens looked around at the sleeping children and wondered who they were and why they had been brought to Braeden. He supposed the Vampire King had another insane idea he was putting to the test and these two were somehow part of the plan.

'I should go.' Pickens said. 'They won't sleep long.'

'Stay safe.' Ratman said. 'And keep me informed.'

Pickens nodded and transformed back into a rat. He crept closer to the children and sniffed, familiarising himself with their scent. Max suddenly snorted in his sleep startling the rat and Pickens ran off into the nearest tunnel.

*****

Back on the streets above, Thebe had gleaned all the information she needed from the homeless boy and was confident she would have the twins in her clutches before the end of the day.

*****

Several hundred miles east of Braeden Peter and Shayla were discussing the latest complication to arise on their journey.

'They were pretty clear at the ferry terminal.' Peter said. 'No dog or pets of any kind. They have to be quarantined for six months.'

Shayla bit back her retort. Titan was neither a pet nor a dog.

'We'll have to go back.' Shayla said.

'Can't he fly back?'

'In broad daylight?'

Peter said nothing. He looked at Titan, who stared back at him with a look of disdain.

'Can he do that thing where he disappears?' Peter asked.

'What thing?'

'You know, that thing he does when he shimmers out of sight.'

'That's only a temporary shift.' Shayla replied. 'He can't do that indefinitely.'

'Then he can't come with us.'

'Titan won't leave.' Shayla said.

'Did he say that?' Peter replied.

'No. I know he won't leave. So do you.'

Peter ran his hand through his hair in exasperation.

There is an alternative. Titan said.

Shayla frowned.

'What did he say?' Peter asked.

'That there's an alternative.' Shayla said.

'I'm all ears.'

Peter watched Titan and Shayla look at each other, conversing in their minds, and wondered what possible alternative there could be other than turning around and driving Titan home.

'Right, let's do it.' Shayla said finally. 'We need to find somewhere off the road where we won't be seen.'

'We passed a small wooded area a couple miles back.' Peter said. 'Would that be any good?'

'That'd be perfect.'

Peter turned the car around and headed back west. Whatever Shayla was planning to do would be revealed soon enough, there was no need for him to bombard her with questions.

Fifteen minutes later Peter, Shayla and Titan were standing away from the car, among the trees and broken, graffiti covered picnic benches.

'You need to stand back and give us some room.' Shayla said. 'Titan and I are going to merge….'

'Whoa! Wait a moment!' Peter said holding his hands out in the universal stop sign. 'You're going to what?'

'Merge, meld.'

'What?…'

Peter was lost for words, his head whipped back and forth from Shayla and Titan.

'It sounds….insane! And dangerous.'

'It's perfectly safe.' Shayla said.

'Have you done this before?'

Shayla hesitated.

'You've never done this before?!' Peter said sharply before Shayla could reply.

'Titan assures me it's safe and I trust him.' Shayla said putting her hand on Peter's arm.

Peter took a deep breath and exhaled slowly.

'Explain it to me.'

'It's a bit like the shift thing he does.' Shayla said. 'But he can't do that for extended periods of time. As we're both part angel, we can occupy the same space.'

'Like possession?'

'No, and yes.'

'That's helpful!' Peter replied sarcastically.

'It's my body and I would still be me. Titan would be, how can I put it? Travelling with me and give me extra strength if needed.'

'But you're in control?'

'Absolutely.'

'And when we get back home?'

'We reverse the process and Titan and I separate.'

'I don't know about this.' Peter said taking his wife's hands.

'I can't send him back home.' Shayla replied. 'He wouldn't go anyway. This way he comes with us and I could definitely use his sharp instincts. We're going to need his extra strength especially if we have to fight our way out of any situation.'

Peter looked away.

'You know I'm right.' Shayla said.

Peter looked back at his wife and shook his head.

'I don't like it.'

'But…'

Peter put his finger on Shayla's lips to stay her words.

'I don't like it.' Peter repeated firmly. 'But I trust you, and Titan, which is why I'm agreeing to it.'

Shayla kissed her husband firmly before stepping away from him and facing Titan.

'What do we do?'

Titan said nothing. He grew in size, lifted his body and stood up on his hind legs, placing his front paws on Shayla's shoulders. The surrounding trees, although sparse prevented anyone from witnessing the event. People would have thought it odd to see a woman and an extremely large wolf-like hound embracing.

Shayla stepped towards him and put her arms as far around his body as she could, resting her head against the soft fur on his neck. Titan rested his head on his paw until his face touched the birth mark on Shayla's shoulder, the mark of the Archangel Michael.

Peter watched in silence as Shayla and Titan both began to shimmer, then glow. The light grew brighter, like the sun reflecting off a window and Peter had to shield his eyes and momentarily looked away. It was all over in seconds and when the light receded, Peter dropped his hand from his face, only Shayla stood before him.

'I'm guessing it worked.' Peter said walking towards her. 'How do you feel?'

Shayla turned to face him and smiled.

'Good.' Shayla said. 'Stronger.'

Shayla turned her hands over and back again as if seeing them for the first time, she splayed her fingers and clenched them back into fists. She stretched her arms and summoned her wings which opened out behind her. Her wings were larger than her own and black like Titan's with glints of silver, akin to rows of overlapping swords, their wickedly sharp edges glinting in the light. Shayla retracted her wings and stepped towards Peter.

Peter smiled and looked into her eyes.

'What?' Shayla asked, noting the expression that passed over Peter's face.

'It is still you?' Peter said stoking her face and looking into her beautiful green eyes.

'Yes it's me.'

'Where's Titan?'

'He's here.' Shayla said putting her hand on her heart. 'And in my head.

It's hard to explain. I can feel him, but it's like he's sitting in the corner of the room.'

'Could he take over your body if he wanted to?'

'Yes, if I consent. I'll show you.'

Shayla closed her eyes and bowed her head. When she looked up again, her eyes were no longer green, they were amber.

'There is no need for concern Peterus.' Shayla said with the syntax of Titan. 'Shayla is in control, but like you, I will not leave her side. We should be on our way, time is short.'

Before Peter could reply, Shayla bowed her head again and when she looked back her eyes were green once more.

'When Titan's in control, are you aware of what he's saying?' Peter asked.

'Yes, it's a bit strange.' Shayla paused. 'I'm aware of what's going on but it's like I'm standing right behind myself watching it all happen. Does that make sense?'

'No.' Peter laughed. 'But as long as you feel OK, that's enough for me. We should get going. As Titan said, time is short.'

Shayla held out her hand and before Peter took it he noticed what appeared to be a tattoo on the inside of her left forearm. Shayla followed his gaze and stroked the tattoo with her other hand.

'It looks like a wolf print.' Peter said.

'It's the mark of our symbiosis.' Shayla said.

'Is it permanent?'

'I don't know. Does it bother you?'

'No. I like it.' Peter said taking her hand and kissing it. 'It makes you look like a bad-ass.'

HIDDEN MEANINGS

The library in Braeden held over twenty thousand books, with one of the largest collections of written works and was one of the most beautiful and majestic buildings on the continent. It was a popular tourist attraction but beneath the surface and inaccessible to the public was the Reliquiarium of the wolves and Grimlock was its custodian.

It was unclear who had built the Reliquiarium but the mysterious builders had ensured the safety of everything inside with a powerful magic spell which only allowed wolves to enter. Grimlock felt certain that the magic would prevent harm from fire and flood but hoped his assertions were never put to the test.

Grimlock's office was carefully positioned with a view of the main library from his desk and a door behind him that accessed the Reliquiarium. Grimlock was proud of his position and fiercely protective of the various relics and valuable artefacts. Some of the relics stored beneath the library were centuries old and even with his vast knowledge, some mysteries remained locked even to Grimlock.

The ancient tome Yendor had discovered in the folklore section should have been in the Reliquiarium and Grimlock puzzled over the mystery of this particular book and its contents. Grimlock ran his index finger over one of the ancient pages trying to capture the essence of the message as it was written centuries before.

'What am I missing?' Grimlock grumbled to himself.

Yendor hovered just outside the office, Grimlock could hear him breathing and closed his eyes in an attempt to control his anger.

'What is it Yendor?' Grimlock snapped.

'There are some people here to see you.'

Grimlock opened his eyes, took a deep breath and exhaled slowly trying to control his impatience.

'Show them in.'

Yendor scurried away muttering, something which annoyed Grimlock intensely. He returned moments later with the four visitors. Grimlock had already detected the scent of Roman and Jedrek, but they had brought two strangers with them.

Grimlock remained seated as Roman entered the room. He refused to stand and bow to the Alpha. Roman was used to it and ignored Grimlock's cantankerous ways, but the lack of respect irritated Jedrek.

'You should stand in the presence of the Alpha, you scrawny old bone chomper.' Jedrek said.

'What can I do for you Roman?' Grimlock asked ignoring Jedrek and the two strangers.

'What can you tell us about the prophecy?' Roman said without preamble.

'Which prophecy?'

'Don't be difficult.' Roman replied sharply.

Grimlock glanced down at the book, it was the closest he would ever come to a submission in the presence of his pack leader.

'Should we be discussing this in front of strangers?' Grimlock eyed Milly and Rufus suspiciously.

'They're wolves.' Roman replied. 'What do you know Grimlock? Time is of the essence.'

'I know they are wolves, but some things are best kept away from the eyes of stranger.'

'Now Grimlock.' Roman insisted.

'I'm not happy about this.' Grimlock said scowling.

'Noted.'

Grimlock closed the book he had been working on and put in under one arm. He retrieved a bunch of keys from his pocket.

'Follow me.' Grimlock said.

Grimlock opened the door to the Reliquiarium and motioned for the wolves to enter. Once inside, Grimlock closed and locked the door behind them. He moved to the front of the line and led the wolves along a narrow passageway which ended at the top of a set of stone steps.

'Be careful.' Grimlock said. 'The steps are quite narrow.'

The steps ended at a wall with an inscription carved into the stone.

"Improve yourself by the writings of others
so that you can come by easily
that which others have worked hard for."

Grimlock selected a key and hesitated.

'Is that key made of bone?' Milly asked.

Grimlock ignored the question and looked at Roman.

'Open the door.' Roman said. 'We need as much information as we can get.'

Sighing his displeasure and impatience, Grimlock took the old key and ran his palm across the inscription stopping at the word "easily". The letter 'L' was a disguised keyhole and Grimlock put the key in and turned the letter 'L' on its side. A soft click was followed by a heavy clunk and the stone slab dropped back leaving an opening wide enough for a person to slip inside.

Grimlock stepped inside and placed his palm flat against the wall. The stone glowed in response to his touch. The others followed him inside and as they walked blocks of stone in the walls started to glow with a soft amber light. Milly and Rufus looked at each other but said nothing.

'The light comes from the stones.' Grimlock said noticing the look that had passed between the two strangers. 'I still haven't discovered the origin of the stones, but I'm sure I will. This way.'

Grimlock led them along another short narrow passageway which opened up into a huge underground cavern. Milly and Rufus stopped short and took in the rows of thousands upon thousands of books all stacked in neat rows. Each book contained its own world and answers to life's many questions.

'Wow, that's…..' Rufus blurted.

'Impressive, isn't it?' Grimlock said.

'Amazing!' Milly replied. 'Questions that have been asked for hundreds of years could be answered by the books in this room.'

Milly knew that Gaolyn had seen a lot of things in his lifetime but he never knew of the existence of this incredible library.

Grimlock led them to a desk stacked high with ancient books and scrolls.

'This book.' Grimlock said holding up the tome he had been carrying under his arm. 'I believe is part of a set. I also believe that the prophecy has been written in several books and only when read together will the meaning be fully revealed.'

'What does it say?' Roman asked.

'Nothing.'

'You just said….'

'I know what I said.' Grimlock snapped. 'Do you really think I'd have the most precious items and ancient text lying around for all to see in the library upstairs!'

Roman bit back his retort and sighed.

'Wait here!'

Grimlock left them standing around the desk while he walked off in search of the book he needed. The room seemed to respond to his movements and soft amber light illuminated the way as he walked between the stacks.

Milly and Rufus conversed telepathically.

This place is exactly like the crypt at Lemington Street. Rufus said. *Not the books of course, but the stone entrance and the glowing walls.*

And that key is definitely made from bone. Milly replied.

The same mysterious builders?

Has to be.

Grimlock returned several minutes later with a large book.

'This book contains copies of the ancient texts.' Grimlock said placing it carefully on the desk.

He opened the book and hesitated moving his hand lightly across the page.

'I've translated some of it, but I'm missing something.'

'There's blood on the page.' Milly said.

'And you are?' Grimlock asked.

'Milly.'

Grimlock looked at Roman for an introduction and an explanation.

'This is Milly and her brother Rufus.' Roman said. 'Their nephew and niece have been kidnapped, and brought to the City by some form of magic. They were caught up in the spell trying to rescue them.'

Grimlock sensed that Milly was something other than a wolf and felt his hackles rising.

'There's something different about you.'

'There is definitely blood on that page.' Milly repeated ignoring the comment.

'I'm sure young wolf I would detect blood on the page. There's nothing wrong with my senses. Don't be fooled by this human form. I am not infirm!'

'And I can assure you sir, there is blood on that page.' Milly said, her syntax undeniably Gaolyn's. 'I have a heightened sensitivity towards blood and your werewolf senses may not be able to detect it. Nonetheless, it is there.'

Grimlock fumed at the young wolf's insolence but said nothing further. Rufus smiled at his sister's feistiness and glanced at Jedrek who smirked. Jedrek was always looking for ways to aggravate his pack brother.

'Why would there be blood on the page, unless.....' Grimlock whispered, more to himself than the others. 'Invisible ink.'

'Diluted blood could have been used as invisible ink.' Milly said.

'I thought lemon juice was used.' Roman said.

'Depends on the circumstances.' Rufus replied. 'Bodily fluids are often used, particularly in prison, saliva, sweat, urine, s...'

'We get the picture.' Milly said holding up her hand for Rufus to cease his explanation. 'The writer used diluted blood, his own I expect.'

Grimlock frowned again at Milly who held his stare defiantly.

'We need ultraviolet light to read this. Jedrek! Go to the back to that stack.' Grimlock said pointing the way. 'And bring me a light. It should be sitting on top of a box.'

'Get it yourself!' Jedrek replied.

'Bring me the ultraviolet light. NOW!'

Jedrek muttered something unpleasant in his own language and stomped away to find the light. He returned moments later with the lamp.

'Anything else sir?' Jedrek asked thrusting the lamp into Grimlock's outstretched hand.

Grimlock ignored him and snatched the light. Jedrek rolled his eyes and Rufus laughed at the exchange.

'What are you thinking?' Roman asked. 'Hidden message in the margins?'

Grimlock said nothing. He switched on the light and held it close to the edge of the page.

'There's nothing there.' Jedrek said leaning in for a better look.

'I can see that!' Grimlock snapped impatiently.

'Perhaps the cypher is nearer to the text.' Milly said.

Grimlock moved the lamp closer to the centre of the page illuminating the text. As he brought it closer to the prophecy, two numbers appeared next to each verse.

'What does that mean?' Roman asked also leaning in for a closer look.

'It means that in verse one, only lines one and three are relevant.' Grimlock said.

'And in verse two, lines two and four.' Milly finished.

Grimlock looked at Milly and almost smiled.

'Reading lines one, three, two and four changes the whole meaning.' Grimlock said. 'An excellent diversion. Now the prophecy reads;

"Lycan Angel's greatest light,

Encroaching darkness, demon sent,

Take a stand or lose this fight.

Destroys us all, not just mankind."

'It still doesn't mean anything to me.' Jedrek said.

'That's because you're a simpleton!' Grimlock said.

Jedrek growled, bared his teeth and stared at Grimlock.

'Enough! Both of you!' Roman commanded.

Jedrek nodded and stepped back to stand next to Rufus.

'Even the discarded lines have relevance.' Grimlock said. 'They make another verse. When read this way, the prophecy reveals a completely different meaning.'

'Aren't all prophecies open to interpretation?' Roman asked. 'If you look hard enough you can make a prophecy fit any situation.'

'True.' Grimlock replied. 'But I don't believe that's the case here. The other lines, which I believe are actually the first verse reads as follows;

"Technologies birth in Gaia's night.
will usher in, mankind's lament.
Holding death within plain sight,
Enters the brain and enters the mind."

'I'd say technology was definitely the downfall of mankind.' Rufus said. 'It all started with mobile phones, "holding death within plain sight" has got to be referring to that. Then came the stick-on medical patches and the implants in the brain.'

'Parallax was definitely the technology that ushered in, mankind's lament.' Milly said.

'I agree.' Grimlock said. 'We need to analyse the remaining text. The other book was misplaced and stored in the folklore section. I believe someone went to great lengths to keep it hidden and to keep the set of books apart.'

'If the book contained information that someone didn't want discovered. Why not just destroy it?' Jedrek said.

'You should never destroy books.' Milly gasped.

Grimlock scowled at Jedrek.

'About eighty years ago, another idiot with your mentality burned books in the streets instead of reading them. Remember how that turned out!'

Jedrek and Grimlock stared at each other darkly, neither one prepared to give any ground.

'Let's get back to the prophecy.' Roman said authoritatively.

'The "encroaching darkness" in the second line has to be referring to the vampire dominance of the City.' Grimlock said.

'And if Arcane isn't a demon I'd be shocked.'

Milly and Rufus said nothing but exchanged thoughts telepathically.

'Tell me.' Grimlock said, his sharp eyes missed nothing.

'Our nephew and niece are twins.' Rufus said.

'Wolves?'

'Not entirely.'

'Spit it out!'

'The twins were born from the union of our Alpha and…' Milly paused. 'A non-wolf.'

'That's impossible.' Grimlock said.

'Apparently not.' Roman added.

'Only another wolf would be strong enough to survive such a union and bear offspring. What's the mother's parentage?'

Rufus and Milly looked at each other, reluctant to discuss Shayla with a stranger.

'You're going to need our help to find the twins.' Roman said. 'Grimlock is part of my pack, you can trust him.'

'She's heir to the throne of Fey.' Rufus said. 'Her mother is the

Queen.'

'And her father?'

'The Archangel Michael in a human host.'

Grimlock sat down in the chair at the desk. No-one spoke for several minutes. Grimlock appeared to be deep in thought. Roman and Jedrek both looked shocked at the revelation that an archangel had been able to father a child. Eventually Grimlock broke the silence.

'The conception of a half angel would be impossible unless there was already a half demon in the world.' Grimlock said. 'It's essential to maintain the balance. What's you're Alpha's lineage?'

'Silver claw.' Milly said.

'Descended from the first Alpha. Royalty, hmmm….' Grimlock said tapping his index finger against his lips.

'We believe the reference "Lycan Angel" means a specific wolf and angel, since the words are both written with a capital letter, making them pronouns.' Milly said.

'And the "greatest light" relates to the twins, their named Max and Elena.' Rufus finished.

Grimlock sat back in his chair again and rubbed his chin thoughtfully.

'Has the mother ever killed a demon?'

'Not that we know of.' Rufus said looking at Milly who shook her head. 'Why?'

'Then the demon child is behind this.'

'I bet my hide it's Arcane!' Jedrek said.

'I agree.' Grimlock replied. 'The name itself means darkness. Arcane wants to kill the angel.'

'Why?' Rufus asked.

'Potentially, she's as powerful as he is, and what better way to bring her to him than kidnapping her children.'

'Why would the Vampire King support Arcane's personal schemes?' Roman said. 'Arcane is duplicitous, but Barumar misses nothing.'

'Did you say Barumar?' Rufus asked.

'You know him?'

'I've heard the name.' Rufus said looking at Milly.

Roman nodded.

'Barumar thinks the blood of the Fey will give him power, hence the lunar hunts.' Grimlock said. 'He's always searching for those with the blood of the Fey.'

'All vampires believe the blood of the Fey is powerful.' Milly whispered. 'But it's so much more…'

The wolves all turned to look at Milly, none more mistrusting than Grimlock. Rufus shook his head at his sister.

'They believe the blood allows them to walk in the day light.' Milly continued a little flustered.

'How do you know this?' Grimlock asked.

Milly regained her composure.

'Don't be fooled by this human form.' Milly said repeating Grimlock's words. 'I look young, but I listen and learn.'

'The King's an idiot.' Grimlock said. 'But I've no doubt Arcane's told him the children are part Fey, that would be enough to gain Barumar's support.'

'We have to find them first.' Rufus said.

'We will.' Roman said putting his hand on Rufus's shoulder. 'We'll search together.'

Rufus nodded in gratitude.

'It's wonderful news!' Grimlock exclaimed standing up.

'What are you talking about?' Rufus said irritably.

'Don't you understand?' Grimlock said excitedly. 'Max and Elena!

The clue is in their names! The prophecy!'

'Straighten your tongue and speak plainly!' Jedrek said.

'Greatest light! They're a weapon against the encroaching darkness!'

Everyone looked at Grimlock.

'They're children!' Rufus said in disgust. 'Not a weapon. I'm done listening to your ramblings old wolf. I'm going to find Max and Elena.'

'I'm coming with you.' Milly said.

'No.' Roman said. 'You'll wait and follow my orders.'

Rufus went to speak and Roman held up his hand to silence him.

'Think. You're strangers here and would arose too much suspicion. I said we would help you and we will. It makes no sense for the two of you go to off on your own, you'd be arrested and killed before the next sunrise. You believe your Alpha is on his way here, right?'

'Definitely.' Rufus replied. 'I've been trying to contact him since Milly and I got here, but he must be too far away.'

'Have you been able to contact your nephew?'

'No. He's too young. He's got enough to deal with coping with his first change.'

'Then we wait.'

'How long?' Milly asked.

'One more day. Then we make our own plan.' Roman said. 'Either way, we need to know where they are.'

*****

Tomas and Kristyna Nebojsa had never been blessed with children of their own, but they were foster parents to many. The runaways and the homeless all found their way to Tomas and Kristyna's home eventually to enjoy a hot meal, love and the warmth of a family, albeit temporary. None of the street children stayed longer than a few hours, although during one of the coldest winter nights three or four had slept in the living room next to the fire but they were all gone straight after breakfast.

Kristyna thought back to when she and Tomas had cancelled their trip on the day of the pulse and thanked the Divine. Had they continued, their plane would have fallen from the sky and they would most likely have died and she and Tomas would never have had the chance to help the street children of Braeden.

Tomas and Kristyna would have loved to do more, but they did as much as they could. While the children ate and warmed themselves by the fire, Kristyna would make repairs to their clothes and she and Tomas would try to engage them in books and reading before they disappeared onto the streets and back to the hiding places they favoured.

They would have adopted all of the children and crammed them all into their little house, but even if that were possible, they knew the children would never stay. Every day Kristyna make a large pot of vegetable stew and baked cookies, these she piled high on a plate and displayed them in her kitchen window, a sign to the children that she was home and a hot meal awaited anyone who wanted it. One child would appear at the back door while another kept watch across the street, hidden in the shadows, this was their usual routine and Kristyna knew that as soon as one visitor left with a cookie, another would appear in his or her place.

Hidden from sight but with a view of the house, Yosef, Max and Elena watched as an older boy left with a cookie in hand.

'Are you sure it's safe?' Elena whispered.

'Of course!' Yosef replied. 'I've been coming here for a while. Kristyna's food is delicious. And it's daytime, no cold ones.'

'I'm not sure about this.' Max said. 'I think we should wait in the sewers, back underground.'

'Trust me.' Yosef said. 'Tomas and Kristyna may have some warmer clothes.'

'Why would they?'

'Because they're good people. They've been feeding us, giving us clothes when they have them and trying to take care of us all for a while. They haven't got any kids. I think that's why they do it. They would never hurt us.'

'If you think they're OK, that's good enough for me.' Elena said.

Yosef smiled and Max looked doubtful, his instincts were telling him this was a bad idea, but Elena seemed convinced and Yosef had kept them safe so far.

'OK.' Max shrugged. 'Let's make it quick.'

The plate of cookies sat in the window, in clear view and the witch Thebe waited in the shadows and watched. The homeless boy returned to her with cookie in hand, his eyes not quite focused.

'I have no more use for you.' Thebe said to the boy taking the cookie from him. 'Forget you have ever seen me. Go.'

The boy turned and ran as if his life depended on it.

Thebe looked back towards the house and smiled, exposing her ruined teeth as the trio stepped out from their hiding place and hurried to Kristyna's kitchen door.

CAPTURE

Yosef stood in the doorway, Max and Elena behind him.

Kristyna smiled warmly at Yosef. Although she cared for the other street children who came to her house, Yosef was her favourite and she looked forward to his weekly visits. She and Tomas had discussed adoption but she had never been able to pluck up the courage to ask Yosef if he wanted to live with them permanently. Kristyna was afraid that such a suggestion would frighten Yosef and he would run away. It would break her heart if she never saw him again. Instead she went the extra mile with Yosef, buying warmer clothes and sturdy shoes, telling him they were cast offs.

Yosef was an intelligent boy and knew he received extra special treatment, which he gratefully accepted although he played his part by appearing taciturn in front of the others. During his visits Yosef would often think about how nice it would be to live in a warm house and be part of a family. Then he would bring his thoughts back to reality knowing that Kristyna and Tomas were not his parents, he lived on the streets, free and able to do as he pleased. When he was of a mood, his reticence wasn't entirely fake.

'I see you've brought some friends.' Kristyna said looking at Max and Elena.

'Is that OK?' Yosef said shyly.

'Of course, come in and warm yourselves, I'll get you something to eat.'

Max and Elena hesitated and stood in the doorway.

'Don't be shy.' Kristyna said. 'Come in.'

Max glanced at Elena who nodded, both of them grateful they could understand Kristyna's words and equally afraid to speak for fear their foreign accent would give them away as strangers. Yosef led the way and all three sat at the kitchen table.

'I haven't seen you two before.' Kristyna said placing a bowl of soup in front of them.

'They've been living in the forest.' Yosef said quickly.

Kristyna nodded. She was certain Yosef's two new friends were not from Braeden, their clothes looked slightly out of place but she couldn't quite put her finger on what it was, and she certainly didn't believe they'd been living in the forest, but she said nothing. The street kids survival depended on their secrets and she knew better than to press for details.

'Are you warm enough?' Kristyna asked Yosef. 'That coat looks a bit thin.'

'I'm OK.' Yosef replied picking at the hole in the sleeve.

'Hmmm…'

Unconvinced, Kristyna left the room and returned minutes later with three woollen garments.

'These might be a bit big for you.' Kristyna said handing a woolly jumper to each of them. 'But they'll keep you warm.'

Max nodded his thanks as he took one of the offered garments. Elena smiled and quickly pulling the jumper over her head.

'I told you she was nice.' Yosef said quietly.

Kristyna watched the three of them, but appeared not to, busying herself at the kitchen counter buttering bread and slicing cheese. Placing the food in front of them she smiled at Max and something flashed beneath his calm expression and Kristyna wondered what they were afraid of, or who they were running from.

Yosef stood up suddenly, the other two followed his lead.

'Leaving so soon?' Kristyna asked unable to keep the sadness from her voice.

'Can't stay.' Yosef said through a mouthful of food.

'Are you sure you've had enough to eat?'

Yosef picked up the remaining bread and crammed it into his pockets.

'Take these.' Kristyna said scooping up the cookies and offering them to Yosef.

Yosef hesitated and Elena stepped forward, taking the cookies. She spoke perfectly in Kristyna's language with no trace of an accent.

'Thank you.' Elena said.

Kristyna was captivated by the strange girl with her fair complexion and blond hair. She had beautiful blue eyes trimmed with long lashes. Her eyes held a gentleness and warmth and her delicate face looked as if it has been crafted by angels.

'You're welcome.' Kristyna replied.

Elena broke eye contact when Max touched her arm. They spoke telepathically.

'We have to go.' Max said. *'Every one of my senses are telling me to run.'*

'From her?' Elena said glancing at Kristyna.

'Not her, but…something….I can't explain it.'

'Then we run.'

* * * * *

Thebe watched from the shadows as the trio emerged from Kristyna's doorway. Using a concealment spell, Thebe took a step forward and called to the children.

'HEY!'

Elena turned towards the sound of the voice just as the figure disappeared from view around the corner of the building opposite Kristyna's house.

'Uri?' Elena said.

'Elena!' Max shouted but Elena had already began to run towards the mysterious figure.

'Wait!' Yosef yelled but it was too late.

Max went in pursuit of his sister leaving Yosef alone. Kristyna put her hand on Yosef's shoulder to comfort the boy but he shrugged himself away from her and ran after his two friends.

CARCERALIS

Arcane stood behind the parapet wall and looked out over the river and the City. He was cold but the roof top afforded him privacy. The King had taken to bursting into Arcane's room whenever he desired, giving orders, making demands, he was less inclined to venture outside. The roof top had become Arcane's sanctuary.

His hand strayed to the amulet he wore around his neck and he ran his index finger over the surface of the black crystal at the centre. There was a time he was forced to hide the pendant from prying, questioning eyes and so using magic he had disguised it to look like a tattoo on his chest but now he wore it in plain sight. Drawing on the Faerie power locked inside the crystal gave him a feeling of euphoria, followed by deep contemplation. It also temporarily suppressed Eversor and Arcane was addicted.

Arcane leaned against the parapet and stared out at nothing, his mind occupied with thoughts of disposing of Barumar completely, but this presented him with a conundrum. Should he kill the Vampire King thereby ridding himself of the annoying parasite but risk losing his influence on the City officials and other vampires? Or should he find a way to exercise more control and render Barumar nothing more than a figurehead? These were the questions Arcane contemplated in the moments that followed the euphoria.

The effects of the Faerie power were dissipating, Arcane could feel Eversor's presence, the demon was like a worm burrowed into his brain. Arcane hated it.

The power of the Fey put Eversor to sleep and it struggled and pushed through the temporary imprisonment until finally exploding into Arcane's mind.

You are addicted to the power of the Fey. Eversor said angrily.

Arcane said nothing.

Eversor hated Arcane.

'I have to completely control the Vampire King.' Arcane said aloud. 'It's either that or kill him.'

'Kill him.' Eversor replied.

'If I kill him, I lose my influence. The other vampires won't follow my commands.'

'You trap yourself with your own limited mind.' Eversor said. 'You already possess the power to control the idiot King. Are you not the son of the Shadow Lord? Next time you're with the King, we will speak to him together. I have the power to magnify the vampire skill of persuasion.'

'The delusional?'

'Together we can, and will, control all vampires.'

Arcane smiled and wrapped his hand around the pendant. Concentrating once again he drew upon the Faerie power inside, the euphoria flowed through him and he felt the demon fade.

The chains of suppression wrapped around Eversor's mind.

Arcane hated Eversor, and Eversor hated Arcane.

*****

Wren was the first to open her eyes, the others laid around her still struggling with the effects of the fatigue. The attacks were becoming more frequent. They barely had time to recover before it washed over them again, draining their strength and zapping them of energy. Wren heard Oren groan and knew he'd pushed himself up into a sitting position.

'Is everyone OK?' Oren asked.

'Fantastic.' Gardenia replied.

'Peachy.' Kealoha added.

'Still here.' Radha said.

Wren didn't move or reply. In the first few seconds after the fatigue passed over, she liked to try and convince herself that her life was normal again and she was back at home in her own bed.

'Wren?'

'Yes Oren, I'm still here.' Wren replied irritably.

'Dreaming about home?'

Wren ignored the question. She didn't want to think about home, the contrast in worlds upset her too much and she had only spoken of it once since arriving in this dreadful place and then only by way of introducing herself to the others. Wren recalled that it was Radha who had asked her which element she favoured.

'I don't know what you mean.' Wren had responded vaguely.

'We're all Fey here.' Radha had said.

Wren remembered looking at the group, all of them waiting to hear whether she could be of any use to them, or at least that's how she chose to remember her first day.

'Air.' Wren said wrinkling her nose at the foul smell that wafted up from a nearby pool.

'Can you push that awful stink away?' Radha said with a smile.

'Sure.'

Wren had manipulated the air and sent the repugnant odour in the opposite direction.

'It's hot!' Wren said wiping her brow with the back of her hand. 'I'm used to the sun, but this is something else.'

'Where are you from?' Oren asked.

'What's with the interrogation?' Wren replied.

'Just trying to be friendly.' Oren snapped before turning away.

'Oren.' Radha called after him, but Oren had turned his back on them.

Radha turned her attention back to Wren.

'Don't mind Oren, he's a bit short tempered.' Radha said. 'It's this place.'

'I'm from…' Wren paused. 'A place where it's always sunny, but not like this.

'If you've got a good memory of home hang onto it.' Oren said turning back.

'I bet you've just been talking to a man called Cane.' Radha said.

Wren said nothing.

'Arcane?' Radha asked.

'How did you know?' Wren asked.

'He's why we're all here.'

Wren thought about the man who had suddenly started talking to her as she walked to work. Although he was friendly Wren didn't like the way he had been so forward and chatted to her as if they were old friends. Even when she took a different route to work, he would join her a day or so later. Wren loved the fragrance of the orange trees that lined the route she took to work, and the stranger who'd inserted his presence into her daily walk had become annoying. Wren stopped walking and decided she would tell him politely, but firmly to leave her alone.

'I realise I've been walking with you for some time and haven't even introduced myself.' he'd said.

Wren looked at him as he held out his hand in friendship.

'Arcane.'

'Listen.' Wren said shaking his hand. 'You seem like a very nice person, but I prefer to walk alone.'

As Wren made eye contact with Arcane his eyes had turned black and the next thing she remembered was waking up in an unfamiliar place, with a woman she now knew as Radha, looking at her.

Wren pushed the memory aside and sat up. She looked around, everyone was up on their feet and she wondered, not for the first time, why they looked to her to lead them. Radha had been there the longest, surely she should have been the leader? And then there was Gardenia, the second longest resident.

Either one of them could lead? Wren thought.

But Gardenia had once confided in Wren that she felt afraid most of the time, even though she didn't show it. She had wandered alone for days after arriving in this world. As an earth element Gardenia had been able to find something to eat. Bitter tasting roots had keep her alive, but she had been about to give up when she had finally found Radha; they were now close. Gardenia didn't consider herself strong enough to lead, but she was eager to follow.

It was during that quiet conversation that Gardenia had told Wren about Oren and Kealoha. Fire and water elements respectively, they were already friends and had been taken at the same time. Gardenia suspected they had been up to no good when they were taken, but that was just her suspicion.

'Nobody's asked them.' Gardenia has whispered conspiratorially.

Wren looked at her companions, focusing on each one of them. She was the last to arrive, the other four were already friends and she thought of herself like the fifth wheel, in a manner of speaking. She had always preferred her own company and avoided being drawn into friendship groups. Perhaps that's why the others looked to her to lead, but she had no idea where she was going, or if there was a way out of this place, whatever this place was.

All five of them were descendants of the Fey with control over the elements, but none of them eager to manipulate the elements in the disembowelled, barren, landscape that surrounded them.

The blasted trees and withered brush that grew out of the earth, dry and twisted like the hands of ancient corpses offered no protection from the incessant heat of the day. The days were long, the sun a fireball in the sky and ash and noxious gases hung in the air. The earth was stained with blood, excrement and the remnants of once living beings destroyed by fearsome creatures thought to only exist in folklore but indigenous to this world, and the air carried the sour stench of death and decay.

Water sat in stagnant, fetid pools, and parasitic insects twice the size of mosquitoes buzzed around looking for a tasty body to feast upon. Wren batted one away from her face before it had the chance to rest upon her skin and feed. When it buzzed back again she clapped her hands together crushing the insect between her palms. Wrinkling her nose in disgust, Wren wiped her hands against the earth to remove the parasite's oozy, splattered remains.

Clean water was hard to find and appeared to move on a daily basis forcing the group to search for the latest clear spring.

The night time temperatures plummeted to a depth of cold Kealoha referred to as colder than the freezer in the meat packing warehouse he had worked in. The shelter of a cave and the weak warmth of the fire provided by Oren did little to keep the cold from penetrating their bones.

The deep, intensity of a roar vibrated in Wren's mind and bones. The overgrown beast that stalked them every day was the size of a fully grown tiger, powerful and all muscle, sinew and hate with wings whose points were as sharp as spears. Wren recalled seeing a picture in a book of a Manticore but never believed such things existed, but it was the closest description she could think of.

'The Manticore's awake.' Wren said jumping to her feet.

The others didn't question her. Wren felt the vibrations in the air before any of them and her skill gave them a head start and had saved their lives on several occasions.

'We need to find cover before the fatigue comes again, we can't get caught out in the open.

'We'll head for those rocks.' Gardenia said. 'We should find shelter there.'

'And more water.' Kealoha said. 'I can feel it.'

'OK. Let's move.'

The five elementals ran in the direction of the rocks and prayed to the Divine they made it to shelter before the Manticore or the fatigue caught up with them.

*****

Arcane knew exactly what the world was like inside the pendant. He'd created the prison using the genetic memories of the Shadow Lord of the Cruciamentum. As much as he hated Eversor, it was the demon who had led him to the discovery of the pendant.

Eversor's knowledge of the pendant was as clear to Arcane as his own memories and those of the Shadow Lord and he thought back to when he had first become aware of its existence.

Arcane considered what he had learned from Eversor and the details flooded his mind like one of his own memories.

He knew that when Princess Allandrea and the Elementals destroyed the black moonstone and sent the Shadow Lord into the oblivion, they almost razed the Regency Theatre to the ground. The clean-up operation was extensive and the Shadow Lord's parting gift, the hell hound that killed Talis Quinn was taken to the nearest crematorium for incineration. Knowing that one of his father's creatures had killed at least one of the elementals brought a smile to Arcane's face.

Arcane absently stroked the pendant. The crystal, a perfect sphere, made from the crystallised eye of the creature from the Cruciamentum. Its body had turned to ash at the crematorium but the eyes remained.

A cold wind blew across Arcane's face as he stood on the parapet momentarily distracting him from his thoughts. He shivered and stepped back closer to the wall which afforded him some shelter. Eversor's knowledge of the origin of the crystal was clear in Arcane's mind.

Melvin Stiggins. Arcane mused, no longer trying to separate his own thoughts from Eversor's knowledge. *A particularly disagreeable and untrustworthy employee.*

Arcane laughed, but the sound was lost, whipped away by the wind.

Melvin Stiggins had discovered one of the crystals whilst cleaning out the furnace and had put it in his pocket. Using money earned through ill-gotten gains, he had the crystal mounted into a diamond shaped pendant which he gave it to his wife. A hideous thing which she'd hated and put away in a jewellery box out of sight. Years later her daughter Trudi had taken the pendant from her mother's jewellery box. She too thought it was ugly but felt drawn to it and wanted to possess it. She wore it from time to time to work. It was during one of those times that Arcane first saw it.

Arcane frowned when he recalled the time he had resided in a psychiatric facility. He used the name Cane and had crossed paths with Trudi Stiggins. Eversor had recognised the black crystal at the centre of the pendant and insisted Arcane needed it.

Arcane had found Trudi's pitiful attempts at teasing tiresome and had ignored her, pretending to be in a pharmaceutical haze but one day fuelled by Eversor's desire for the pendant, Arcane turned on Trudi and threatened to hurt her and her family when he was released from hospital.

'Trudi Stiggins was an idiot!' Arcane said aloud. 'But I wiped that stupid smile from her face.'

Arcane smiled to himself as he recalled the memory of Trudi Stiggins. The delight he had seen in her eyes as she pitifully attempted to torment him and the satisfaction he had felt when he had turned on her and saw the terror in her face. Arcane had allowed Trudi to see the eyes of Eversor, the memory of Trudi's terrified expression still delighted him.

'Here. Take it.' Trudi had said. Her hands shaking as she removed the pendant and gave it to Arcane.

Trudi thought she had paid for her family's protection, pleading for

Arcane not to hurt her. Arcane had no interest in Trudi or any of the Stiggins family, he only felt contempt.

After the incident, Trudi quickly forgot about the terrifying eyes she had looked into and quietly seethed at having her pendant stolen and being threatened. She planned for her brother Kurt to pay a visit to Arcane to teach him a lesson but the following day Arcane escaped from the hospital and she never saw him again.

After escaping the confines of the psychiatric facility, Eversor educated Arcane in the power of the crystal. Once Arcane discovered that being born of the Shadow Lord gave him the inherent knowledge, and the power to use the crystal, there was no stopping him. He was able to extract the Faerie subconscious from his victims and imprison them within the pendant. Incarcerated in the crystal prison he could torment the Fey and draw on their power, but the power was finite however and Arcane knew that every time he drew on the power either to control the elements or enjoy the euphoria, he drained the life of the Fey trapped inside. Sooner or later they would expire but he was too deep into his addiction to stop.

Arcane was convinced the offspring of his nemesis with their combination of angel, wolf and Fey DNA were the key to infinite power.

He stepped away from the wall and turned from the parapet. He would find the witch. She had one more day to locate the children and deliver them to him. If she failed, he would use Eversor's power to destroy her.

* * * * *

Three of the elementals were already in the shelter of the cave but Gardenia and Kealoha were lagging behind, the fatigue already pulling at them.

'Run!' Wren yelled.

Gardenia and Kealoha made it to the rocks and the others pulled them inside where they collapsed to the floor.

Wren manipulated the air to lift the larger rocks and Oren and Radha moved them into place at the mouth of the cave, blocking the path of the manticore.

'That was close.' Gardenia said breathlessly. 'I could barely lift my legs.'

'It's like trying to run through syrup.' Oren said. 'I don't think I can do this much longer.'

'We have to keep going.' Radha said.

They all sat quietly for a moment catching their breath. Eventually Kealoha spoke.

'Do you think if we die in here we die outside?'

'No.' Radha replied firmly. 'But the part of us that's Fey will die.'

Radha paused.

'We'll never feel whole again.' Radha said.

Any further discussion was silenced by the scratching and roaring of the manticore on the other side of the rocks.

'Is there another way out of this cave?' Wren asked.

'I'll take a look when my legs don't feel like lead.' Oren said.

'We should all rest while we can. The rocks will hold that thing back for a while.'

The ground was hard and uncomfortable but their limbs felt too heavy to move and the five companions laid down where they were and waited for the weariness to wash over them.

'Perhaps it'll get bored and wander off.' Radha said before her heavy eyelids closed and she succumbed to the exhaustion.

The next time they awoke, there were only four.

WELCOME

'Finally!' Shayla muttered through gritted teeth. 'Ten miles to Braeden. I thought we'd never get to this wretched place.'

'Is that you or Titan talking?' Peter asked stretching and yawning.

Shayla was driving and quickly glanced at Peter before returning her attention to the road.

'It's me. Titan's impatience is fuelling my own. Sorry, I didn't mean to wake you.'

'How long have I been asleep?'

'Not long, an hour at most.'

'Where are we? On a back road?'

'There's a diversion from the main road, all traffic is being directed through the forest.'

'What traffic?'

Peter sat up straight and looked around from within the car.

'We're the only car on the road.'

'I know.' Shayla glanced at Peter again. 'Someone knows we're coming, this diversion is for us.'

Peter put his hand on Shayla's shoulder and squeezed gently, she turned her head slightly and kissed the back of his hand.

'What do you think? Road block, check point, broken down vehicle?'

'Doesn't matter what they do.' Shayla said with a smile. 'We're getting our children back.'

'Together.' Peter affirmed.

It was less than three miles before Peter's keen wolf eyes saw what appeared to be a road traffic accident.

'Ah! Two cars and a truck blocking the road following a collision.' Peter said sarcastically. 'How predictable and incredibly boring.'

Several men and women in uniform appeared to be moving in pointless circles around the supposed broken down vehicles.

'A lot of police for a minor accident.' Shayla remarked.

'They'll detain us until nightfall.' Peter said.

'I'll turn the car around and find another way.'

'Don't bother. They'll have sealed off the road.'

'It's still daylight.' Shayla said slowing the car. 'No vampires.'

'Not yet, but they'll come.' Peter replied. 'These minions will delay us by pretending they don't understand us and we'll have to wait for their superior to arrive who speak the common tongue.'

'What do we do?'

'Play the game.' Peter said.

'Their superior will be a vampire?' Shayla asked, already knowing the answer.

Peter nodded.

'And he or she won't turn up until nightfall. You ready to fight when they do?'

'Definitely.'

Peter was out of the car before it came to a full stop and quickly took in his surroundings. Two Officers standing beside an overturned car watching him, another two trying to hide behind the truck and two more straight in front. The two officers closest to Peter and Shayla's vehicle strolled towards him talking in their own language and gesticulating for him to stay back. He didn't understand their words, but he understood their body language, they were wary of him. He inhaled and smelt their fear.

'They're being very cautious.' Shayla whispered now standing beside Peter.

'They're expecting someone dangerous.' Peter replied winking at her.

'They're afraid.'

Peter stepped forward, hands held high at the side of his head, his body language saying he didn't want any trouble.

'Is there another way around?' Peter asked.

One of the Police Officers replied in harsh tones that Peter didn't understand, his right hand unclipping the holster of his sidearm.

'He said we have to stay back.' Shayla said stepping up next to Peter.

'I'm getting that.' Peter said frowning. 'I don't need to understand the language to know what this one's thinking. The hand on his gun tells me everything. Do you understand them?'

Shayla nodded.

'Must be my Angel DNA.' Shayla said quietly. 'The two over there, by the car on its side, are muttering something about keeping us here and…oh!'

'What?'

'The two trying to hide just said they'll kill us if we try to leave.'

'They can try.' Peter said. 'I smell six different scents, these humans are the only creatures here, nothing else, but if we hang around til nightfall these woods will be crawling with vampires. I say we subdue them now, move these cars and get to the…..'

Before Peter finished speaking Shayla launched herself at the nearest Police Officer delivering a roundhouse punch to the right side of his head. As his legs buckled, Shayla used her own momentum, brought her fist in towards her chest and landed an inward elbow strike to the left side of the other Officer's head. Both Police Officers eyes rolled back, their legs crumpled and they fell to the ground unconscious.

Peter didn't hesitate. He moved with lightning speed and rendered the two Police Officers furthest away and the two trying to hide behind the truck unconscious before they unholstered their guns. In minutes all six were disarmed, laid side by side out of sight and restrained with their own handcuffs. Shayla took their keys and Peter crushed their sidearms with his hands, breaking them apart like children's toys.

'We're supposed to be working together.' Peter said.

'I knew you'd get to them before they unclipped their guns. Are you angry with me?'

'No, but you were reckless.'

Shayla paused and looked away.

'I'm sorry.' Shayla said looking back at Peter. 'I desperately want to find Max and Elena and this …'

'Ambush?'

'This ambush really annoyed me. I suppose I let my anger and desperation take over.'

Peter hugged his wife and kissed the top of her head. As they embraced Peter reached out with his mind and using his werewolf telepathy, spoke with Rufus for the first time since the night the twins were taken.

'I've just made contact with Rufus.' Peter said.

'What did he say? Are Max and Elena with him?'

'They're at a place called Mike's Cafeteria.' Peter replied only answering Shayla's first question. 'In the centre, not far from the clock tower.'

Shayla knew her husband well enough to know that her children were still missing and her heart sank. It was too much to hope that the twins were safe with Rufus and Milly and that she was heading for a happy reunion.

'Let's go.' Peter said sensing Shayla's change in mood. 'I'll move one of these cars out of the way so you can drive through.'

Five minutes later they were back on the road heading to the City.

*****

Pickens watched from the shadows as the four wolves left the library. Usually he remained hidden and kept a safe distance from humans and other creatures, especially wolves, but he was desperate. He would have to be in human form to speak with the Alpha. He knew where they were heading, the safest place for wolves was Mike's Cafeteria, that and they were always hungry. Pickens kept a safe distance downwind all the while looking for a suitable place to change into human form. Finally he found what he was looking for between two buildings in a small alleyway, a large stinking bin full of waste, some wooden boxes full of rags and other items for disposal and smelly enough to keep most people away and out of sight. Pickens changed into human form and rummaged around in the boxes until he found what he was looking for. Dressed only in an old pair of trousers and a thin summer jacket with a flowery pattern, he straightened himself up and made his way barefoot over to the Cafeteria.

* * * * *

Rufus and Milly sat opposite Roman and Jedrek at the same table they had used hours earlier at breakfast time. The cafe was quiet with one other couple at a table by the window.

'Tourists.' Roman said inclining his head in the direction of the only two patrons before returning to his coffee.

Roman had the sensation of being watched and looked up. Outside the window looking back at him was a small thin man he didn't recognise. It was clear the man had some information he wanted to impart but was hesitant about entering the cafe, Roman made eye contact and beckoned him to come inside. The man looked around quickly and sniffed the air before heading to the door and entering the Cafe.

As the door opened, Jedrek's head snapped up.

'Rat.' Jedrek muttered.

Roman was already on his feet, his hand on Jedrek's shoulder keeping him in place.

'Welcome friend.' Roman said gesturing for the man to sit. 'Come and join us.'

Pickens quickly took in his surroundings before approaching the table. He was cautious and pulled up a vacant chair giving him a straight line to the door.

'Coffee?' Roman asked.

Pickens shook his head.

'Water then?'

Pickens nodded and smiled.

'Witty, water for our friend please, and some bread and cheese.' Roman said sitting back at the table. 'You have information?'

Pickens nodded but said nothing.

Roman had only encountered a wererat once before in his life and knew they were secretive and understandably cautious around wolves.

'My name is Roman.'

'Pickens. I'm known as Pickens.'

'This is Jedrek, Rufus and Milly.'

Pickens nodded to each in turn.

Witty brought a glass of water, a fresh pot of coffee and a plate of bread rolls and cheese to the table. Roman broke one of the rolls and offered half of it to Pickens, a gesture understood by all, one of friendship and safety. When the Alpha shared his food, the pack knew that the guest was afforded every courtesy, safety and protection of the pack until the Alpha indicated otherwise. Pickens took the bread and nodded in gratitude.

'In your own time.' Roman said.

Pickens gulped down the bread and cheese as if he hadn't eaten for a while and Roman waited patiently for him to speak.

'You seek the twins.' Pickens said looking directly at Rufus and Milly.

'You know where they are?' Milly replied. 'Can you take us to them?'

Pickens shook his head and picked up the glass of water.

'Speak!' Jedrek said slamming his hand on the table.

Pickens started, spilling his water. Roman frowned at Jedrek and shook his head in warning.

'Can you tell us where they are?' Rufus asked gently sensing Pickens agitation at being surrounded by a four werewolves.

Pickens returned the glass to the table and composed himself.

'The witch has them.' Pickens said. 'At the palace.'

Milly sat back in her chair and stared at Pickens. Pickens sat upright and stared back at Milly equally appraising and holding her gaze.

'Are the tunnels still accessible?' Milly asked.

'If you can navigate the labyrinth.' Pickens replied. 'Do you know the tunnels?'

Milly shrugged trying to appear casual but she sensed the wererat knew more about her than she was comfortable with. Pickens inhaled and exhaled slowly, something wolves also did in human form when detecting a scent.

'Many new tunnels have been built.' Pickens said a smile playing on his lips. 'Since you were last here….vampire.'

Milly said nothing but continued to stare at Pickens.

'Some tunnels were never completed.' Pickens continued. 'A lot of dead ends if you don't know the way.'

'Could you show me the way?' Milly said.

'Possibly.' Pickens said.

Milly was about to ask Pickens how he knew the identity of the vampire that was now part of her, but was interrupted.

'Peter's here.' Rufus said suddenly.

'Your Alpha?' Roman asked.

'He and Shayla are a few miles outside the City. I've told them to come here. I hope that was OK.'

Roman nodded.

'I've also got to tell them Max and Elena are prisoners of a witch who works for the Vampire King.' Rufus paused.

'What?' Milly said.

'And that the king is Barumar.'

Milly's face dropped.

'Exactly.' Rufus said.

THEBE

Hazel Volger was a pretty child and upon reaching adulthood became a beautiful young woman with straight black hair framing an oval face of exquisite symmetrical features with dark eyes and full red lips. Shorter than average with a perfect hourglass figure Hazel was stunning and irresistible to all around her, except perhaps for one; her mother.

The childhood of this woman was a sad, sad tale filled with cruelty and torment with long years of suffering at the mercy of her mother. Salvia had despised her child from the moment she was born. Years of criticising, put downs and beatings had driven away any confidence that Hazel might have had in herself and although the beatings ceased when she grew up, the fear was always with her.

Returning home from the local market where she worked one day, Hazel had turned down an alley to take a longer route home as she still lived with her mother at that time and although her mother was now elderly and posed little threat to her she still seemed to maintain a hold of power over her forged from the years of torment and home was a place that Hazel was in no hurry to get to.

On this particular day she had ventured just a little way down the alley when she saw a group of men who appeared to be making menacing intentions to a small young man. Perhaps they were intending to rob him. Hazel turned on her heels and was about to run in the opposite direction when she heard the first of the screams. Glancing back what she now saw was the young man with his hand outstretched in the air and gesticulating whilst the group of would be attackers were on their knees. They began to sob and beg forgiveness as the young man said a strange word and opened the fingers of his hand. The other men were cast backwards to the ground and they picked themselves up and ran from the man in Hazel's direction. They did not even look at her as they ran past her. Laughter brought Hazel's attention back to the young man behind her.

'I'm sorry about that.' laughed the young man.

'What happened?' Hazel asked. 'I thought you were about to get robbed for sure.'

'Magic.' said the young man. Seeing the puzzled look on Hazel's face caused him to elaborate. 'Most folk call it magic but that is such a generalist term, it's actually so much more than that.'

'Magic.' Hazel intoned slowly.

She looked at the stranger again; looking more closely this time; taking in his features and appraising him to herself.

'My name is Vallendor.' said the young man extending his hand. 'Don't worry, I will not harm you.'

She could not explain why but Hazel felt drawn to the man as if he were someone she had known for a very long time. Someone who felt… friendly? She reached out her own hand.

'My name is…'

'Is?' Vallendor added.

'Thebe. My name is Thebe.'

'Thebe. I like that name; it sounds quite exotic.'

'I bet you never get robbed or beaten with a power like that do you.'

Vallendor raised an eyebrow. 'Well, let us say it would take more than the likes of them.'

'What I mean is I bet you never get scared of something like that.'

It was now Vallendor's turn to look at her in the same manner.

'You are a strange one aren't you. I think that I have seen you at the market before when I have been on errands for my master.

'You live nearby?' she asked.

'I reside within the Mage Academy Northside.' he gestured.

'You're a Mage? Of course you are. I've never met a Mage before. Oh I would love to be a Mage, that way nobody would mess with me. Boom, pow.'

As she spoke she mimicked his previous hand movements at imaginary opponents and the two of them began to laugh until the tears were rolling down their cheeks.

After little more than a month, Hazel, who now called herself Thebe after a young Empress she had once heard a story of and liked the sound of was enrolled into the Mage Academy herself. She had never had the courage to leave her mother all these years until now but there was something about Vallendor and this power he had used that called to her on a higher level. She knew that she had to have and wield this power for herself and she knew that if she did then she would never be scared or afraid of anyone ever again. Even being in the proximity of the magic had changed something in her. Hazel had finally left her that day; long live Thebe.

The Mage Academy was unlike anything she could possibly have imagined. She was enrolled into the school with a recommendation from her new friend Vallendor and the masters there seemed to like her. She absorbed everything that she could not just mentally but physically as well and in time she became one of the most gifted students of the academy. Her thirst for knowledge was insatiable; Thebe learned, practised and continued to practise. She prospered and the feeling of the magical energies she practised strengthened and revitalised her in ways she could hardly believe possible.

Then one day she was asked to go back to the market on an errand that was usually given to others when she happened down an alleyway similar to the one she had met Vallendor in some five years previously when she came upon a scene that sent shocking vibrations down her spine. There in the doorway of a crooked looking house was a woman who was scalding who Thebe supposed was the woman's daughter. She was shouting at her and shaking her violently. The young girl was crying and looked over towards Thebe. The look on the little girl's face still haunted her today.

'Don't you dare look away from me when I'm talking to you, you horrible little brat.' said the woman as she began to hit the child repeatedly over and over.

Something inside Thebe snapped that day; perhaps a doorway in her mind that had blocked out the worst of her tormented childhood or the barrier her mind had put up to stop herself from recalling those memories is unknown. One thing that was certain was that this was a turning point in

Thebe's life, and for the very first time since being able to control magic for herself she began to think dark thoughts.

It was the screaming pitch of the young child that brought her back to reality and as she began to take in her surroundings Thebe was aware of the fact that she had somehow been in some kind of trance and as she looked down upon the screaming child she was suddenly aware that the child was not screaming because of the beatings from her mother but at what her mother had become.

There in front of Thebe was what could only be described as an abomination. What was once the girl's mother was now unrecognisable as a withered mass of shrivelled flesh that looked as if it was burning from some invisible flame. The flesh melted from the bones and yet there was still a wailing exhalation from what was once a mouth. This thing was still alive. Far from snapping her out of this dark zone, the sight before Thebe caused her to act and with a gesture of her hand the now unrecognisable blob of charred flesh before her exploded like a balloon. The child ran for her life and Thebe was overcome with an emotion that staggered her. She struggled as this new feeling caused her to sway and stagger and she reached out her hand to steady herself on the bloody wall beside her until she gave it a word. That word was joy.

The discovery of the power within her fuelled by her darker emotions was intoxicating and for a while Thebe enjoyed the blissful ecstasy she felt when encapsulated by her new found powers. The magic took her to a level of happiness she had never felt. Thebe began to volunteer to run errands to the market where she listened for heated arguments and watched for signs of trouble so she could intervene. Thebe told herself that what she did was righteous, some people deserved to be punished for their actions, all the while refusing to accept that the real reason for using her magic this way was because she enjoyed it.

Word of a mage exacting vigilante justice reached the highest levels of the Mage Academy and Thebe was eventually expelled and banished from the local village, but the most painful punishment of all was the look of betrayal on Vallendor's face. He had believed in her, stood up for her and encouraged her to become more than she ever could have imagined. She would never forget seeing the hurt and disappointment in Vallendor's eyes as he turned away from her for the last time.

For decades Thebe travelled from village to village adopting the guise of a crippled beggar woman, her face hidden in the shadows of her hooded cloak. With a few whispered words Thebe was able to ensure the kindness and generosity of the villagers. She was never hungry or without a warm room and a comfortable bed to sleep in but she never spent too long in one place and was completely forgotten by everyone when she left.

As villages grew into towns and cities, Thebe found life much easier. She no longer had to hide beneath her cloak and the advancement of technology brought her out of the shadows. People were too busy looking down at the little devices they clutched in their hands to take notice of a disfigured old woman. Even after the pulse people rarely gave her a second look, especially in Braeden. They were all too busy scurrying about their daily business and trying to avoid the vampires to pay much attention to an old woman.

As Thebe walked through a crowd, people moved to one side to let her pass, the dark magic within creating an aura around her. People felt rather than saw the aura and were both afraid and repelled by it. In the market Thebe would fill her basket with groceries and the person behind her would offer to pay for her goods as well as their own. Nobody ever recalled seeing the old crone, they would only question why their own shopping was so expensive. Thebe enjoyed the power she could wield, but she was never careless. The discovery of supernatural creatures had made her cautious. Thebe found them annoyingly resistant to magic and thereby more difficult to manipulate and control. The malefic magic exacted a higher price when dealing with such beings, the loss of two toes on her left foot was a constant reminder.

Thebe no longer maintained the ruse of a beggar woman, she walked upright with the aid of a walking cane which she spitefully used to knock against the shins of passers-by or to trip them up just for the enjoyment of seeing them wince and curse. None of them challenged her, most apologised for their own clumsiness at having put their legs in her way. Although larger towns and cities afforded Thebe some anonymity she preferred to keep her distance. In one way or another they were all descendants of the people who had banished her from her own village, they were all sheep and she despised them.

Her small house on the outskirts of Braeden was deep enough into the forest to be overlooked by almost everyone. The arrival of Arcane's messengers a week earlier had been both a surprise and an irritation; she found the very fact that Arcane was aware of her existence perplexing and the demon within him terrified her.

What Arcane had demanded of her was costly, but he had since supplied her with recompense for the task. Thebe ran her fingers across the contours of her face and wondered what she looked like. The life-force she had stolen from the young homeless people Arcane had provided as sacrifices for the magic had only smoothed some of the ridges, the payment barely sufficient for bringing the children of his nemesis to Braeden.

Thebe looked at the two beautiful children, unconscious, restrained and helpless in the dungeon of the palace and hated them. Whatever Arcane wanted them for was no concern to her, their youth and beauty alone was enough to earn them pain and punishment. How easily they had fallen for the illusion spell, especially the girl. She had been so keen to chase after what she believed to be her beloved friend and the boy stupid enough to follow. During the spell to bring the children to Braeden, Thebe had seen enough of the old she-wolf to create an illusion of her face.

'Good enough to fool you!' Thebe said looking at the sleeping girl.

The boy began to stir and Thebe stepped back out of sight into the shadows.

The pounding in his head brought Max fully awake. The pain felt like someone had taken a knife to his skull. He squeezed his eyes shut and willed the pain to go away, but it stayed. He opened his eyes again, Elena was asleep next to him, the knock she had taken to the forehead a deep shade of purple and crusted with dried blood. Max had no doubt that Elena would awake up to a similar headache. He lifted his hand to rub the back of his neck, the metal wrist cuff and chain clanked as he moved and he frowned. The metal burned and chaffed his skin; it was silver.

Max looked around and recognised the stone room with its candles and chains bolted to the walls. It was a dungeon, the one he had seen in the cave during the rite of passage. Somehow he and Elena had ended up in the very place Uri had tried to save them from. Max tried to recall the details, his brain felt foggy, the details vague, the last thing he remembered was leaving Kristyna's kitchen, then he remembered the crone.

Elena had run from the house having caught a glimpse of Uri, or at least what she thought was Uri. Max had run after her knowing in his heart it was a trick but unable to leave Elena to run into the trap alone.

The Uri illusion, always just out of reach, had led them along the streets and into a narrow alleyway. The crone had turned, dropped the mask of Uri, and hit Elena square in the face with a blast of magic, knocking her off balance. Max had tried to fight, his werewolf strength should have been more than enough to deal with an old woman, but this woman had possessed a magical strength that he was not prepared for and so she had grabbed Max and Elena and thrown them into the back of a small van. A sickening stench had filled the back of the van rendering Max and Elena unconscious. The next thing Max knew, he was waking up with a pounding headache.

Recalling the stench inside the van Max felt suddenly nauseous. The sound of Max's dry retching brought Elena fully awake and she turned to look at her brother.

'Are you OK?' Elena asked rubbing her forehead.

Max continued to retch for a few moments and the chains on Elena's wrist jangled as she moved.

'These chains are stinging.' Elena said.

'Silver.' Max replied as the retching finally subsided.

'What is this place?'

'The dungeon Uri tried to save us from.' Max said turning back to look at his sister.

Elena looked down at her hands.

'I'm so sorry.' Elena said. 'I thought it was Uri.'

'I know.'

'I thought she'd come to take us home. How could I have been so stupid!?'

Elena started to cry and Max shuffled closer and put his arm around her, the wrist cuffs finding a new piece of skin to burn, Max gritted his teeth.

'Don't cry. At first I thought it was Uri.' Max said. 'I'd do anything to be at home right now. I wanted it to be real just as much as you did.'

'How did we get here?' Elena said sniffing.

'Some kind of gas in the back of the van I guess.' Max replied, his stomach turning at the thought of the putrid smell.

'What happened to Yosef?'

'I don't know.' Max said. 'I'm sure he followed us but as he's not here I'm guessing he was lucky not to get caught.'

'I hope he's OK.'

'Me too.'

Elena looked at Max who smiled and put his other arm around her and hugged her.

'We'll get out of this.' Max said. 'I promise.'

Max looked over Elena's shoulder and saw the light reflecting in the eyes of someone hiding in the shadows. The crone stepped forward and smiled. It was the same evil smile Max recognised from the cave and he knew he and Elena would not be getting out of the dungeon any time soon. His stomach clenched once more and he muttered the words his father had once said to him.

'Bravery and fear go hand in hand….never let the fear rule you.'

Max focused on his breathing and steadied his heart rate. He knew that they were in the presence of evil.

PAIN AND PUNISHMENT

'The elusive angel twins.' Arcane said stepping into the light.

Max looked at the man as he approached and wondered how long he had been watching. Elena pulled away from Max's shoulder and turned to face Arcane, her usual look of defiance on her face.

'My name is Arcane and you're a wolf.' Arcane said looking directly at Max.

Max said nothing.

'And what are you?' Arcane asked Elena.

'The one who's going to rip your heart out!' Elena replied.

'Really?' Arcane laughed. 'I don't think so child. Look at your position.'

'We'll see.' Elena said contemptuously.

Arcane laughed and the witch cackled. The sound made Elena wince and she broke eye contact and looked away.

'What an interesting pair you are.' Arcane said looking at the twins. 'Part angel, part Fey, part…..other, an impossible mixture of species, but here you are.'

'What do you want with us?' Max said angrily.

'Almost nothing.' Arcane replied cryptically. 'You have a little something I can use, but you're simply the bait.'

'For what?'

'Your mother. The only way to bring her here was to kidnap you.'

'What do you want with our mother?' Elena asked.

'To kill her of course.' Arcane replied.

Elena's eyes widened in shock and Max tightened his arm around her shoulder.

'I'll destroy you if you hurt my mother.' Max said. 'If my father doesn't tear you apart first.'

'I thought your sister was going to rip my heart out.' Arcane mocked. 'Make up your minds, is she going to kill me first or you?'

'One of us will kill you.'

Arcane stepped closer to Max, the whites of his eyes turned pure black, his iris glowed red and his features contorted into a malicious sneer. Max was looking back at the face of Eversor.

'Neither of you will succeed.' Eversor said.

Arcane's face reverted back to his normal features and he looked from Max to Elena.

'I see you.' Elena whispered. 'The darkness.'

'What are you babbling about?' Arcane snapped.

Elena looked at Arcane, her eyes fixed, in a trance-like state.

'Encroaching darkness demon sent, will usher in mankind's lament, holding death within plain sight, take a stand or lose this fight.'

Arcane frowned. Elena snapped out of her trance.

'It's you.' Elena said. 'You're holding the demon inside you.'

Arcane stepped back momentarily unnerved and although the shift to fear and back was instant, both Max and Elena saw it. Max hadn't heard the words before and wondered where Elena had read them and what the full impact was. Was she growing into her powers? Now was not the time to discuss it.

'I tire of this.' Arcane said. 'Witch! Make them stand up.'

Thebe stepped forward her hands outstretched towards the twins.

'Statum.' Thebe commanded.

Max and Elena both stood up straight. They were young and fairly easy to control but Thebe knew that as with all supernatural beings they were more resistant to magic, especially spells and commands intended to restrain or hurt them and would soon prove more challenging.

Restrained by Thebe and the silver chains Max and Elena stood erect in front of Arcane. He stepped closer and put his hands on Elena's shoulders and looked into her eyes. His eyes turned black as he looked into her soul, trapping the Faerie part of her consciousness. Arcane stared into Elena's eyes and inhaled deeply. He felt the power of the Fey rush to his head and savoured the temporary high before he transferred it to the black gem in the centre of the amulet he wore around his neck. The transfer complete he released Elena and repeated the same procedure with Max. Max did not know what he was doing but he did not resist. His fate would be no different to that of his sister.

Arcane staggered back from the twins, unsteady from the infusion of Faerie power he had just taken.

'You are….' Arcane left the sentence unfinished and turned away.

'What do you want me to do with them?' Thebe asked. 'I don't intend to stay here forever!'

Arcane waved a hand dismissively as he walked away.

'I have no further use for them.'

'What of the mother?' Thebe asked.

'She'll come whether they're alive or dead.' Arcane said as he ascended the stone steps. 'Do as you please.'

Thebe released her hold on the twins but they remained standing, both staring back at her brave and defiant.

'So boy, you're a wolf.' Thebe said menacingly. 'Let's see.'

* * * * *

'Are you OK child?'

Elena heard a female voice speaking to her and wondered where it was coming from.

'She's coming around.' the voice said. 'You're alright little one.'

Elena opened her eyes to see a woman with long silver hair, pale skin and light grey eyes looking down at her.

'My name is Radha, I'm a friend.'

'Where am I? Where's Max?' Elena asked sitting up. 'Where's my brother?'

Elena looked at the people around her. Standing next to Radha was a younger woman, slender with smooth dark skin, long dark brown hair and friendly brown eyes, she smiled at Elena as she spoke.

'My name is Wren. Your brother is fine. As for where you are, I'll explain later. Can you walk?'

Elena nodded.

'Good, 'cos we have to get moving.' Wren said with an air of authority that reminded Elena of Uri.

Elena stood up and Radha placed a steadying hand on her back.

'The boy's waking up.'

A large muscular man with auburn hair was kneeling down beside Max and another woman whose hair and body were as white as snow was standing over them. Elena looked at the man who had spoken then glanced back at Wren.

'That's Oren and Gardenia.' Wren said nodding in their direction. 'Oren, get him on his feet. We need to find shelter.'

Oren helped Max to his feet and soon the six of them were running.

'Where are we?' Max asked Elena as they ran. 'I feel…strange.'

'Me too. I don't know where we are, Wren said she'd explain later.'

Oren fell back and drew level with Max and Elena as they ran.

'Make sure you keep up.' Oren said. 'We're too exposed here.'

'Are we running to your camp?' Elena asked.

'We don't have a camp, we have to keep moving.'

Far out to one side, the silhouette of a winged creature standing on a hill caught Max's attention and Elena turned her head to look.

'We're not in our own world are we?' Elena said.

'The heat and the ice aren't the worst things in this place.' Oren replied.

Before Max and Elena could ask anything further Oren ran on ahead to catch up with Wren. Elena and Max kept pace with their four new friends as they ran through the withered trees and brush that surrounded them.

*****

Queen Thana paced up and down in her room waiting for nightfall. Against Barumar's orders, which he said were in place for the Queen's protection, Thana had slipped out of the Palace every night unaccompanied. Thana enjoyed the freedom of hunting in the forest and she could survive perfectly well on rabbits and other small animals, as could all vampires, though most chose not to. Thana didn't want to feed on human blood, she had lost that desire when she started to regain her humanity, but in recent years she had shamefully succumbed to the luxuries of life at the palace and drank whatever was prepared for her without a thought for its origin.

Since the meeting with Sheriff Reidar, Thana had felt unsettled and not only because of her feelings for her former lover. The news of twins in the City had reminded Thana of another set of twins and her heart clenched at the painful memory.

The daylight was almost gone, Thana could feel it in the air and she grabbed her cloak, pulling the hood down to hide her face. She opened the door carefully and quietly, there were no guards outside of her room, she would have sensed them and she was the Queen after all, not a prisoner, but she was still cautious, Arcane had spies everywhere. The distant, muffled sound of a child crying out in pain caught her attention, her acute hearing heard the anguished cry and Thana knew beyond any doubt that the twins were in the palace dungeon and by the sound of the cries and screams, they were being tortured. Thana heard the sound of bones breaking and the boy cried out again, a girl's voice shouted and pleaded for the torment to stop.

Thana moved with vampire speed. The flames in the wall sconces flickered as she arrived at the top of the stone steps that lead down to the dungeon.

Thana flew down the steps and took in the scene in front of her. An old crone stood with her back to Thana facing a boy and a girl, both chained. The boy was a wolf and the witch was using magic to trigger his werewolf change and reverse it before completion. Snapping and reshaping bones was part of the process and the witch was taking great delight in seeing the boy suffer the agony of the transformation. The girl was begging the witch to stop which only seemed to enhance her desire for cruelty.

Thana had committed transgressions over the centuries but in her state of near repentance, the sight of such brutality sickened her.

'STOP THIS AT ONCE!' Thana commanded.

The witch spun around, startled by the intrusion. Thana called for the guards and two vampires of her own personal guard were at her side in an instant.

'What's the meaning of this?' Thana asked the witch. 'Speak!'

The witch paused before responding. Thebe was powerful, but smart enough to know that she was no match for a millennial vampire and two vampire guards.

'Your majesty.' Thebe replied. 'I was….'

'I saw what you were doing.' Thana replied. 'Is it necessary to torture these children? They could have been subdued by any one of us and coerced into telling us everything.'

'You don't understand, your Highness. They are very dangerous. Arcane…'

'I might have known Arcane was behind this.'

The witch nodded but said nothing, she had already given away too much information. Arcane, or rather the demon within him would kill her if she revealed anymore.

'Do you have the King's permission to torture children?' Thana asked.

Again, the witch said nothing, she glanced at the twins and back to the Queen.

'I didn't think so.' Thana said. 'Guards, take her.'

'Take me where?' Thebe asked.

Thana stepped closer to the witch and looked at her.

'Be grateful I haven't killed you.' Thana said. 'You're a repulsive creature, the thought of feeding on you turns my stomach. Now get out of my sight.'

Thana nodded to the guards and Thebe didn't resist when they took an arm each and started walking her towards the stone steps.

'Shall I inform the King your majesty?' one of the guards asked.

'No. I'll see to it.'

The guards and the witch winked out of sight. Thana remained still until she was certain they were out of the lower levels of the palace. She turned to looked at the twins, they were beautiful, blond haired and blue eyed, they stared back at her with wide frightened eyes. Thana sniffed the air, the boy was a wolf and possibly the girl too, but they were something else, fragrant and intriguing, but unidentifiable. Whatever special capabilities they did or didn't possess, Thana knew she had to get the twins out of the palace before the witch went bleating to Arcane or he discovered they were gone, whichever came first.

Barumar would have heard their cries, although the sound of suffering would have probably made him smile and Thana hoped he would not have the inclination to investigate. Arcane, however, was a different matter.

'Don't be afraid.' Thana said knowing how empty her words must have sounded. 'My name is Thana and I'm going to get you out of here.'

'This is a trick!' the girl said recoiling.

'No. We're all getting out of here. What are your names?'

'Elena.'

'That's a lovely name, it means light.'

'Why do you want to help us?' the boy asked his eyes full of suspicion.

'Because I need to escape from this place too.'

'Why? You live in a palace.'

'It's still a prison.' Thana replied. 'Just with better rooms.'

Thana smiled and was rewarded with a half-smile from Elena. The boy didn't smile but he held out his hands.

'My name is Max and you need to unlock the chains.' Max said.

Thana found the keys and released the twins, the silver cuffs stinging her hands. The welts on Max's wrists were raw and bleeding but there was no time to clean and bandage his wounds. Thana suspected that his wolf DNA would heal him now that he was released from the silver shackles.

'Come to me.' Thana said holding her arms wide. 'I promise I won't hurt you.'

Max and Elena looked at each other before stepping forward. Thana pulled them close and held them in a tight embrace. The memory of another set of twins rose to the surface, there was no time to lose. Thana wrapped her cloak around both children and held them tight.

The same wall sconces flickered once more as Thana ran from the dungeon with the twins.

Arcane stood behind the parapet wall and looked out over the river and the City. Movement along Draven Bridge caught his eye and he smiled.

'Look.' Arcane said to no-one but Eversor. 'The wolves have kidnapped the Queen.'

Arcane hurried to find the King, his plan finally in motion.

TREASON

Sheriff Reidar's residence sat on a hill on the opposite side of the Nejelski River. Reidar loved the architecture, especially the first floor balcony with its columns. The house was sited on what was once a vineyard and Reidar was drawn to its ancient appearance, large gardens and isolation. He was as far away from the palace and the City as it was possible to be, whilst maintaining the position of Sheriff.

Reidar retained a small number of employees, loyal human staff who tended to the house and gardens during the day whilst he slept and vampire guards at night, none of whom resided in the house. Reidar guarded his privacy and the vampire guards had their own quarters in one of the outbuildings.

Standing on the balcony Reidar heard the whisper of movement and inhaled a familiar scent. He moved quickly and intercepted his visitor just as his armed guards emerged from the trees.

'What are you doing here?' Reidar asked.

'I had nowhere else to go.' Thana replied.

Reidar could hear the desperation in her voice, the guards edged closer sniffing the air, Thana was not alone.

'What have you done?' Reidar said looking at the children hiding beneath Thana's cloak.

'I know coming here is treason.' Thana said. 'But I need your help. There's no-one else I can trust.'

'I'm loyal to the sovereign.' Reidar replied. 'And you are my Queen.'

'Arcane's witch was torturing the boy. I had to save them Reidar, I couldn't leave them, I had to save the twins this time.'

Reidar nodded his understanding and put his arm around Thana's shoulders.

'Bring them inside.'

Reidar dismissed the guards who melted back into the shadows and ushered Thana and the twins into the house.

'This is Max and Elena.' Thana said opening her cloak. 'These are the twins the wolves are looking for.'

'I won't harm you.' Reidar said. 'You are under Thana's protection and you have my word.'

The twins stepped out from under Thana's cloak. They looked sceptically at Reidar and glanced back at Thana.

'Sheriff Reidar is a very old friend.' Thana said.

'I'm a man of honour, you can trust my word.' Reidar said.

'You're not a man anymore, you're a vampire.' Max said.

'Some things never change. My word of honour is one of them.'

Max stared at Reidar and nodded, it was Reidar who broke eye contact first.

'You're safe here.' Thana said.

'For now.' Reidar said. 'When Barumar discovers you've left the palace, this is the first place he'll look. We need to get you all somewhere more secure.'

'He won't look for me tonight, he barely notices me anymore.'

'You can't be certain.' Reidar said. 'It was Arcane's witch that was torturing the boy, he's bound to go back and check on her progress.'

'Barumar doesn't know the twins were in the palace, if he did they'd be dead already.'

Reidar nodded but said nothing, he felt with absolute certainty that Arcane was playing a longer game and couldn't help but feel that Thana's rescue of the twins was part of a more elaborate plan.

'Even if that's the case, I'd feel better knowing you and the twins were somewhere else.' Reidar said. 'You're all vulnerable here.'

'What do you suggest?' Thana asked.

'Take them to the wolves.'

Thana gasped and Reidar stepped forward cupping her face in his hands.

'My love.' Reidar said. 'The wolves are looking for them. They'll be safer with their own kind. I have an understanding with the Alpha…'

'But…'

'I'll die before I let them hurt you.'

Reidar kissed Thana passionately and Max and Elena looked at each other in awkward silence.

'Do I have time to use the bathroom before we go?' Elena asked.

Reidar stepped back from Thana and disengaged from her embrace.

'Of course.' Reidar replied clearing his throat.

* * * * *

After the initial greetings and introductions Peter asked Rufus to bring him up to date. Between them, he and Milly had given Peter and Shayla the news that they had located the twins, but they were prisoners of a witch and being held at the palace of the vampire king.

Rufus was pleased to see his Alpha, but the rage in Peter's eyes was at a level Rufus had never seen before and he bowed his head and waited for Peter to speak.

'Breathe.' Shayla whispered to Peter. 'Save the rage for rescuing the twins.'

Roman stepped in between Rufus and Peter and put his hands on Peter's shoulders.

'We'll get your children back.' Roman said. 'Together. My pack and I will fight beside you.'

Peter nodded his gratitude and controlled his breathing, clenching and unclenching his fists he waited for the rage to subside, something it had taken years of practice to do, it would be all too easy to let the wolf inside him loose, but he had made that mistake in his youth, a memory he lived with and regretted.

'Come.' Roman said squeezing Peter's shoulders. 'Let us talk somewhere more private.'

'Tell me more about the City.' Peter replied.

Roman understood the subtext in Peter's reply and lightened his speech for the benefit of the other patrons in the cafe.

'Braeden has many interesting sights for you to enjoy brother. Let's have a drink and I'll tell you all about the City.'

Roman released his grip on Peter and led the way to the back of the cafe, nodding to Matyas to join him. He opened a wooden door near the kitchen and indicated for everyone to step inside. Peter led the way, Shayla and the other wolves followed. Roman detained Jedrek at the door.

'Fetch Grimlock and tell him to bring all the plans and blueprints.'

'He won't come.'

'Tell him it's not a request.'

Peter looked around the basement, it was larger than he had expected.

'It takes in the whole footprint of the courtyard above.' Rufus said. 'Including the tree.'

Rufus spoke to Peter using werewolf telepathy.

There's another way out. Trap door behind the rowan tree. Tunnels extend across the whole City. A lot of silver and ash wood reinforcement. All vampire repellent.

The end of the tunnels? Peter asked.

Secure and tricky to open but not impossible.

Easier if you have the vampire skill to become mist. Milly said.

One thing at a time. Peter responded.

Roman sensed the wolves communicating. Werewolf telepathy developed between pack members and Roman was thankful that eavesdropping was not possible especially with some of the conversations he'd had with his own pack. Instead he ignored the wolves and turned to Shayla.

'Can I get you anything, your Majesty?' Roman said.

Shayla frowned.

'I know you're heir to the throne of Fey.' Roman said.

'How do you know that?' Shayla replied, then shook her head. 'It doesn't matter. No thank you. I'm fine.'

Shayla smiled and folded her arms across her body. She shivered, the basement was cold.

'Here.' Milly said wrapping the shawl she had coerced from a street vender around Shayla's shoulders. 'You need this more than I do.'

'Thanks.'

'There's a hat to match if you want it.' Milly said winking at Shayla.

Shayla smiled and shook her head.

'We can speak freely down here.' Roman said commanding everyone's attention.

'The city feels overrun with vampires. How many are there?' Peter asked.

'Too many.'

'How do I get into the palace?'

'Jedrek will return soon with another of my pack who has the blueprints of the sewers and plans of the palace.'

'What of the King who has my children?' Shayla asked.

'All I can tell you about Barumar is he's insane.'

'Barumar?' Peter said. 'Did you say Barumar?'

'You know him?' Roman asked.

Peter inhaled and exhaled deeply, his rage never far from the surface.

You failed to mention the vampire king's name! Peter said glancing at Rufus.

Rufus shrugged but said nothing.

'A member of my pack removed his head decades ago.' Peter said. 'He should have turned to ash.'

'How is he still alive?' Roman asked.

'He must have been wearing a token.' Milly said. 'I've heard that reanimation is possible, but it's rarely successful, at least that's what I heard.'

'If Barumar knows they're your children….'

Rufus instantly regretted his words and let the sentence hang in the air. Shayla looked stricken and Peter shot Rufus a warning look.

'I don't think the king is behind this.' Roman said quickly. 'There's enough humans and wolves in the City to keep him entertained. Using magic to kidnap children doesn't fit.'

Matyas remained silent throughout the conversation but suddenly spoke in Roman's mind, Roman nodded.

If the children are part Fey, Barumar would have supported any scheme to bring them here.

'What did he say?' Shayla asked.

'Arcane, the king's advisor is most likely responsible.' Roman lied.

'You're lying.'

Roman looked uncomfortable but continued after a momentary pause.

'He said Arcane controls the city through the king. It sounds more like his kind of thing to employ the services of a witch.'

Shayla's frustration overwhelmed her. Fuelled by her own anger and Titan's strength Shayla unleashed her rage. Her huge black and silver wings materialised behind her, their razor sharp edges shiinged as they unfolded. The wing tips, like three long, pointed black fingers, grabbed Roman by the throat and pinned him against the wall of the basement. Shayla's eyes turned amber, the timber of her voice deepened and she spoke with Titan's voice.

'Do not lie!' Shayla said through sharp elongated teeth. 'Tell me what he said.'

Roman remained perfectly still but said nothing. Matyas growled deep in his throat and moved to intercept but Roman held up his hand to stop him.

'Matyas said, if the children are Fey, Barumar would have supported any scheme to bring them here. I know your children are Fey.' Roman said. 'My intention was to spare you more pain and not destroy any hope you have.'

'Shayla.' Peter said gently. 'Roman is not our enemy.'

Peter stepped forward and whispered in Shayla's ear.

'Titan, release him. Meldainiel, my angel, let him go.'

Shayla blinked and her eyes returned to their usual green. Releasing Roman, Shayla retracted her wings and they phased back out of sight.

'My apologies.' Shayla said quietly.

'None necessary.' Roman replied. 'You're upset about the children, I understand that. Those formidable wings were a surprise, to be sure.'

'I let my anger get the better of me.'

'How did you know I was lying?' Roman asked. 'I'm usually very good at it.'

Roman smiled and his eyes twinkled with mischief and Shayla felt herself relax and smiled back.

'I always know when someone is lying.'

Shayla looked at everyone in turn, surprise and shock registered on all of the faces around her. Peter took her in his arms and stroked her hair.

'Save the rage for rescuing the twins.' Peter said. 'Isn't that what you told me?'

* * * * *

Arcane wasted no time in finding the King and now he watched as Barumar set about destroying everything in Queen Thana's room. Barumar slammed his fist down onto the writing table, smashing it to pieces, he shouted, stomped his feet and ripped the door off its hinges and threw it against the wall. He turned to Arcane, hard eyes staring, his face contorted in rage.

'Tell me again.' Barumar said.

'It was the wolves my liege.' Arcane paused, relishing the moment. 'With the help of the witch, I acquired two Fey children for you, for the next lunar hunt. The children must have been known to the wolves.'

'Why?' Barumar said. 'Why would they risk taking the Queen. How did they overpower her? It makes no sense.'

'The witch must have betrayed me and helped the wolves break into the palace. Queen Thana was obviously their real target. The wolves have gone too far my King. The children are nothing, but they have taken your Queen. This cannot be ignored.'

Barumar paced the room and Arcane waited in silence, his expression revealing nothing.

'Even if the Queen went willingly…' Arcane said.

'What are you saying?' Barumar snapped. 'Thana would never betray her own kind.'

Arcane paused again, knowing that if he gave the king just enough information, Barumar would jump to the inevitable conclusion.

'Of course not, but Sheriff Reidar…'

'Even after twenty-five years, after all I've given her, she's still in love with that fool.' Barumar said.

Arcane looked down at his feet playing the part of reluctant informant before leading Barumar one step further.

'The Sheriff has also been seen in the city.'

'He's the Sheriff, where else would he be?' Barumar asked.

'I know he has been meeting with the wolves in secret…'

'I should have known.'

'This is treason my king.' Arcane said.

'No.' Barumar replied. 'This is war.'

And there it was, just as Arcane had planned. Eversor was impressed by the level of evil Arcane had sunk to. King Barumar had declared war on the werewolves. The City streets would run red with the blood of the innocent citizens of Braeden.

Arcane and Eversor smiled.

WORLD WITHIN A WORLD

'There.' Wren said pointing to a small building in the distance. 'We'll rest there.'

The derelict stone building hid among the trees, stubbornly refusing to die. The walls were no more that the same rock and dirt that surrounded it, yet no storm had succeeded in reducing it to rubble. The walls were firm and the thick dust covered glass from the single window was intact. It was a refuge for the six inhabitants.

The six companions had stopped to catch their breath but without another word they all recommenced running towards the place Wren had indicated. The building was the largest of three surrounded by gnarly trees with large black leaves. From a distance the trees looked dead but upon closer inspection their leaves appeared waxy, not dry and papery, and the thick tree roots spread out wide from the base of the trunk in search of water.

Wren set everyone a task and Max and Elena were sent to collect wood for a fire and commanded to keep at least one of the adults in sight at all times. They talked quietly whilst picking up fire wood.

'How do you feel?' Elena asked.

Max shrugged but said nothing.

'Talk to me Max.'

'I feel strange.' Max replied finally. 'I can't feel the wolf anymore.'

'What?'

'I can't explain it. It's like..'

'You're not quite you anymore.'

Max nodded and kicked absently at a protruding tree root disturbing a small creature which looked like a squirrel, or a rat with no tail. It was grey like the stones of the surrounding earth with small blunt ears and black eyes. Max and the squirrel stared at each other, one inquisitive, the other in fear. As the creature made a dash for alternative cover Oren caught it in his two large hands and swiftly broke its neck.

'Dinner.' Oren said holding the squirrel's limp body up for Elena to see.

'Seriously?' Elena said feeling nauseous again.

'They don't taste that good, and there's not much meat on them, but it's all there is. Let's go, we'll find water beneath that tree with the black waxy leaves, but we'll have to dig for it.'

Max and Elena carried what little firewood they could find and walked either side of Oren.

'I overheard you talking.' Oren said. 'We all feel different in here.'

'Why is that?' Max asked.

'Only the part of you that's Fey is trapped in here. It's hard to explain.' Oren said rubbing his hand over his stubbly chin which never seemed to grow any longer.

'Is this what it feels like to be pure Fey?' Max asked.

'I'll let Wren or Radha explain, they're better at this than me.'

Inside the building, Oren made a fire and placed a couple of small skewered creatures over the flames to cook. Max ran his hand along one of the stone walls and studied the hair-line cracks as if they hid some secret meaning. His eyes flickered over the rest of the building and at Elena and his four new companions sitting by the small fire before he spoke.

'What is this place?' Max asked. 'Why don't I feel right?'

Radha looked at Wren who nodded.

'It's a prison.' Radha replied. 'You feel different because it's only the Faerie part of your consciousness that's been trapped. Your physical bodies are still outside, but you'll feel differently out there too, as if part of you is missing.'

'How's..?' Max began.

'That possible?' Radha finished the sentence for him. 'I'm sure you've met a man called Arcane?'

Max and Elena nodded.

'I met Arcane a long time ago.' Radha continued. 'I thought he was my friend, but I discovered too late how wrong I was.'

'Who is he?' Max asked.

'He's the son of the Shadow Lord and just as evil.'

'The Shadow Lord?' Max said. 'I've heard the story of how he was defeated. Were you one of the elementals that fought with my father?'

'Yes.' Radha nodded.

'Wow!' Elena said. 'One of the Elementals. You must be really brave.'

'Not really.' Radha said recalling how the battle with the Shadow Lord had affected her so badly that she had abandoned her friends and lived in a pharmaceutical haze for a few years.

Radha became aware that everyone was waiting for her to continue the explanation and she pushed the memories aside and looked at the twins.

'As I was saying.' Radha said. 'This is a prison world.'

'How do you know this?' Max asked.

'I'm an awakener.' Radha replied. 'Or at least I was outside. It's how I know things. Arcane has genetic memories from his father. This world is a replica of the place the Shadow Lord was incarcerated in for centuries by the Fey. We're trapped in a world of Arcane's creation, inside the crystal pendant he wears around his neck. He uses this place to punish us, as revenge for his father, at least that's what I think.'

'There's a darkness inside that man.' Elena said quietly. 'I saw it.'

'There is.' Radha replied reaching out for Elena's hand. 'It was the demon who showed Arcane how to use the crystal and draw on its power.'

'Is there a way out?' Max asked.

'We haven't found one yet.' Wren replied.

'Doesn't matter how far you travel north, south, east or west.' Oren said. 'Eventually you come to a solid black wall. It's impenetrable.'

'Nothing's impenetrable.' Max replied.

'I admire your spirit.' Oren said.

'Has it always been just four of you?' Max asked.

'No.' Oren said shaking his head sadly. 'There were five of us until recently and there have been others.'

'Where are they?' Elena asked with the innocence of youth. 'Are they hiding somewhere else?'

Radha glanced at the others. Oren bowed his head, Gardenia and Wren remained silent.

'I'm not going to lie to you, this is a terrible place.' Radha said looking from Elena to Max. 'We're hunted by the abominable creatures that Arcane has created to torment us, many have fallen.'

'Including your friend?' Elena said her eyes full of tears.

'No.' Radha replied her voice catching in her throat

Max and Elena looked around at each of their companions in turn.

'Arcane has learnt to draw on the power of the Fey.' Wren said finally. 'It leaves us weak and vulnerable. One night five of us laid down to sleep and in the morning Kealoha was gone.'

'He ceased to exist?' Max asked.

Wren nodded.

'If you die in here, do you die outside?' Elena asked.

'I don't think so.' Wren replied. 'But you'll never feel quite the same again. As Radha said, you'll always feel as if part of you is missing.'

'There's got to be a way out of here.' Max said defiantly. 'I *will* feel whole again.'

'I admire your tenacity.' Wren said. 'But I'm afraid it's hopeless.'

'My father wouldn't give up.' Max said. 'And neither will I.'

Elena stared straight ahead, her eyes fixed on something only she could see.

'Nothing is forever.' Elena said with a wisdom beyond her years. 'Hopelessness is merely the fog that surrounds us at this moment. The light will burn through and show us a clear path. I'm sure of it.'

Nobody spoke for several moments and Max contemplated again whether Elena's strange turn of phrase and her trance-like stare was a manifestation of a new power.

'Will that path be good or bad?' Wren asked breaking the silence.

'Fifty-fifty.' Max replied. 'I like those odds.'

Oren clamped his hand on Max's shoulder and gave an encouraging squeeze but said nothing.

'Rest while you can.' Wren said. 'We have to move at first light.'

* * * * *

Thebe hurried from room to room in her small house gathering essential belongings and stuffing them into a bag. Queen Thana's intervention of Thebe's torture of the wolf-boy had been unfortunate and she wondered to herself how much more there was to both children, now she would never know. She admonished herself at how clumsily she had revealed Arcane's name, he would surely make her the scapegoat in this matter. Thebe considered herself lucky that the vampire guards had only escorted her out of the palace and left her at the end of Draven Bridge.

Her mind raced, where should she go, and how much time did she have before the vampires came knocking at her door?

Thebe stopped suddenly. She thought back over her long miserable life. For years she had hidden in the shadows, constantly moving from village to village, she was tired of running.

'Why should I run?' Thebe said to herself. 'They should be running from me.'

Her mind raced again, this time in a different direction. Thebe made the decision to run no more.

'I'll need help.' Thebe said looking around at the scattered items in the room.

Thebe picked up a ragged piece of cloth.

'Perhaps a stitch golem.' Thebe said thoughtfully, turning the cloth over in her hands.

An idea blossomed in her mind. The mud and silt from the riverbed would made an excellent medium and there was more than enough to make herself not one, but two golem protectors. When the vampires came for her, Thebe would be ready.

Thebe grabbed her cloak and walking cane and hurried out of the house leaving the door unlocked, she wouldn't be returning.

ENEMY AND FRIEND

Max felt as if he had only just closed his eyes and now Elena was shaking him.

'Max, wake up!' Elena said, her voice urgent. 'Wren says we have to move quickly.'

'What time is it?' Max said yawning and stretching as he stood up.

'I don't know.' Elena said. 'It's hard to tell.'

'What's going on?'

Max looked at Elena quizzically; Elena shrugged.

'The creature that was following us yesterday.' Oren said from his position by the door. 'It's found us.'

'What is it?' Max whispered.

'A manticore.' Wren replied. 'At least that's what I call it.'

A deep growl and the scratching of claws against the door froze everyone in place. Max and Elena looked to Wren who put her finger to her lips for them to remain quiet.

Wren took a deep breath and nodded to Oren whose hand remained poised on the handle of the door. Wren manipulated the air in the room and directed their scent towards the window directly opposite the door, pushing the air out through the smallest cracks. The creature reacted, sniffing and snorting, its huge feet could be heard shuffling outside and moving away.

Wren nodded again at Oren who quietly opened the door with one hand and produced a fireball in the other. He was first out of the door, hurtling a fireball at the creature. Gardenia followed, whipping up a maelstrom of earth and rocks creating a wall between them and the beast.

'Run!' Wren said pushing Max and Elena out of the door. 'Stay with

Radha, run and don't look back!'

Gardenia, Wren and Oren rained earth, air and fire down on the manticore. The creature backed away, its own hunt temporarily forgotten by the assault. Oren threw missile after missile of fire and Gardenia manipulated and moved twisted tree roots to tangle around the manticore's feet, restricting its movements. Oren set a ring of fire around the creature who roared out its anger, saliva dripping from its razor sharp teeth. The manticore opened its wings and beat them against the flames, the fire began to retreat. The earthly shackles wouldn't hold a creature of such strength for long and Wren, Gardenia and Oren were soon running as fast as they could catching up with Radha, Max and Elena.

Radha held onto Max and Elena, pulling them along, but the children struggled to keep up the pace, the fatigue ever present in the prison world washing over them, drawing what little energy they had.

'We have to put as much distance as possible between us and that thing.' Wren said. 'Pick up the pace.'

'I can't go on.' Elena said, her breath wheezing in her chest.

'You must!' Radha said pulling at her. 'We can't stop! Nothing will hold that thing for long.'

'Let me go.'

Elena pulled her hand free and staggered to a stop.

'Elena!' Max cried pulling free from Radha and returning to his sister.

'I'm sorry Max.' Elena said. 'I'm too tired. You go on with the others.'

'I'm not leaving you.'

Wren and the others stood away from the children their heads turning from the horizon and back to the children, all of them torn between the instinct to survive and the pull to save the twins.

'Keep going.' Gardenia said. 'I'll go back and help them along.'

Gardenia jogged back to where Max and Elena stood side by side.

'Come on, you can make it. There's always another ridge of rocks or a cave or something and we usually find somewhere to hide.'

Elena shook her head.

'I feel so tired.'

'I know how you feel.' Gardenia said. 'I'm tired too, but we have to keep going.'

Gardenia smiled and Max and Elena nodded. A deep, loud roar caught everyone's attention and Gardenia pushed Max and Elena until they began running again.

The manticore broke free from its bonds, leaped over the remaining flames and pursued its prey.

The beast stood on the horizon and let out a roar; a raw sound that started deep within its body, the sound pushing out into the air with so much force it could be heard for miles.

Gardenia glanced behind her, her heart pounding in her chest. She recalled seeing wildlife shows as a child and remembered one in particular where a lioness ripped a gazelle apart. Now running across a barren landscape with nothing more that the clothes she stood up in and the ability to manipulate the earth and rocks around her, the idea of tearing flesh seemed to grip her attention more strongly. She imagined the intense pain of her own flesh being torn from bones and felt sick. Gardenia ran faster and hoped they all had the strength to reach shelter.

The beast roared again and began moving, its powerful limbs eating up the distance between them. Max and Elena looked behind them to see the manticore gaining ground.

'Keep moving.' Gardenia yelled. 'Don't look back.'

Before Max and Elena could turn back around the manticore leapt into the air, using its wings to aid its momentum; its powerful jaws wide open exposing wickedly sharp canine teeth. The beast moved in a perfect arc and as its feet touched the ground, its mouth clamped on the back of Gardenia's neck forcing her to the ground.

For a split second Gardenia made eye contact with Elena before mercifully losing consciousness. Max and Elena stopped and stood frozen in fear. They watched horrified as the manticore's canines pierced Gardenia's windpipe and surrounding blood vessels, her heart still pumping once life giving blood into the torn arteries, flowed down into Gardenia's lungs and if she wasn't already dead from a broken neck she would have drowned in her own blood.

The manticore unclamped its jaws from Gardenia's throat and looked up at the twins. It stood with one of its huge paws on Gardenia's back. The purpose of the kill wasn't for food as with most carnivores, the creature hunted for sport.

'We need to run.' Max whispered tugging at Elena's hand.

Elena stood immobile.

'Elena!' Max cried.

The beast licked Gardenia's blood from its muzzle and stared directly at Elena.

'I'm sorry Max.' Elena said her eyes transfixed on the manticore.

Max looked at the beast who stared back at his sister, he knew there was no way they could out run it. He understood they were the next target. Resolved, he took a deep breath and stood beside his sister.

'I'm not leaving you.' Max said reaching for Elena's hand. 'We came into this world together, we die together.'

Elena glanced at her brother and took his hand, a jolt of electricity passed through them as their fingers touched.

'What's happening?' Max and Elena said in unison.

Both felt a heat rising from the pit of their stomachs as the angel light from within burst forth and surrounded them. In that instant Max and Elena awoke to infinite possibilities and an understanding of each other beyond their human, Fey or wolf comprehension. Their bodies transcended the confines of flesh and bone and merged to become something far greater and more powerful than any world had ever seen.

Wren, Oren and Radha stood a short distance away, all three traumatised by the death of Gardenia, wanting to run but none of them able to look away. The beast seemed to hesitate, or was it deciding which of the children to kill first?

Oren produced a fireball.

'We're too far away.' Wren said staying his hand.

'I'll move in closer.' Oren replied. 'I can't just stand here.'

'Something's happening?' Radha said blinking her eyes rapidly. 'The beast isn't moving and there's a light coming from the twins.'

As the three companions watched Max and Elena, a light emitted from their clasped hands. The light grew larger and brighter encompassing both their bodies. The twins bodies glowed with a brightness that would have made fresh snow look dull and grey, a brightness to rival the sun in the prison world. Wren, Oren and Radha shielded their eyes for fear of going blind, when they opened them again Max and Elena were gone and a single being stood in their place and it was speaking to the beast. Speaking in a voice of dual tones, the words it spoke easily carried to their ears.

'Angry creature all alone, we are all so far from home, let our eyes hold you still, we bind you now unto our will.'

The manticore tilted its head to one side and blinked its eyes slowly.

Large wings unfolded behind the mysterious newcomer and it spoke once more to the beast.

'See us now as friend not foe, sleep until we let you go.'

The beast stepped away from Gardenia's body, turned a full circle and settled itself down on the ground. The manticore folded back its wings, put its head on its two huge front paws and closed its eyes.

Whether drawn by curiosity or some unknown force, Wren, Oren and Radha walked towards the mysterious stranger that had taken the place of Max and Elena. The newcomer turned around and smiled, it was the most beautiful creature any of them had ever seen, neither male or female but a mixture of both.

'What happened to Max and Elena?' Wren asked glancing from the sleeping manticore to the stranger.

The stranger replied with a voice that sounded like the most beautiful song they could ever imagine.

'We are Max and Elena.'

'I don't understand.'

'We are Elemax.'

Elemax stood tall and confident, body muscular but slender and completely silver, covered with smooth and shiny, downy silver fur, from the top of the head to the tips of the toes. Piercing blue eyes and long silver lashes looked out of an ethereal face framed by long silver hair like spun silk. The silky straight hair hung down at the back between two large wings, the feathers varied in shade from light grey at the centre out to silver and almost white at the tips.

'What are you?' Wren whispered in awe.

'You're so beautiful.' Oren said breathlessly.

Radha went to speak but hesitated.

'Are we an Angel?' Elemax said as if reading Radha's mind.

Radha nodded but said nothing.

Elemax glowed with a light from within and walked towards the three of them with an animalistic grace of effortless and fluid movements.

Radha looked at Elemax and could see this creature was entirely beautiful and could only have been crafted by The Divine. When Elemax walked, the ground seemed to recognise its footsteps, softening beneath its toes and the air moved to assist it forward. Radha felt in her heart that every molecule Elemax breathed was alight with something else.

Elemax's face was flawless with a disarming smile that lit up its eyes. Wren, Oren and Radha couldn't help but smile back. To stand in Elemax's presence was to feel like they had been warmed by the summer sun regardless of the time, place or the season.

Elemax held out one of its hands towards Wren who took it in her own. The hand was beautiful, precise and elegant with long slender fingers and pointed spear-shaped metallic nails that shone like living silver, the grip strong.

'Do not be afraid.' Elemax said smiling at all three of them in turn.

Radha didn't fully understand what had happened to Max and Elena, not yet. Radha had sensed when they first appeared in the prison world that there was something more to the twins than being part Fey. Given the animalistic movements of Elemax, Radha suspected the twins were also part wolf, but what else? Why had she thought Elemax was an angel? Was it possible? Perhaps their mysterious DNA combination and their heightened fear of the situation had triggered the merging of the two as a protection.

It's certainly a different response to the usual fight of flight reflex. Radha thought.

Radha stared at Elemax, there was more to see than the superficial beauty. Elemax was strong and the blue-eyed gaze held a steely determination. She felt the answers to all of her questions were on the tip of her tongue and her mind grasped at what she knew and what she suspected, but the answers wouldn't come, at least not for the moment.

'What are you?' Radha asked repeating Wren's earlier question.

'We are the wolf-angel.' Elemax said staring back at Radha with challenging eyes. 'We are here to save you.'

REUNION

Tempest opened the door to the cafe's basement and almost flew down the steps towards Roman. They spoke quickly in their own language, Roman frowned and shook his head. Tempest nodded and returned to the cafe closing the door behind her. Matyas moved to the foot of the stairs and stood with his arms across his chest, clearly barring the way.

Peter and his pack used werewolf telepathy to communicate.

What's going on? Rufus asked.

Visitors. Milly replied

Who?

She's being deliberately vague, she suspects I can understand her.

Vampires. Peter said. *I can smell them and…*

Peter sniffed the air and looked towards Shayla.

'Max and Elena.' Shayla said inhaling.

Peter nodded and held out his hand to Shayla, she took it and they made their way to the stairs and the exit above. Roman held up his hand to stop them.

'Out of my way.' Peter growled. 'I know my children are upstairs.

'Listen to me.' Roman said firmly. 'They're not alone.'

'I know. Vampires.'

'One of them is known to me and can be trusted.'

Peter inhaled deeply holding in his anger but said nothing.

'Reidar has brought your children here because it's the safest place for them, with their own kind, but he has done this at great risk to himself. I have given my word that he will not be harmed.'

'OK.' Peter replied.

'I am Alpha here. Reidar and his companion will not be harmed.'

'I understand.' Peter said. 'Can I see my children now?'

'Of course.' Roman replied. 'Tempest, bring them downstairs.'

With her acute wolf hearing Tempest had only been waiting for Roman's command and immediately opened the door and ushered the vampire Sheriff, his companion and Max and Elena downstairs into the basement. Matyas stepped to one side and the twins ran to Shayla's outstretched arms. Shayla pulled them close and kissed them, Max, Elena and Shayla were all crying with relief at being reunited. Peter gathered his wife and children to him and the family stood together for a few minutes enjoying that brief moment in the safety of Peter's arms. Rufus and Milly moved towards them and the pack huddled closely to each other. The circumstances of the twins abduction, the strange city and the two vampires with them, momentarily forgotten in the euphoria of the reunion.

It was Milly who broke away first and stepped towards the Sheriff, recalling Gaolyn's memories of his friendship with Reidar.

'Thank you old friend.' Milly said clasping his hand and shaking it. 'You know this is treason?'

'I know.'

Reidar's companion threw back the hood of her cloak, revealing a face Milly had only seen in the memories of Gaolyn and not for many, many years.

'Thana!' Milly said embracing the Vampire Queen. 'It's been so long.'

Thana stiffened at Milly's embrace.

'My apologies.' Milly said releasing Thana.

'There was no time to tell you.' Reidar said putting his arm around Thana.

'It's alright.'

Milly stood still before Thana as she raised her hand to touch Milly's face.

'I don't know you, but I know your eyes.' Thana said.

'You are as beautiful as the day we first met.' Milly replied.

'Gaolyn?' Thana whispered.

Milly nodded. Rufus watched with concern as his sister exposed her throat to the vampire and he growled. Thana stepped in closer to Milly's neck and inhaled.

'How is this possible?' Thana asked.

'Sanguinaria ritual.'

'I've never heard of a success between species.' Thana said stepping back and frowning.

'We were the first.'

'Do you know these vampires Milly?' Peter asked.

'Yes. I'm sorry.' Milly replied. 'Introductions; Reidar; Thana; this is my Alpha, Peterus Maximus. Peter, may I present Reidar and Thana. The three of us are very old friends…er...were…er…you know what I mean.'

Reidar and Thana inclined their heads towards Peter who responded in kind, nobody moved.

Everyone in the basement watched the exchange between Milly and the vampires. The silence was broken by Jedrek bursting through the door to the basement, Tempest hot on his heels, Grimlock bringing up the rear. Jedrek leaped to his Alpha's side baring his teeth.

'You brought the Sheriff down here?' Jedrek asked incredulously.

'He brought Peter's children to us.' Roman replied.

'You know who that is right?'

Roman looked more closely.

'You brought the Vampire Queen here!' Roman said to Reidar. 'Are you trying to start a war?'

'Thana is not your enemy!' Reidar said stepping in front of Thana. 'She saved the children.'

'Wanted them for herself did she?' Jedrek spat, his body beginning the transformation to warrior form.

'You idiot dog!' Reidar said baring his fangs at Jedrek. 'We've brought the children to you. Why would we do that if we wanted to hurt them?'

'Why would the Queen betray the King in this way?' Roman said desperately trying to keep control of the situation.

'The witch was torturing the boy!' Thana said. 'I couldn't bear it! I stole them away from the palace and took them to Reidar. I didn't know where else to go. It was his idea to bring them to you, he said the wolves were looking for the twins and would protect them. I'm beginning to wonder if it was such a good idea, you're all such savages!'

'KILL THEM!' Jedrek raged.

Peter pushed Shayla and the twins behind him and stepped up next to Roman. Jedrek's transformation was underway and Rufus was also bearing his teeth and extending his claws in response to the perceived threat. Grimlock stood at the foot of the stairs barring the exit as Matyas took up position near his Alpha the werewolf rage permeating into each and every one of them. Reidar and Thana stood facing off the wolves, their sharp fangs exposed.

Standing back with his mother and sister, Max watched events unfold, the situation was spiralling out of control, neither side would prevail.

Max pushed away from the relative safety at his mother's side and stood between the wolves and the vampires, arms extended, hands up in the universal stop sign.

'STAND DOWN!' Max commanded 'ALL OF YOU! NOW!'

Wolves and vampires all looked at Max.

'STAND DOWN!' Max repeated.

'Max, get out of the way.' Peter commanded his son.

'No father. I won't allow any of you to hurt Reidar and Thana.' Max replied looking at each of the wolves. 'Listen to me!'

Max's sudden intervention had shocked both sides and the vampires now stood silently, fangs retracted. The wolves tamped down their rage, but remained alert and ready.

'Let the boy speak.' Grimlock said stepping forward.

Peter nodded encouragement to his son.

'We wouldn't be here without Reidar and Thana.' Max said. 'If Queen Thana hadn't gotten us out of the palace Elena and I would be still chained up in the dungeon being tortured or worse. They've both risked their lives.'

'And we thank them for their service.' Jedrek said sarcastically. 'Now let's send them on their way.'

'NO!' Max replied firmly. 'Sheriff Reidar and Queen Thana will not be harmed.'

'On who's authority?' Jedrek asked frowning.

'My own. Elena and I are in their debt. They saved two lives and two lives are owed.'

'Step away from the blood suckers pup.' Jedrek said menacingly.

Peter stepped in front of Jedrek and shook his head.

'No.' Max said. 'I owe them my life. I stand with them.'

'I admire your courage.' Reidar said. 'But why would you do that?'

'Because it's the honourable thing to do.' Max said with a shrug.

'Spoken like a true Alpha.' Grimlock said suddenly.

'Reidar and Thana saved my sister and I and in doing so betrayed their king.' Max said. 'They brought us here, to wolf territory where they thought we'd be safe. They shouldn't be punished for that, at least not by us.'

Jedrek growled but nobody spoke. Encouraged, Max continued.

'They could have killed us, none of you would have known, but they didn't. Like I said before, Elena and I owe them a life debt. Two lives for two lives.'

Max glanced at Elena who nodded.

'Elena and I claim the lives of Reidar and Thana and as such, they will not be harmed.'

'A great leader knows when to take a life and when to spare one.' Grimlock said. 'At last, I have found my Alpha.'

Roman stood in stunned silence as Grimlock dropped to one knee in front of Max.

'In the words passed down from the first Alpha.' Grimlock said. 'By the blood that sustains me I pledge you my life. I stand as your servant, friend and brother. Let me always be at your side in peace and in war, from now until my last breath. We are pack.'

Grimlock remained on his knee in supplication and lifted his chin, exposing his throat to Max.

Max had been educated in the pack pledge of allegiance and knew the appropriate response. He had anticipated saying the same words to his father once he had completed the rite of passage. Max recalled the stories of how the early pack Alphas had killed wolves whose hearts were not true and their pledges insincere. Nowadays wolves were seldom killed but sent on their way and forced to live alone, never knowing the closeness and protection of a pack. There were some who chose the solitary life but most wolves yearned for family.

Max looked at Grimlock who waited patiently for his fate. It was for Max to either accept him, or kill him.

Max placed his left hand on Grimlock's shoulder and his right hand on his own heart as he accepted the pledge.

'I accept your service brother……?'

'Grimlock.'

'Brother Grimlock. Stand. We are pack.'

Grimlock lent forward and whispered to Max 'At this point we embrace as brothers.'

The new Alpha and his first pack member embraced as brothers. Peter's heart swelled with pride at his son. Max released Grimlock and looked around awkwardly.

'Max.' Reidar said stepping forward. 'If I may.'

Max looked at the vampire Sheriff quizzically as he too dropped to one knee. Grimlock stood at Max's side.

'I am not a wolf and therefore cannot make the same pledge as Mr Grimlock here, but on my honour of the Knight I once was, you have spared my life and that of my companion. My life is yours to command. I pledge my sword to you.'

Reidar looked at Max and lowered his voice to a whisper, a futile gesture in the presence of so many with acute hearing.

'You can check with Milly if I can be trusted and whether my word is true.' Reidar said before bowing his head and waiting for Max's decision.

Max looked at Milly who nodded.

'I accept your sword and your service.' Max replied. 'Stand..er..please?'

Reidar stood to attention and bowed before Max before stepping back to Thana's side.

The room was silent as the wolves looked from one to the other. Rufus and Peter spoke using werewolf telepathy.

What just happened? Rufus asked Peter

Max has accepted Grimlock's pledge. Peter replied. *He is Alpha of his own pack now.*

Wow! He's a very young Alpha.

My ancestor, the first Alpha was only young and… Peter said leaving the sentence hanging.

'That was so cool.' Elena said excitedly.

Max returned to his mother and Elena. Shayla hugged her son who squirmed when she kissed him in front of everyone.

'Mum!' Max said through gritted teeth, his face turning red with embarrassment.

'Max speaks the truth.' Roman said taking back control of the room. 'Reidar and Thana will not be harmed.'

Roman stared at Jedrek who reluctantly nodded and bowed his head.

'So *now* you kneel?' Roman said turning back to Grimlock who shrugged.

Everyone laughed, the tension in the room completely dissolved.

'Tempest, bring food and wine.' Roman said. 'We will share a meal.'

Everyone in the basement understood that Roman's commands to share food and drink was an indication that the Alpha was welcoming Reidar, Thana and the twins as guests and they would all enjoy the safety and protection of the pack.

'I cannot eat this food.' Thana whispered to Reidar.

'A small bite of the bread will be enough.' Reidar replied. 'Can you drink the wine?'

Thana nodded.

Tempest returned with Witty and two trays of food, wine and water.

Shayla looked over each of her children, checking them for injuries, most were superficial but there was something different about them.

'How do you feel?' Shayla asked.

'OK.' Max said vaguely.

'Strange.' Elena replied.

'How so?' Shayla asked.

'I don't know.' Elena said. 'It's just a feeling…'

'…That you're not quite yourself.' Max finished. 'Me too.'

'And I've got this pain in my head.' Elena said. 'And zig-zagging lines in one eye.'

'It sounds like a migraine.' Shayla said looking into Elena's eyes. 'Perhaps you should lie down.'

'I can see things too.'

'What things?'

'Burnt trees and lots of dust.' Elena said. 'It's like…..um…looking through a broken window.'

'I think you're both exhausted.' Shayla said. 'And dehydrated.'

Elena and Max both nodded.

'What happened in the dungeon?' Peter asked moving in closer. 'And I don't mean with the witch.'

Peter had his suspicions about what had transpired and had no wish for Max to relive the details.

'There was a man called Arcane.' Elena said.

'He had a pendant.' Max said. 'And black eyes.'

'And a demon inside him.' Elena added.

'How do you know that?' Peter asked.

'I could see it.' Elena replied matter-of-factly.

'What did he do?' Shayla asked.

'He stared at us, his eyes turned black and then he stepped back.' Max said.

'What else?'

'Nothing else.' Max said. 'He staggered a bit like he was drunk and then left.'

'He said the witch could kill us if she wanted to.' Elena said. 'He said it didn't matter if we were dead, you'd come anyway.'

Elena's eyes filled with tears and she broke down and cried. Shayla pulled her daughter close and hugged her.

Max held himself upright blinking back tears. He was an Alpha now and wanted to appear strong. Rufus could see Max struggling to hold back his emotions and went to him, grabbing him in a rough bear hug and lifting him off the floor.

'Good to see you Max.' Rufus said.

'Ger-off!' Max replied fighting against him and breaking free. 'One day I'll be too big for you to pick up!'

'Ha! But not yet!'

Rufus put his arm around Max's shoulder and pulled him roughly towards the food.

'You must be starving!'

'A bit.'

Peter stood on the other side of Max and smiled at his son.

'I'm proud of you.' Peter said. 'And so very glad to have you back.'

REVEALED

Roman shared bread and wine with Reidar and Thana. Having overheard their conversation, Roman had brought out an uncooked rabbit to enable the vampires to eat something. Sharing his food also let the pack know that they were his guests and not to be harmed, at least until he said otherwise. Roman watched Max with his parents and sister, he was a very young wolf, barely more than a cub.

Roman was aware that Reidar and Thana had moved closer.

'The boy is unusual.' Reidar said also looking at Max.

'Indeed.' Roman replied.

He wondered what Grimlock had seen in the boy to cause him to kneel and pledge his allegiance to Max as his Alpha and why the vampire Reidar had offered his sword but these questions would keep for another time.

'What do you think Barumar's next move will be?' Roman asked his eyes still fixed on Max.

'I'm sure Arcane engineered this whole thing to start a war between our species.' Reidar replied. 'He'll be whispering in the King's ear, convincing him you've kidnapped the Queen.'

'Arcane couldn't have known I would save the twins!' Thana said.

'Oh he knew.' Reidar replied.

Roman nodded thoughtfully, he suspected the same thing.

'Tomorrow night then.' Roman said. 'We'd better be ready.'

'I'll fight with you.'

'No.' Roman said firmly looking Reidar in the eye. 'You and the Queen need to stay out of this.'

'You don't trust me?' Reidar said.

'I do, but others may not follow my lead. When they're in warrior form, the rage takes over and they'll see any vampire as an enemy.'

'I understand.' Reidar said.

'You and the Queen will stay here.'

'Underground in your prison?' Thana said.

Reidar put his arm around Thana and pulled her close to him.

'It's not a prison my love.' Reidar said. 'It's a safe house. The wolves have brought us here for safe keeping. I would do the same in their position.'

'What will happen to us should you prevail?' Thana asked.

'The vampires that survive will need their Queen and those that visit will need a strong, sensible Sheriff to keep them in line.' Roman said. 'I see the two of you fulfilling these roles.'

'You have our thanks and our gratitude.' Reidar said.

Thana didn't respond immediately, she was distracted by the twins and their mother.

'Doesn't he Thana?'

'Yes, of course.' Thana said distracted. 'My thanks. May I speak with the children?'

'If their mother permits.' Roman said.

Shayla felt the weight of Thana's stare and met her gaze. The two women stared at each other for a long moment before Shayla nodded for Thana to approach. Thana moved slowly so as not to scare Shayla and the twins and stopped in front of Shayla. The two woman stood in awkward silence, it was Thana who spoke first.

'I couldn't help but overhear Elena saying she felt unwell.'

'Probably exhaustion. Thank you for saving my children. I'm very grateful, but why *did* you save them?' Shayla said coming straight to the point.

'I was turned as a young woman.' Thana replied. 'I never had children of my own. There was a set of twins, many years ago that I tried to save. I failed.'

Thana looked away as if recalling the memory. Her expression was one of pain and Shayla felt pity for the woman, she understood all too well how it felt to lose your children.

'I'm sorry.' Shayla said, not knowing what else to say.

Thana pushed her memories aside and smiled at Shayla.

'You are part Fey.' Thana said. 'But the twins smell different. Arcane must have done something to them before I got there, a spell perhaps?'

'Elena mentioned a pendant…'

Shayla's voice trailed off and she took a deep breath. She could feel Titan's hackles rising inside her and found it difficult to concentrate on what she was saying. Milly stepped up next to Shayla, thinking that her knowledge of Gaolyn's memories might help the conversation.

'Shayla, it's unusual to see you without Titan.' Milly said. 'How did you convince him to stay behind.'

'Oh he's here!' Shayla replied pinching the bridge of her nose with her thumb and index finger.

Milly frowned.

'What's wrong?' Peter asked coming to his wife's side.

'It's Titan.' Shayla replied. 'He wants to speak.'

Milly's eyes widened.

'He's right here!' Milly said inhaling. 'Is it a cloaking spell?'

'Not exactly.' Shayla said.

Peter looked at Shayla. Titan was clearly asserting his will and Shayla was holding him back.

'He's trying to tell me something.' Shayla said.

'Then let him speak.' Peter said. 'There's no point fighting him, it's obviously important for him to fight you like this.'

'I'm not sure how this is going to go.' Shayla said. 'The wings could come out again.'

Peter kissed Shayla on the cheek and took a step away, nodding for the twins to do the same.

'You might want to stand back.' Peter said to Milly and Thana who both complied.

The wolves had stopped eating and all eyes were on Shayla, Peter smiled and nodded his encouragement.

Shayla closed her eyes and bowed her head. Huge black and silver wings materialised behind her, with razor sharp edges that sounded like clashing blades as they unfolded. Roman had already seen the wings and recalled the pointed wing tips like long fingers that had pinned him to the wall of the basement and absently touched his throat.

Shayla opened her eyes which had turned amber and looked around the room at everyone present. When she spoke it was with Titan's voice.

'Elena is neither exhausted nor suffering a migraine. She is seeing into another world. The pendant Arcane carries is made from the crystallised eye of a creature from the Cruciamentum.'

'How is that possible?' Peter asked.

'The creature that killed Talis Quinn was incinerated but its eyes survived. One was mounted into a pendant.'

'And the other?'

Titan didn't respond.

'What does this pendant do?' Peter asked.

'It's a prison. As the son of the Shadow Lord, Arcane would know how to use the crystal.'

'Wait! What? The son of the Shadow Lord?' Peter said.

'Yes Peterus, the son of the Shadow Lord.'

'How is that possible?'

'You repeat yourself Peterus.' Titan said.

'But…'

Shayla as Titan stared at Peter with impatience but said nothing further.

'I see.' Peter said. 'Balance.'

Peter looked at his Shayla and understood completely that she existed because of the necessity for balance in the universe. The Shadow Lord had sired a child which had enabled the Archangel Michael to do the same.

'What does this crystal do?' Max asked.

'It extracts the essence of the Fey from those of Faerie descent. This part of them is imprisoned within the crystal. As the creature came from the Cruciamentum, the prison world would resemble its home.'

'But surely Arcane wouldn't have the power to use the crystal in this way?' Peter said. 'He's only a half-demon.'

'A demon resides within him.' Titan said. 'The demon would have given him the power.'

'He has a darkness inside him.' Elena said. 'I saw it.'

'I saw it too.' Thana whispered recalling the way he had looked at her when she had threatened him.

Thana put a comforting arm around Elena's shoulders and Titan growled, fuelled by the Shayla's protective instincts. Peter looked at Titan and shook his head. Thana removed her arm and stepped away. Max took her place beside his sister and held her hand.

'Why extract the Faerie part of someone?' Max asked.

'The power of the Fey would suppress the demon and drawing the essence of the Fey would give Arcane a feeling of euphoria which would be hard to resist, but the power is finite and eventually he would need more.'

'Like a drug addict?'

Titan nodded.

'Is that why I don't feel right?' Max asked.

'Part of you has been taken.' Titan said. 'Until that part of you is released, you will never feel whole again.'

'You said the power was finite.' Max asked. 'What happens when Arcane uses up what he has?'

'That part of us is lost.' Elena said. 'Isn't it?'

Titan smiled sadly and nodded.

'Why can I see inside the crystal and Max can't?' Elena asked.

'Your angel DNA.' Titan replied.

'Max is angel too.'

'But he has always manifested more as a wolf than an angel.' Titan said. 'Whereas you Elena, have yet to come into your full power. You see things sometimes don't you? And know things?'

Elena nodded.

'Arcane believes the offspring of his nemesis with their combined DNA of angel, wolf and Fey are the key to infinite power.' Titan said.

'But he's wrong.' Elena said.

'Yes he is.'

'Is there a way to break out?' Max asked.

'There is a way to break free, but you will have to work together.'

'Elena and I will be able to break free from the prison?' Max said smiling.

'There are other prisoners inside, you will need their help to survive.' Titan said bluntly. 'And in this world, you and Elena will need to be closer to the crystal in order to weaken it.'

Titan paused before continuing.

'Arcane wears the pendant, always. Sometimes it is disguised as a tattoo on his chest. You will have to be in the same room or face to face with him. Your mother will not let you go alone and Arcane knows this.'

'This has been Arcane's plan all along.' Roman said to Peter. 'Kidnapping your children ensured their mother would come to him. The war between wolves and vampires is an unexpected turn of events, one I am sure the king is happy with.'

'And the chaos demon inside Arcane.' Elena said quietly.

The room fell silent once more.

'How do you know this?' Reidar asked looking at Titan.

Titan looked at Reidar and growled before replying. He understood that the vampires had saved the twins and Max had asked for them to be spared. He could feel Shayla cautioning him to show restraint and for her sake he would allow them to live, for now and not because they were under Roman's protection in the basement. Titan's loyalty was to Shayla and the twins alone. He was not bound by werewolf traditions.

'I am a Halo Hound.' Titan replied curtly.

Without further explanation, Titan retracted his wings and closed his eyes. When they opened again they were green showing that Titan had relinquished control back to Shayla.

'What does that mean?' Reidar asked.

'It means he doesn't have to explain himself.' Shayla replied. 'To you or anyone else for that matter.'

Shayla returned to Peter and the twins and sat down, she needed to think. Max and Elena stayed beside her and Peter stood beside them. Shayla put a protective arm around Elena's shoulder and pulled her close. Elena put both hands on either side of her head, her eyes closed tightly against the pain. Max sat the other side of Elena feeling helpless.

'Is it getting worse?' Shayla asked. 'Let me look at you.'

Elena said nothing, but turned towards her mother and opened her eyes.

'Is it painful when you open your eyes?'

'No. Only my head.' Elena replied. 'I can't see properly, it's easier to close my eyes.'

'Can you see anything?'

'Sometimes zig-zags, other times…mmm….a desert.' Elena said wincing against the pain.

Over the years Shayla had learned how to focus the healing power of the Fey. According to Titan, the power to heal came easily to her mother and grandmother but Shayla was only half Fey and the process took more concentration.

Shayla pulled Elena close to her again and laid her palm against the side of Elena's head, rubbing her thumb softly against her hair. Shayla called on the healing power and felt the warmth of the energy begin to spread through her whole body. She concentrated and moved the heat down her arm and into the hand that stroked Elena's head transferring the healing energy to her daughter.

Max watched as Elena's face relaxed and knew the pain had subsided. Shayla looked up and smiled at her son, but continued to stroke Elena's head. After a few moments Elena opened her eyes and looked at her brother.

'Better?' Max asked.

Elena nodded.

'Is your vision still blurry?' Max asked.

'A little bit, but I can see….faces.'

'Whose faces?' Max asked. 'Ours?'

'No. Strangers.'

Max looked confused and glanced at his mother who said nothing.

'I'll show you.' Elena said suddenly grabbing Max's hand.

As soon as their hands touched a jolt of electricity passed through them. Shayla kept her arm around Elena, her other hand reached for Max who took it. The three of them made a circle of divine energy, Shayla's more concentrated angel DNA providing the conduit.

'What's happening?' Max said.

'I don't know.' Shayla replied holding both children tightly.

Max felt a heat rising from the pit of his stomach and his body glowed briefly with an internal light. In that instant Max and Elena's mind became one; they saw with one vision and for the briefest of seconds they were both aware of infinite possibilities and an understanding of each other.

As their minds connected, Max felt as if he was transported to another world. He saw the desert Elena had spoken of and the faces of strangers with perfect clarity as if they stood in front of him. He felt as if he was looking through someone else's eyes but at the same time, he was aware as if it were his own eyes. He looked around for Elena, he could sense her but not see her, only his surroundings and the strange place and people. He felt simultaneously connected and disconnected to the other world and his twin. The connection only lasted a second and was instantly gone but the images and feelings remained.

Shayla felt the energy subside and looked at her children in turn, understanding that something had happened to the twins but not exactly what; her main concern was for their welfare.

'Are you both alright?' Shayla asked.

Max and Elena nodded.

'What just happened?' Shayla asked.

'We connected.' Elena said matter-of-factly.

'I saw it.' Max said, then paused. 'That place felt awful and the people looked afraid and…'

'Tired and sad.' Elena finished.

Max nodded.

'It's as Titan said.' Elena explained. 'The part of us that's Fey is trapped in a prison and the other people in there are prisoners too. We have to get out before we die in there.'

'We will.' Max replied squeezing Elena's hand that he was still holding.

Elena looked thoughtful for a moment before speaking again.

'Do you think that our Fey selves inside are aware of us out here?'

'I don't know.' Max shrugged. 'I'm getting a headache just thinking about it.'

Max and Elena laughed. Shayla watched them silently.

* * * * *

'How long will it sleep?' Wren asked glancing back over her shoulder.

'The beast will sleep and wake up as it naturally would in its own world.' Elemax replied. 'We will be long gone before that happens. Lead on.'

Wren led the way and Elemax and the elementals walked in silence for some time before Oren stumbled. Elemax caught his arm as he fell and looked into his eyes.

'It's this place.' Oren gasped. 'It sucks the energy out of you. There used to be more of us.'

'Where are they now?'

'Gone.' Oren said sadly. 'They just disappeared.'

Elemax helped Oren to his feet.

'You have seen the crystal that Arcane wears around his neck.' Elemax said.

Oren recalled the last memory he had of his life before waking up in this world. He had met a man calling himself Cane. He was good looking and very charming and he and Kealoha had been happy to sit and chat with him. Oren recalled seeing Cane's necklace and had even commented that it was unusual.

'The pendant is made from the crystallised remains of a creature from a place called the Cruciamentum. This world is a replica of the Cruciamentum.'

'We know all this.' Oren said irritably, the pain of losing his friend Kealoha still cut like a knife and Oren suppressed his sadness with anger. 'Radha told us this world is a replica of the Shadow Lord's prison. We're trapped in a world created by his son Arcane and he uses this place to punish us.'

'Do you want to escape this place?' Elemax asked.

'Of course.' Wren said.

'More than anything.' Radha added.

'I don't want to die in here.' Oren said.

Elemax looked thoughtful.

'What would you do?' Elemax asked. 'All of you? Would you return to your wretched lives?'

Wren, Oren and Radha looked at each other but said nothing.

'Radha.' Elemax said. 'Would you continue to hide in a fog of pharmaceuticals, denying who you are? Your friends could really use your help. Cassie has been lost without your friendship, as have you.'

Radha blushed and looked down at her hands.

'And you Wren.' Elemax said. 'Would you return to your old life?'

'Possibly.' Wren replied tentatively.

'Stealing.'

'It wasn't stealing!'

'There are other ways to earn a living.' Elemax said frowning.

Wren looked away shame-faced.

'Oren?' Elemax said. 'Would you seek help in controlling your anger?'

'I.....'

'Has this place taught any of you anything?' Elemax asked in a somewhat angry tone.

Wren, Radha and Oren all looked uncomfortable but remained silent. Each wondering how Elemax knew about their lives before they met inside the crystal, but the prison world had taught them never to be surprised at anything.

'I want to go home.' Radha said finally.

'We all do.' Wren said putting her arm around Radha.

'I want to be whole again and live a normal life. I don't want to die in here.'

Elemax nodded and moved to stand behind the elementals as they huddled together. Silver wings extended around them in a protective shield and Elemax looked up to the sky. Stretching out both hands Elemax whispered something inaudible and a pulse of light shot from each palm and hit the sky above. Clouds spread across the sky as far as their eyes could see. The sky glowed briefly behind the clouds as if the sun had broken through a storm on a winter's day and the elementals squinted in the sudden brightness, then the light faded and the day settled into a semi-twilight.

'How do you feel?' Elemax asked Oren.

'Better.' Oren smiled. 'Thank you. What did you do?'

'A temporary shield until we reach the outer walls.' Elemax replied. 'The dark force that has taken the lives of your other companions will not be able to touch you, but we are still trapped in this prison. We must move quickly before the creator of this world thinks of new ways to torment us.'

KILL THEM ALL

At the same time that Reidar and Queen Thana arrived at Mike's Cafeteria, Barumar sent messengers around the City calling for every vampire to gather at the palace. The king had an important announcement and every vampire was compelled to attend.

The palace courtyard was pandemonium. Arcane stood in the shadows and scanned the faces of the assembled crowd. This wasn't a crowd of fine upstanding citizens, this was a gathering of vampires hungry for blood and vengeance.

Arcane had a fleeting thought that if the sun were to suddenly shine on the palace courtyard and incinerate the hoard of gathered vampires, the collective ash would fall like snow on the surrounding City.

The vampires jostled for the best position, snapping and hissing at each other and asking if it was a public execution and if not, why not? A ripple went through the crowd and the word went around that this was a call to war.

'Where is the witch?' Barumar said suddenly appearing at Arcane's side.

'She has betrayed us sire.'

Barumar sighed impatiently.

'Without the witch's spell to cover the sun, we have no choice but to wait for nightfall.'

'I will find her and kill her.' Arcane said.

'I will send others to kill her.' Barumar said. 'You will remain at my side. You are my Advisor.'

Arcane said nothing.

'You're afraid.' Barumar said.

In a crowd Arcane usually enjoyed the freedom of anonymity and the ability to move around unseen. He fixed his eyes on the crowd below; he had never seen so many vampires gathered together in one place and his stomach clenched in fear. The mood of the vampires swirled in unseen currents beneath the dark expressions of their faces. Even with the strength of Eversor, this many vampires would tear him to shreds.

'They will not harm you.' Barumar said.

'Do they know that?' Arcane asked.

Barumar bit into the inside of his own wrist and two rivulets of blood ran down his forearm. He wiped the blood across Arcane's forehead and across both cheeks.

'I have marked you as my pet.' Barumar said. 'No one will touch the property of their King.'

Arcane stood rigid, repulsed by the action. Barumar turned away from him and stepped out onto the balcony to address the seething mass of the undead.

When the king stepped out, the crowd ceased their jostling, shouting and baying for blood and fell silent. Even the young vampires, eager to be set free from the imposed restrictions on their feeding contained themselves to listen. They knew their enemy, this was the moment they had waited for; the wolves had to go.

Barumar stood like a celebrity before adoring fans and announced, with feigned regret that the fragile truce that had existed between the vampires and the wolves in Braeden has been broken.

'The wolves have kidnapped the Queen.' Barumar said. 'This is a most heinous crime. One that cannot go unanswered. The wolves have declared war on our species, and how do we respond? How do we answer that declaration?'

The crowd remained silent and Barumar paused.

'WE WILL ANSWER THEM IN BLOOD!'

From his place in the shadows Arcane heard a blood-chilling sound, like the low snarling of many voices, it grew louder and louder until it became a muttering roar. He stepped out from the shadows and looked down at the courtyard below. Barumar waited for the noise to subside before proceeding.

'Tomorrow night! As daylight falls, I command all vampires to flow through the streets of Braeden and purge this City of the disease that has held us at bay for too long!'

Barumar paused once more.

'KILL THE WOLVES! KILL THEM ALL!'

Hundreds of voices erupted in jubilation and the fate of thousands of innocent men, women and children was sealed.

Arcane fled from the balcony, returned to his personal chambers and vomited.

Eversor's earlier rage at the vampire's audacity to mark Arcane with his blood evaporated, replaced by elation at what had just transpired; chaos and destruction were the purpose of its creation.

Arcane laid on the floor of his chambers for some time, weak from his body's purging. His mind wrestled with a conscience he didn't know he had, over whether the vampire situation that was unfolding and which he had manoeuvred was what he had really intended. The sight and smell of so many vampires caused his stomach to clench once more and he reached for the pendant, eager to wrap himself in the euphoria and escape the nightmare.

Closing his hand around the crystal, Arcane drew on the power of the Fey within and felt.....nothing. Pushing himself into an upright position, he clasped the pendant more tightly and concentrated but still he felt nothing.

'How can this be?' Arcane said aloud.

'The power is finite.' Eversor replied. 'Perhaps you have exhausted your supply.'

'No!' Arcane whispered in panic. 'The children are special, their power should be infinite.'

Arcane stood up and looked at his reflection. The whites of his eyes turned black, his iris glowed red and his features contorted into a malicious sneer, the face of Eversor.

'You cannot suppress me this time.' Eversor said. 'You are weak and pathetic. Vomiting in fear when you should be rejoicing in our success.'

Arcane's eyes and face reverted to its usual good looks.

'So many vampires….'Arcane said.

Arcane's features switched from his normal appearance and back to the demonic, black eyed stare of Eversor as he conversed with his reflection.

'Blood will run like a river through the City in the wake of chaos and destruction.' Eversor said.

'I only wanted the half-angel.' Arcane said.

'Do not fear. She will die like everyone else.'

'She's mine to kill!' Arcane snapped. 'I have to find her first.'

'Do you have a plan?'

'You're going to help me.' Arcane said staring back at his reflection.

Eversor remained silent. Arcane wrapped his hand around the pendant once more and concentrated but the power of the Fey was not forthcoming.

* * * * *

The witch Thebe stood back and admired her work. The creature's humanoid body was made entirely from mud and detritus from the river. It wore no clothing and could not speak or make any vocal noise. Once animated, weighing around five hundred pounds it would walk with a slow, clumsy gait, but its power would be devastating. It would feel no pain and would remain energised as long as she lived and Thebe had no plans of expiring any time soon.

Thebe had created a golem once before from rags. She recalled the memory of how it had terrorised one of the Villages that had shunned her but the process had left her weak. Thebe wondered how much truth there was in the legend of the Golem of Braeden. According to the legend, the priest who created the golem used mud and clay from the river, just as Thebe had done. The priest named the golem Yosef but Thebe had no intention of naming her creature. The stories conflicted over whether the priest lost control of the golem or whether the golem fell in love and when rejected became a violent monster. Another story said the Golem was a young child who roamed the City streets keeping a watchful eye and reporting back to its master. Thebe didn't care which ending of the story was true, her golem would obey her commands, its purpose would be clear.

Thebe wrote the incantation on a piece of paper, rolled the spell into a small scroll and placed it in the golem's mouth. The creature closed its mouth, stood up and waited.

'Your purpose is to protect me.'

The golem nodded.

'We are leaving the City. Kill everyone and everything that comes near me.' Thebe said. 'Kill them all.'

Thebe led the golem away from the river and headed back towards the old part of the city. The original town square, before the city had grown and sprawled, was located in what was considered to be the poorer end of town. Most businesses had moved to the new square and only a few small shops remained with tired looking cafes facing in on the square. Between a closed down restaurant and a bakery was an old stone archway that led back towards the pauper cemetery. Thebe led the golem to the archway and stopped.

Thebe looked at the sky and scowled, she needed moonlight for what she wanted to achieve and hoped her power would be strong enough. She spoke the words carefully.

'Realm to realm through space and time,
air to water thus combine.
In shadows veil at end of night,
the moon reveals her modest light.'

Thebe paused and traced her gnarled hands over the symbols engraved into the stone and using dark magic, recited the words to force open a gateway.

'The day is high, the moon is low,
draw from the lives that ebb and flow,
One traveller and a beast of mud
Accept their sacrifice of blood.'

Nothing happened for a few seconds and the few people milling around the street stopped and looked towards the old crone. Their attention drawn by the large creature made of mud standing inert beside her.

Thebe cursed under her breath, it was taking too long.

Suddenly, a veil of mist formed in the archway and began to swirl, air and water combining and turning in a slow circle. Everything fell eerily silent as if the universe was holding its breath, then a blast wave of intense pressure expanded outward from the centre of the water hitting the people in the street and throwing them backwards. Unable to breath, they all clutched at their throats, their eyes wide in fear.

Thebe gave no thought to the innocent passers-by whose lives she had stolen. As the gateway opened before her, Thebe took the golem by the arm and led him through the swirling vortex into another realm.

The authorities would later discover more than twenty people lying dead in the street, with no visible signs of what happened to them.

* * * * *

Grimlock handed the plans of the city and the detailed plans of the underground sewer system to Roman who spread them out before him.

'Is this all of them?' Roman asked.

'No!' Grimlock replied. 'Jedrek stressed the urgency of the matter and as you were holding my feet to the fire, I only picked up the most useful plans.'

Roman sighed impatiently but said nothing.

'Is there another way into the palace?' Peter asked.

'The sewer system.' Grimlock replied handing a rolled up plan to Peter. 'There are a couple of tunnels that run beneath the river.'

'Milly and I used the tunnels to get from here to the square.' Rufus said. 'We can plan a route.'

While Peter studied the plan of the sewer tunnels, Roman studied the plan of the City.

'Most of the vampires are on the other side of the river.' Roman said finally. 'They'll swarm into the City across the bridges. We need to funnel them onto one bridge, narrowing their line of attack. Which means we need to take down the other two bridges and leave only Draven Bridge. It's the strongest point on this side for our defence, *and* the most direct line to the palace.'

Grimlock unrolled another set of plans, each showing the original design of the bridges that spanned the Nejelski River.

'We only need to bring down one or two key points. Any one of these bridges will fall if you target the right place.' Grimlock said pointing to various places on the design sketch. 'These are the weak points.'

'How do you know this you old bone muncher?' Jedrek asked.

'I have studied many things over the years.' Grimlock said. 'Engineering being one of them.'

'Why?' Jedrek said.

'Unlike you, I like to keep my mind as sharp as my claws.'

'And your tongue.' Roman said sharply. 'Can we focus?'

The room felt silent and Roman returned to the plans.

'Can you set the explosives?' Roman asked.

Grimlock raised one eyebrow, smiled and nodded.

'Excellent. Jedrek will go with you.' Roman said. 'And bring Karayan and Lorcan back here. Brief them on the way.'

Jedrek moved towards the exit and stopped when he realised Grimlock was not following. Grimlock looked to Max and Max looked at his father.

'You're his Alpha son.' Peter whispered. 'He seeks your permission to go. Personally, I think it's a good plan but the decision on whether you allow Grimlock to follow Roman's orders is yours.'

Max felt uncomfortable but he stood up straight and spoke clearly.

'Grimlock. Roman has more experience in these matters than I. This is his territory we should follow his lead.'

'Understood.' Grimlock replied.

Roman winked at Max, conveying his gratitude in an imperceptible nod. Max looked at Peter who smiled encouragement to his son.

'How many wolves can you call upon?' Reidar asked Roman as soon as Grimlock and Jedrek had left.

Roman looked around the room and back to Reidar.

'There are eight in my pack.' Roman said.

'I will fight, as will Rufus and Milly.' Peter added.

'I too will fight.' Shayla said.

'So will I.' Max said.

'And me.' Elena finished.

'This is it?' Reidar said incredulously. 'Any army of what, fourteen? Two of which are children? There are hundreds of vampires in Braeden and the surrounding area. Barumar will call them all to war. Arcane also has the witch and whatever dark magic she brings.'

'A wolf in warrior form is worth fifty vampires.' Roman said.

'You'd better hope so.'

Roman thought about the small group of wolves; all of them would fight to the death and in all likelihood none of those gathered in the basement would see another sunrise but he kept those thoughts to himself. The twins had been reunited with their parents and Roman gave no further thought to Pickens, the wererat and his promise to return.

Beneath the City, unseen and ignored by both wolves and vampires, Pickens prepared for the coming battle.

OLD FRIENDS

The man called himself Elliot but that wasn't the name his mother had given him. He swung a sword once, but that was in another life. He preferred the simpler life he now lived with his wife, self-sufficient in their little cabin in the forest. Elliot looked around his garden which he had created to resemble his original home where he had grown up. Sometimes he missed it, but not often. After many years Elliot and his wife had decided to stop travelling and settle in one place. Neither of them liked crowded places and big cities, and the highlands at the edge of the forest that most people shunned due to the harsh winters and mild summers suited Elliot and his wife just fine and Elliot had happily put his sword away in favour of the axe and garden tools.

The black bird watched from its perch high in the tree as the man swung his axe and split the log in two. As the man placed another small log onto a tree stump and lifted his axe, the bird squawked. The man looked up and smiled before returning his attention to the log in front of him which he split with one powerful swing. The season would be turning soon and the leaves would start to fall from the trees. He needed a good supply of wood to see them through the winter. Once the leaves had fallen, winter would be upon them. Elliot thought the first snow would be earlier this year, the winters had become much colder and longer since the pulse.

Elliot had built the cabin himself using hand tools. The hard work kept his muscles toned and his body strong. The cabin was small but adequate for their needs with a small kitchen area just off the main living room and a mezzanine floor where they slept. The elevated level took advantage of the rising heat from the fire during the winter. The Nejelski river began its journey north of the cabin and Elliot and his wife made use of the river for water and washing.

Having observed the man for long enough, the bird took flight and swooped down, landing on the tree stump in front of Elliot. The bird tilted its head to one side as if appraising Elliot's shirtless body, his muscles glistening with sweat in the autumn sunshine.

The bird's form shimmered and shifted into the shape of a woman, slim with stunning blue eyes, dark hair and smooth brown skin. She stood completely naked. Myshka, his wife was a Morphian, sometimes referred to as a shape shifter.

'Are you going to stand there all day?' Elliot asked.

'Maybe.' Myshka replied. 'But only if you're going to stand around shirtless.'

Elliot's smile widened and he grabbed his shirt and wrapped it around her, thinking that she was just as beautiful as the day he had first laid eyes on her.

'Come here.' Elliot said holding her close. 'You'll catch a cold.'

'I've got my love to keep me warm.'

'You're such a sweet talker.' Elliot laughed.

Myshka stood on tip toes and kissed him pulling the shirt around herself. The day wasn't particularly cold in spite of the breeze but still she shivered.

'Let's get you inside, I'll make some tea.' Elliot said.

Before they reached the door of the cabin a large golden eagle swooped just above their heads and landed in the garden next to the cabin. The bird stood almost forty inches tall with a broad wingspan of over seven feet. The dark brown plumage was broken only by the golden feathers on the back of the crown and nape of the neck, but Elliot's attention was mainly on the wickedly sharp talons and beak.

'Welcome Medwin.' Elliot said.

The eagle bowed its head, shimmered and transformed into a broad muscular man standing at six feet, five inches with dark skin, dark brown eyes and a smooth bald head. He was also a Morphian and Myshka rushed forward to greet him.

'Medwin.' Myshka said hugging him. 'It's been so long. How have you been?'

'Well. It's good to see you too.' Medwin paused.

'What is it?' Elliot asked.

'I'm sorry to be the bearer of bad news.' Medwin said. 'I have a message for you from Pickens.'

Myshka and Elliot exchanged a look.

'The City's in trouble.' Medwin continued. 'Hundreds of vampires are set to ravage the city, the wolves are outnumbered, even with the new comers. He said it's time you moved on, if the city falls there'll be no stopping them, they'll tear right through the forest and with their speed they'll be on you in minutes.'

'Are you leaving?' Myshka asked.

Medwin nodded.

'Where are you going?' Myshka asked.

'As far away from Braeden as possible. You should do the same, take what you need and go, now.'

'Is Pickens staying in the City?' Myshka said.

'He's staying to fight.' Medwin replied.

'What?'

'I don't know what he thinks he can do, but he's insisting he's staying.'

Myshka turned to Elliot.

'We have to help him.' Myshka said. 'Without Pickens I never would have found any other Morphians. I can't let him fight alone.'

'Don't be crazy!' Medwin said. 'This is not a fight you can win. It's going to be a slaughter as it is, don't risk your life.'

Elliot said nothing and stood silent for a while thinking about his past life and how he had been glad to put away his sword. In all the years they had travelled and finally settled near Braeden, Elliot had always known that nothing was permanent. Life in the forest cabin was temporary, he was a soldier and always would be.

'You said this day would come.' Myshka said as if reading Elliot's thoughts.

'I'd hoped to be wrong.' Elliot replied. 'But now that it's here, there's no running away.'

Elliot took his wife's hand and brought it to his lips and kissed her fingers. He loved Myshka and had made a vow to always be at her side.

'I made a vow to you my love.' Elliot said. 'Where you go, I go.'

'Thank you.' Myshka said squeezing his hand.

'You'll never reach Braeden by nightfall on foot.' Medwin said. 'Myshka can shift into a bird but not you Elliot.'

'I can shift into a horse and take us both to the City.'

'I don't doubt your strength.' Medwin said. 'But you'll be tired by the time you get there and in no shape to fight.'

Elliot and Myshka said nothing, both considering their options. Medwin ran his hand across his bald head in exasperation.

'I'll take you.' Medwin said. 'I must be an idiot!'

Myshka went to speak and Medwin held up his hand to silence her.

'Get your things quickly.' Medwin said. 'Before I change my mind.'

Medwin's body shimmered and he shape-shifted into a magnificent chestnut coloured stallion. The stallion reared up onto its hind legs and dropped back down pounding his front feet impatiently on the ground.

Elliot ran into the cabin and opened the storage chest containing his armour and sword from his old life. He thought about his early life and put his armour on, it glinted in the light. Elliot picked up his sword and remembered the oath he had sworn and who he was. He was a Knight of Feylore, a trained soldier and protector and one of the best Knights ever to wield a dragon blade.

Stepping from the cabin he saw that Myshka had already transformed into a beautiful golden mare. She stood next to Medwin and tossed her head impatiently, Eli mounted the stallion and held onto his mane.

'Run Medwin.' Elliot said. 'Let your feet take flight.'

*****

Uri growled in frustration. She had taken to meditating in the ritual cave every day since the twins disappeared trying to make sense of what had happened and to implore the spirits of the elders for some guidance but so far the cave had given up no secrets and the spirits remained silent.

Uri opened her eyes and looked around momentarily disoriented. The world came flooding back to her senses, she could hear the wind rustling the trees outside the cave and smell the earth beneath her. She wondered how long she had been meditating and her growling stomach told her she had missed at least one meal, which was unusual for a wolf. She thought about returning to the pack and getting something to eat and drink, she was thirsty, but in the end decided to try and contact the elders once more.

'Perhaps the hunger will sharpen my other senses.' Uri muttered to herself.

Closing her eyes again she let the noise of the world, like radio static, fade away and concentrated on the sound of her own heartbeat; nothing.

'This is useless!' Uri said angrily.

Uri knew that fasting sharpened her senses and enabled a deeper meditation but her hunger and thirst had only succeeded in making her more irritable.

'Patience was never your strongest attribute.'

Uri looked up to see the spirit of Rusty standing before her.

'It worked!' Uri said. 'Finally.'

'You've done nothing.' Rusty said. 'I chose to come here because I need to speak to you.'

Uri scowled, even more irritated at her lack of success and Rusty laughed.

'Trying to contact the elders is not an easy task.' Rusty said his ethereal form shimmering.

'I know. I've been trying for days.' Uri paused. 'If the elders weren't going to answer my call, why have you come?'

Rusty's spirit form disappeared and reappeared again.

'The connection is weak.' Uri said. 'You said you needed to speak to me. What's going on? Is it Peter? Has he found the children? Do you have news?'

'The balance is in danger of tipping the wrong way.' Rusty said vaguely.

'What does that mean for our kind?'

'It could mean the end.' Rusty said.

'What can I do? What can the *wolves* do to stop it?'

Rusty disappeared once more leaving Uri alone in the cave.

'Rusty?' Uri called out to the darkness.

No reply was forthcoming; Uri waited.

Hours passed and Uri lost all sense of time and space. She fell asleep from exhaustion and woke with a start, only to find herself still alone in the ritual cave. Her neck ached from where her head had lolled to the side and she rubbed the muscle absently with hand.

She felt nauseous and hungry at the same time and thirsty, her tongue felt like the bottom of a leather shoe. She licked her lips, they were dry and cracked. She felt uncharacteristically cold and a shiver ran through her entire body lifting the hairs on her head and arms. Her eyes felt gritty from a lack of sleep and her body ached from sitting in the same position for too long, but she waited, knowing that she was close to finally making a connection with the spirits.

'Please talk to me.' Uri whispered to the universe.

Uri saw her breath as she spoke and shivered again. The temperature in the cave had dropped significantly since she had spoken to Rusty almost a day earlier.

Uri closed her eyes and folded her hands in her lap. She tried to focus her mind but her thoughts were a jumbled mess of images and feelings.

At first the spirit's presence was no more than a chill in the air and Uri wondered whether the cool breath she felt was nothing more than the outside breeze having shifted direction. Uri opened her eyes, the air in front of her shimmered as if being warped and twisted. A soft, pale, silvery light illuminated the cave and Uri saw a form take shape, the spirit smiled and bared its teeth taking a step closer. It was someone she recognised.

'Hello Rusty.' Uri said. 'I wasn't sure you were coming back.'

'I'm not alone.' Rusty said smiling

Another form took shape beside Rusty. The spirit materialised and Uri instantly knew who it was from the stories passed down from Alpha to Alpha. She remained seated in respect of the one who had come to see to her. Although with the cataracts Uri's eyesight was poor, she clearly saw the large wolf with the silver fur and blue eyes that towered over her as she sat in the cave, his paws the size of dinner plates with long, sharp claws made of living silver. Never had she seen such a resplendent visage as Maximus, the first Alpha who stood before her in full wolf form, Uri bowed her head in reverence.

'Events are balanced on a knife edge.' Maximus words sounded clear in her head. 'Uri, the Great spirit pack needs your help.'

ALLIES

At the same time that Roman was pouring over the plans of the City, Grimlock was planting explosives onto one of the bridges spanning the river; Elliot, Myshka and Medwin were galloping at full speed towards Braeden.

Elliot expected they would reach the outskirts of the City before sunset. As a Fey in a different world he had command over the elements and manipulated the air adding flight to Medwin and Myshka's feet. They had agreed that Medwin would accompany them as far as the City limits, Elliot and Myshka would then make their way into the centre of the City to find Pickens.

When they arrived, Myshka and Medwin still in the form of horses, rested their heads on each other and whinnied. Elliot knew they were communicating their goodbyes and stepped away to give them a moment of relative privacy. Medwin shape-shifted once more into a golden eagle and bobbed his head to Elliot. Elliot responded with a small bow of thanks and Medwin took flight, his seven foot wingspan would quickly take him far from the City.

Myshka shifted into human form to speak and Elliot immediately wrapped his cloak around her naked form.

'I asked Medwin if he knew where Pickens would be.'

'And?' Elliot asked.

'He said Pickens had been typically vague but that I should be able to find him. I'm not entirely sure what that means.'

'Perhaps he'll leave a sign, something only you or another Morphian would recognise.'

Myshka nodded.

'We can walk from here.' Elliot said looking at the sun, now low in the sky.

'That'll take too long, besides….' Myshka said glancing down at herself, naked beneath Elliot's cloak. 'I'll carry you. That was the original plan.'

Before Elliot could argue, an explosion, followed by two more almost simultaneously, caught their attention. Myshka shifted back into the form of the golden coloured mare and nudged Elliot to hurry.

*****

The two vehicular crossings either side of Draven Bridge allowed access to and from the City Centre to the Council buildings and the Palace on the west side of the river in a one-way system. The bridge down river provided access for vehicles from the centre to the west side and the other bridge up river of Draven Bridge gave exit from the west side to return. Draven Bridge had been pedestrianised for decades to preserve the cobbled stones. The west end of Draven Bridge led directly to the Palace via an extremely steep and uneven narrow road, still known as the Kings Road. It would be from that high point that the vampires were expected to stream down and onto the bridge and into the City, if Grimlock was able to destroy the other two.

Grimlock and Jedrek stood beneath the bridge, Jedrek watched as Grimlock set the last explosive.

'How will this work exactly?' Jedrek asked.

'The charges have been placed on three key joints. When detonated, the structure should fall straight down into the river. What you might call energetic felling.' Grimlock laughed.

'What about the cars?'

'That's why you're here.'

Jedrek shook his head and held out his hands waiting for Grimlock to explain.

'Assume wolf form and stand at the end of the bridge.' Grimlock said.

'And do what?'

'I don't know!' Grimlock snapped. 'Snarl, howl, do a dance, I don't care, just stop anything coming onto the bridge or they'll end up in the river with the rest of the debris.'

Jedrek sighed but transformed into wolf form as requested.

'Hurry!' Grimlock said. 'The charges are all in place. When this one comes down we have to bring down the other. With the help of the Divine we won't get caught before completing the task.'

Jedrek ran to the end of the bridge and faced the oncoming traffic. The first vehicle to spot the large, brown wolf swerved to avoid him and with a screeching of brakes, stopped side on to the bridge. The car behind hit the first vehicle in its side shunting it forward creating a barrier. Both drivers exited their vehicles and began shouting at each other and pointing to the various dents and scratched on their cars. Jedrek slipped out of sight in the chaos and changed back into human form and waited for Grimlock to join him.

'Good work.' Grimlock said.

The drivers were still arguing when Grimlock threw the switch. The first charge in the middle of the bridge exploded and the other two followed simultaneously. The bridge imploded and fell straight down into the river as expected.

'That was absolutely spectacular!' Grimlock exclaimed.

Jedrek looked at him momentarily speechless, then they both laughed.

'Let's get the other one down.' Grimlock said.

Jedrek and Grimlock ran past the two drivers who stood dumbfounded looking at the gap across the river where the vehicular bridge had stood seconds before.

Reaching the other bridge Grimlock quickly got to work setting the explosives.

'You've seen what I've done, do you think you can set the other explosive?' Grimlock asked Jedrek.

'Sure.'

'Then go. Once I'm done here I'll join you at the other end.

'That end?' Jedrek asked pointing towards the opposite side of the river.

Grimlock nodded but didn't look up from his work.

Both wolves worked quickly and soon all charges were in place and Grimlock joined Jedrek at the palace end of the bridge.

'There's no traffic.' Jedrek said.

'Probably because the other bridge is down, nothing can get over and anyone entering the city wouldn't be able to get back.'

'Right.' Jedrek paused. 'Can I blow this one?'

Grimlock handed Jedrek the detonator.

'Wait until we're…..'

Grimlock's words were cut off by the noise of the explosion and the bridge imploded and collapsed into the river.

'IDIOT!' Grimlock yelled.

'What?'

'You were supposed to wait until we were on the other side! That's what I was trying to say. Now we're stuck here on the vampire infested side of the city!'

'Oh.'

'Oh indeed hothead!'

Jedrek looked embarrassed.

'I'm sorry. I got carried away. I didn't think.'

'That's your problem.'

'How are we going to get back?'

'No idea! You think of something genius!'

*****

Everyone in the basement of the cafeteria felt the vibration of the explosion and ignored it. They even ignored the second explosion, but when they felt a low vibration, then rumbling, followed by the sound of scratching, they all looked at Roman.

Roman sniffed the air and recognised the scent.

'Wait here.' Roman commanded. 'Matyas. With me.'

'I'm coming with you.' Peter said in a tone that brokered no argument.

Roman nodded and ran up the stairs to the cafe, Matyas and Peter close behind. Outside Roman looked in the direction of the River. People had stopped in the streets looking around for the source of the explosions and turning to each other for explanation. Drain covers began rattling and people stepped away looking both bewildered and frightened. The three wolves ran in the direction of the rumbling sound, the vibrations felt strongest in the Town Square.

All three looked around as a young woman screamed. From the drain next to her feet, the grate lifted off the road and flipped on its side and from the sewers poured hundreds of rats, a mass of brown furry bodies with black beady eyes and writhing tails. People jumped back out of the way of drains and manhole covers and ran into doorways. The rats flowed through the streets like a muddy river, spreading out across the square. They moved outwards towards the side streets and alleyways not deviating from their course, thousands upon thousands of rats flowed in a stampede, all moving with a single purpose.

Roman, Matyas and Peter watched as the rats moved in a frantic brown wave, thousands of tiny claws scratching against the stone beneath their feet, climbing over one another, then falling back down into the flow of their furry brothers and sisters.

'Pickens.' Roman whispered.

'Who's Pickens?' Peter asked over low roar of the scratching and rumbling.

'A wererat. He had knowledge of your children.' Roman said. 'He promised to return this morning, but as the children came back last night, I never gave him another thought.'

'Which one is Pickens?' Peter asked.

'I am Pickens.'

At the sound of his voice all three wolves turned around. Pickens stood slightly in the shadows in one of the alleyways. Roman, Matyas and Peter went to him, the sea of rats parting as they walked across the street and closing again behind them.

'The scent of so many of my brothers and sisters enabled me to pass by all three of you undetected.' Pickens said with a slight smile.

'Are you leaving the City?' Roman asked.

Peter didn't understand the language Pickens was speaking but when he pointed back towards the streets, Peter turned his head and understood what was happening. The rats pouring onto the streets has caused people to run for shelter, anywhere they could find.

Pickens spoke again and Roman translated for Peter.

'He says rats will always make people run. With rats on the city streets people will stay in their homes.'

'Smart move.' Peter said. 'This could save hundreds of people.'

'As long as people stay in their homes, they should be safe.'

'How did you find him?' Peter asked.

'He found me.'

Turning back to Pickens, Roman spoke in their native tongue. Pickens replied, transformed into a large brown rat and scurried off to join the tsunami of brown fur that was still streaming into the City.

* * * * *

As they entered the City, Myshka came to a sudden stop nearly throwing Elliot. Thousands of rats were pouring down the streets and Myshka struggled to avoid stepping on them.

'Head for the square if you can.' Elliot shouted over the noise of the scratching, squeaking and chattering.

The rats parted way and Myshka galloped onwards.

Upon entering the square the sight wasn't much different. Hundreds and thousands of rats poured up from the sewers, lifting drain covers and scurrying across the stones, all heading towards the residential areas.

Myshka stopped in the middle of the square and reared up, the hooves on her front feet pounding the air.

* * * * *

Above the scratching and rumbling Peter heard another new sound and detected a familiar scent.

'Where'd all these rats come from?' Rufus asked.

Peter looked at Rufus and Milly, faithful as ever, the siblings were never far from each other's side, nor his in times of trouble.

'You were both told to wait.' Peter said.

Rufus shrugged, Milly ignored the comment, her attention elsewhere.

With a nod, Roman led the way back towards the town square, the others followed and the rats once more parted way for the wolves.

Reaching the square, Matyas exclaimed something in his own language at the sight in the middle. A golden mare rearing up on her hind legs, her front feet pounding the air, clearly disturbed by the presence of so many rats and on her back sat what looked like a Knight in silver armour brandishing a sword.

'Fey.' Milly whispered as she sniffed the air.

A large brown rat rose up on its hind legs, using its tail for support its whiskers twitching, it looked straight at the horse and rider.

'Is it me, or does that rat standing on its back legs look bigger than the rest?' Rufus asked.

LOCAL TROUBLE

Barumar had held court all through the night, stirring up the young vampires and revelling in their adoration and blood lust. Arcane had remained by his side as commanded.

The vampires gathered within the safety of the palace walls most of them asleep wherever they could find a space. Daytime made them weaker and less inclined to be active and Arcane felt slightly more comfortable moving among them. Some hissed as he walked by, but most ignored him. Even Arcane had to admit that Barumar's marking of him as the King's pet had its advantages, however demeaning the act had felt at the time.

At dawn when the King had finally given orders for all to rest and gather their strength for the fight, Arcane made his way to the Courtyard and the palace gates beyond, desperate for some fresh air after the confines of the palace and the fetid stench of the undead.

At the sound of the first explosion Arcane called the human guards who patrolled the gates during the day, and commanded them to send whatever Police the King owned to investigate. Suspecting the wolves of this latest trouble, the Police were advised to use silver bullets.

'Find out what's happening and who's responsible.' Arcane said. 'Report back to me at once!'

'Should we detain them?' the head of the guards asked.

'No. Stop the rioting. Use deadly force.'

The guard nodded to his men who radioed through to the City Police; vehicles were immediately dispatched.

* * * * *

Myshka stopped pounding the air and stood still.

'Is that Pickens?' Elliot asked looking at the large brown rat standing in front of them.

Myshka bobbed her head up and down as if nodding.

Elliot looked across the square and saw five people staring them, three he recognised instantly and raised his sword.

The sound of sirens filled the air.

'What now?' Roman asked rhetorically.

Two Police cars entered the square at speed, too quickly for the rats to move out of the way and many were crushed under the wheels before the cars skidded to a halt. Several armed officers got out of the cars, guns pointed at Elliot, Myshka and the wolves. A disembodied voice sounded over a loud speaker from one of the cars. Peter and Rufus didn't understand the words, but they could guess the context from the harsh intonation of the voice. Milly quickly translated.

'EVERYONE STAY WHERE YOU ARE. YOU ARE ALL UNDER ARREST. YOU WITH THE SWORD. GET OFF THE HORSE AND DROP THE WEAPON.'

Elliot had a good idea what the police were asking him to do and swung his leg over Myshka's back and jumped down to stand beside her. He put his arm under her head and stroked the side of her face, keeping his sword in his right hand. Leaning forward he whispered in Myshka's ear.

'Go with Pickens.'

Myshka shook her head from side to side in irritation.

'This is going to get ugly. Please go with him.'

Elliot rested his head against hers, all the while stroking her face.

'Find me later. Follow the scent of the wolves.'

Elliot stepped back and Myshka bobbed her head. Her body shuddered, shimmered and shrunk and she transformed into a rat and stood beside Pickens. Elliot kept his eyes on her for as long as possible before she joined Pickens and the river of rats that were still scrambling out of the sewers and heading towards the side streets.

As soon as the horse disappeared in front of them the Police opened fire.

Elliot was full Fey and although he hadn't controlled the elements of this world for many years he had not lost the ability to do so. As the bullets flew towards him, Elliot held up his left hand, palm facing out in the universal stop sign and manipulated the air to form a barrier. Most of the bullets from the handguns hit the barrier of air as if it was a brick wall, the impact sending out ripples until each bullet's ripples merged with the other before they dropped to the floor in front of Elliot. The Police kept firing and walking forward, closing the distance.

It had not been Elliot's intention to kill anyone but forced into a situation of life or death the techniques of his former training returned to him and Elliot twisted the Dragon Blade in his hand and deflected the stray bullets that made it through the barrier back towards the Police. The ricocheted bullets off the blade killing them all.

It was over in seconds. The driver of one of the police cars, the only survivor of the mobilised task force and the owner of the disembodied voice, slammed his car into reverse and with a screech of tyres sped out of the square and away from the carnage.

Peter crossed the square and headed towards Elliot.

The flow of rats from the sewers had slowed to a trickle and by the time the other wolves crossed the square to join Peter, they had all disappeared from sight.

Peter held out his hand to Elliot who took it and Peter pulled Elliot to him in a rough hug.

'You look well Eli.' Peter said. 'I hadn't thought to see you again. Was that Myshka?'

'Yes it was. Eli. I haven't gone by that name for quite some time. I use Elliot now. New world, new identity, you know how it is.' Elliot said with a shrug.

Elliot looked at Rufus and Milly.

'There's something different about you Milly.' Elliot said. 'I don't remember you having blue eyes.'

'You know this man?' Roman asked before Milly could respond.

'Roman, this is…Elliot.' Peter said. 'Elliot, meet Roman, the Alpha of the Braeden pack.'

Elliot and Roman shook hands.

'Elliot is an old friend.' Peter said.

'And ally.' Elliot replied.

'Then you are welcome.' Roman said. 'But we should get off the street. More police will be coming.'

Roman led the way back towards Mike's Cafeteria, Elliot followed. He looked around once before going inside knowing and trusting that Myshka was somewhere safe.

* * * * *

Grimlock and Jedrek were still standing at the end of the bridge looking down at the river when the sound of sirens filled the air.

'If the police catch us we're dead.' Grimlock said his eyes quickly scanning the area looking for somewhere they could hide.

'What's wrong? Afraid to fight you old bone chomper?' Jedrek asked.

'Never! But don't be a fool. We won't have a chance to fight, they'll have silver bullets. They can pick us off from a distance.'

A shrill whistle caught their attention and both wolves spun around. Pickens stood at the mouth of one of the storm drains below, beckoning them towards him.

'We'll have to move further up and jump in.' Jedrek said. 'The river will carry us back towards the drain. Let's hope the rat's strong enough to haul us in.'

A police car pulled up alongside them with a screech of tyres and the smell of burning rubber filled the air. Two officers exited the vehicle, firearms already drawn. The sound of gunfire from across the river drew everyone's attention and Jedrek grabbed Grimlock's arm.

'Go!' Jedrek said. 'Now while they're distracted. I'll draw them away.'

Before Grimlock could reply, Jedrek pushed him over the edge of the wall into the river. The last thing Grimlock heard before his head went under the cold water of the Nejelski River was Jedrek's voice and the sound of single gunshot.

'Can I help you?' Jedrek said.

'Stand where you are!'

One of the Police Officer's fired a warning shot at Jedrek's feet small particles of debris jumping into the air as it embedded itself into the stone.

Jedrek glanced down to the river in time to see Grimlock scrambling into the mouth of the storm drain with the aid of Pickens, the wererat.

Jedrek took a step closer to the police officers. In human form the wolves were stronger than most people and Jedrek could feel the wolf rising and transformed somewhere between man and wolf, making him even stronger while maintaining the outward appearance of a man, for the most part. His eyes, always the first and last thing to change turned an animalistic yellow. His hands grew larger and his fingernails turned to claws and when he spoke his voice was more guttural.

Jedrek stood facing the armed Officers, his hands in his jacket pockets. He felt the block of explosive material, malleable in his left hand and wrapped his fingers around it, squeezing the plastic putty-like substance into a ball. He felt for the blasting cap in his right pocket; nothing. Jedrek's heart sank, the explosive block was useless without it.

'Hands where I can see them.' The officer commanded.

As Jedrek starting to pull his right hand out of his pocket his clawed fingertips touched the top of the blasting cap. He smiled and spoke to Grimlock using werewolf telepathy.

Do you still have the detonator?

There was a pause before Grimlock responded and Jedrek pictured him checking his pockets and prayed to the Divine that Grimlock hadn't lost it when he fell into the river.

I have it.

I have one block left. When you hear fire in the hole blast it.

Fire in the hole?

Always wanted to say that. Jedrek smiled to himself.

Do what you have to and join me. There's a way across the river. We'll be needed for the fight.

'Hands where I can see them!' The Officer commanded again.

Jedrek slowly took both hands out of his pockets and held them in front of him discreetly pushing the blasting cap into the ball of explosive material and activating it.

'I don't want any trouble.' Jedrek said taking another step closer to the young Officer.

'Hands above your head.'

Jedrek stepped closer again and raised both hands above his head, the long fingers of his left hand curled around the ball of explosive making it appear as if he was clenching his fist above his head.

This was the part of any hunt Jedrek loved the most, seconds before striking. The Police Officer was young and frightened, his heart beating fast in his chest, Jedrek smelt the mixed odours of sweat and fear and waited. The radio on the officer's shoulder crackled with static and when the Officer's eyes flickered towards it Jedrek pounced, grabbing the man's chin in his large right hand, twisting and snapping his neck. As the body dropped, Jedrek grabbed the gun and shot the nearest officer between the eyes in one swift movement.

For a second the whole world froze in place. Jedrek stood side on facing the two police cars with his right arm outstretched pointing a gun, a ball of explosive in his left hand. Two officers stood beside their car, guns pointing at Jedrek, their mouths slack in shock at just seeing two of their colleagues killed. Four officers standing beside the open doors of the second vehicle had guns trained on their target. Jedrek roared, shattering the paralysis of time and leapt into the eye of the storm.

The police opened fire, silver bullets zipping through the air. Jedrek moved quickly and tore open the throat of the nearest man to him. He was quick but not fast enough to dodge bullets and he felt the small silver missiles pierce his body. Guns set to automatic fire, the Police closed in around him forming a tight circle. When Jedrek dropped to one knee they ceased fire and once again time seemed to stand still.

In the silence, a strange sound filled the air and the Police looked each other for explanation. The sound continued until one of the officers recognised what it was.

'He's laughing!' The office said incredulously.

Jedrek could feel the life draining from him, each bullet hole oozing dark, congealing blood, the silver preventing any regeneration and he spoke to Grimlock once again.

Ready, you old bone chomper?

Ready.

Standing in the relative safety of the storm drain, Grimlock heard

Jedrek roar and the following gunfire and didn't have to be there to know what was happening. He and Jedrek were pack and he felt his brother's pain. He knew the police would pursue them and Jedrek was buying time for Grimlock to escape. Suddenly Jedrek's voice sounded in Grimlock's mind asking him if he was ready.

Grimlock closed his eyes and controlled his breathing, waiting for what would be Jedrek's final command.

Ready. Grimlock replied.

Jedrek raised his head and looked at the faces of the police surrounding him. He struggled to speak and spat a mouthful of blood and saliva onto the nearest pair of boots. Holding up his left hand Jedrek thoughts communicated to Grimlock at the same time as he spoke aloud.

'Fire. In the hole.'

The head of the blasting cap began blinking and Jedrek held out his hand towards the Police and closed his eyes. Sharp intakes of breath, the scent of panic and the scraping of boots in a futile attempt at escape were the last things he heard.

Grimlock and Pickens felt the vibration of the explosion in the storm drain and Grimlock bowed his head.

Goodbye my brother. Grimlock thought.

Pickens put his hand on Grimlock's shoulder.

'This way.'

* * * * *

In the basement of the cafe, the faint sound of a third explosion cut conversation short and Roman closed his eyes. Peter knew from Roman's body language that one of his pack had been killed and understood his pain. Although Rusty had died a warrior's death, Peter still felt the sorrow of his loss all these years later.

Roman and Matyas stood away from everyone, joined in their grief but both aware there was no time to grieve properly for Jedrek. If any of them survived the night they would grieve as a pack, or join Jedrek in the afterlife.

*****

'There's nothing more to be done here.' Pickens said.

They walked along the dark, damp storm drain. Pickens led the way, obviously familiar with the tunnels, Grimlock followed, deep in thought. He and Jedrek had bickered constantly but they were pack and the loss of his wolf brother cut like a knife. The tunnel narrowed and the air turned colder as Pickens stopped before a sharp decline.

'We travel in our natural form from here.' Pickens said. 'Quicker.'

Grimlock nodded but said nothing.

They transformed; Grimlock to wolf, Pickens to rat.

There were other rats in the tunnel and several scampered past them. Grimlock cursed himself that he hadn't considered the tunnels.

The vampires could come up anywhere. Grimlock thought to himself irritably.

Pickens scurried along, his scent ripe to Grimlock's heightened wolf senses. Grimlock followed at a steady pace. In wolf form he was unhampered by the darkness of the subterranean passages, which was fortunate when Pickens came to a sudden stop in front of him at the branch of one of the tunnels.

The tunnel entrance was blocked from floor to ceiling with hundreds of rats. Small, medium and large bodies, all standing on top of each other to form an impassable wall of teeth, claws and fur. Grimlock looked at the entrance of the tunnel, mouth agape, tongue lolling, he had never seen so many rats in one place and he understood why Pickens had stopped.

Enough to deter any vampire. Grimlock thought.

Grimlock's spirits lifted in spite of his grief, Jedrek would have approved, as much as he'd hated rats. Pickens and his kind were a formidable force when brought together and Grimlock leaned forward and nudged the wererat with his muzzle in a gesture that said everything.

Pickens led on and as they turned a corner Grimlock could see the silhouette of a tall man and a cat waiting for them, Grimlock followed Pickens leaving the rats to their business.

SHOCK NEWS

Back home in Plym City, Uri stood and waited for Scara, her sister and Alpha of the pack in Peter's absence, to process what she had just been told. It was a lot to take in and Uri herself was still coming to terms with what she had agreed to do.

Maximus, the first Alpha had asked Uri to join the spirit pack as the Alpha female and elder. He said Uri was the most powerful elder there had been in many years and the pack needed her. As much as Uri loved Peter and the pack she missed being able to run and hunt. The injuries she sustained in the fight against Parallax had left her crippled and her vision poor. As an injured wolf Uri knew that in the wild she would have died. The first Alpha's offer had made her feel alive in a way she hadn't for a long time and she yearned to return to an active existence, full of danger, excitement and purpose. The price was her physical form and Uri was happy to shed the restrictions of her corporeal body. She would be as formidable as she had been in her youth and Uri saw this offer as a chance to live again.

Uri looked at her sister, even with impaired eyesight she could see her sister was close to tears, she waited patiently.

'I'm tired Scara.' Uri said sighing. 'I've done so much but the world has moved on without me. I'm a relic.'

'You're the pack elder.' Scara said. 'What are we going to do?'

'When Milly returns she'll take my place as elder.'

'If she returns.'

Uri raised one eyebrow but said nothing, Scara broke eye contact.

'Is she ready?' Scara asked looking back.

'More than ready.' Uri replied. 'I've been instructing her and with Gaolyn's memories spanning almost a millennium, what she doesn't know now she'll never know.'

'I don't want to lose you.' Scara said.

'You won't be losing me little sister. I'll always be with you.'

'But it won't be the same.'

Scara turned away hiding fresh tears.

'Listen to me Scara.' Uri said. 'Look at me.'

Scara turned back and faced Uri.

'All these years since the pulse I've been living with the pack, relying on their charity for every meal when I should be out hunting. Training Milly, communing with the spirits and advising Peter has kept me feeling like part of the pack, but for me it hasn't felt like living.' Uri paused. 'I've been waiting to die.'

Scara said nothing, she understood the sub-text in Uri's words, it was more than the inability to hunt.

'When will you go?' Scara asked.

'As soon as you give me leave to do so.' Uri said smiling. 'As acting Alpha, I seek your permission to go. And your blessing.'

Scara pulled Uri towards her in a tight hug and whispered in her ear.

'I love you Uri. You don't need my permission to go.'

Scara held Uri at arm's length.

'But as Alpha, you have my permission to join the spirit pack. And my blessing.'

'Thank you.' Uri said, tears filling her own eyes. 'Will you stay with me during the ritual and ascension?'

'It will be my honour.' Scara replied. 'Peter won't be happy.'

'He'll get over it.'

* * * * *

Meanwhile, back in Braeden….

'This is madness!' Roman exclaimed. 'Suicide!'

'I have to do this.' Peter said. '*We* have to do this. You heard what Titan said. The only way to heal my children is to get close enough to Arcane.'

'You know he wants your wife dead!'

'He can try, and…'

Peter held up his hand as Roman went to interrupt.

'…I have an old score to settle with Barumar. Who knows? Perhaps killing the king will stop the war.'

'That's incredibly optimistic of you.' Roman replied sarcastically. 'The old adage of cutting the head off the snake.'

Roman ran his hand through his hair and sighed impatiently, a gesture often done by Peter who understood the Alpha's dilemma. What Peter was proposing split the already small werewolf force in two leaving only Roman's pack to fight against a hoard of vampires on Draven Bridge.

Although exasperated, Roman understood the need for Peter to save his children, body and mind.

'How are you planning on getting into the palace?'

Peter looked to Rufus.

'Through the tunnels.' Rufus said pointing to the trap door.

'It's a maze down there.' Roman protested.

'I'll follow the stench of the vampires.' Rufus replied.

'But..'

Roman paused and looked down at the trap door.

'Did you hear that?' Roman asked looking around the room.

A second knock on the trap door confirmed what Roman thought he heard and alerted everyone else. All eyes fixed on the access door of the escape tunnel. Nobody moved and another knock, louder and more urgent this time spurred Roman to move. He heaved the trap door open and looked down into the blackness of the escape tunnel, every fibre of his body ready to fight.

The roar of a wolf echoed from inside the tunnel

'Stand back.' Roman commanded.

Roman stepped back from the opening and Grimlock leapt into the room landing softly on all four paws. He turned a full circle and transformed back into human form.

Grimlock leaned over the trap door and held out his hand. A small hand reached up and grabbed it. Grimlock lifted the boy easily out of the tunnel and set him down.

'Yosef!' Elena exclaimed running towards him.

The two youngsters hugged as Max joined them.

'I'm glad you're ok.' Yosef said looking from Max to Elena. 'I saw the witch take you. How did you get away?'

Elena and Max exchanged a look but said nothing. Yosef suddenly saw the two vampires standing away from everyone else and looked terrified. Roman put his hand on the boy's shoulder.

'No-one will harm you. You have my word.'

Yosef nodded but did not look convinced.

'Who are you?' Roman asked the boy. 'Where did you come from?'

'I'm Yosef. I've been hiding in the tunnels.'

'Do you want to give me a hand up?' a gruff disembodied voice yelled from the tunnel.

Grimlock leaned in again and held out a hand. A large hand took it and Grimlock heaved the man out of the tunnel, his overcoat flapped out behind him like a cloak and hanging onto the end of the cloak was a cat. Both man and cat landed softly on the floor and looked around as if their entrance into the room was the most natural thing in the world.

'Ratman!' Max and Elena said simultaneously.

'Myshka.' Elliot said smiling as the cat ran for cover.

'Grimlock?' Roman said stepping forward.

'I've brought friends.' Grimlock said. 'And news.'

Elliot followed the cat and returned seconds later with his arm around a woman who was busy pulling his cloak across her body.

'Who are you people?' Roman said irritably.

'I am known as Ratman.'

'How do you know this tunnel?'

'I know all of the tunnels.'

Ratman stepped up to Roman and put his hand on his shoulder.

'We don't have time for long explanations. I'm sorry for the loss of your wolf brother, know that he died a warrior's death. You have already met Elliot, this is his wife Myshka, she's a Morphian.'

Roman looked at Myshka.

'You were the horse then the rat in the square?' Roman asked.

'And a cat.' Myshka replied. 'We came to the City to help Pickens, he's a friend.'

'I've met Pickens.'

'I can tell you exactly what's going on.' Ratman said turning from Roman to address everyone in the room. 'But first, Yosef come here.'

Yosef went to Ratman and stood before him. Ratman dropped to one knee bringing him eye level with the boy.

'I need you to go to Tomas and Kristyna.' Ratman said.

'I don't…'

'No arguments.' Ratman said.

Yosef stopped talking and listened.

'I have a job for you.' Ratman said. 'I want you to make sure that Tomas and Kristyna and as many of their neighbours as possible stay in their homes tonight. Tell them the rats are still in the streets and it'll be morning before the situation's under control. Can you do that?'

'Yes.' Yosef nodded. His eyes strayed to the vampires. 'And the cold ones?'

Ratman put his finger under Yosef's chin and turned his head back to face him.

'Don't worry about them. Tell Tomas and Kristyna not to open their door for anyone.' Ratman said. '*Anyone.* Pickens has done a good job mobilising his forces. The fear of rats getting in, should stop people opening their doors. Will you do this for me?'

'Yes.' Yosef said.

'Good boy.'

Ratman stood up to his full height and put his hand on Yosef's shoulder. The boy looked up at him waiting further orders.

'Stay with Tomas and Kristyna tonight, keep them safe.' Ratman winked at the Yosef conspiratorially.

Yosef nodded and smiled. He took one last look at Elena and smiled again. When she returned his smile Yosef blushed and looked away.

'Go now.' Ratman said.

Yosef ran to the steps of the basement and was gone.

'Now all we need is a bit of good fortune.' Ratman said. 'Pickens sending his rats into the streets was a stroke of genius.'

'The rats are blocking all of the tunnels across the City.' Grimlock said. 'The vampires will have no other choice but to use Draven Bridge.'

'There you have it!' Roman said turning to Peter. 'All the tunnels are blocked. There's no way you can get into the palace. I'm sorry Peter, we need to stand and fight together, I know you want to try but you have your children back alive and well, that's all that matters.'

Roman looked at Peter triumphantly; Peter said nothing, it wasn't all that mattered. He stood still, jaw clenched holding in his anger, not trusting himself to speak. He wasn't sure if he was angry at Roman or the unfairness of the situation. Max and Elena had been returned to him, but part of them remained trapped at the palace and the only way they would be fully restored was to destroy Arcane's pendant. And what of Barumar? The mad vampire king who needed to be destroyed once and for all.

Shayla watched as Peter inhaled and exhaled slowly, a sign that he was controlling his anger, a technique she had also adopted since merging with Titan. Shayla had never understood the extent of Titan's impatience and or how easily irked he became. Only now did she fully appreciate his frustration and irritation when situations thwarted his, and her plans.

'Pickens will open the way for Peter, Shayla, the twins and whoever else wants to go with them, to pass through and close the tunnel behind them.' Ratman said.

Roman rounded on Ratman, his eyes turning yellow as the wolf's temper rose to the surface.

'That'll split our small force in two! You may as well kill us now! You're condemning us to death with this madness!'

'Calm yourself wolf.' Ratman commanded, his own voice dropping to a deep growl.

'*I* am Alpha here.' Roman said.

'You are not *my* Alpha.' Ratman replied.

Something flashed across Ratman's eyes that Roman hadn't seen before and didn't quite understand, but he stood his ground.

'Grimlock told you he had news, so listen.'

'I'm listening.' Roman said through gritted teeth.

Roman didn't know where Ratman had come from or who he was, but he knew instinctively that he was ancient. Whatever Ratman was Roman sensed he wasn't evil, nor was he an enemy. Roman communicated to his pack to stand down and waited to hear what Ratman had to say, but didn't fully pull back the wolf inside him.

* * * * *

The Palace guard had just informed Arcane that the vehicle bridges were destroyed when they heard the third explosion. The crackle on the guard's shoulder radio and the look on his face as he listened through the earpiece told Arcane that something had happened to the investigating police officers. He cursed under his breath and walked away.

Arcane summoned two of Barumar's vampire guards.

'Did you find the witch?' Arcane asked.

'There's no sign of her in the palace or any of the underground rooms.'

'You were ordered to find her and kill her.' Arcane said. 'Did you search her house?

The vampires looked at each other.

'Problem?'

'It's daylight.'

'Take a car. They have tinted windows, do they not?' Arcane asked.

The vampires hesitated.

'NOW!' Arcane said. 'By order of the King.'

The two vampires nodded and left.

Arcane looked at one of the paintings in the hallway, his eyes not on the painting, but on his own reflection in the glass.

'You should have gone yourself and killed the crone.' Eversor said.

'I know.' Arcane replied.

*****

Shortly after, the vampires arrived at Thebe's house and sat in the car.

'Do you smell that?' Sasha asked.

'Smells like rotten eggs.' Vernon replied. 'But she always smelt like that.'

'It's not that, it's something else. I don't like this.'

'I don't think she's there.'

'Me neither.' Sasha said.

'Feels like a waste of time.' Vernon said. 'But we'd better check inside.'

'I agree. Let's get it over with.'

The trees screening the house provided little shelter from the early afternoon daylight. Dressed head to toe in thick black clothing with gloves and hooded jackets, the two vampires pulled the hoods as low as possible for minimum skin exposure.

'The door's unlocked.' Sasha said glancing at Vernon and pushing the door gently.

Thebe had set a booby-trap and Vernon felt a rush of heat. He grabbed the back of Sasha's jacket yanking her to one side as purple flames ripped through the house incinerating everything it touched. The vampires retreated but the purple flames followed them, seeking them out. Sasha caught a lick of flame to the side of her face as she and Vernon got into the car and slammed the doors. Vernon started the car and sped away as the house exploded, eventually outrunning the flames.

'That's no ordinary fire.' Vernon said. 'The old witch set a trap.'

'You think!' Sasha said wincing at the pain. 'It's not healing!'

'It will when you feed.'

Sasha gave him a withering look and Vernon drove on in silence.

'What now?' Vernon said.

'Head back into the City, try and pick up her scent.' Sasha said. 'She can't have gone far.'

Vernon stopped the car and looked at Sasha.

'What?' Sasha asked.

'There's little chance of finding the crone in the City. She rigged her house to blow up, don't you think she can hide her scent? If we go back empty handed the King will send us for a walk in the sun, you know that right?'

'What do you suggest?' Sasha asked.

'We keep driving, away from the City.'

'We'll be executed for treason.'

'Only if we get caught.'

Sasha contemplated the reality of their situation before finally responding.

'Drive. Get us out of here.'

DIVIDED

'You will not fight alone.' Ratman said.

'I've recalled Loran and Karayan which makes a total of seven to defend the City.' Roman said.

'Seven you say.' Ratman said rubbing his chin thoughtfully. 'Then you are fortunate!'

'I'm losing six good fighters!'

'Eight.'

'I'm not including the children.' Roman said glancing at Max and Elena.

'You also have two vampires.'

Roman paused before replying.

'They will not fight with us. Max owes them a life debt which must be honoured. If they fight alongside the wolves their presence would cause confusion. No. They will stay here.'

It was Ratman's turn to pause before speaking.

'Six are leaving. Six must be replaced.'

Roman thought about responding that if Peter and Shayla weren't going on their fool's errand and taking their pack with them, and the handy with a sword newcomer and his wife, there would be no need to replace six fighters, but he said nothing. Instead he seethed.

'You know of the spirit pack?' Ratman asked.

'Of course.' Roman replied. 'But how do you know of the spirit pack?'

Ratman waved his hand dismissively and Roman inhaled and exhaled slowly, his patience was barely keeping his anger in check. Ratman wasn't a wolf but he seemed to know a lot and yet he explained nothing.

'Only the elders can commune with the spirit pack.' Roman said.

'I am an elder.' Ratman said. 'Tonight they will fight with you.'

'You're an elder?'

'Yes.'

'I don't believe you. You're not wolf.'

'Do not call me a liar.' Ratman paused and glanced at the faces around him. 'There is far more in the multiple universes than you will ever know.'

Roman stared at Ratman, whose expression gave nothing away.

'When did you speak to the spirit pack?' Roman asked.

'You ask too many stupid questions!' Ratman snapped. 'Either accept what I am offering or don't! Your choice.'

Roman hadn't felt reprimanded in such a way since his own father had been Alpha of the Braeden pack; the feeling was uncomfortable. He thought about Ratman's offer.

'How can they fight with no physical form?'

Ratman closed his eyes and sighed.

'As I said, there is more in the universe than you will ever understand.' Ratman replied. 'They can cause pain and injury without corporeal form. They can bring chaos and confusion. Each one of the spirit pack has the strength and ability of ten wolves. Do you want their help, or are you too arrogant to accept?'

Again Roman had the uncomfortable feeling of being chastised and having no other options available he nodded.

'I accept your offer and their help.'

'Excellent.' Ratman said. 'Now that you've seen sense, is there any chance of some food?'

Roman nodded to Tempest who gave Ratman a full plate.

'Who are you?' Roman asked. 'Where did you come from?'

'I have told you. I am Ratman and I came from the tunnel.' Ratman said rubbing an apple on his arm until it shone. 'Did you not see me?'

Ratman inspected the apple and paused again before taking a bite.

'I'm…..complex.'

Peter and his pack look at each other quickly and back to Ratman.

'You're not….?' Peter began.

'Finban.' Roman finished.

'Fishbone?' Shayla questioned.

'Fishbone? Why would I want a fishbone?' Ratman said shaking his head and biting into the apple. 'Fishbones are for cats.'

Ratman winked at Myshka, who was now wearing some of Tempest's clothes, she scowled. He looked at the apple again, this time with unseeing eyes, his thoughts elsewhere.

'Although, there's one of us who calls himself Fishbone.' Ratman said. 'Or was it Frank? Hmmm…'

Ratman continued eating, when it was clear he had no more to say on the subject, Peter turned to Shayla.

'We should get going.' Peter said putting his hands on Shayla's shoulders.

'Peterus Maximus.' Ratman said using Peter's full name.

Peter looked at the mysterious Ratman.

'Fire walker. Do not look so shocked. I know more than you can imagine. You will need both the living silver and internal fire when you face the king. Barumar has acquired a few gifts of his own.'

'I will finish him this time.' Peter replied.

'Take no chances and remember the Mortem Dormitabius.'

'I will.'

'Go now before sunset. Keep to the south tunnels. One will bring you up under the chapel.'

'There's a chapel in a vampire palace?'

Ratman sighed impatiently.

'It's unused and hopefully unguarded.'

Ratman turned his gaze towards Milly.

'The vampire will show you the way.'

Milly shuffled awkwardly and averted her eyes so as not to meet the gaze of the Braeden wolves.

'Isn't that right Gaolyn Lancing?' Ratman said. 'You know the way.'

'That's right.' Milly said looking back at Ratman. 'I know my way around the palace.'

Peter glanced at Roman who said nothing further. Peter decided explanations were best saved for another time.

'Princess.' Ratman said. 'Shayla Meldainiel. Once inside, Arcane will come for you. Don't let him distract you with his evil words.'

Shayla listened both concerned and afraid and confused as to who Ratman was and how he knew her name.

'Encroaching darkness, demon sent.' Ratman said staring at a space in the corner of the room.

'You're quoting the prophecy.' Shayla whispered. 'What does that mean?'

'Take a stand or lose this fight. Enters the brain and enters the mind.' Ratman continued. 'Destroys us all, not just mankind.'

Ratman shook his head and returned his attention to Shayla.

'Beware the darkness inside him, it is more powerful than even he realises. It has its own purpose. Of that you should be most afraid. Destroy the pendant, heal the twins, everything else will fall into place. Now I will speak with Titan.'

Before Shayla could ask a question she felt Titan's consciousness in her mind, he wanted to hear Ratman's message for himself. Shayla closed her eyes and opened them again slowly. Her eyes had changed colour and Titan looked at Ratman through Shayla's eyes.

'Hello Titan.'

'Ratman.'

'You must not let the darkness in.'

'I won't.' Titan replied.

'Whatever it takes, do not let it in. *You* must remain in control.'

'I understand.' Titan replied.

Ratman smiled but his eyes looked sad.

'I know you do.'

Titan relinquished control back to Shayla and Ratman turned to the twins putting a hand on each of their shoulders.

'You are more than you realise.' Ratman said. 'Stay together. Work together. You can turn the tide. Remember, Lycan Angel's Greatest Light.'

Max and Elena both nodded but said nothing. They also wondered who Ratman was and what his words meant.

'Are you Fishbone's brother?' Elena asked in her usual forthright manner.

Ratman laughed and pulled the twins towards him and hugged them tightly whispering something in their ears. As he held them at arm's length Max and Elena nodded.

'Good.' Ratman said. 'Go now.'

Grimlock had been silent for some time but as Peter and Shayla moved towards the trapdoor to the tunnel he stepped towards Max.

'You are my Alpha. My place is at your side.' Grimlock said.

'I know.' Max replied.

Max looked at Grimlock and spoke with a maturity beyond his thirteen years.

'My father and his pack are leaving because they must, I have to go with him. I need you to stay to represent our pack. Will you fight alongside Roman in my stead?'

'Of course.'

'I will join you as soon as I am able.'

Grimlock inclined his head towards his Alpha and Max, slightly unsure of the correct response, nodded his head in return.

Rufus was the first to move and jumped down into the tunnel, followed by Milly, then Peter. Max and Elena, a little hesitant, followed their father with Shayla close behind. Myshka leaped into the tunnel closely followed by Elliot.

Once all eight people had gone Matyas replaced the trap door, plunging the tunnel into darkness.

'I'll take point. Rufus said. 'I've been this way before.'

Before following Rufus, Shayla held onto Max and Elena.

'What did Ratman say to you?' Shayla asked.

'He said shine brightly.' Max replied.

*****

Karayan and Loran were making their way back to the cafeteria as quickly as possible, dodging rats who still littered the streets. They walked side by side, the need for stealth no longer seemed necessary and Lorcan took human form rather than posing as Karayan's dog. A front door opened as they passed by.

'Where did all these rats come from?' the woman asked through the gap in the half open door.

'I heard the sewer is flooded and all the rats are coming up to escape.' Karayan replied. 'I'd stay inside if I were you and keep the doors locked until tomorrow.'

The woman looked at them suspiciously.

'We're on our way home now.' Lorcan said picking up what Karayan had started. 'You know what the City officials are like. It'll take them until morning to sort things out.'

'Ha! They'll meet and talk about it first!' the woman scoffed.

'Day after tomorrow then.' Lorcan said laughing.

'You got that right!'

The woman laughed although suspicion remained in her eyes.

'Have a nice evening.' Karayan said.

The woman nodded and closed the door, the wolves heard the click of the lock and the sliding of a bolt.

'We'd better hurry.' Lorcan said.

Rounding a corner and only one street away from the cafeteria the wolves stopped dead in their tracks, alerted by a familiar and foul stench. Lorcan and Karayan looked at each other knowing exactly what lay in wait for them, the smell of dead flesh never getting any easier to stomach.

Ambush. Lorcan said telepathically.

How many? Karayan replied.

Can't say. Too many.

The wolves knew they would not make it to the cafeteria; a side street in Braeden was where they would make their last stand.

The vampires stepped from the shadows fully armed and dressed in full black biker's leathers, complete with crash helmets and leather gloves. All skin covered, faces obscured by dark tinted visors, the wolves saw only the reflection of their own faces.

Lorcan inhaled and glanced at Karayan.

I know brother. Karayan said. *Silver ammo.*

Warn Roman.

Roman! Karayan said. *Ambush.*

Both wolves transformed into warrior form, neither concerned with humans seeing them. The Dementium would take care of the human perception but the situation had gone too far to worry about any humans seeing the confrontation and their possible descent into madness, it was more likely nobody would survive to talk about seeing monsters in the streets.

We die fighting. Lorcan said saliva dripping from his razor-sharp teeth.

Kill as many as possible. Karayan replied.

As the vampires took aim, both wolves leapt, teeth bared, claws slashing. The sound of bullets echoed in the street before silence returned, the scurrying rats the only witnesses to the aftermath.

*****

Roman clenched his fists and roared. He looked at Ratman, pain evident in his eyes.

'The spirit pack will come.' Ratman said.

Reidar understood from Roman's reaction that the vampires must have attacked early and Roman had lost more of his pack. He put his arm around Thana holding her close and wondered just how honourable a wolf was, whether an Alpha kept his word and if he and Thana would now be killed for being vampires. As Roman stepped forward, Reidar put his hand on his sword.

'It's started.' Roman said finally.

'I'm sorry.' Reidar replied.

Roman held his gaze for a few seconds before he nodded and turned away.

Ratman stepped forward and put his hand on Roman's shoulder.

'I'm sorry for your loss.' Ratman said. 'Pickens and I will fight with you.'

'Thank you.' Roman replied. 'We should go and make our stand.'

*****

Peter and the others heard Roman's roar from inside the tunnel and all stopped.

'Barumar sent a group out before sunset to attack the wolves, to throw them off balance.' Milly said.

'You don't seem surprised.' Peter said.

It's what I would have done. Milly replied but not aloud.

'Let's keep moving.' Peter said. 'Rufus. Get us out of here.'

INTO BATTLE

The tunnel was completely dark rendering everyone blind except Rufus. With his ability to see into the afterglow he led the way along the same route he and Milly had taken previously to escape Roman's basement.

A dim light from the sewer turned the tunnel to a dark grey and Rufus knew they were approaching the portcullis that would lead them to the sewers. The widened tunnel allowed Peter to walk side by side with Rufus.

'Watch your step.' Rufus said. 'The floor dips down here.'

'How much further?' Peter asked.

As if in answer, the floor dipped again and Peter and Rufus stopped at the head of four stone steps.

'Ash wood and silver.' Rufus said pointing to the portcullis. 'Last time there weren't this many rats running around.'

Rufus transformed into warrior form to open the portcullis. This time it was Peter, not Milly who held the gate open for everyone to pass through, dropping it back in place with a resounding clang. As he held the gate, Peter watched the rats bustling along the tunnel, all headed in the same direction.

'We went this way last time.' Rufus said pointing along the tunnel.

'The rats are gathering there.' Peter said. 'What did Grimlock say about the rats blocking the tunnels?'

'I think the rats are trying to stop us from going that way.' Myshka said. 'This is Picken's doing. He's trying to help us. We should follow their lead.'

'Ratman said to keep heading south.' Peter said. 'The rats are going south anyway, we might as well follow them.'

The eight companions followed the rats as they moved along the southward tunnels. As they headed downwards to one of the passages beneath the river Elena held her hand to the side of her head in an attempt to push back the pain. The stabbing pain in her head and the visual disturbance was getting worse the closer they drew to the other side of the river. Max sensed his sisters anguish and held her hand as they walked in silence towards the palace, suppressing his own fear of the unknown.

After what seemed like an hour, although there was no real way of telling, the trail of rats trickled away to nothing and the eight companions were alone in the tunnels. The rats obviously sensed more danger on the other side of the river and had sensibly opted to stay away.

'We're close.' Rufus said. 'I can sense evil, it feels like it's everywhere.'

'Because it is.' Peter replied.

'Peter!' Shayla exclaimed as Elena stumbled and fell.

Peter rushed to his daughter's side as she lay on the floor holding her head and shaking. She was crying quietly in spite of the pain trying not to make too much noise.

Shayla cupped Elena's face in her hands.

'Look at me Elena.' Shayla said.

'It hurts.' Elena said her eyes full of tears.

'I know darling. Look at me.'

Elena looked into her mother's green eyes, Shayla's hands either side of Elena's head, she traced small circles on Elena's temples with her thumbs. Shayla maintained eye contact and gently massaged Elena's head, her hands glowing faintly in the dim grey tunnel. The glow dissipated as quickly as it had appeared but in its wake Elena seemed much calmer and had stopped shaking.

'Any better?' Shayla asked.

'A little. It still hurts but not as bad.'

Peter and Shayla exchanged a look and Peter knew that Shayla's healing touch was only a temporary fix and the pain and convulsions would soon return.

'We're not far now.' Peter said. 'I'll carry you the rest of the way.'

'No.' Milly said kneeling beside Elena. 'You should stay up front with Rufus. I'll carry her.'

Milly picked Elena up and held her close as if she was a very small child. Elena put her head on Milly's shoulder.

'Rest if you can little one.' Milly said stroking the back of her head. 'You'll be back to normal soon enough.'

Elena didn't respond but Milly felt Elena's body relax in her arms.

We need to move fast. Peter said to Milly and Rufus. *We have to find Arcane and smash that pendant as soon as possible.*

The unspoken sub-text that the convulsions and pain could kill Elena if she wasn't fully restored soon was not lost on the wolves. Max also heard the conversation in his own mind, the werewolf telepathy a new development, he felt sick to his stomach at the thought of losing his twin sister, but said nothing.

Rufus was correct in that they weren't far from the palace and even the non-wolves smelt the nauseatingly offensive odour of dead flesh.

Turning her face towards Elena, Milly whispered in her ear.

'Do you think you can walk now?'

'Yes.' Elena said in a quiet voice.

'Good girl.' Milly said setting Elena down on her slightly unsteady legs.

Max was at his sister's side instantly to support her.

'This tunnel connects to another, which leads directly to the drain at the back of the chapel.'

Milly moved to the front and led the way, soon all eight companions were standing in a circle looking up at a grate, beyond which was the chapel.

'I've been expecting you.' a voice called from somewhere above. 'Join us.'

Shayla looked at Peter and frowned questioningly, her arms around her children.

'Barumar.' Peter said quietly.

'How?' Shayla asked.

'Arcane knows who you are.' Peter said. 'Which means he knows who I am. If I were in his position, I'd have told the King to expect us. There's no more need for stealth.'

'Titan and I will fight.' Shayla said.

'I can fight.' Max said stepping forward.

Peter put his hand on his son's shoulder and looked him in the eye.

'Stay here. Protect your sister and Myshka.' Peter said. 'They're the most vulnerable. They'll need you.'

Max nodded.

Peter stood directly beneath the grate and transformed his hands and claws into living silver.

'I'm coming up!' Peter shouted as he leapt up bursting through the grate in the floor.

Milly and Rufus were right behind him and the three wolves stood in a line facing the front of the chapel. Peter looked around, there were vampires sitting in the pews their faces now turned towards the wolves, fangs exposed, some of them hissing and spitting. Peter ignored them all, his attention on the one at the front, dressed in a long black clerical cassock.

'Welcome!' Barumar said, his arms outstretched. 'And all of you still in the sewer. Come and join us. I *insist.* No-one here will harm you.'

Peter and Rufus stood their ground while Milly helped everyone else out of the tunnel. When Shayla and the twins emerged a ripple of excitement ran through the assembled vampires and Shayla pushed the twins slightly behind her. At the appearance of Myshka and Elliot, him being full Fey, the vampires began snapping and thrashing around in their seats, their senses overwhelmed by the scent of the Fey, their blood lust at an all-time high. It was only their obedience to Barumar that held them in place, although his grasp was tenuous.

Peter stepped slightly ahead, flanked by Rufus and Milly. Shayla stood beside Rufus and Elliot drew his sword and stood beside Milly. Glancing at Elliot's Dragon Blade, Gaolyn's memories of his own Greatsword surfaced in Milly's mind and she quickly looked around the chapel. There were no ancient suits of amount on display, the empty shells of knights holding their broadswords in front of them, but her eyes alighted on a large processional cross. Milly calculated from the base to the tip it was approximately six and a half feet long, an ideal size for a wolf in warrior form. She would snap off the base and use it as a blunt sword, the ornate silver and jewelled cross forming the hilt. The jewels would cut her hands and the silver would aggravate the wounds, but not before she had skewered a few vampires and relieved them of their heads. Milly smiled exposing her teeth.

Behind them Max stood in front of Myshka and his sister feeling the wolf's rage pushing against his human body trying to get free. He could feel his whole body tingling as his skin began to pull tight, his teeth elongating and shrinking back in his gums. His muscles flexed beneath his skin and he felt a grinding sensation in his bones as they waited in anticipation to break and reshape into a new form. Unlike the first time he transformed, Max fought against the change and held the warrior and the wolf in check.

Shayla noticed movement at the front of the chapel behind Barumar and knew the dark haired man who was sneakily trying to slip away, was Arcane. Arcane looked and made eye contact, Shayla's rage bubbled up insider her. Her eyes fixed on the man who had kidnapped her children, she also wanted to punish the witch, but Arcane would have to suffice. Titan's thoughts sounded in her head to attack and kill him. Shayla concurred but her own rage was tempered by the thought that she needed to find the pendant and destroy it in order to heal her children.

The tension in the air was palpable, vampires and wolves balanced on a knife edge, both sides waiting for the command to engage.

Barumar's arms were still outstretched as he stood at the opposite end of the aisle to Peter. Suddenly, he screeched, a high pitched, piercing sound that caused wolves and vampires to wince. All eyes turned to Barumar and the sound of bones snapping and reforming filled the air. Barumar elicited another ear piercing screech before transforming.

Standing at the front of the chapel stood an abomination that Peter had heard about in legend but had never seen, a man-bat. Barumar's face had changed to bat-like features, pointed ears and nose with sharp front teeth shaped to slice skin and exceptionally long fangs, dripping saliva. His eyes were completely black and his limbs were covered in thick black hair. His feet resembled a bird of prey, the talons glinting silver in the flickering light of the candles. Huge, powerful leathery wings stretched out behind him which he flexed extinguishing the candles and plunging the chapel into darkness.

Barumar flew down the aisle, talons outstretched and pierced through each of Peters shoulders. The creature clenched its feet and flew upwards taking Peter with it. The sharp bony protuberances on this thing's wings shattered the stained glass domed window of the chapel and Barumar carried Peter up into the night sky and away.

This was the signal the vampires had waited for; they attacked.

EVIL TIDE

Roman stood with the remainder of his pack at the end of Draven Bridge. Matyas, his second in command and oldest friend stood by his side, Tempest stood on the other. Grimlock and Witty stood slightly behind Tempest and Matyas and Ratman and Pickens behind them, the seven forming a phalanx.

At the other end of the bridge stood a crowd of around five hundred vampires.

'What are they waiting for?' Tempest asked.

Roman shrugged but said nothing.

Grimlock turned to Pickens and thought of how much Jedrek would have hated standing side by side with a rat.

'Who'd have thought a werewolf and a wererat would be fighting side by side?' Grimlock said.

'How about *we're* done for!' Tempest snapped.

'Silence.' Roman commanded.

Even in the gloom Roman could see the crowd waiting; but this crowd was not armed with clubs, stick and stones, it was armed with sharp fangs, long nails, evil and cruelty.

'I hope you're right about the spirit pack.' Roman said to Ratman.

Before Ratman could respond, Roman transformed into warrior form and the other wolves followed suit. Pickens transformed into his own warrior form leaving Ratman as the only one standing as a human.

Draven Bridge was too narrow for all vampires to move at the same time and when they eventually made their move the bottle neck would slow and focus their attack. Movement at the end of the Bridge caught Roman's attention as he stood, teeth bared ready to engage the first flood of vampires.

The two wolf statues beside the tower, their motion caught as they leapt at their prey, appeared to be moving. Large stone jaws fixed open revealing sharp stone teeth moved barely more than a millimetre but Roman saw it. In human form Roman may have dismissed the movement as a trick of the light but in warrior form his senses were extremely heightened and he knew the movement to be real.

'The spirit pack comes!' Ratman shouted somewhat joyously.

Both statues moved again with a fluidity that defied their stone bodies. They turned and leapt down from their perches and stood side by side blocking the end of the bridge. Four other ghostly figures materialised beside the wolves, three in warrior form, the fourth stood beside Roman as a human. The spirit took the shape of a woman in her forties, slim with short cropped blond hair with a no-nonsense expression on her face. She spoke to Roman fluently in his own tongue.

'You don't know me Roman, I am Uri, formerly Elder of Peter's pack, now Alpha of the Spirit Pack. We have come to help you.'

In warrior form Roman could not speak but his thoughts were clear in his head and Uri understood every word.

You are most welcome and not a second too soon. Roman said.

Uri smiled.

'Rusty and Long Fang are the ones animating the statues. As Alpha, I will stand with you, Gannek will stand with Matyas, Sheba and Pippa will stand with Tempest and Witty.'

Sensing that Grimlock had something to say, Uri turned towards him cutting into his thoughts before transforming into warrior form herself.

'I have someone here for you Grimlock' Uri said.

Grimlock did not mistake the spirit in warrior form that materialised next to him, the recognition was bitter sweet. Jedrek stood beside his former pack brother, now much larger as a warrior than when he took corporeal form.

A high pitched screech sounded from across the river and a rustle of movement swept through the crowd of vampires at the other end of the bridge.

As Alpha of the spirit pack, Uri's howl could be heard on the outskirts of the City over five miles away and all wolves responded with a howl of their own.

A second screech filled the air and a huge winged creature appeared in the night sky above the palace carrying something. This was what the vampires were waiting for, they moved en-masse towards Draven Bridge and the City of Braeden. Roman, the Alpha, roared and the wolves responded, standing their ground against overwhelming odds and the approaching tide of the undead.

The spirit pack brought the full force of their unlimited power to bear creating a barrier between the wolves and the City and as the first wave of vampires dashed against the stone bodies of Rusty and Long Fang they were torn to pieces.

The vampires flowed across Draven Bridge like an oil spill from a broken tanker, many climbing over each other and the statues along its length trying to get ahead of the crowd. Driven by bloodlust alone they looked for ways around the wolves to the City beyond and its citizens, full of warm, fresh blood.

*****

Kristyna felt nervous but couldn't explain why. There was something in the air and her instincts were screaming at her to find a quiet corner and hide. She told herself she was being silly and when she heard the knock at the front door she stood still in the middle of the hallway momentarily frozen. A second knock, more urgent this time accompanied by a muffled plea for help broke Kristyna's paralysis and she moved to answer it. Keeping the chain across on the door as was her usual precaution, Kristyna opened the door and looked out through the gap into the bloodshot eyes of a young woman. The woman smiled revealing long sharp fangs but Kristyna didn't notice, she was mesmerised by the woman's eyes.

'Open the door.' the woman said. 'Invite me in.'

The tone of the woman's voice was almost musical to her ears and Kristyna nodded and smiled. Closing the door enough to slide and disengage the chain Kristyna remained transfixed by the strange woman's stare.

'NO! DON'T OPEN THE DOOR!' Yosef yelled running up to Kristyna and slamming the door closed, breaking eye contact between Kristyna and the woman outside.

Kristyna blinked and shook her head as if waking from a dream and looked at Yosef.

'Don't let anyone in.' Yosef said.

'But she needs help.' Kristyna replied. 'She had blood on her face.'

'It's not her blood.'

Kristyna looked at Yosef quizzically but said nothing. Until recently she didn't want to accept the fact that vampires might actually be real but she'd lived in Braeden long enough and heard enough stories to deny it no longer.

'Help me!' the stranger shouted pounding on the door. 'Open the door!'

Yosef shook his head and Kristyna pulled him to her, wrapping her arms around him protectively.

The pounding stopped and Kristyna exhaled a breath she didn't realise she was holding. The shattering of glass moved Kristyna to action and she ran towards the sound, Yosef only a step behind. Entering the kitchen

Kristyna saw the woman from the front door, her face at the broken window and Tomas in the centre of the room transfixed by her stare. Kristyna moved towards Tomas and inadvertently looked at the woman.

'Open the door.' the woman said. 'Please.'

Yosef stood in front of them tugging at their sleeves, trying to pull their attention to him and away from the vampire but his efforts were futile. Both Kristyna and Tomas were caught in the vampire's delusional and they nodded enthusiastically.

'Invite me in.' the vampire said, her smile wide in her blood stained face.

Yosef looked around the kitchen desperate for something he could use to break the eye contact and the vampire's hold on Tomas and Kristyna. His eyes alighted on the bread knife on the draining board and the drying cloth, he grabbed both.

Tomas and Kristyna both moved slowly towards the door. Yosef stood in front of them blocking their way to the door. He suddenly realised how much he loved them and he began to cry.

'I'm sorry.' Yosef said through his tears.

Slashing the bread knife across Tomas's forearm was one of the hardest things he'd ever done but it worked. Tomas instinctively put his other hand on his injured arm and looked away from the vampire and down at the cut which was now bleeding.

'Let me in!' the vampire said salivating at the smell of fresh blood.

Yosef dropped the knife and threw the cloth over Kristyna's face breaking her eye contact with the vampire and pushed her with all his might. Kristyna fell into Tomas knocking them both off balance and Yosef ran at them again propelling them out of the kitchen and away from the open window. Yosef closed the kitchen door and pushed a chair under the handle before turning to face the vampire.

'Open the door boy.' the vampire said sweetly. 'Invite me in.'

'No.' Yosef replied.

The vampire exposed her sharp fangs and hissed and spat at Yosef.

'OPEN THE DOOR!' the vampire commanded.

'NO!' Yosef said firmly. 'Your tricks don't work on me cold one.'

The vampire tried to reach through the open window, but her cold dead hand stopped against an invisible shield. The rock had broken the glass but she could go no further without an invitation. She held Yosef's gaze for a brief second her eyes full of questions as to how the boy was impervious to the vampire delusional, before screaming in rage and disappearing into the night.

Petrified by fear, Yosef stood in the middle of the kitchen shaking and breathing hard.

'Yosef!' Kristyna and Tomas yelled together.

Yosef pulled the chair out from under the handle and opened the door falling into the open arms of Kristyna.

'I'm sorry, I'm sorry.' Yosef said through a fresh onset of tears.

'It's ok.' Kristyna said holding him and kissing the top of his head.

'You need to cover all the windows.' Yosef said looking at Tomas.

'We will.' Tomas said.

Tomas put his hand on Yosef's shoulder in much the same way as Ratman had done earlier.

'We owe you our lives. Thank you son.' Tomas said. 'Will you help me cover all the windows?'

Yosef nodded and smiled.

Kristyna didn't know how Yosef knew the woman was a vampire nor how he had known what to do, but she would be eternally grateful that he'd saved their lives. She pulled him to her again as much for her own comfort as for his.

Yosef didn't protest, he felt safe in Kristyna's arms and Tomas had called him "son", he liked the sound of that and thought he could get used to it, but first they all had to survive. Staying away from all doors and windows was the key to surviving the night. The vampire was the first of many who would try and get into the house and Yosef knew that others would likely open their doors willingly to the cold ones and would not be so fortunate.

*****

As soon as the Barumar creature flew up through the shattered glass dome of the chapel, Peter changed into warrior form. Larger and much heavier he expected Barumar to lose his grip but the werebat merely adjusted its talons pushing them in and under Peter's collar bones holding him firmly. The searing pain in Peter's shoulders confirmed the talons were actual silver and not just a trick of the chapel's candlelight. Recalling Ratman's earlier warning, Peter realised he should have expected the unexpected but living silver was a wolf's gift, not a vampire's.

Barumar flew up into the night sky over Draven Bridge. From his *disadvantage* point Peter could see the hoard of vampires rushing towards the City. Swarming over each other like a colony of ants emerging from a disturbed anthill, they spewed across the cobbled stones towards Roman and his pack at the other end. Peter saw the two huge wolf statues moving among the flood of vampires, crushing and tearing them limb from limb and opaque, ghostly warrior wolves, he assumed to be the spirit pack, fighting side by side with the Braeden pack.

Fuelled by rage and pain Peter transformed his own claws into living silver and reached up. Grabbing the bottom of one of Barumar's thick wings he slashed with his other hand, over and over until the wing hung like a ripped sail. Barumar tried to flex his wing but the tattered remains were unresponsive and he loosened one taloned foot. Peter moved quickly and grasped Barumar's leg, twisting and breaking it eliciting a high pitched screech from the werebat. Barumar opened the talons on his other leg, Peter hung onto the tattered wing until they were directly over the Nejelski River before letting go and plunging into the black cold waters below.

THE CHAPEL

As soon as the extinguished candles rendered the chapel completely dark, the wolves moved into action. Rufus was in warrior form before Barumar shattered the glass dome above taking Peter with him. He looked into the afterglow to enhance his already sharp vision and to him, the room was as bright as a summer's day and he howled in rage.

Anticipating the vampire attack when Barumar took Peter, Milly concentrated and dissolved into a fine mist. In this particular vampire form everything around her appeared to move in slow motion, typical vampire speed reduced to nothing more than a slow walk. Milly swirled through the slow moving forms and coalesced behind them to stand in the very spot Barumar had vacated seconds before. Transforming again, but this time into werewolf warrior form, Milly used one powerful foot to smash the base of the processional cross. Flipping it around, she stood holding her make-shift sword, lifted her chin and howled in response.

'Protect your sister and Myshka!' Shayla said to Max before extending her wings.

Shayla's large black and silver wings opened with a "shiiing" as the feathers, like rows of overlapping swords, moved across each other to extend outwards. Shayla held her fists in front of her face in a fighting stance and the top edge of her wings mimicked the motion like an extra set of limbs, the fiendishly sharp edges of the feathers tilted outwards. Lifting off the ground, Shayla spun in a circle, extending her arms and wings and simultaneously decapitating several vampires at the front of the attack. Opening the wings to their full extent Shayla flew to the front of the chapel and landed behind Milly. In the chaos Arcane had managed to slip away and Shayla turned and stood beside Milly ready to fight, she would find him later.

Max transformed into a warrior for the first time, his clothes shredding and falling to the floor. Although young, in warrior form he stood at around eight feet tall, muscular, strong and completely silver. Unusual for a werewolf, Max retained his blue eyes which looked out in rage at the vampires. He stood in front of Elena and Myshka and extended his silver, razor sharp claws and when he opened his mouth to howl a deep, teeth rattling Alpha's roar shook the room and every vampire felt the vibration to their very core.

Elliot stood his ground next to Rufus, Dragon Blade in one hand, his other hand held up to manipulate the air to form a barrier between himself and the vampires. The wall of air wouldn't stop them, but it would slow them enough to balance the odds. The sound of Max's roar vibrated through Elliot's bones and he felt sure he sensed momentary hesitation in the vampires' momentum.

Approximately one third of the hundred or so vampires gathered in the chapel turned towards Milly and Shayla; confident in their numbers they charged.

Milly planted her feet firmly, holding the make-shift sword in both hands. Gaolyn's memory of how heavy his Greatsword felt in his hand flashed through her mind and his sword skills resurfaced as if they were her own. Milly held her sword in one powerful hand and twirled it around in long practiced battle form before thrusting the ragged wooden end straight through the head of the first vampire to reach her, impaling it against another who was too close behind. Milly pushed the first vampire with her foot extracting the weapon in one swift movement, a second kick threw both bodies back into the crowd.

Shayla pulled her wings closer to her body and lifted off the ground flying towards the vampires. Tilting the sharp edges of the wings outwards, she spun around in a circle gradually increasing in speed, the feather blades beat the air like a small tornado and sang a low hum to the vampires that moved towards her. The vampires, driven by their blood lust, especially for the blood of the Fey paid no heed to the double-edged blades that whipped through the air. Shayla waited until she was within arm's length of the vampires grasp before tilting the bottom edge of her wings out horizontally. The edge of the wings cut with surgical precision, decapitating and dismembering as they moved. Extended arms fell to the floor, fingers still twitching, heads rolled along the stone floor, their faces frozen in expressions of shock and surprise.

At the other end of the chapel Rufus moved in to engage the first vampire wrapping his elongated fingers and claws around its head pulling it to one side exposing the neck. Rufus sank his sharp teeth into the cold flesh and pulling with his other hand, ripped the head from the body. He discarded the severed head and spat the foul tasting blood into the face of the next vampire momentarily blinding it before punching his fist straight through the vampire's torso and pulling out its un-beating heart.

When the first dead vampire's body began to smoulder, Elliot took advantage of the presence of fire and manipulated the flames to burn hotter and brighter. Combining his power over air and fire, Elliot directed the flames like a flame thrower, into the path of the vampires. They thrashed and flailed as the flames took hold, knocking into each other causing more confusion. Elliot moved in with the Dragon Blade bringing real death to the undead.

Max took advantage of his surroundings, picking up one of the pews in front of him, he moved in a sweeping motion landing a solid blow to the head of one vampire knocking it backwards. As it stumbled, Max leapt forward pushing the vampire onto its back and making a fist he pounded it into the vampire's head and body, smashing it to a pulp.

Everything happened so quickly, no more than a few minutes, but to Myshka it felt much longer. Myshka had pulled Elena into her arms, holding Elena's head to her chest, so she could not witness the carnage, her own head also turned away, her eyes tightly closed. When Elliot touched her shoulder, Myshka flinched.

'It's over.' Elliot said. 'There's nothing to see.'

Myshka opened her eyes, Elliot stood in front of her. Myshka moved her head to see the chapel beyond. Small fires still burned, black smouldering lumps littered the floor which she assumed were the remains of the vampires. Elliot's face was scratched and bleeding, but nothing that wouldn't heal. The wolves had returned to human form and were also bleeding but their faces looked triumphant. Shayla was standing beside Max who remained in warrior form, both were looking at Elena and Myshka.

Elena moved and Myshka released her hold to allow the girl to look around. Elena scrambled to her feet and ran to her mother's arms. Shayla extended her wings again and wrapped them around both her children. Within the safety and comfort of his mother's embrace Max transformed back into human form and Shayla held the twins tightly until Rufus spoke.

'Is everyone alright?' Rufus said.

Shayla released her children and retracted her wings, everyone was nodding. Rufus chuckled and Shayla turned to look at Max, the boy was naked.

'Until you get your crystal that's gonna happen every time.' Rufus said.

Max blushed and moved his hands to cover himself.

'Use my cloak.' Elliot said offering the garment to Max who accepted it gratefully.

'We need to find Arcane.' Shayla said still a bit breathless from fighting. 'Fast.'

Shayla had her arm around Elena who was holding her head again and wincing in pain.

'We need a wolf's senses.' Max said.

'I'll change.' Rufus said.

'No. I'll do it.' Max replied. 'I know what he smells like. I can find him and being in wolf form it won't matter that I'm naked.'

'Are you sure?' Shayla asked.

'Positive.' Max said.

Shayla looked at Rufus who nodded.

'OK.' Shayla said. 'But stay close. I don't want you going on ahead and trying to take him on by yourself.'

Max rolled his eyes.

'I'm serious.' Shayla said firmly.

'I know.'

Max took a few steps away from his mother and sister, his nakedness forgotten, and dropped to his hands and knees. A wave of pain ripped through his body, but this time he was expecting it and breathed slowly and deliberately through the pain. In the quiet of the chapel, the sound of bones snapping and reshaping filled the air. Max's fingernails grew into sharp claws, the skin peeled back on his fingers and toes as his hands and feet transformed into paws. Silver-grey fur sprouted all over his body, his mouth extended into a snout and his teeth grew into sharp pointed fangs.

The transformation took no more than a minute and when complete Max shook his whole body from head to toe and stretched into all four legs, familiarising himself with his wolf form. Max lifted his head and sniffed the air.

'The last time I saw Arcane he was standing with Barumar over there.' Shayla said pointing to the front of the chapel. 'He must have escaped through a hidden doorway.'

'One of the larger stones is hinged and opens onto a narrow passageway.' Milly said recalling Gaolyn's knowledge of the palace. 'The old kings and queens used it as a quick exit from the chapel, probably so they didn't have to engage with their subjects. It runs parallel behind the walls on this level, then splits in two, one leads to the study that overlooks the gardens, the other has steps down to the lower levels and the stables.'

Milly looked at her companions, none of whom questioned her knowledge of the palace, before continuing.

'Either passage leads to an exit. My instincts tell me Arcane will head to the gardens. Max's nose will be able to tell us for certain.'

Max turned and led the way to the altar end of the chapel, the others followed. Wood panelling and curtains now covered the stones and Milly pulled the curtain aside and pushed one of the large stones. It moved easily and the stone door eased inwards opening out into a dimly lit passageway. Max pushed past everyone to be first into the tunnel, sniffing the air he easily caught Arcane's scent.

Holding Shayla back, Rufus took point right behind Max. Rufus was Peter's second in command and Shayla followed without argument. Elena and Myshka were in the middle of the group, followed by Elliot, sword still drawn and Milly brought up the rear, closing the stone panel behind them. When the tunnel split Max paused momentarily. He turned to look at Milly and tilted his head to one side before taking the path that led to the garden; Milly smiled to herself.

*****

When Barumar had changed into a creature of his nightmares, Arcane had taken the opportunity to run. Eversor the demon wanted to stay and fight, but Arcane's need to survive had over ridden Eversor's control and now from their hiding place in the unkempt gardens of the palace Eversor agreed that if the half angel survived the vampires she would undoubtedly come looking for Arcane.

Fleeing the chapel Arcane had exploded from the tunnel into the empty study and out into the garden, shocked and relieved to find no vampires, their attention was focused on Draven Bridge and the City and its inhabitants beyond.

The small formal garden, a gift from a long dead king to his queen, had once been beautiful and lovingly attended by servants who knew the difference between weeds and flowers and how to care for them. Flowers no longer grew in the contaminated soil, even the resilient weeds had forsaken the garden and the fountain that once trickled into a pool full of fish stood dry, the fish gone the way of the human king.

Arcane stood in the shadows, imagining all the ways in which he would kill his nemesis.

Eversor on the other hand imagined possessing and controlling the half angel which would eventually enable him to possess a full angel, The Deceiver.

They waited.

THE ARENA

Peter broke the surface of the cold river water within seconds of plunging in and he immediately swam for the river bank. The wounds in his collar bone aggravated by the silver, were already healing but not as quickly as he would have liked. Reaching the bank, Peter pulled himself out of the water and in three powerful leaps he was up over the river bank and standing on the side of the road down river from Draven Bridge.

Several vampires, stragglers at the back of the hoard turned to look at Peter as he took up a fighting stance but none moved. Barumar landed on the road opposite Peter, his damaged wing making for an awkward landing. The leg Peter had broken hung limp and useless from Barumar's body and he stood with both wings outstretched behind him. Barumar tried to fold his wings, but the tattered limb refused to comply and Barumar screeched in rage baring his long fangs.

Peter looked at his enemy, damaged and broken but still formidable and with an army at his back if he decided to call them. Sensing their master's need, the vampires moved slowly towards the two combatants. Forming a circle they created an arena in which the werewolf and the werebat would have their final showdown.

Peter assessed his opponent.

Barumar had a broken leg, but the other was strong and deadly. His wings were two additional limbs. The top of each wing, hinged at the shoulder, elbow and wrist appeared to be bone and Peter had no doubt they were strong enough to inflict a hard blow. The top end of each wing tapered off into three points, like long sharp fingers but unlike Barumar's feet, these fingers did not appear to be silver. Peter's mind was racing, recalling stories and legends of werebats and their abilities. How could this vampire Barumar also be a werebat? But there was no time to dwell on this right now. He knew that it was possible to transform his whole body, not just his claws, into living silver and he had to assume that Barumar could do the same. The only question was whether Barumar had mastered the skill or whether like Peter, the claws were as much as he could manage.

Peter kept his eyes fixed on the centre of his opponent's chest, using his peripheral vision to anticipate Barumar's next move. Some warriors looked into the eyes of their opponent but the eyes could be deceiving. In any event, Barumar's eyes were now completely black and would give nothing away. Peter would have to rely on his skills as a warrior. Peter watched and waited for Barumar to make the first move.

Barumar flapped his wings but the damage only lifted him a few meters off the ground, but it was enough to fly over Peter's head. Barumar used his silver talons to lash out but Peter anticipated this move and blocked the incoming blow. Turning his hand to grip the ankle, Peter twisted Barumar's good leg and grabbing the broken leg that hung loosely in the air he ripped it from its knee joint. Flipping the dismembered limb around, Peter swung the leg at Barumar's lower abdomen. The silver claws ripped three deep gashes into the werebat's flesh spilling blood into Peter's face. Barumar screeched and flapped his wings to shake free from the werewolf's grip. Briefly blinded by his enemy's blood Peter shook his head to clear his eyes. Barumar pulled his leg free from Peter's grasp and lifted higher off the ground. Peter leapt into the air trying to pull Barumar back down but Barumar turned and swiped at Peter with the edge of one of his wings. The sharp bony fingers raked across Peter's shoulder and neck. Barumar turned in the air and the silver talons of his remaining leg gouged deep into the left side of Peter's head. The werebat turned again pulling the talons across Peter's face. The silver burned, slicing the skin up his cheek and through his left eye.

Blood poured down Peter's face from the rents in his neck and face and the lid closed over his severed eye. Barumar circled overhead screeching, the delight evident in the tone of the werebat's cries.

The circling vampires closed in eager for their chance to assist in bringing death to a werewolf, his end clearly in sight.

Peter sensed the vampires closing in, their master circling overhead like a vulture. When death comes, werewolves all dream of a warrior's death and Peter was no different. He knew that Rufus and Milly would protect Shayla and the twins with their lives if necessary and he hoped taking Barumar down would somehow save Shayla and the twins. Peter took a deep breath and prepared himself to fight.

Suddenly he recalled Ratman's words.

"You will need both the living silver and internal fire when you face the king…..remember the Mortem Dormitabius."

'ORDIS…' Peter began.

Peter stopped and shook his head in frustration, the words had to be precise. Peter looked at his enemy, the abomination circling overhead. He clenched his fists, concentrated and in warrior form spoke two words loud and clear.

'MORTEM DORMITABIUS'

*****

'We're not getting anywhere!' Oren grumbled.

'I agree.' Radha said. 'Everything looks the same. I'm sure we've passed those gnarly trees before.'

'We have!' Wren said. 'We're going around in circles.'

All three looked at Elemax.

'This is a prison.' Elemax said. 'What did you expect?'

'I thought…' Wren hesitated.

'That our appearance would change your circumstances?' Elemax finished.

'I suppose so.'

'There is little we can do in here.' Elemax said. 'Until the other halves of us draw near, we are almost as powerless as you.'

'That's it then!' Oren said throwing his hands up in exasperation.

'Patience.' Elemax said. 'We said almost…..'

The unfinished statement hung in the air, Elemax looked down to the ground.

'What?' Oren asked.

'Silence!' Elemax commanded holding up one slim hand. 'Do you hear that?'

Wren, Oren and Radha listened and shook their heads, Elemax continued to look down.

'There!' Elemax pointed to the earth.

Small stones moved against each other, minuscule movements, barely noticeable, then the stones became more agitated, jiggling, dancing and bouncing off each other. Thin cracks appeared in the ground beneath the stones and a rumble sounded deep within the earth which they felt rather than heard.

'Ourselves draw near.' Elemax said smiling. 'We must hurry to the wall, time is short.'

Elemax started running and the others followed hopeful that this new turn of events signalled an end to their imprisonment.

* * * * *

Rufus pushed open the stone door and stepped into the study. His sharp senses detected no vampires but a human scent hung in the air. Max pushed past Rufus to stand in the middle of the room and sniff the air. Max immediately went to the half open glass door that led into the garden.

'Wait.' Rufus commanded.

Max obeyed and stood looking out on the garden while the others emerged from the secret passage. Elena held her hand to the side of her head as soon as she stepped into the study and Shayla led her to one of the big armchairs to rest.

'What's the plan?' Elliot asked.

'You all stay here.' Rufus said. 'I'll go outside and drag him back in.'

'He could be gone.'

'No he's hiding.' Milly said. 'His scent is strong.'

'It's me he wants.' Shayla said. 'I should go outside and see if I can lure him out.'

Max growled.

'I agree with Max.' Rufus said. 'He could kill you as soon as you step outside the door. We need the pendant to heal the twins. No. You stay here. Milly and I will go.'

Milly used the vampire ability to dissolve into mist and moved slowly over the ground so as not to arouse suspicion.

From his hiding place Arcane saw a man he assumed to be a werewolf, step out of the study. There was no attempt at stealth he simply stepped out into the garden and looked in the direction of Arcane's hiding place.

'Come out.' Rufus said. 'I only want to talk.'

Arcane remained silent and still. He watched the wolf take another step into the garden.

'I can help you get out of here.' Rufus continued, wisps of mist swirling around his feet and dissipating into the garden. 'I can get you of the City. What do you say? Can we talk?'

It's a trick! Eversor said in Arcane's mind.

Of course it's a trick! Arcane snapped. *I'm not a fool!*

While Arcane and Eversor argued, the mist suddenly coalesced and Milly stood in front of Arcane eye to eye. Grabbing hold of the front of his shirt, Milly pulled expecting to easily drag him out into the middle of the garden. He was surprisingly strong and resisted however Rufus had joined her and the two wolves pulled Arcane out of his hiding place. They shoved him towards the open door of the study.

'If you kill me the children will die!' Arcane said stumbling.

Max ran out of the study and pushed Arcane to the floor with his front paws. Arcane landed on his back and Max stood over him, both front paws on Arcane's chest pining him to the ground. He recalled how he had told Arcane in the dungeon that he would destroy him if his father didn't tear him apart first. Max bared his teeth and growled.

Looks like I got here first. Max thought.

Arcane momentarily shrank back before Eversor took control. The demon lifted Max and threw the wolf aside as if he were a small puppy. Max landed heavily on his side on the rough, dry earth and yelped in pain.

Shayla ran blindly out into the garden, her only thought was for her injured son. Arcane knew instantly that this woman was the half angel and he scrambled to his feet pulling a knife from his boot as he did so.

The world seemed to slow down as the wolves watched Arcane run towards Shayla, the blade low. Shayla turned to face him holding her fists up in front of her ready to fight, her wings responded to the oncoming danger and extended around her in a protective shield.

Less than three feet apart Arcane stopped short. His back arched and his arms opened wide. His hands opened dropping the knife and his fingers splayed open. Arcane's head tilted back and his face looked up at the night sky, he screamed in pain. Shayla took a step back but remained in a fighting stance.

Suddenly Arcane's head snapped back to face Shayla, he looked at her, his eyes full of hatred and contempt and completely black. Shayla looked back at him horrified and saw the demon inside. Arcane's black eyes began to glow and two beams of fire shot out and hit Shayla in the eyes, connecting the half angel and the half demon in a flaming tether. They both stood shock still while Eversor transferred from Arcane to Shayla. The connection glowed fleetingly at the centre before exploding and disappearing, throwing Shayla one way and Arcane the other.

In the aftermath Shayla and Arcane both lay still and unconscious in the garden. Max padded over to his mother and Elena came out of the study in spite of the pain in her head and stood beside him. Rufus moved closer to protect Shayla and the twins and Milly knelt down beside Shayla to take closer look.

'Her eyes are moving.' Milly said.

'Is she dreaming?' Rufus asked.

Milly put her hand on Shayla's head and closed her eyes for a few seconds in the way Uri had instructed her.

'No. She's fighting something.' Milly said.

Elliot and Myshka had followed Elena when she left the study and now stood beside Arcane. Rufus turned to face them and nodded towards the prone body of Arcane.

'Is he dead?'

Elliot turned Arcane over and felt his neck for a pulse.

'No. Just unconscious.' Elliot said.

'Search him for weapons.' Rufus commanded. 'And a pendant.'

Elliot nodded.

'What happens now?' Rufus asked turning back to Milly.

'We wait.' Milly replied.

Max turned a full circle and settled down at his mother's side, his furry head resting on his paws. Elena laid down next to her mother and pulled her close as Shayla used to do when bad dreams had woken Elena in the night when she was a very young child.

'Come back mummy.' Elena whispered in Shayla's ear. 'Come back.'

*****

Shayla stood in the middle of a cage. She looked around and wondered how she had gotten there. The last thing she remembered was staring into the eyes of the demon who possessed Arcane. Shayla shook the door of the cage even though she already knew it was locked. She looked out of the prison cell and into a darkness that swallowed the dim light around her, there was nothing except her and the bars.

'Half angel.' a voice sounded from the shadows.

'Who's there? Who are you?' Shayla said.

'Eversor.'

'You're a demon.' Shayla said.

'You're a half angel.'

'What do you want?'

'Chaos and destruction.'

Shayla said nothing.

'Do you know where you are?' Eversor asked.

'No.'

'We are in your mind. This is all you are now. Your body and mind are no longer yours to control. You will exist here until you wither and die.'

The demon laughed, a terrible sound that Shayla felt in every cell of her body. She was trapped inside her own consciousness, a prisoner in her own mind and the demon had control. Shayla shook the door of the cage again in desperation.

'There is no escape.'

The demon moved closer to the cage but Shayla couldn't make out any shape or features, it was more of an intense feeling of evil and malice. She recalled the dreams she had of her mother when she was young. Her mother fighting a demon so that she could escape to safety, but the demon was always hidden.

'The demon of your memory.' Eversor said. 'What other painful memories can we explore?'

Suddenly Shayla was overwhelmed by dark negative emotions. The feelings of loss and abandonment she felt when recalling the memory her mother. The shock and confusion of meeting Parallax inside the virtual world. The dread of what might happen to Peter as he was carried away into the night by the creature, and the terror of losing her children.

The feelings of hopelessness and despair produced a physical pain in her chest as if her heart was breaking and Shayla put her hand to her heart in agony.

Eversor laughed and dug deeper into her memories, tearing at her psyche, torturing her with her own emotions and triggering the limbic system in her brain, stimulating only the flight, fear and freezing up actions.

Eversor laughed again and suddenly stopped.

Silence.

The pain of her memories and the psychological torture suddenly gone, Shayla held her breath, her hand pressed against her chest in an attempt to relieve the ache in her heart, she listened.

Another sound emanated from the shadows, a deep reverberating growl.

'How is this possible?' Eversor asked.

A dark menacing shape moved towards the cage and a pair of amber eyes glowed brightly in the gloom. Titan emerged from the shadows and bared his teeth at the demon, his thoughts audible.

'You are not welcome here.'

ONLY ONE VICTOR

As soon as Peter spoke the words the circling vampires stopped, dropped to their knees and started digging holes with their hands. The sudden urge to go to ground and find cover from the perceived approaching dawn overwhelmed them. Some began smashing their fists into the road, ripping up the asphalt and digging holes to hide in, their movements slow and fluid as though they were overcome with fatigue. Their futile efforts were in vain and in a few seconds every surrounding vampire lay sleeping. Peter didn't know how long they would be rendered unconscious but the situation gave him the opportunity to deal solely with Barumar.

Barumar was not impervious to the command, but neither was he so easily put down. The werebat landed clumsily on the road; shredded wings struggled to balance a one legged damaged body. Peter lunged but the werebat dissolved into mist as his long fingers reached where Barumar's neck should have been.

Sensing the coalescence of the vampire behind him, Peter spun around to face Barumar, once again in human form with no trace of injury. Peter snarled and assessed the situation. Barumar looked arrogant and was twisting a large signet ring on his left hand. Slight movement to the side of Barumar caught Peter's attention and one of the sleeping vampires suddenly stood up and transformed into a werebat, also undamaged. This time, instead of lunging at his enemy, Peter stood his ground and waited for either Barumar or his avatar to attack first.

With all of his senses in overdrive, Peter missed nothing and when the werebat moved to extend its wings Peter was on it. Holding it with both his mighty hands Peter ripped out the werebat's throat with one powerful bite. As the head lolled to one side, Peter ripped open its chest and pulled out the heart. Peter dropped the destroyed body to the ground and once again turned to face Barumar. The vampire king was laughing.

Peter glanced at the werebat, the body dissolved into mist and returned to Barumar. Another sleeping vampire started twitching, stood up and transformed into a werebat. This time the creature leapt into the air and unfolded its wings before Peter could reach it, hovering just above Peter's head. Folding back its wings and stretching out its legs the werebat attacked. Sharp silver talons dug into Peter's chest opening huge gashes.

Blood poured from Peter's wounds as the werebat twisted and pulled trying to tear muscle from bone. The silver talons burned and Peter roared in agony and rage.

Peter's own claws were silver and he slashed the legs and abdomen of the werebat with both hands. The creature screeched and flapped its wings, the pointed tips slicing at Peter's shoulders and back. Peter stopped slashing and opened his arms. He bent his legs and leapt into the air closing his muscular arms around the werebat's wings and squeezing. The sound of snapping bones could be heard above Barumar's laughter as Peter crushed the creature's wings. The werebat struggled against the werewolf who held it in a strong bear-hug. Both combatants hung in the air for a second before gravity pulled them both back to the ground. They landed, werewolf on top, his colossal strength having crushed the chest of the werebat.

Peter held the creature as it made a final attempt to fight, knowing its end was near. The werebat thrashed its head from side to side, fangs grazing Peter's arms but doing no significant damage. Peter opened his jaws ready to tear out the werebat's throat and finish it, but hesitated.

This will never be over. Peter thought to himself. *Each reincarnation learns from the last. Barumar will keep sending this creature until it knows my every move.*

Peter looked at the werebat and saw the full moon reflected in its black eyes.

Living silver. Peter thought. *But how?*

Peter focused on the pain in his silver inflicted wounds, the deep slashes across his shoulders and back, the chunks of flesh torn from his chest and the burning pain on his face and the loss of his left eye from the werebat's silver talons. He focused on the reflection of the full moon, his own rage and the searing pain and as the werebat's thrashing weakened, Peter felt the metamorphosis begin. He stood up holding the werebat by the neck, silver creeping up his forearm from his claws slowly turning his body into that of a living body of pure silver.

Barumar sensed something was happening and began his own

transformation into mist but as he began to lose coalescence Peter reached out with his other hand clamping his long silver finger s around Barumar's throat, halting the vampire's transformation.

Living silver made its way up Peter's hands and arms to his shoulders and across his chest. The sensation was new, akin to the pain of transforming from one wolf form to another but with an added burn. It was nothing that he couldn't handle however and the feeling gave him an extra sense of focus.

As the final cells of Peter's body transformed into silver the werebat crumbled into dust and fell through his fingers. Peter looked at Barumar through silver eyes and saw fear. Barumar clawed at Peter's hand and slashed at his body with his long, sharp nails but every blow resulted in more pain for the vampire as his skin touched the silver and burned. Peter slowly closed his hand burning through Barumar's neck like a hot knife through butter. The vampire king choked and spluttered.

For Rusty. Peter thought as his hand closed into a fist separating Barumar's head from his body.

As the vampire king's body dropped to the ground the sleeping vampires began to stir answering Peter's earlier question as to how long the Mortem Dormitabius would last.

Peter held Barumar's head by the hair, it was beginning to smoulder. Peter looked up at the full moon.

Fire walker. Peter thought. *But how?*

Peter had always felt the werewolf rage as a white hot anger and had learned to let the heat flow through him during the transformation, but tonight he felt different. Whether it was the living silver, the full moon or the adrenaline rush of finally vanquishing an old enemy, Peter didn't know, but what he did know was that the rage inside him was burning like an inferno.

Lifting the smouldering head of the vampire king aloft, Peter focused on the heat inside him. Suddenly his hand was ablaze but the flames felt cool. The fire from his hand encapsulated Barumar's head incinerating the dead flesh and bone, turning them to ash. As the ashes fell from Peter's hand, so did the flames but the vampires had already ran away leaving him alone on the road.

Something sparkled in the light of the dying flames and Peter bent down and picked up Barumar's large signet ring. This time there would be nothing left to chance and Peter ignited the flames once more, melting the ring.

Only the living flame could be hot enough to achieve this. Peter thought recalling the mysterious Ratman's words.

With the vampires gone and their king destroyed, Peter transformed back into human form and the pain in his wounds rushed up to meet him. Tearing a strip off his shirt, Peter wrapped it around his head over the ruined eye and ran towards the palace, his only thought was for his family.

*****

Titan paced slowly back and forth in front of Shayla's cage, his eyes fixed on the darkness. The demon hadn't spoken since Titan appeared and Shayla naively wondered if it would simply leave now that it had discovered Titan's presence, but the thought was fleeting. Her mind raced, she argued with herself as to whether she should be thinking at all. Surely the demon would know everything that it was in her mind.

Calm yourself. Titan spoke to Shayla alone. *The demon has entered your body and your mind, but it does not control you completely. It was not expecting another presence.*

I thank the Divine for you Titan. Shayla replied. *I don't know what I'd do without you.*

I am a halo hound, you are my soulmate.

Titan said nothing more.

From the darkness came a sound, somewhere between a grunt and a snarl and a sound like heavy limbs moving across a concrete floor.

Whatever form the demon had taken, it wasn't graceful, it was massive. When it stepped to the edge of the circle of light, Shayla took a step backwards inside the cage. The creature was terrifying. It resembled an overgrown tiger, powerful and muscular, short wiry black fur completely covered its body and it looked at Shayla and Titan with red eyes glowing with hatred and malice. Saliva dripped from a mouth overpacked with huge sharp teeth.

Titan stopped pacing and faced the beast, hackles raised over powerful muscles. He had grown in size to match his enemy and bared his teeth. Before the pulse Shayla had seen footage of illegal dog fights and had been horrified by the violence and destruction; the scene before her reminded her of this causing an unpleasant nausea to fill her body. Just before Titan attacked the demon beast, his thoughts sounded in her head.

Look away.

Shayla closed her eyes and crouched down into the corner of the cage trying to make herself as small as possible. An ear-splitting roar made her wince and the sound of snapping jaws filled the air. Shayla squeezed her eyes tightly and put her hands over her ears but the sound of crunching and claws scraping the floor was deafening. She felt the air moving around her as the two huge adversaries fought, she felt powerless. This was her body and she should be able to do something, but she was paralysed by fear.

A crack followed by a yelp broke through her paralysis and Shayla opened her eyes to see that it was the demon that had yelped. Held by the neck in Titan's powerful jaws the demon thrashed and broke loose falling back and slamming hard against Shayla's cage. The rattle of its breath rattled the bars of the cage and Shayla wished she could help Titan in some way, by holding onto the demon or drawing on her Fey and Angel powers but this was not the physical world, only her consciousness and Shayla realised that she had taken for granted the Fey and Angel powers her entire life.

Titan attacked pushing the demon tight against the bars of the cage and Shayla closed her eyes against the sight. Even covering her ears didn't block out the snarls and groans, nor the grinding and crunching of teeth against bone. Titan and the demon fought against the cage, Shayla heard a snort and felt hot breath on her face and she hoped that when she pictured Titan's face up against the demon's body ripping into the creature, that was what was happening.

Titan and the demon moved away from the cage and a shrill utterance caused Shayla to open her eyes again. Titan stood half over and half on the demon beast, his feet pinning the creature to the ground, his jaws around the demon's throat ripping and tearing. The demon was weakened but managed to shake and pull itself free from Titan's grasp.

We need to send it to the oblivion before it regains its strength. Titan said.

How? You need a doorway.

Shayla looked at the cage she was sitting in, a door stood right in front of her and suddenly Shayla knew what she had to do and the words that would open the doorway to the oblivion. Titan's memory of when he had saved Allandrea from the Shadow Lord bloomed in her mind.

Say it now! Titan commanded.

No! You could get pulled in with it. Shayla pleaded.

The demon's breath rasped, its body shuddered.

NOW! Titan's thoughts sounded aloud.

Tears streaming down her face Shayla held her hands in front of her and said the words that would open a doorway and save her from the demon.

'Full moon's light and Gaia's grace, banish evil from this place. Perpetual night, no warmth or sun…..'

Finish it. Titan said.

'…exile to oblivion.'

Two beams of light shot from her hands, hitting the bars of the cage. The bars contorted and pulled apart and a mist formed in the opening, churning in a slow circle. The mist turned to water and swirled in a vortex increasing in size until the entire doorway of the cage became a portal to another realm.

The demon's body shifted, pulled along the ground by invisible forces. It staggered to its feet and tried to walk backwards its claws scraping the ground. Eversor roared in rage and pain and fought against the pull of the vortex moving away slightly before sliding back, each time closer to the churning water. Shayla watched willing the demon towards the doorway, but its will was strong and little by little it gained more ground.

Titan turned his head to look at Shayla.

Live. Save the twins.

Titan turned back, opened his wings and pounced on the demon. Clamping his jaws firmly on its neck Titan dragged Eversor to the doorway. Titan brought his wings around his body and the bladed feathers formed a shield, the demon thrashed and the sound of its claws screeched against the metal of Titan's wings.

'No!' Shayla cried knowing her protest was futile.

The vortex pulled Eversor, body first into the oblivion. The demon struggled and tried to tear itself free. Titan held fast and the further Eversor fell into the swirling water the weaker it became.

Shayla watched, not wanting to take her eyes off her beloved Titan and wishing with her whole heart that she could save him. A faint light appeared above Titan's head. Shayla recalled her sister had once said Titan had a halo and finally Shayla could see it. Titan's halo was glowing brightly, lighting up the darkness all around him.

'I love you!' Shayla cried through her tears.

I love you. Titan replied.

The last thing Shayla saw was an intensely bright light which forced her to close her eyes. When she opened them again the door to the cage was wide open and she was alone.

Shayla wanted to cry, her heart was breaking but a voice was calling her.

'Save the twins.' Titan had said.

Shayla took a deep breath and stepped out of the cage.

* * * * *

'Shayla.' Milly said. 'Can you hear me?'

Shayla opened her eyes and looked up at Milly who smiled in relief.

'Let me help you up.' Milly said pulling Shayla to her feet. 'What happened?'

'I'll tell you later.' Shayla replied her eyes full of tears.

Milly nodded but said nothing.

Shayla looked at the twins and was grateful to see them both again. Max was still in wolf form and she knelt beside him and put her arms around his furry head and hugged him. Shayla opened one arm to Elena who moved into her mother's embrace. Closing her arms around her children, Shayla noticed the wolf paw tattoo was still on her left forearm and smiled. Titan would always be a part of her.

FREEDOM

'There!' Wren said pointing ahead. 'The wall.'

Another deep rumble signalled the approach of another earthquake and the elementals looked down for the first signs of a new crack in the earth. The shocks had become more violent, the earth moving like a wave on the ocean. Deep ravines opened in the ground swallowing trees and boulders then closed leaving no trace that anything was ever there.

The sky above grumbled in response to the ground and iron grey clouds rolled towards them. Forked lightning flashed in the distance and the four companions squinted in the momentary brightness.

'This place is determined to kill us.' Radha said.

'Not today.' Elemax chimed, their musical voice sounded quite out of place in this nightmare prison.

The ground shuddered once more and whilst the others struggled to stay upright, Elemax seemed to glide heading for the wall. In the calm between shocks, the others caught up to Elemax and soon all four stood at the wall.

'Put your hands on the wall, like this.' Elemax said demonstrating.

They all placed their hands on the wall, palms down.

'What now?' Oren said. 'It's a solid wall.'

Wren and Radha looked at each other, then at Oren.

'What?' Oren mouthed silently.

Oren exhaled impatiently but said nothing further.

Wren shook her head and turned her attention back to the wall, the surface smooth against her hands. She wondered, and not for the first time, exactly what Elemax was going to do now they had reached the outer limits of their prison world.

'Will this reveal a hidden door?' Wren asked.

'Patience.' Elemax replied.

Elemax spoke softly in a voice with dual tones, the words inaudible, both hands pressed against the black crystal wall.

The sky grew darker as the storm drew close. They waited.

'I can feel vibration in my fingertips!' Radha said.

'It's probably aftershock from the earthquake.' Oren said irritably.

'No.' Elemax said. 'The wall weakens.'

* * * * *

Elena was whispering and Shayla pulled back to look at her daughter. Max tilted his head to one side also listening.

'What did you say?' Shayla asked.

'Not today.' Elena said quietly.

'What about today?'

Elena was looking at nothing in particular, her eyes fixed trance-like on a distant place.

'I see the other world. There's a storm overhead and the ground is shaking.' Elena said.

Elena reached out to Max and put her hand on his head. Max stepped closer and put his head down, Elena put her forehead against her brother's head and spoke.

'Ever present prison wall, surrounding darkness one and all. Hear our voice the angel call, crack and tremble, crumble fall.'

Max lifted his head and Elena looked into his eyes and smiled.

'The wall weakens.' Elena said.

Shayla glanced up at Milly who shrugged her shoulders.

Arcane laid completely still on the ground, eyes closed, listening. He was on his side, the damp and cold from the ground permeated his clothes, he felt chilled to the bone. He held himself still trying not to shiver. He could hear the girl child muttering something and dismissed it. Instead he tried to focus on the whispered conversations.

'We should kill him and be done with it.' a woman said.

'I agree.' replied another female voice. 'But we need him.'

As long as they need me, they'll keep me alive. I can still get away. Arcane thought to himself smugly.

Arcane ignored the remainder of the conversation, he needed to escape, but how? This was usually the time Eversor would input thoughts and possibilities, but Arcane felt different. An evil so strong Arcane could barely contain it, was now gone. He knew that he was never really in control and did not mourn the loss, but Eversor's will had been the driving force of almost everything Arcane had done. He had achieved so much, gained power and influence and for that he was grateful. The demon had twisted his way of thinking and Arcane was confident the lessons he had learned from Eversor would help him find a way out of his current predicament.

Arcane thought about what he had seen when he looked the half-angel in the eyes, she was full of light. He was almost within arm's reach of her and would have cut her throat if Eversor hadn't interfered. The demon had taken over and the last thing Arcane remembered was flying backwards through the air.

Even lying still, the agonising pain in his back reminded him of the exchange. He should have known the demon had its own agenda all along and Arcane cursed himself for being so arrogant and assuming he was in control. The demon had been playing him the whole time.

Arcane's thoughts returned to the power of the Fey. It had been the only thing that silenced Eversor long enough to allow Arcane to think for himself. He wanted that power now, *needed* it to ease his troubled mind and to soothe the pain in his body. He craved the euphoria he felt when drawing on the power from the crystal. Arcane moved his fingertips and touched his chest hoping to find the pendant. A man's voice spoke making him start.

'Looking for this?'

Arcane remained still, feigning sleep.

'Cut the pretence. You've been awake for some time. Don't think I didn't notice.'

Realising any further attempt at subterfuge was pointless, Arcane opened his eyes and pushed himself up into a sitting position. He winced as pain flared in his back and hips. The voice belonged to a tall, slim man with short dark hair. The man was wearing armour, a sword at his side. He was also holding Arcane's pendant in his left hand.

Arcane assumed the pendant had become visible when the demon had left his body. The power to disguise it as a tattoo no longer his to command.

'I asked you a question.' Elliot said closing his hand around the pendant and putting it into his pocket.

Arcane said nothing. Even without the demon, Arcane was cunning and resourceful. He looked around assessing the situation.

The half-angel stood with the twins, the girl holding her mother's hand. The wolf next to her he knew was the boy. Another woman stood with her, slim and petite with piercing blue eyes. Arcane did not know if she was human, wolf or something else and he didn't care for the way she was looking at him. He assumed it was her that said they should kill him. The man with his pendant looked like a soldier, and his manner suggested he was proficient with the blade he carried, another woman stood next to him, she too regarded Arcane with contempt.

'I don't have time for this.' another voice said from the shadows.

The tall, strong man Arcane had seen from his hiding place in the garden and had correctly assumed was a wolf walked up to him. Grabbing and twisting the front of Arcane's shirt, the man pulled him to his feet in one swift movement. Arcane's toes barely scraped the floor as the man dangled him in front of his face, holding him at eye level.

'Listen to me and listen well.' Rufus said. 'I'd much rather snap your neck and kill you right now, but you might be of some use to us which is why you're still alive.'

Arcane remained silent. He was astute enough to know when to keep quiet. The wolf was not to be antagonised.

'You'll do exactly as I say.' Rufus continued. 'Step out of line once and I'll kill you.'

Arcane's eyes flickered towards Shayla and the twins.

'Look at me or anyone else in a way I don't like, I'll kill you.' Rufus continued. 'Breathe in a way I don't like, I'll kill you. Do you understand?'

Arcane nodded but said nothing.

Rufus released his grip on Arcane's collar and pushed him. Arcane landed hard, agonising pain shot through his body causing him to cry out involuntarily.

'I see you've found your voice.' Rufus said with a smile that didn't reach his eyes.

Arcane looked at the wolf and the others surrounding him, he gritted his teeth against the pain and stood up slowly.

'Whatever you did to the twins, you will reverse it.' Rufus said.

'I didn't do anything to them.' Arcane lied. 'It was the witch.'

'Do not lie to me.' Rufus growled. 'This is not the time to try my patience.'

Arcane paused and wondered if he was resourceful enough to get out of this, or whether he was completely out of options.

'We don't have time to wait for him to be compliant.' the woman with the blue eyes said as she walked towards him.

The woman stared into Arcane's eyes and smiled revealing very sharp teeth, Arcane flinched.

'You're wasting your time Milly. I doubt the coercion will work on him.' Shayla said. 'He's half demon.'

'Are you a vampire?' Arcane asked.

'I'm your executioner.' Milly replied. 'If you don't do as you're told.'

'I thought he was going to kill me.' Arcane said nodding towards Rufus. 'And not so long ago the boy was going to destroy me if his father didn't tear me apart first and the girl said she'd rip my heart out.'

Arcane paused and looked around.

'You can't all kill me.'

Milly moved closer to Arcane as if she was going to kiss him.

'Yes we can.' Milly said menacingly.

Milly snapped her jaws at Arcane who took a step backwards and cleared his throat nervously.

'I need the pendant.' Arcane said.

'Why?' Milly asked.

'I…um..'Arcane paused.

The power to use the crystal was Arcane's and not from Eversor. He was the son of the Shadow Lord, the power was inherent. The half-angel was part Fey, perhaps the soldier too, although he couldn't be sure. If he could convince them to give him the crystal he could take their power which might be enough to enable an escape.

'To reverse the magic.' Arcane said.

Milly stepped back from Arcane and returned to Shayla and the twins. Arcane looked away smiling smugly. The children would have told them what happened in the palace dungeon. They would have no option but to give him the crystal.

Elliot stood with Myshka, he had taken a few steps away when Rufus had stepped in to give Arcane his final warning. He frowned and put his hand into his pocket, retrieving the pendant.

'What?' Myshka asked seeing the puzzled expression on Elliot's face.

'It's buzzing.' Elliot said opening his hand. 'I mean vibrating.'

'And glowing.' Myshka said.

They both looked at the crystal which had the faintest light at its centre. The light pulsed in time with the vibration.

'I don't know what's happening, but you can't let him have it.' Myshka said closing Elliot's fingers around the pendant. 'He wants it too badly.'

'I know.' Elliot said.

Elliot looked again at Arcane, he clearly wanted the pendant and not to reverse any magic and help the twins. Although Elliot did not know how the crystal worked, he knew that Arcane was desperate for it.

Elliot had seen this sort of behaviour before, Arcane was an addict. Whatever power the pendant gave, Arcane needed it. Perhaps the crystal gave Arcane feelings of warmth and contentment, or the power to subdue the demon that possessed him, bringing a blissful moment of control and domination. Whatever the crystal pendant did for Arcane it took a piece of him, little by little. Elliot was certain that whatever Arcane wanted the crystal for, it was not going to be good for any of his company.

'You want this?' Elliot said to Arcane.

Elliot held out his open hand to Arcane, the pendant vibrating and glowing in his palm. Arcane nodded and took a step forward.

'Here!' Elliot said throwing the pendant high into the air.

Arcane lunged forward arms outstretched to catch it, the desire and desperation to possess the pendant evident in his eyes.

Movement caught his attention and everything seemed to move in slow motion. Arcane saw the soldier unsheathe his sword, leap and walk on steps made of nothing but air. An inherited memory from his father sprang to mind of another soldier who had been made to fight in a crude arena against the Almas and Arcane suddenly knew where he had seen the armour before. This soldier was a Knight of Feylore like the one who had stabbed his father in the chest.

'No!' Arcane cried out.

Elliot brought the dragon blade down in a swift arc slicing through the pendant. As he hit the ground, Elliot segmented the air in practiced form before returning the blade to its sheathe at his side.

The pieces of the pendant landed on the dead grass and bright light burst from the two halves encompassing everyone around it and momentarily lighting up the garden before fading and winking out.

*****

The dim daylight of the prison world suddenly grew brighter. The storm clouds dissolved and the sun burst through bringing the barren landscape into even sharper focus. The blasted trees and withered brush, like twisted hands reached out from the dry earth. The earth rumbled and a large crack opened in the ground and the withered trees fell into the ravine. The crack opened again and ran towards the four companions at the wall.

'Remember the lessons you have learned from this place when you are free.' Elemax said.

'We're gonna die!' Wren said.

'Close your eyes and keep your hands on the wall.' Elemax commanded.

They all complied, squeezing their eyes tight against the sudden brightness of the day, hearts pounding in their chests.

The crack in the earth met the wall and ran up through the crystal beneath their hands, splintering out into smaller cracks across the surface.

The reverberating booms from the earth and the cracking of the wall was deafening but they all heard Elemax speak over the roaring of the protesting earth.

'Ever present prison wall, surrounding darkness one and all. Hear our voice the angel call, crack and tremble, crumble fall.'

*****

Arcane picked up the pieces and held the two halves of the crystal, one in each hand. The pendant mount was twisted and the chain broken. His key to the power of the Fey gone forever. Rage burned through him like fire, twisting and distorting him with hate. He looked at the half-angel and her children, he despised them. They were all responsible for the pain and anger he felt. Her kind, the Fey had killed his father, it wasn't fair that he shouldn't have his revenge. Arcane dropped the useless crystal pieces and heedless of the wolf's earlier warning, lunged at Shayla.

Shayla stepped in front of the twins. Her large black and silver wings materialised and wrapped around her in a shield. As Arcane ran at her, the pointed tip of her right wing like three black fingers grabbed him by the throat halting his assault. Arcane's eyes widened in shocked surprise. He met Shayla's steely glare as she held him.

The sharp edges of her wings glinted in the moonlight and the pointed tip of her left wing came forward punching through Arcane's chest and sliding smoothly between his ribs straight into his heart.

Arcane grabbed the end of Shayla's wing and twisted, snapping off the point. Shayla cried out and dropped Arcane. He sank to his knees, the broken shaft of the wing tip lodged tight.

Arcane had no memorable last words. The Shadow Lord's memories flooded his mind as he struggled to breath. A broken bone shaft had killed his father, ironic he was to suffer the same fate. The sum of his life had been one evil deed after another with no reward.

He drew a ragged breath and fell forward, landing face down on the ground. He had imagined his confrontation and victory over the half-angel for so long his dying thoughts had trouble accepting defeat. He wondered if he would join his father in the oblivion or whether he would simply cease to exist. Arcane took one last rasping breath and died. The Shadow Lord and his heir were no more.

Max, still in wolf form, nudged at Shayla and she put her hand on his head.

'Mum?' Elena said slipping her hand into her mother's.

'He was a bad person.' Shayla said.

'No mum, your wing.' Elena said.

Shayla looked at the broken wing tip and winced as they disappeared behind her. She felt no joy at taking Arcane's life, no matter how evil he was, but he had kidnapped her children and had attempted to kill her.

'It'll heal.' Shayla said. 'Let's find your father.'

SHINE BRIGHTLY

Peter reached the main entrance to the palace at the same time Rufus was leading the others out and Shayla ran to him.

Shayla gently touched Peter's cheek below his bandaged eye. Peter shrugged and put his hand over hers.

'Arcane?' Peter asked.

'Dead.' Shayla said.

'What else?'

'Now's not the time.' Shayla said her voice breaking as she held back her grief. 'I'll tell you later.'

Shayla cleared her throat.

'Barumar?'

'Dead.' Peter replied. 'But that's not the end of it. I had hoped killing Barumar would have taken the legs out of the vampire invasion of the city, but his death has done nothing to stop them. They're frenzied, in chaos, relying on their overwhelming numbers to defeat anything in their path. More vampires are pouring in from the surrounding countryside from both sides of the river.'

Shayla glanced at the twins, then back to Peter.

'We're not getting out of this are we?' Shayla said tears in her eyes.

Peter shook his head and looked at Rufus and Milly.

'We make our last stand here.'

'Agreed.' Rufus and Milly said simultaneously.

'I'm with you.' Elliot said drawing his sword. 'I will protect Shayla and the twins for as long as I am able.'

'Thank you.' Peter said.

Elliot stood to attention and nodded his head to Peter.

'I'm a Knight of Feylore, it's my duty to protect the royal family and my honour.'

'I stand with my husband.' Myshka said. 'I'll take the form of a wolf and fight. Although I won't have your strength I will have strength enough'

Max transformed from wolf to warrior and stood, battle ready, in front of his father. Elena stood next to Max a determined look on her face.

'I was going to ask if you could fly out of here with the twins?' Peter said.

'I think Max and Elena have made their decision.' Shayla said. 'We fight.'

Peter held her at arm's length and looked into her eyes.

'Hold back as long as you can.' Peter said.

Shayla nodded and Peter smiled sadly before transforming into warrior form. Milly and Rufus followed his lead and Myshka shimmered next to Elliot and shifted into the form of a timber wolf and bared her teeth.

Vampires stepped out from the shadows and surrounded the small group of wolves and companions. They outnumbered the group at least five to one and they moved in slowly, hissing, spitting and snapping like wild, rabid animals, the wolves snarled in return. Both sides bared fangs and teeth and snapped at the air waiting for the other to make the first move. Eventually Peter howled, Rufus and Milly replied and the wolves attacked.

Max felt a mixture of fear and exhilaration. His wolf DNA was urging him to join the attack but he was still also a young teenager, inexperienced; unsure, and he hesitated. He could feel his heart pounding in his chest and fought the other urge from the primitive part of his brain to run. Fighting these vampires would be his rite of passage, his first and last fight. Max howled in response to his father. He was afraid but he was ready.

Elena stood rigid, petrified, her heart beating so hard in her chest she could hear it pounding in her ears. She stared at the faces of the vampires as they edged closer, tightening the circle. In response to the situation, Elena had undergone her own change. Her teeth had grown larger and sharp claws had replaced her fingernails, her eyes had turned animalistic yellow. Her mind filled with thoughts of Yosef and Ratman. The time in the tunnel felt like such a long time ago. She hoped Yosef was somewhere safe and she thought that she would probably never see him again. Elena thought about Ratman. He reminded her of Fishbone, they were both strange and….

The words of the prophecy flooded Elena's mind. Some of it lost in the passing down of stories from tribe to tribe. The translation skewed in the writing and re-writing of books throughout the years. In a sudden flash of understanding, Elena spoke the words aloud.

'Lycan Angel's greatest light,
Encroaching darkness, demon sent,
Take a stand or lose this fight,
Divine Almighty Power is lent.

In reflex to her racing heartbeat, Elena's hand shot out towards Max.

'Max!' Elena said. 'Shine brightly!'

Max took his sister's hand and as their hands locked the twins remembered everything that had happened in the prison world. Max looked at Elena and a jolt of electricity passed through their hands and into their bodies. Both felt heat rising from the pit of their stomachs just as it had in the prison world and angel light burst from within them. Once again, but this time in the physical world, their bodies transcended the confines of flesh and bone and merged in a blinding flash of light.

The first wave of vampires hesitated in the sudden brightness and were felled by the attacking wolves.

Shayla turned to look at her children and a new being stood in the spot previously occupied by Max and Elena. Tall, muscular and completely silver, covered with smooth, shiny silver fur. Two large wings of light grey, silver and white feathers with a wingspan to rival Titan, stretched out behind them.

'Elemax.' the being replied to Shayla's unspoken question.

Piercing blue eyes looked out of Elemax's ethereal face.

'Lycan angel's greatest light.' Elemax said.

'Shine brightly.' Shayla whispered in sudden understanding.

Elemax flexed their wings and took flight soaring up into the night sky. Bright against the blackness, their colossal wings beating the night air, their silver head catching the moonlight as they rose higher.

As the night sky lit up with the intensity and brightness of the midday summer sun, Shayla shielded her eyes.

* * * * *

Elemax flew higher, the city shrinking with every downbeat of their wings. They could see everything. Roman and his pack battling the tirade of vampires crawling over Draven Bridge. The vampires were spacing their attack to wear the wolves down; eventually exhaustion would become the wolves enemy and the vampires would destroy them one by one. Even with the help of the spirit pack, they wouldn't survive.

On the other side of the river the vampires flowed in from the surrounding forest like black water from a broken jug, all heading for the city to slaughter and feed. Peter and his pack valiantly fought each new surge of vampires.

They could see vampires streaming through the city streets, others crawling over roofs and buildings, all with evil intent. The sound of screams and cries for help reached their ears and Elemax was outraged at the taking of innocent lives for no reason other than to kill.

Reaching a height of over one thousand feet Elemax held their position in the air.

'Shine brightly.' Elemax said recalling Ratman's words.

The angel light within broke free lighting up their whole body, turning night-time to daytime. Divine light exploded across the sky and shone as brightly as the sun on a hot summer's day. Anyone looking up would have been forced to shield their eyes.

Every vampire on Draven Bridge was caught by the light. The vampires on the ground stopped in their tracks, burst into flames and exploded into ash.

Elemax's light illuminated the sky and the city of Braeden was awash with its brilliance. The stream of vampires in the streets and on the buildings dissolved into black ash. The light lasted only a few seconds before winking out, returning the city to night-time once again.

A wind blew in from what seemed like nowhere and swept the ash from the city streets and the bridge, whipping the remains of the vampires upwards where it dissolved without a trace.

Vampires at the edge of the light were fortunate enough to survive. Their numbers depleted, most turned and ran, seeking shelter. The foolish few, too crazed with blood lust were quickly taken care of by the wolves of the spirit pack.

From either side of the river the wolves looked up to the sky. Roman and his pack reverted to human form and Roman turned to see Ratman looking up at the sky smiling.

Peter returned to human form and stood beside Shayla, his arm around her shoulder. Both looked up to the sky. With the extinguishing of the light, and their destiny fulfilled, Elemax returned to their original form.

The Nejelski River and the stone statues of Draven Bridge grew in size and shape as Max and Elena hurtled towards the ground faster than they could have ever imagined.

FREEFALL

There was a moment of dizzying confusion as the wind hammered their faces, then they realised, they were free falling. The air rushed past as Max and Elena accelerated faster and faster towards the ground. The City lay before them like a model, some areas alive with lights, but it was too dark to make out individual houses, only the lights that mirrored the night sky.

Max reached for Elena and for a second their hands clasped and they fell in tandem. Draven Bridge grew bigger as gravity pulled them fiercely towards the statues and stones below.

Their bodies twitched and jerked as they fell and the wind pulled them apart twirling them like leaves in the autumn. Elena called out to Max but the wind tore the words away as soon as they left her lips. Her hair whipped about her face and her eyes felt as if they were being sucked back into their sockets.

Time seemed to slow down as they fell; the twins knew they would hit the ground in seconds and it would hurt; or maybe nothing would ever hurt them again.

When the sky went dark, Shayla uncovered her eyes and looked up, there was no sign of Elemax. Shayla scanned the night sky, a few wispy clouds skidded across the face of the moon.

'There!' Elliot cried pointing, his sharp Fey eyesight catching movement in the sky.

She looked left and right and stopped. Her blood ran cold and her stomach lurched. She saw two objects falling to the ground, her children. Shayla opened her wings and glanced at Peter, they both knew she had to try and save them.

'Wait!' Elliot said. 'You'll never reach them, they're moving way too fast. Take me.'

'What?'

'If I can get closer, I can move the air which might just push them away from the bridge.' Elliot said.

Without hesitation Shayla grabbed Elliot's hand and flew up into the sky. Since merging with Titan her wings had changed, grown bigger and Shayla was never more grateful for their additional strength than she was at that moment. Shayla offered a silent prayer to the Divine for the lives of her children and for Titan's power that was now part of her.

Elliot held on tight to Shayla's hand as they ascended into the dark night sky above Draven Bridge. Extending his right hand, Elliot concentrated and manipulated the air, pushing it towards the twins as they hurtled towards them. He felt the wind rushing past and moved it in the direction of Max and Elena, also praying to the Divine that he was strong enough.

Shayla and Elliot felt their prayers were answered when the twins seemed to move away from them. Elliot's efforts had not slowed their descent, only changed their trajectory. Max and Elena were headed for the icy waters of the Nejelski River.

In the seconds of free fall, Elena felt surprisingly calm and thought that she would probably never know whether she was more angel than wolf, or neither. Max had always manifested as a wolf and had never been in any doubt as to what he was and that one day he would be an Alpha. Elena, on the other hand, had only shown wolf-like traits, nothing more. She felt a strong gust of wind pushing her and she looked at Max wondering if he felt it too.

Elena had a sudden epiphany. She was Elemax. Max was Elemax. The being they had become was both of them, lycan and angel. Everything they are merged into a single being, once and for one divine purpose. With this realisation two large wings, feathers varying in shade from light grey at the centre out to silver and almost white at the tips opened out behind her. The wind no longer rushed past her, Elena halted her descent and floated in the air.

Max felt the wind pushing him and he looked at his twin, her face serene. For a second they were together, frozen in the air, then she was whipped away. He saw silver wings unfold behind her and realised that it was him who had been pulled away, he was still accelerating towards the ground. The bridge was no longer his destination and he was grateful. The river, like a black snake drew closer and Max transformed into warrior form hoping the extra strength might in some way help him survive the fall.

Elena pulled her wings close to her body, streamlining her shape and dived steeply like a Peregrine falcon to catch up with Max. Dropping at a speed of almost two hundred miles an hour Elena closed the gap between them. Reaching Max, Elena wrapped her arms around his body and held on tight, opening her wings for deceleration, but it was not enough, they were too close to the water. Elena pulled her wings around both of them and the twins plunged into the river head first.

Shayla and Elliot landed on Draven Bridge and looked over the edge. Peter and the others ran to the same spot. The twins impact point still visible on the surface of the water.

When the twins plunged into the water their momentum carried them deep down into the river. Elena adopted an aquatic version of flight and swam towards the surface. She swam under Draven Bridge pushing hard against the water heading for the surface. The strong current of the Nejelski River pounded and pummelled their bodies, the current pulling them in the opposite direction. Pulling her wings tightly around herself and Max, Elena fought the current, determined to win the battle. Eventually the river released its grip on the twins and they broke the surface. Elena extended her wings and lifted them both into the air.

'I'm going in.' Peter said climbing up onto the side wall of the bridge.

Before Peter could dive into the river, Elena exploded from the water on the other side of the bridge, her arms still around her brother, now back in human form. Elena beat her silver wings and landed them both safely on the bridge. Elena released her grip on Max and almost collapsed to her knees in exhaustion.

Peter and Shayla ran to their children and hugged them fiercely. Rufus and Milly, unable to hold back joined them. Elliot and Myshka stayed to one side.

Myshka shifted into human form but remained covered in fur.

'How?' Elliot asked looking his wife up and down.

'Secret.' Myshka said winking at him.

'I didn't know you could that.'

'There's still so much about me you don't know.'

Elliot smiled and hugged her.

By the time Roman and his pack reached the centre of the bridge, the group had broken apart leaving Peter, Shayla and the twins at the centre. Everyone stood together bearing cuts and bruises from the fight with the vampires, only Ratman appeared to move without injury.

'Are you all OK?' Roman asked.

'You?' Peter asked taking in Roman's battered appearance.

Roman laughed.

Elena's wings were wrapped around her body like a silver cloak. The transformation of both children had left them naked. Milly had given Elena her coat, saying she did not feel the cold, but Elena still shivered in the night air and the wings were comforting.

Ratman stepped forward and offered his coat to Max.

'This is the second time I've had to give you my coat!' Ratman said. 'I hope you're not going to make a habit of it!'

Max shrugged and took the coat, no longer self-conscious but the night air was cold and he suddenly felt very tired.

Roman looked around. Ratman seemed to read his mind.

'The spirit pack have returned to the afterglow.' Ratman said. 'Once the balance tipped the other way, their assistance was no longer required.'

Roman looked around as if to confirm Ratman's words. The two statues at the end of Draven Bridge were back in place, their stone faces once again watching over the City. Roman thought their posture had changed slightly but not enough for ordinary citizens to notice. He turned his attention back to Ratman and nodded.

'Wounds need attending.' Roman said. 'We should return to the cafe. Reidar and Thana need to know what's happened here.'

Everyone followed Roman back to the cafe. Frightened faces appeared in windows as the group passed the houses but nobody opened their doors. Any vampires not caught and destroyed by the light had fled the city, for now.

When they reached the cafe, Pickens and Ratman had already disappeared into the shadows. Inside, Roman led the rest of them straight to the basement and unlocked the door.

It was empty. Roman looked at the others, nobody spoke. Finally Milly stepped forward.

'They left as soon as you were gone.' Milly said.

'The door was locked.' Roman said.

'The tunnel. It's not as vampire-proof as you think. Reidar and Thana have the ability to become mist. The sting of the silver and the ashwood is tolerable to older vampires.'

'You knew!' Roman said. 'But said nothing!'

'I suspected. Did you really expect them to wait in a wolf's lair for your return?' Milly said.

Roman looked angry but said nothing; he was tired. A scent caught his attention and he sniffed the air, vampire. He turned towards the open door of the basement and the scent.

'You spared our lives. You kept your word.' Reidar said from the top of the stairs.

'I'm pleased you survived.' Milly said. 'Thana?'

'Safe.' Reidar said.

Reidar surveyed the company of wolves and companions and finally made eye contact with Roman.

'Nothing more is expected of you.' Reidar said. 'I hope our truce remains.'

Roman didn't answer immediately. He was angry, he'd been duped, but eventually he conceded that he would have done the same thing if their positions had been reversed.

'It does for now.' Roman said with a sigh. 'But there have to be changes. Keep your kind under control and we won't have a problem.'

'Perhaps we can discuss details another time?' Reidar said. 'I'll deal with the city officials, if that's acceptable to you.'

Roman nodded and Reidar disappeared in the blink of an eye.

Wounds were tended and bandaged and Rufus and Milly insisted they would keep watch for the remainder of the night. Wolves, angels, Fey and Morphian all rested together close to the roots of the rowan tree in the centre of the basement of the cafeteria.

Peter didn't sleep at all. Instead he watched over his family. Thankful they were all alive and together. At dawn as the sun rose on a clear crisp day over the City of Braeden, he stood with Rufus and Milly in the courtyard of the cafeteria his eye closed and his face upturned towards the light.

AFTERMATH

Twenty-four hours later, Mike's Cafeteria was closed to the public for a private party. Not that any of the citizens of Braeden were looking to have an evening out. Many were reeling from the previous night, devastated by the loss of family and friends.

Everyone who had fought the vampires joined together for a victory feast. Wolves have voracious appetites and the food kept coming, but even werewolves eventually have their fill. Satiated and content the conversation turned to events the previous night. Most had sustained wounds that would leave permanent scars, some more visible than others.

An eyepatch would be a permanent reminder of Peter's battle with Barumar. His wounds would heal, but his eye wouldn't grow back and those caused by the werebat's silver talons would take a little longer.

Peter sat in a corner, facing the main entrance, his back to the wall surveying the room. Never totally comfortable in a crowded room, he sat slightly away from the others. He looked around, surveying the damage each had sustained, starting with his own family.

Shayla's cuts and scratches were mainly superficial and would be gone in a few days. She looked tired having spent hours alongside Elliot healing some of the deeper wounds the wolves had sustained. Shayla had not yet allowed herself to grieve for Titan and Peter wondered if perhaps she had not completely accepted he was gone.

The twins looked exhausted but otherwise undamaged. Both children were changed by their experience. The innocence of youth swept away, replaced by an assured knowledge that evil had many faces. From now on, they would always be on their guard.

Peter gave thanks again to the Divine for saving his wife and children. He was still trying to understand the full extent of what had happened; how they had become this being called Elemax. Peter had many questions, but he would wait for Max and Elena to mention it first. When they were ready to talk, he was ready to listen. Peter was still incredulous that in a couple of weeks Max had become an Alpha.

Grimlock sat beside Max, the two engaged in conversation with Elliot and Myshka. Peter could have listened, but chose not to. Instead he looked around the room at the rest of the company.

Roman and Matyas were also engaged in conversation and drinking wine. Roman had lost the top of one ear, but his hair would cover the damage and Matyas had always looked somewhat battered, Peter thought there was little visible change.

Rufus and Witty sat together, their conversation much more intimate. Both were smiling and laughing together. They had become close, slipping away when they thought nobody was looking. Everyone knew, but all pretend not to notice, that Rufus and Witty were spending time together in the forest, either in wolf form running, or simply enjoying each other's company.

Pickens sat in the opposite corner from Peter also watching the room. Peter made eye contact and nodded, a kindred spirit, uncomfortable in the company of too many people. Unlike Rufus and Witty, Pickens had the uncanny ability to slip away into the shadows unnoticed and Peter knew that before the end of the evening the wererat would be gone.

The door of the cafe opened and Milly entered followed by Reidar. Milly had spent some time with Reider and Thana saying they understood her in a way the Wolfpack couldn't. Milly was a complicated hybrid needing the company of wolves and vampires. She might never have the opportunity to speak to old friends of Gaolyn's and reminisce again. No matter how many years passed by Milly would always feel the pain of losing Gaolyn although she seldom spoke of it.

Tempest came out from the kitchen as Milly and Reidar stepped into the room. She growled and slammed the plate of food down onto one of the tables.

All conversations stopped and Milly stepped forward, standing between Reidar and Tempest but said nothing. Peter sat upright, as did Rufus.

'Your kind aren't welcome here!' Tempest snapped.

'Silence!' Roman said glaring at Tempest. 'I say who is welcome, not you.'

Tempest stood her ground defiant. Roman growled deep in his throat and Tempest eventually bowed her head and took a step backwards.

'Welcome Reidar.' Roman said. 'Share my food and wine.'

'Thank you.' Reidar said. 'But I won't stay. I came to update you.'

Reidar looked at Tempest and held her gaze for a second before continuing.

'As you and I discussed last night, I've spent several hours with the city officials convincing them to accept our version of what happened last night.'

'*Our* version?' Tempest said.

'The one Reidar and I agreed upon last night.' Roman replied.

The tension was palpable and Reidar hesitated.

'Did they believe you?' Roman asked.

'Yes.' Reidar said. 'Rats gained access to many houses causing people to panic and run into the street where they were overwhelmed. Drawn by the smell of blood, a bear came in from the forest attacking and killing people. Stray dogs ran wild through the streets in the chaos. Some people were bitten.'

'Stray dogs?' Tempest exclaimed looking to Roman. 'What of the vampires?'

'Nobody wants to believe there are vampires.' Roman said. 'People accept that rats, bears and dogs could be responsible.'

'Typical vampire! He sold us out!' Tempest said angrily.

'No.' Roman said. 'This is what we agreed.'

Tempest went to speak but after a look from Roman she thought better of it.

'I've told the city officials to advise people to stay out of the forest.' Reidar continued. 'You and I know there's no bear but it's useful for them to believe there is. It's probably a good idea not to roam the streets in your natural form for a while, but at least you have the forest.'

'That's good.' Roman said. 'Are you and Thana staying in the City?'

Reidar nodded.

'The council were happy that Thana has succeeded Barumar and I've been asked to represent the Queen in council business.'

'I can't listen to this!' Tempest said.

Tempest stormed out of the room and returned to the kitchen. Reidar looked uncomfortable.

'Do we still have a truce?' Reidar asked.

'Keep your people in line and we won't have a problem.' Roman replied.

Reidar turned to Pickens.

'The council want to flood the drains with some sort of phosphine gas. Can you get your kind out for a few days until they've done?'

Pickens nodded.

'I've convinced them not to start until tomorrow morning.' Reidar said. 'I'm sorry. It was the best I could do.'

'That's plenty of time.' Pickens said. 'We'll be gone.'

'Give it a few days and you can come back.'

Pickens smiled and stood up.

'I'll walk you out.' Myshka said also standing.

'I should go.' Reidar said.

As Pickens and Myshka stepped out through the door, Ratman stepped in. Ratman's hair lifted off his face in the draft caused by Reidar's exit.

Tempest returned from the kitchen, her eyes blazing in anger.

'We shouldn't be making alliances with that filth!' Tempest said. 'We should be killing them, as we're meant to!'

'As Alpha I make the decisions.' Roman said. 'We live in this City, we protect the citizens. If we are at war with the vampires, innocent people will be caught in the crossfire.'

'Collateral damage.'

'That is not who we are.'

Tempest paused gathering her thoughts.

'Then we should be moving from city to city eradicating all vampires.' Tempest said.

'What are you talking about?' Roman asked.

'The twins!' Tempest replied pointing to Max and Elena. 'They're the greatest weapon I've ever seen. We could rid the world of vampires!'

Peter stood up, his anger rising. He stepped in front of his family and faced Tempest.

'My children are not a weapon.' Peter said quietly.

Elsewhere in the room Rufus and Milly had moved themselves into position to defend their pack if necessary. The room went quiet and everyone looked at Max and Elena.

'What do you say?' Roman said looking at the twins.

Elena looked at Max and shook her head.

'No.' Max said. 'We don't want to do that again.'

'There's your answer.' Roman said turning back to Tempest. 'They choose not to.'

'Then they should be made to!' Tempest said.

'Who's going to make me?' Max replied angrily. 'You!'

'If I have to.'

Tempest's anger triggered the start of the change, which she kept under control but her eyes still changed to an animalistic yellow and her teeth elongated. Max responded to the threat, his teeth and claws extending.

'ENOUGH!' Ratman commanded. 'Sit down and listen.'

Ratman's voice reverberating in everyone's ears. The wolves felt their anger dissolve, transformations reverse through no action of their own. Something in the tone of his voice held an authority greater than all of them. Everyone returned to their seats and turned their attention to Ratman.

'The power was finite.' Ratman said. 'Even if the twins had agreed, it is not possible.'

Tempest sighed impatiently and Ratman addressed her directly.

'What was your plan?' Ratman asked. 'Travel the world, kill all vampires?'

'Something like that.' Tempest muttered.

'How were you going to force the twins to become your instrument of destruction?'

Tempest said nothing.

'Exactly.' Ratman said. 'You couldn't. The power was not theirs to control; neither was it anyone else's.'

Ratman looked around the room and addressed everyone.

'It is not for any of you to decide what becomes of the vampires. This city was out of balance. Elemax fulfilled their purpose and balance has now been restored. The job of the wolves is to maintain that balance.'

Ratman looked at Max.

'I have something for you.'

Max went to take a step forward but Peter put his hand on his son's shoulder and held him back.

'Relax Peterus Maximus.' Ratman said. 'I mean no harm.'

Peter stood his ground.

'Shayla Meldainiel.' Ratman said with a sigh. 'Hear my words and tell them if I am lying. I mean your children no harm.'

'He's telling the truth.' Shayla said.

'Thank you.'

Peter smiled at his son and let him go. Max stepped up to Ratman.

'Your rite of passage was interrupted.' Ratman said. 'Nevertheless, you have been tested. Tested to the extreme and survived. You have also shown wisdom and proven yourself as a leader. You have earned this.'

Ratman opened his hand to reveal a black crystal threaded onto a leather cord. Max looked at the crystal and back to Ratman.

'The remains of Arcane's pendant.' Ratman said. 'Part of it. This part has been re-purposed for you.'

'How?'

Ratman frowned and waved his hand dismissively but didn't answer. He merely offered the necklace to Max again. Max felt a little unsure and glanced at his father. Peter nodded and Max took the necklace. Ratman leant forward and whispered into Max's ear.

'You won't need to borrow my coat anymore.'

Max laughed and put the necklace over his head.

'Thank you.' Max said proudly.

'Elena. I have something for you too.' Ratman said.

Elena stepped forward with confidence and stood next to her brother. Ratman opened his hand again to reveal another crystal threaded onto a leather cord, this one was white.

'You have also been tested.' Ratman said. 'And have earned this. The other half of Arcane's pendant.'

'It's white.' Elena said. 'Arcane's necklace was black.'

'It has been re-purposed for you.'

'I don't understand.'

'Remember what I said about balance? Max's crystal serves one purpose, yours another.'

Ratman paused and put a large hand on each of their shoulders. He looked them in the eye.

'Night and day. Good and evil. Balance.'

Max and Elena nodded their understanding. Ratman smiled, patted them on the shoulder and released them.

The twins returned to their parents and the others gathered around to look at the crystals and to congratulate them on surviving their rite of passage. All earlier tensions forgotten.

Only Shayla was aware of Ratman's departure. Hugging her daughter, she looked over Elena's shoulder and saw Ratman turn and take a quantum step into another part of the universe. As his foot touched the ground the mysterious Ratman disappeared.

EPILOGUE

Two years later….

Max and Grimlock stood together on the east side of the Nejelski River looking at the construction of the new vehicular bridge. Max could hear the sounds of machinery and the voices of crew chiefs shouting orders to the people working on various sections of the construction.

'We need to get it finished as soon as possible. Draven Bridge has been opened again for vehicles but it's not ideal. It was pedestrianised years ago for a reason.' Grimlock said glancing at Max. 'Traffic damage.'

Max nodded.

'This bridge will be better than the last one. There's still a long way to go.' Grimlock continued. 'But I'm pleased with the progress.'

'How long before it's finished?' Max asked.

'With the help of the Divine and two policemen, probably another year, maybe two.' Grimlock said with a smile.

'It was the right decision asking you to stay.' Max said. 'Who better to oversee the rebuild of the bridges than the person who brought them down.'

'I wasn't happy when you asked me to stay in Braeden and represent our pack in your stead. You're my Alpha, I should have gone with you, but I have to admit.' Grimlock paused and looked at Max. 'I'm thoroughly enjoying this project.'

'You've done an amazing job Grimlock.' Max said.

Grimlock smiled and looked out over the construction.

'I must say I've been surprised and impressed by Sheriff Reidar.' Grimlock said.

'How so?'

'It was Reidar who persuaded the council to make funds available for the construction of this bridge.'

'Isn't that easy for him to do with the delusional?' Max asked.

'He hasn't used it, as far as I know.' Grimlock said. 'Never expected to be impressed by a vampire, but I suppose he's not like most of them.'

Max said nothing for a while, but eventually he asked Grimlock the question that had been on his mind for the last two years.

'Why did you bow to me as your Alpha?' Max asked. 'I was a kid, still am I suppose.'

Grimlock turned to Max.

'Age has nothing to do with it.' Grimlock said. 'You showed remarkable courage standing up to Jedrek in defence of two vampires you didn't really know anything about.'

'They saved my life.' Max said. 'And Elena.'

'But wolves and vampires are sworn enemies and you didn't know the vampires' real motive.'

'I know, but Thana and Reidar went to incredible lengths to save my sister and I and put themselves at risk returning us to the wolves. Whatever their motives, both our lives were saved, therefore two lives were owed. At least that's how I saw it.'

'And you were prepared to defend your decision.' Grimlock said.

'Absolutely.' Max replied firmly.

'Jedrek could have killed you.'

'I know that.'

'But you still stood by your decision.'

'It was the right thing to do.'

'That's when I saw what you really are.' Grimlock said. 'Courage, wisdom and integrity. It was....what do young people say....um....aha! It was a no-brainer!'

'I don't think anyone says that anymore.' Max laughed. 'But thanks for the compliment.'

Max and Grimlock turned back to the construction of the new bridge, standing together in companionable silence.

The rumbling sound of a car engine caught his attention and Max turned his head in the direction the approaching vehicle. The afternoon sun peeked out from behind the clouds to glint off the shiny white bonnet of a nineteen sixty vintage Silver Cloud drop-head coupe. The car pulled up alongside Max.

'Are you ready?' Rufus asked from behind the wheel.

'Yes.' Max replied. 'Grimlock?'

'I'm going to stay a while longer.' Grimlock replied. 'Go.'

'Thank you.'

Grimlock bowed his head to Max.

'You will always be my Alpha.' Grimlock said.

'And I'm proud to have you in my pack.' Max replied.

Max got in the car and Rufus leaned his head out of the driver's window to speak to Grimlock.

'Hey Grimlock! Next time I visit, I want to see this thing finished!'

Grimlock laughed.

Rufus revved the engine and drove away. Grimlock watched the car until it disappeared from sight.

Rufus and Max arrived back at the cafe to find Dyaniika, the newest member of Roman's pack, waiting for them. She couldn't speak any of the common tongue but Max was able to understand her words perfectly, just as he had understood Yosef on his last visit.

'Problems?' Rufus asked.

'No.' Max replied. 'She's saying there's someone here to see me.'

Rufus and Max went inside and to find none other than Yosef waiting for him.

'Yosef!' Max exclaimed grabbing the boy and hugging him.

'It is good to see you.' Yosef said.

'How did you know I was here?' Max asked.

'Ratman told me.' Yosef paused. 'I had also hoped to see Elena.'

'I know.'

'She'll come back again one day.'

Yosef nodded his understanding.

'Will you give her this letter?' Yosef said handing Max an envelope.

'Of course.'

'I have sent other letters and Elena has replied.' Yosef said his face flushing. 'If you take the letter it will arrive quicker.'

It was Max's turn to pause. The night before he left home Elena had stayed up late writing. She must have known Yosef would meet Max on this trip.

'Elena had the same thought.' Max said pulling a crumpled envelope out of his pocket. 'Um….sorry....it got a bit crushed.'

Yosef smiled. He was thirteen years old now, his clothes no longer dirty and torn. He looked happy and was obviously well cared for.

'How are Tomas and Kristyna?' Max asked.

'Great!' Yosef replied.

Yosef looked around the room to see who might be listening and leaned in closer to Max.

'I had to move in with them.' Yosef said lowering his voice. 'To protect them, you understand.'

Max nodded. Roman had already told him how Yosef had saved Tomas and Kristyna from the vampires. Roman didn't know how Yosef was unaffected by the vampire delusional but guessed the mysterious Ratman had something to do with it. Yosef was happy to stay with them and Tomas and Kristyna Nebojsa had officially adopted Yosef a few months later. However, it was also clear Yosef wanted to keep up his appearance as a self-sufficient street kid.

'I understand completely.' Max said winking at Yosef conspiratorially.

Rufus watched Max and Yosef in animated conversation from the other corner of the cafe, his wolf hearing missing nothing. He smiled to himself.

'Fatherhood looks good on you.' Roman said sitting down next to him.

'She's quite a handful.' Rufus replied looking at Witty who was holding their daughter in her arms, who in turn was squirming.

'Uri. An unusual name.'

'She's named after our pack Elder.' Rufus said. 'I mean former pack Elder.'

'I know. I met her.' Roman said. 'Alpha of the spirit pack. A formidable wolf. Great fighter.'

'It's only now that I have a cub of my own that I understand why she used to get so frustrated with Milly and I when we were young.' Rufus said smiling. 'She's into everything, and so quick! We've nicknamed her Zippy!'

Roman and Rufus watched baby Uri as she fought against Witty's embrace, determined to have her own way. Eventually she succeeded and Witty set Uri on the floor where she proceeded to crawl under and around the tables and chairs.

'Witty and I went up to see Elliot and Myshka to say hello, and introduce them to baby Uri, but the place was empty.' Rufus said. 'Looked like it's been empty for a while.'

'They left to look for more of Myshka's people.' Roman said.

'You saw them before they left?'

'Elliot came to see me. He said they might be back one day but I doubt it. I think they only stayed close to Braeden as long as they did because of Pickens.'

Rufus smiled. He recalled that Elliot, or Eli as he once was, had set out with Myshka a long time ago to help find other Morphians. Eli had always said Fey was his home and he felt unsettled in this world, it would seem he still felt that way.

Dyaniika brought coffee to the table her eyes on Roman. Eventually Roman looked up at her and smiled. Dyaniika's cheeks flushed pink and she walked away.

'Fatherhood may be something you'll have to get used to some day.' Rufus said raising one eyebrow quizzically.

Roman laughed but said nothing.

'What happened to Tempest?' Rufus asked changing the subject.

'She left Braeden not long after you.' Roman said.

Roman sat quietly for a few moments thinking. Rufus waited.

'Tempest wasn't happy with some of the agreements I had to make with Reidar.' Roman said.

'How are things with the Sheriff and Queen Thana?' Rufus asked.

'As good as they can be between wolves and vampires. Reidar and Thana are old vampires, they've seen pretty much everything. They both understand the necessity of working with us and the humans to stay alive. The Queen keeps to herself and the council love it! Having a reclusive Queen across the river seems to attract the tourists and all they see is the money coming in.'

'The city feels different.' Rufus said.

'There's nowhere near as many vampires.' Roman replied. 'And Reider keeps his people on a tight leash. I can't ask for much more than that.'

'But it wasn't good enough for Tempest.'

Roman shook his head sadly.

'Tempest wanted to find and kill every last vampire in the city and beyond. She didn't understand that there has to be balance and living in a City requires a certain amount of compromise. She kept in touch for a while, but it's been a few months since I've heard anything.'

'Do you know where she is?' Rufus asked.

'Oh yes.' Roman said smiling again. 'I keep track of her movements. Tempest is still part of my pack, but for now she needs time alone. I'm giving her that time until she's ready to come home.'

Baby Uri finally made her way to Rufus who picked her up and hugged her. She yawned and rubber her face against Rufus's chest. Rufus gently stroked her hair, the same deep brown colour as her mother.

'She's got your eyes.' Roman said.

'Everyone says that.' Rufus said looking at his daughter proudly.

Uri slowly opened and closed her eyes a few times, then fell asleep to the sound of her father's heartbeat.

'Thanks for the use of the car.' Rufus said. 'I brought her back in one piece. Not a scratch.'

'Yes you did. Thank you.'

'Did you manage to find me something else to get us back home?'

'I did.' Roman replied.

Roman dangled a set of keys in front of Rufus.

'A gift for Uri.'

Rufus frowned. Roman was offering him the keys to his vintage car.

'I fought alongside your Uri.' Roman said. 'I might not be here today if not for her. I cannot give this give to Uri, so I give to *baby* Uri instead.'

'Seriously?'

Roman laughed at the confused look on Rufus's face.

'Yes. Serious.' Roman said. 'But you will have to drive and take good care of it until she is older.'

'Thank you.' Rufus said taking the keys.

'It's nothing.' Roman shrugged.

*****

The sunshine was warm and Wren turned her face towards its brilliance. Even with her eyes closed the world was bright behind her eyelids. After an interminable amount of time in the prison world with its blistering sun and dry heat, Wren still wanted to live in a place that enjoyed sunshine almost every day.

'You'll never get any work done with your eyes closed.'

Wren smiled and opened her eyes.

'Hello Oren.' Wren said. 'It's good to see you.'

'You too.' Oren said.

'How did you find me?'

'I guessed you'd want to be somewhere sunny.' Oren said. 'Back where you used to live. I managed to track you down, eventually.'

'How have you been?'

Oren shrugged. Wren thought he looked tired.

'Not sleeping?' Wren asked.

'No.' Oren said shaking his head.

'Working helps.' Wren said. 'At the end of the day I'm too tired to think about anything.'

'Sounds good.' Oren said.

Oren scuffed his feet on the ground kicking up dust and dirt, he seemed lost. Wren walked towards one of the orange trees and stood beneath the shade of its leaves. Oren followed.

'What are you doing here Oren?' Wren said.

'I thought we could hang out.' Oren said. 'You're one of only two other people in this whole world who understands what I'm feeling.'

'Did you find Radha?'

Oren nodded.

'Radha's doing good. She has family, people she can turn to. They offered me a place to stay but it didn't seem right. I'm not good with new people.' Oren paused. 'And I wanted to find you.'

Wren said nothing for a while. Seeing Oren again reminded her of the terrible time they had spent in the prison world, the people they had lost and how close they came to dying there.

'You looking for work?' Wren said finally.

'Could be.' Oren said smiling.

'Maybe you should stick around a while. It's hard work, the pay isn't great and the living accommodations are basic, but you get a meal every night and trust me, after a day in the fields, you'll sleep like a baby.'

'Thanks Wren.' Oren said.

'No problem. You can start right away if you're up for it.'

'Absolutely.'

'Come with me.'

Wren linked her arm through Oren's and led him along the path towards the farmhouse. His presence was comforting. Wren didn't realise until seeing him again just how much she needed a good friend.

'I don't know the first thing about being a farm hand.' Oren said quietly as the old Farmer descended the steps to greet them.

'Wing it!' Wren whispered. 'Like we always do.'

*****

'Tea?' Cassie asked offering Radha a cup.

'Luminosa?' Radha asked.

Cassie nodded and smiled. Radha took the offered cup of tea and settled back into the armchair.

'Thinking about Oren?' Cassie said.

'Are you able to read my thoughts again?' Radha asked.

'I didn't need to. You had a faraway look about you. I guessed.'

Cassie settled into the armchair opposite Radha.

'I hope he's found Wren.'

'Perhaps he'll send word when he has.' Cassie said.

'Maybe.'

Radha blew across the surface of the hot liquid and took a small sip of tea. She looked around the small but familiar room with its leather chairs relatively unchanged since the first day she had come to Hampton Hall. Over the years the walls had been repainted but always in a similar shade of beige and unlike in the days of Talis Quinn where the walls had been bare, there were now black and white framed photographs of Talis Quinn and Grace Redman. The old mirror still hung above the fireplace with the photograph of Lady Ophira in its silver frame and the carriage clock on the mantle.

'It's like stepping back in time sitting here.' Radha said.

'Familiarity is good.' Cassie said.

'Cass….'

'Don't.'

'I was going to say…' Radha said.

'I know what you were going to say.' Cassie said. 'You don't need to say anything.'

Radha sipped her tea and smiled at Cassie, who returned her smile.

They sat in silence, the old carriage clock ticked away the seconds as they two friends drank their tea.

I'm sorry. Radha said telepathically, something she hadn't been able to do for a long time.

For what?

Everything.

I knew you'd come back. Cassie replied.

Thanks for not giving up on me.

Cassie sat forward in her chair and took Radha's hand.

'Never.' Cassie whispered. 'I love you.'

'I love you too.'

Cassie and Radha sat back in the armchairs and looked out of the large south facing window. The setting sun low in the sky giving the walls a golden glow that slowly turned to orange. In the frames on the opposite wall the faces of their mentors Talis Quinn and Grace Redman watched over them.

* * * * *

A week later Max, Rufus, Witty and baby Uri were back home after their trip to Braeden. The rest of the pack had lots of questions about the city and the Braeden pack and Sandy immediately began pestering Rufus to borrow the new car. Rufus flatly refused. Shayla was just pleased to have her family back together again. Shayla watched Max interact with the others, he had matured so much in two years. Elena slipped both arms around her mother's waist and hugged her.

'Can we go now?' Elena asked.

'Yes.' Shayla replied kissing the top of Elena's head.

Max and the other wolves would be eating and catching up for some time. Shayla and Elena slipped away.

They walked away from the house, across the clearing and into the surrounding trees. They hadn't gone far when Elena gasped at what she saw. Shayla had told her what to expect, but Elena had never imagined such beauty.

Queen Albezia stood before them, pale as the silver birch tree and as elegant as ever. Elena looked at the Queen of the Arbocans, part of her unable to believe what she was seeing. The Queen's green face and neck covered with triangular shaped markings like silver birch leaves. Her hair made up of slender branches heavy with yellow-brown and green catkins.

'Hello Elena; my angel-child.' Queen Albezia whispered in her soft voice.

'H.h.hello.' Elena said. 'I'm pleased to meet you.'

'And I you.'

'You're so beautiful!.' Elena said, her initial nerves forgotten.

Queen Albezia laughed and took a step closer to Elena.

'Are you ready?' Queen Albezia asked holding out her silver arms.

Elena nodded.

'Then take my hands.'

Shayla watched as Elena placed her hands in the Queen's upturned palms as she had done so many years before.

'Close your eyes angel-child and meet your grandmother.'

Completely trusting the Arborcan Queen, Elena closed her eyes and surrendered herself to the feeling of detachment. She saw through Queen Albezia's eyes and looked at a woman with ruby red hair and green eyes. The woman looked like Shayla but older, her red hair streaked with grey, Elena knew it was her grandmother, Queen Allandrea of Fey.

'Thank you Queen Albezia for making this possible. Hello Elena, my name is Allandrea and I'm your grandmother. I'm also the Queen of Fey which makes you and your brother royalty. You're young and I probably shouldn't be saying this but…'

Allandrea paused and looked around as if to check no-one was listening. Allandrea looked and stared into Queen Albezia's eyes. Elena had the sensation of Queen Albezia nodding and Allandrea continued.

Elena squeezed Queen Albezia's hands and listened to the rest of her grandmother's message. Shayla watched the changing expressions on Elena's face, from amazement, to frowning and finally nodding her head. Shayla instinctively knew the message was not a simple one of greeting and her stomach clenched.

When Elena finally opened her eyes she stared at Queen Albezia for a long time.

'That time is not upon you yet.' Queen Albezia said releasing Elena's hands.

'What happened?' Shayla asked. 'What did your grandmother say?'

Elena looked at Shayla, her expression unreadable.

'She said.' Elena paused. 'That one day I will have to cross over to Fey and rule.'

Shayla put her arm around Elena, still only fifteen years old but mature beyond her years.

'Tell me everything.' Shayla said.

* * * * *

Peter sat opposite Milly in the large, round cavern in the cave where Max would have taken his rite of passage, had events not interfered, a small fire between them.

'Why didn't you return to Braeden?' Peter asked. 'I know you need the company of vampires as well as wolves. I would have understood if you had wanted to go.'

Milly paused.

'I cannot live in two worlds. I made that decision last time we were there. I said my goodbyes to Reidar and Thana.' Milly said. 'This is my home. My place is with the pack.'

'I'm pleased you have chosen to stay with us.' Peter said. 'I'm proud to have you as pack Elder.'

'Are you ready?' Milly asked.

'Yes.'

'She might not come, but I'll try.'

'Thank you for giving me this chance.'

Milly closed her eyes and Peter closed his one good eye. Neither of them had eaten in a while, fasting enabling a heightening of the senses and increasing the chances of contacting the spirits. Peter felt a shift in the air and wondered if his hunger was tricking him into thinking something was happening. When he felt a slight chill in the air, he knew Milly had made contact.

The veil between the normal world and the spirit world parted. Peter opened his right eye to see the faint glow of brightly coloured crystals all around them. A pale, silvery light illuminated the cave and the air shimmered in front of him warping and twisting into a form. The form took shape and the spirit smiled baring her teeth. Peter smiled back at the familiar shape of Uri.

'Hello Peterus.' Uri said. 'I wondered when you would call me.'

The spirit of Uri sat down between Peter and Milly.

'It's so good to see you again.' Peter said. 'I've missed you.'

'And I you.'

Uri paused.

'Leaving without saying goodbye was the last thing I wanted, but the opportunity to ascend to the spirit pack was also the *only* thing I wanted. Do you understand?'

Peter nodded.

'How long can you stay?' Peter asked.

'Long enough to answer all of your questions.' Uri said with a smile.

* * * * *

The witch Thebe stepped through the gateway followed by the lumbering golem. She hadn't expected to move on again so soon, but the world she had just fled had no tolerance for magic and the time had come for her to leave. For two years she and the golem had moved from town to town under the cover of night and Thebe wondered if the pattern of her life was to be always on the move. She was tired and looked around at the world they had just entered. The gateway was part of a ruin and Thebe presumed the building had once been a castle. With a bit of work it would suit her needs.

Movement caught her eye, a small individual cowered behind a partial stone wall.

'Show yourself!' Thebe commanded.

The child stepped out from behind the protection of the wall and stood before Thebe. The witch looked at the child, it wasn't a typical human looking child with its curled ridges on the side of its head like flattened horns.

'What world is this?' Thebe asked.

The child cowered, its eyes fixed on the mighty golem next to her.

'Speak!'

'Zodiana.' the child whispered before turning and running.

Thebe let the child go and turned to the golem.

'We have work to do.'

*****

Several hours later Peter returned to the house. Shayla didn't need to ask whether the ritual had been successful, she could see by the contented look on Peter's face that things had gone well. Peter took her in his arms and hugged her.

'We have a visitor.' Shayla whispered in his ear.

Peter released her and Shayla led the way to their kitchen. Sitting at the table was none other than Fishbone.

'The eye patch suits you.' Fishbone said. 'Makes you look like a pirate.'

'Where have you been all these years?' Peter said without preamble.

'It's good to see you too!'

'Peter.' Shayla said putting her hand on Peter's arm and shaking her head.

Peter paused, a little embarrassed by his outburst.

'My apologies.' Peter said. 'It's good to see you Fishbone. It's just that we could have used your help when the twins were taken.'

'Yours isn't the only world that needs my help.' Fishbone said irritably. 'Besides, you had help. More than you realised.'

'I guess we did.'

Shayla poured coffee for all of them and sat down next to Peter.

'I know what happened to Titan.' Fishbone said breaking the awkward silence. 'But you don't have to worry. He's OK.'

'He's alive!' Shayla exclaimed. 'Can I see him?'

Fishbone shook his head.

'No.' Fishbone said. 'He's somewhere you can't visit, not until it's your time. He's taking a well-earned rest. He's got a beautiful garden to roam around in and take regular walks.'

Shayla's eyes filled with tears. Fishbone was talking about the afterlife. She knew in her heart when she had seen Titan's halo that he had not fallen into the oblivion with the demon. Fishbone had just confirmed what she had hoped for the last two years, Titan was with the Divine.

'Thank you.' Shayla said taking Fishbone's hand.

'He's content.' Fishbone said squeezing Shayla's hand. 'Probably pacing the garden waiting for you.'

Shayla laughed through her tears.

'He will always be a part of you. You still have the mark of your symbiosis to prove it.'

'I know.' Shayla said wiping her tears away with the back of her hand.

Peter put his arm around Shayla and pulled her towards him. Shayla leaned her head against Peter's shoulder.

'I don't mean to sound rude.' Peter said. 'But you've suddenly turned up after all these years. Is something wrong?'

Fishbone had a far-away look in his eyes, which always preluded a revelation.

'Do you remember years ago, before you met Shayla, when I said certain events from the past had disrupted time and causality and sped things along.'

'You were referring to Parallax becoming self-aware.' Peter said.

'That's right.' Fishbone said. 'I'd seen a similar chain of events unfold in multiple realms, in multiple dimensions. All worlds destined to move along similar paths.'

'We destroyed Parallax. Peter said.

'You did but….' Fishbone paused before continuing. 'I've just returned from another realm. I followed someone through the gateway to stop him delivering this.'

Fishbone opened his hand to reveal a USB memory stick.

'What's on it?' Peter asked picking it up and turning it over.

Shayla sat up straight and looked at Peter, they both looked at Fishbone.

Printed clearly on one side of the USB stick was one word –

PARALLAX

The End

ABOUT THE AUTHOR

Bex Gooding was born in Devon, England. She currently works as an Administrator having spent over 10 years working in the Legal Profession. An avid reader of all types of fiction, especially loving the escapism into fantasy and horror. Bex still lives in Devon with her husband Peter, their daughter and two Jack Russell Terriers.

OTHER TITLES BY BEX GOODING

Available from Amazon Books

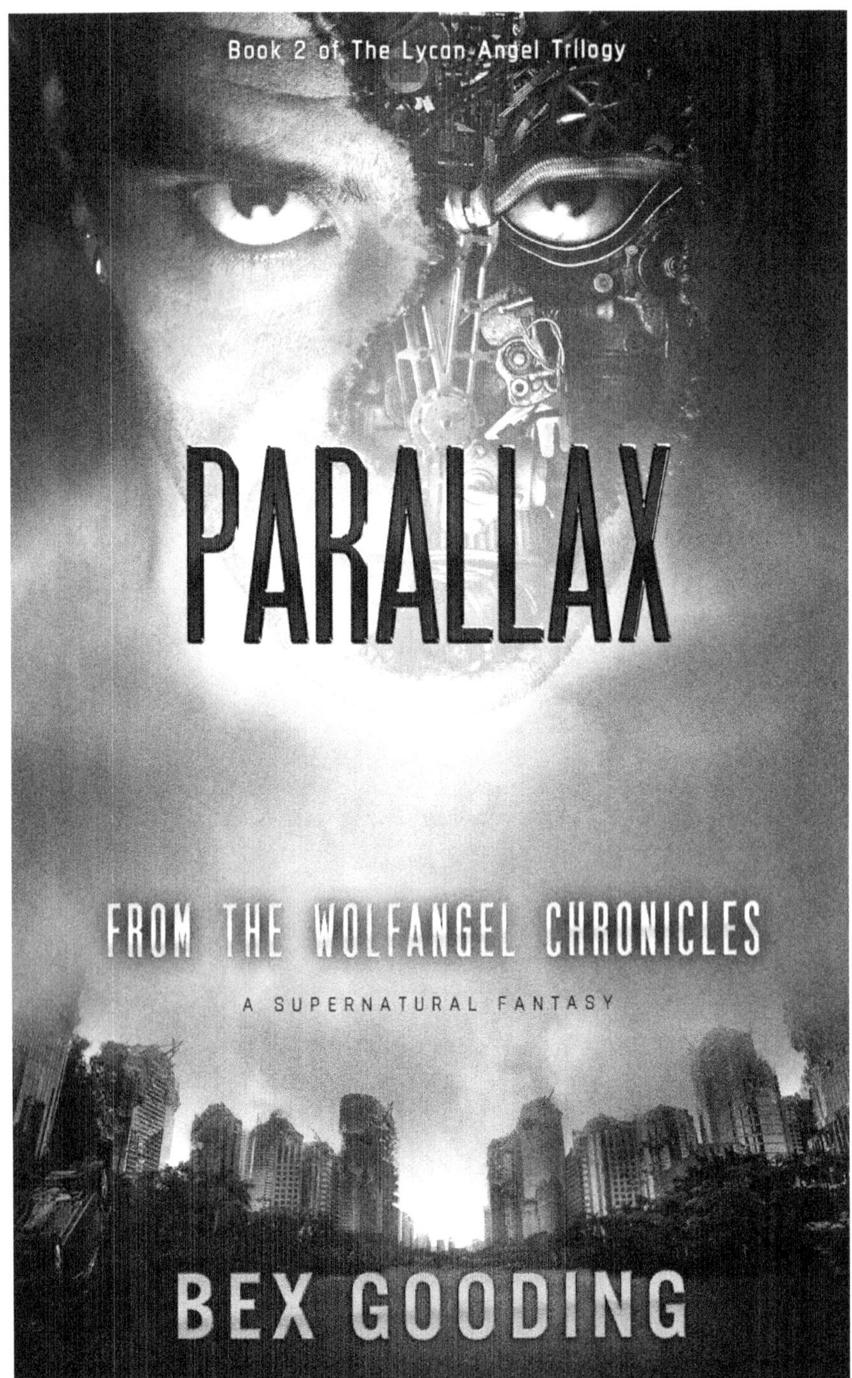
Book 2 of The Lycon-Angel Trilogy
PARALLAX
FROM THE WOLFANGEL CHRONICLES
A SUPERNATURAL FANTASY
BEX GOODING

Tell Me a Story Mr W.O.L.F.

Bex Gooding

A collection of short stories

Printed in Great Britain
by Amazon

82648039R00222